forever
beach

forever beach

SHELLEY NOBLE

wm

WILLIAM MORROW
An Imprint of HarperCollins*Publishers*

FOREVER BEACH. Copyright © 2016 by Shelley Freydont. All rights reserved. Printed in the United States of America. No part of this book may be used or reproduced in any manner whatsoever without written permission except in the case of brief quotations embodied in critical articles and reviews. For information address HarperCollins Publishers, 195 Broadway, New York, NY 10007.

HarperCollins books may be purchased for educational, business, or sales promotional use. For information please e-mail the Special Markets Department at SPsales@harpercollins.com.

FIRST EDITION

Designed by Diahann Sturge

Library of Congress Cataloging-in-Publication Data has been applied for.

ISBN 978-0-06-243906-2

16 17 18 19 20   OV/RRD   10 9 8 7 6 5 4 3 2 1

forever
beach

Chapter 1

Sarah stood just inside the door and watched the bundle of mail slide through the slot. It fell in slow motion toward the floor, where it hit the hard wood and splayed like so many playing cards. Normally she would open the door and wave to the postman, Mr. Reidy.

But not today. Mr. Reidy liked to chat, and today Sarah's stomach was roiling too much to listen. And if she opened the door, Leila would come running on her sturdy little legs, curious to see who it was. Sarah had been jubilant the first time Leila had come up behind her and, holding tightly to her leg, smiled up at Mr. Reidy. It had felt like they were home free, they would become a family, and at last Leila would be safe and loved and would finally learn to trust and love Sarah in return.

Six days a week for almost two years, Sarah had picked up her mail with a sense of trepidation. You never knew when something would change, your life never completely your own. A simple white envelope could set your world spinning out of control. She tried to always be prepared. Maybe today would set them free.

Barely breathing, she stared at the envelopes until she heard Mr. Reidy walk away, across the porch, down the steps, on to the next house. It was a sunny day, she could see that through the windows. The hall was dark, the letters in shadow, mere shapes, but she recognized the envelope she'd been waiting for.

She took a breath, or tried. Her lungs seized up in a war of hope and anxiety. Surely today would be the day . . .

She reached down, watching her hand, not the envelope, trying to imagine herself smiling as she read the letter. *Your petition for adoption has been approved.* Approved. Approved. Approved. She'd been taught that somewhere along the line. Imagine the positive and it will happen. It was a lie, of course, like so much of their optimism, but Sarah still held on to it, thinking one day, one day it would actually work.

Ms. Sarah Hargreave. Her fingers were shaking so much that when she tried to pick the official envelope out of the pile, she only managed to send it sliding across the floor.

She heard the cackle of Snow White's evil queen coming from the living room. Leila's shouted "Mommee" would soon follow. Leila had brought the DVD home from the Wolcotts against Sarah's better judgment. Leila loved the movie, except for the evil queen. Sarah didn't know why she watched it. Sympathetic magic, maybe.

"Mommee!"

Sarah tried to answer, but nerves kept her voice at bay. The letter was in her hand now. She saw the return address, turned the envelope over.

She should go find the letter opener.

She ripped through the flap. Unfolded the paper, a single sheet.

In her mind she read *Your adoption of Leila Rodrigues has been approved,* but the words said, *You are hereby given notice that Carmen Delgado, birth mother of Leila Rodrigues, has petitioned the court for visitation rights and has been approved. You will be contacted by your caseworker to schedule a supervised visit.*

"Mommee!"

Sarah rocked on her feet, leaned back against the wall to steady herself. And slid to the floor.

No. Not again. How could they let that woman have her again? And again. How could they be so cruel?

Sarah started to shiver, or maybe it was the paper shaking as she read it again. Trying to change the words that would promise that Leila would never be mistreated or frightened again. Sarah would be her forever home, and she'd love her forever.

Schedule a supervised visit.

The hell she would. But even as she thought it, she knew she would have to comply. That's the way the system worked.

She could see Leila padding down the hall. She was wearing her pink shorts and *Lady and the Tramp* T-shirt, hand-me-downs from Bessie Wolcott who was a year younger than Leila but looked and acted two years older. Leila had a lot of catching up to do, but she was growing and was beginning to talk in sentences and become the little dynamo she was supposed to be. Sarah could not let all that progress be undone.

"Mommee sad?"

Good God, what could Sarah say? She shook her head. It was a lie, but it was the best she could do.

Leila climbed into her lap and put her little hands on both of Sarah's cheeks.

Her favorite game. A game for younger children, but Leila loved it.

"Kisses, kisses, ki-ss-es . . . Bunny wabbit."

Leila squealed, her body vibrating with giggles against Sarah; Sarah held her tighter. She had to make a plan, call Reesa, her original caseworker, and now her friend. Reesa would know what to do.

"Mommee." Leila pressed Sarah's cheeks.

"Kisses, kisses . . . kisses . . . kisses. Bunny wabbit."

Leila laughed harder and threw her body back, nearly popping out of Sarah's arms. How easily that laughter could turn to sobs and hysterical crying.

She patted Sarah's cheeks with both hands. "Mommee, are you sad?"

"Sad? No. Of course not." *I'm terrified.*

Terrified that Leila will be frightened. Hurt. That she won't understand why Sarah let her go. Again.

"Mommee, you're squeezing too tight."

But Sarah couldn't let go.

I MOVE CLOSER to Nonie. We all know that someone is going to be placed today. They haven't said who, but word gets around. We all try to look our best, clean, neat, without letting the others know that's what we're doing. It doesn't fool anybody, but no one mentions it. Each of us is filled with hope and dread, hope that it will be us and we'll go to a family who loves us—and dread that it will be us and it will be worse than here.

It's safer not to be chosen.

I have a sick feeling in my stomach; somehow I know it won't be me. I try to be strong, tough it out, act like I don't care.

I used to think pick me, pick me. But I've been picked and now I'm back. Now I only look at the floor as if not making eye contact will protect me. Of course, it has all been decided beforehand. No matter how hard we try.

But I can't not look, so I peek quickly, long enough to see Mrs. J's eyes search the room. Slow motion; I know where they're going to stop. Not at me.

I slip my hand in Nonie's. She's older, taller, stronger than me. She's taught me everything I know about the system; she's been here longer. She protects me; no one messes with me when she's here. She's like my sister.

Mrs. J's eyes stop; she's not looking at me. But at Nonie. I can feel Nonie's hand relaxing. I hold tighter, but somehow it slips from mine, and she steps forward like she's at the movies in the ticket line. And it's sort of like that, isn't it. Take a ticket.

Mrs. J has a big smile on her face. "Nonie," she says. "We've found you a home. A very nice home."

Nonie doesn't answer, but I feel her change. She's already left. Like a photo that someone tore in half and I'm the half that was thrown away.

Nonie is the one that's leaving, but I am the one who's gone . . .

"MOMMEE."

Sarah forced herself to relax her arms. She wanted nothing more than to hold on to Leila forever. Never let anyone get near her, hurt her, but she knew she couldn't sit here on the floor and wish the situation away. She'd have to do something.

She should have pushed her lawyer to expedite the adoption papers. He'd warned her that the process from foster to adoption was slow, and she'd taken him at his word. She should have pushed him. Hadn't she learned anything from all those years of being in the system? You can't relax, you have to be alert, watchful; you have to stay in their face, not give any of them an inch.

She took a breath. Leaned her cheek against Leila's little

head. Began to rock and Leila nestled against her chest and sucked her thumb. A bad habit, but she'd worry about braces later; let Leila have her comfort now.

"What about a snack and then we'll see if Bessie and Tammy are home?"

"Bessie." Leila squirmed out of Sarah's lap and pulled on her hand. Sarah struggled to her feet. "Thank you for helping me up."

They walked to the kitchen side by side, Leila's arm stretching to reach her hand. Leila headed straight to the sink and climbed onto her step stool and held out her hands. Sarah turned on the water, and when it was warm, she held Leila up so that she could wash her hands by herself.

While Leila scrambled onto her booster seat at the table, Sarah opened the fridge. They had a routine, and things were going smoothly, well, at least more smoothly than before, the last time she'd been taken from her drug-addicted mother and returned to Sarah.

What did it take for them to figure out Carmen Delgado was not going to be drug free—ever.

Twice Carmen had "straightened" out, tested clean; twice Leila had been put on a reunification track only to be removed again when Carmen failed to stay drug free. Leila would come back to Sarah wary and hurt. And Sarah would have to start again to earn her trust. Why didn't they get that sometimes bio families just didn't work. Just ask the children of drug addicts, like Sarah, those who had been shipped back and forth from some stupid notion that kids belonged with their birth mothers, until it was too late to save child or mother.

"Walk in my shoes, people."

Had she said that aloud? She peered over the top of the fridge door. Leila was watching her.

Sarah smiled and reached into the fridge for an apple. She took a couple of slow breaths and reminded herself not to let Leila sense her fear. Don't think ahead. Fix the now.

Fix the now. Sam had written the words on the front of the fridge over ten years ago. It was still there, three years after his death. Sarah recited it to herself every day. *Fix the now.* He'd been her lifeline since the day she wandered into his clock repair shop and asked for a job, and today she felt adrift without him.

She put the apple on the counter and reached back inside for the almond butter. Closed the fridge door, opened the door of the white painted cabinets, and chose the plastic plate and cup that she'd bought when Leila had first come to her over two years before.

She cut up the apple, sliced off the core, and spread almond butter over the pieces, concentrating on each step, each slice. The swipe of the almond butter across the juicy surface. The wedges carefully arranged in a circle around the plate. *It's important to give the child a sense of order. Consistency makes a child feel safe.*

But today Sarah was doing it for herself.

She poured out a glass of milk and put the glass and plate on the table in front of Leila. It was a small kitchen; you could reach anything you needed with just a few steps. Fridge, stove, counter, wall calendar where they marked school dates, doctors' and therapists' appointments, play dates and special days with colorful stickers.

It was a cozy little house, nestled alongside the little clock store that she owned now that Sam was dead.

Sarah sat down to watch her daughter eat. It was funny. Sam used to stand at the fridge and watch her eat. She thought for sure it was because he thought she was going to steal the silverware. Now she understood what he was seeing.

She never understood why Sam had hired her. He was old and slightly stooped, she guessed from leaning over tiny clock pieces all day. Sarah didn't even know why she'd ended up on that street of colorful gingerbread houses and shops; or in that quaint town that abutted the town where the other half lived.

She'd just aged out of the system, started walking, and had ended up here. She used to walk a lot in those days: to the mall, the Kwikee Mart, the school, the park, but never to the beach. The group home was only about a half hour walk away, and yet she'd never been there.

She wasn't sure she liked the beach, all that space, and that funny feeling that the waves might come all the way up on the boardwalk and snatch her away. Later she learned to appreciate the power and beauty of the ocean, but that day she crossed the street, away from the water. And that's how she found Sam.

He'd given her a soda and asked if she had a place to live. And he taught her how to fix clocks.

Clocks were good. You always knew where you were with clocks. Not the digital kind where the numbers just kept clicking forward until they fell off the end of the earth. But the old kind, whose hands went round and round, always clockwise until they came back to the place they started even though it was an hour or a day later.

Sam had lots of old clocks. The grandfathers, the grandmothers, the ormolus, the cabinets, the pop-up travel alarms. People from miles around brought him their clocks to be fixed. Now they came to Sarah.

But that had come later.

That day he'd checked her ID to make sure she was eighteen, then he gave her a room in his little house. He didn't charge her anything for it. Which made her nervous. The first night, she slept with a knife under her pillow. The second day she went back to the home where she'd stashed her stuff and moved in for good.

Sam had taught her about trust. About love. Had held her hand on the path of her new life.

Oh, Sam, I wish you were here to help me now.

WHILE LEILA ATE her snack, Sarah took her cell to the other room and called Karen Wolcott. The phone rang five times before Karen picked up.

"Hey," she said, and huffed out a breath. "Jenny's at the mall with her friends. The other three are home today and driving me nuts."

"Oh. I wanted to bring Leila over for a few minutes if it's all right."

"Sure. What's one more?"

"I just need to make a phone call." Sarah saw Leila standing in the doorway, an apple wedge in each hand. Sarah smiled at her. Gave her a thumbs-up.

"Is everything okay?" Karen asked. "You sound weird."

"I know. I do, and it's not." Sarah kept her smile glued to her face.

A pause, then, "Little ears?"

"Uh-huh."

"Come on over, I'll put on some coffee."

"Thanks. See you in a few."

Leila packed up her favorite toys, and they stopped in at

the clock store to tell Alice Millburn, who was minding the counter, where they were going. Then they went around to the backyard where her car was parked. Leila was anxious to go, but she balked at actually getting in. Sarah knew that to Leila cars meant she was being shuttled to some new scary place. But Sarah persevered and most days Leila climbed in the backseat willingly.

Not today.

"We can't go to Bessie's until you get in."

"Front," Leila said.

"Little girls have to sit in the back where it's safer for kids. Bessie sits in the backseat."

Leila thought about it. She could be stubborn. Sometimes it was exasperating, but even now when Sarah was anxious to get on the phone to Reesa, she refused to force her into the car seat.

So they stared at each other for a few seconds. Sarah looking down, Leila with her arms crossed and frowning up. Light and dark, Sarah, a strawberry blonde with skin that freckled in the sun; Leila, just the opposite with inky black hair cropped short, and skin that grew deeper and richer at the beach. Yin and yang, different but each incomplete without the other.

And both stubborn. It was inconvenient at times, but Sarah had no intention of letting Leila run roughshod over her. She'd been in Leila's place once. The tough ones started out with an advantage but only if they were able to adapt. Sarah hadn't been very good at it. She hadn't been dropped into the system until she was eight, and she'd never learned to put her best foot forward and keep it there. When she and Nonie were together, it didn't matter. But she hadn't learned to make it on her own until Sam Gianetti had taken her in.

Leila growled, like some cartoon animal, letting Sarah

know she wasn't happy, but finally she climbed into the back and got in her car seat. Sarah clasped her in and gave her a raspberry on her neck before she moved away.

Leila giggled and life was back to normal. As normal as it got for now.

"Sing my song, Mommee."

Sarah smiled over her shoulder. "You are my sunshine . . ."

Chapter 2

Sarah drove west to where the painted Victorian buildings gave way to the newer neighborhoods of town. Karen Wolcott lived in an expanded ranch with her husband, Stu, and their five children. Sarah had met Karen at a support group Karen ran for foster and adoptive parents, and they'd bonded immediately. Their girls played together, twelve-year-old Jenny sometimes baby-sat Leila, and Karen was the person Sarah came to for advice and friendship.

She pulled into the driveway and parked behind Karen's minivan. The yard was littered with ride-on toys, bikes, scooters, and a big basketball hoop on a stand. It was the kind of house that was lively, sometimes hectic, and always welcoming.

Sarah had begun to imagine Karen's girls and Leila someday walking back and forth to each other's houses after school. Trying on each other's clothes, sharing nail polish and all those things Sarah had never done. Now that dream seemed like it might explode in her face.

Don't think that way. Imagine success, imagine success.

Karen was a success story. She'd gotten pregnant at sixteen, and her baby was put in foster care. Amy was almost five when Karen was able to take her back full-time. Then she'd married Stu and he'd adopted Amy, who was now a senior at Rutgers University. Karen was an inspiration to the other parents who often felt confused, inadequate, and alone. And she was a lifeline to Sarah.

Bessie and Tammy came running out of the house as soon as Sarah parked the car.

Leila was pulling on the straps of her car seat, and Sarah hurried to the back to help her get out.

"Oh dear," Karen said, once the kids had run past her and into the house, herding Leila with them. She fisted her hands on her hips. "Girl, you look like you're having a rough day. Come on back to the kitchen."

"You could call it that." Sarah stepped through the door and followed her through the house. She could hear the girls chattering away in the family room. She didn't hear Leila, and she had to fight the urge to go check on her. That was crazy. She had to act normal for both their sakes.

"There's coffee or . . ." Karen opened the fridge and looked inside. "Not much. I have to get to the store today. Let's see. Milk, some disgusting cherry-flavored kiddie drink, ginger ale?"

"Nothing thanks."

Karen swung around. "Okay, girlfriend. What's wrong?"

"They—" Sarah pulled out a chair and sat down.

Karen sat down across from her and frowned. "You're shaking. What's happened?"

Sarah looked toward the door.

Karen went over to shut it, then sat in the chair closer to Sarah. "Spill."

Sarah reached down for her purse and pulled out the letter from child services. Slapped it on the table in front of Karen.

She looked at Sarah, then opened it and read. "I thought her parental rights had been terminated."

"They were."

"It must be a glitch in the system," Karen said, looking at it again.

"Maybe, but it doesn't sound like a form letter."

"What are you going to do?"

"Comply. What else can I do? Jeez. When are they going to get it that Leila belongs with me? I love her more than Carmen ever did." Or could.

Karen sighed. "I know, hon, I know."

"You saw what happened the last two times they sent her back. All the progress she'd made was out the window. She wouldn't talk, wouldn't look at me. The tantrums came back, the nightmares. It took weeks before she began to relax again. And she's been doing so well." Her voice caught. "And I can't even tell her that I don't want her to go."

Sarah was careful to follow the directives in the training session. *Make the visit positive.* Tell her she gets to visit her bio mother and then she'll come back. *Don't dis the bio mother.* Your mother misses you. *Don't promise her a "forever" home until adoption is imminent.* You'll always be welcome here and I'll always love you. *Just make the transition as smooth as possible.* Right.

It went against everything that Sarah felt. Sure kids loved their bio mothers. She even loved hers though she didn't have much of a memory of her, just as a phantom person who appeared and disappeared for reasons Sarah didn't understand until much later. She didn't remember her father at all. Wasn't even sure if she'd had one. A real father.

"It's the rules."

"Yeah, I get that they want to keep families together. But Carmen isn't some poor woman who lost her job and is having temporary housing issues. Or who's in the hospital and needs someone to care for her kids. Carmen is a longtime addict with a string of men who pimp her, or beat her, or both. She's had seven children, and every one of them is in foster care. Her apartment is filthy. I have no idea what she feeds Leila while she's there or if she even feeds her . . . And I'm supposed to make Leila feel good about visiting that?"

"Sarah, they're doing the best they can."

"Yeah, well, I was one of those kids. I survived, but it wasn't until I aged out and wandered into the clock shop that I found my forever family."

She slumped in the chair. "I just want Leila to grow up happy, and safe, and not afraid of where her next meal is coming from."

She wanted that for Leila now. *Now.* Wanted to watch her grow to a height not stunted by malnutrition, gain weight that would be normal if her mother had bought food instead of crack. Feel safe enough to let her personality shine. To not fear Sarah or Sarah's friends. To unconditionally accept Sarah's love.

"I need to make some calls, and I want to talk to Reesa before I do anything. But I didn't want Leila to know because she always gets fretful when one of the social workers comes to the house or we have to meet with the 'team.' I know she's afraid they're going to take her back. And shit—" Her voice cracked. "So am I."

Karen dropped the letter and stretched across the table to clasp her hand. "Take all the time you want. Leila can stay here for as long as you need."

"But you have to go to the store." It was such a stupid thing to say.

"I'll go tomorrow. What's a little mac 'n' cheese and chicken fingers two days in a row? The kids will be ecstatic. Or, heck, we can splurge and order a pizza."

"I can pay for pizza." Sarah reached for her bag.

"Stop right there. This is what friends are for. Go do what you have to do."

"Thanks. I'll try not to be gone long. I'll just say good-bye to Leila, explain that I'll be back."

"Sarah, stop it. She'll be fine as long as you don't act like something's wrong. Go to the door and wave good-bye and leave." Karen touched her arm. "You're the one I'm worried about."

"I know. I have to pull myself together. It's just . . . I was expecting the adoption papers; instead I got a kick to the gut. I don't want her to be scared."

"She won't be, if you aren't." Karen was a sink-or-swim kind of mother, within reason. Let them try, and be there to save their little butts if they got in over their heads.

Sarah was overprotective, tended to hover. Not a healthy way to raise a kid, she knew that, and she planned to work on it just as soon as Leila's adoption was final.

They looked in at the family room, a bright sunny space at the back of the house that was filled with toys, a craft table, a huge media center, a fireplace covered by a glass door, two cats sleeping beneath the chair, and a yellow lab named Casper who was currently serving as a pillow for the three girls watching *Sesame Street* on the huge flat-screen television.

Karen put her finger to her lips and they tiptoed away.

"She'll be fine. Now go." Karen nudged Sarah toward the door, but as they stood on the porch, Sarah pulled out the big Mickey Mouse clock she always carried in her tote. She handed it to Karen. "Tell her I'll be back by the time the little hand is here and the big hand is here."

Karen smiled. "You mean three thirty?"

"Yeah. Sorry. I'm a nutcase. I just can't believe this is happening."

"It's all right. Give me the clock. You have every right to be a little bonkers today. Go get things fixed." Karen gave her a quick hug. "Then come back for some mac 'n' cheese."

"Thanks." At first Sarah thought about just pulling to the end of Karen's block to make her calls, but she might need paperwork, so she drove back to Main Street. Traffic was heavy in the three-block shopping area, and when she got to her driveway, it was blocked by a truck making a delivery.

The hell with paperwork—she needed to talk to Reesa now. She drove straight down the street to the beach, where she found a parking place between two SUVs whose drivers were out sitting on their boards in the almost nonexistent waves, waiting for the big one. She knew exactly how they felt.

She pulled out her cell and called Reesa Davis, left her name and number on Reesa's voice mail, and waited for an incredibly long half hour before Reesa finally called her back.

"I just heard," she said without even saying hello. "I was going to call you."

"How can they do this? Now of all times."

"I have no idea. I'm in my car; I haven't even seen my desk today. I'll check into it as soon as I can. You just stay calm."

"I'm trying." Sarah took a breath. Did she sound like a hysterical mother? Well, she was. They'd been so close to being a family—a legal family—a "forever" family.

"I just don't understand. The termination papers were filed, the adoption papers are in the pipeline. Randy Phelps said it was just a matter of time."

There was silence on the other end of the line.

"What? What's happened? Were you included in the decision?"

"Sarah. I don't have time to talk right now. I have three kids literally starving to death that I need to get into emergency care. I'll get back to you. Don't panic."

"Sorry. I know you're needed everywhere, I just . . ."

"I know, and we will see this through. Now try to calm down and not pass on your agitation to Leila. I'll try to get by sometime in the next couple of days and help you prepare her for the visit."

"Can't we get some kind of stay? You know what happened the last time she went back."

"Evidently Carmen passed the last drug test and has been going, albeit sporadically, to the therapy sessions. And I might as well tell you, she was making rumblings about wanting her children back."

"What?"

"It seems unlikely that she's anywhere close to being able to take care of children. But I thought you should be prepared."

"But I already filed for adoption. She signed the agreement."

"This is just a visit."

"And we know where that leads."

"Not always."

"It has twice already, back to home visitations. Are they going to guarantee that she won't hurt Leila, traumatize her, let her newest boyfriend—and I use the word loosely—abuse her and take her monthly stipend—which is probably what this is all about—and spend it on drugs? Oh, God, Reesa, I'm sorry. I didn't mean to lose it. But it's so unfair."

"I know you're upset, Sarah, and I won't sugarcoat it. You've been through the system yourself, and you know that shit happens. And you know we're obligated to give Carmen a second chance."

"She's had her second chance. What about Leila, what about her chances? Will she make it through a third time without being permanently damaged?"

"Look, I don't know that anything more will come of this, but if it does, you will need a good lawyer."

"You mean not Randy Phelps."

"Randy is perfectly fine in certain cases, but if Carmen insists on going forward with this, it will probably end up in court. I'll bring you up to speed when I see you. But I think you should contact Leila's court-appointed advocate. I think they will try to keep the same CASA for her if it does go to court. And talk to your adoption caseworker. And you should start looking about for an attorney for yourself, someone articulate and persuasive. Just in case."

Just in case. How can this be happening?

"Do you know of anyone?"

"I might. But she's in demand and expensive."

"I don't care. I'll pay what it takes."

"Okay. I'll give her a call, see if she's even interested in looking at your case if—and I stress the *if*—it comes to that. Here comes my police support, gotta go. I'll get back to you." Reesa hung up.

Sarah dropped her cell onto the passenger seat and closed her eyes. *Shit happens.* She'd had a hard enough time finding Randy. The other parents she knew in the foster support group didn't have any recommendations. Most of them hadn't needed a lawyer. And now she needed a better lawyer. And court? What the hell was going on?

How much could this other lawyer cost? Sam had left her all he had. The clock store was doing fine, she was okay financially, but could she pay out thousands and thousands of dollars?

Would it come to that?

Maybe this was just a hitch in the process. Maybe this was Carmen's last hurrah. Maybe she wouldn't even show up for the visit. Maybe she would die of an overdose before then.

Sarah drooped forward, rested her head on the steering wheel, shocked that she would even think such a thing. She just wished Carmen would go away . . .

IT'S BEEN TWO months since Nonie left. I write her every week, but she hasn't written back once. And she promised. Promised. Maybe she's dead and that's why she hasn't written.

"This looks like the real deal," she'd said when she came back to get the rest of her stuff. "Mrs. J says they're rich; he's some big deal in the state government or something. If it works out, I'll ask them to take you, too. Tell them you're my sister."

I tried to smile 'cause we don't look anything alike.

"Just watch your back and hang tough. You can do it. I'll write to you every week."

"Promise?"

"Promise, and you write, too."

"Every week," I told her. I was afraid I was going to cry. Worse. I was afraid Nonie was.

I'd never seen her look like that. She was the tough one, the knowing one. The kick-ass one who didn't take shit from nobody, the one who always had my back

But today, right before she turned away, I saw something I'd never seen before.

Nonie was scared.

I watched her walk away. She didn't look back; I was glad 'cause I didn't want her to see me crying. You couldn't cry, or they'd be in your face, the other kids. But that day I couldn't stop. I can feel them trying to get out of my eyes now. But I push them back, or maybe I just don't have any tears left.

I kept my promise. I write every week. I wait for the mail every day, but nothing comes. Mrs. J feels sorry for me, I can tell.

She's always coming over to me saying, "You're a pretty girl, Sarah, and smart. Don't you worry, you'll get placed somewhere nice, too."

I don't want to get placed. I want Nonie to write and say she's convinced her wonderful, rich new family to take me, too.

"She's probably busy getting used to her new life. Be patient."

I almost laugh. That's one thing you learn if you don't learn anything else. You don't have a choice about being patient . . .

A KNOCK ON the window made Sarah jump. She blinked. She couldn't have been asleep, but she felt disoriented. For a moment she'd been somewhere else, some other time. Being patient. Like now.

Another knock. She turned on the ignition and lowered the window.

Wyatt Monroe braced his hands on the top of the car and leaned in toward her. "Are you all right?"

"Yes. Not really. I don't know."

Wyatt smiled at her, which was more than she deserved. They'd been friends for years. More like friends with benefits . . . until recently. She'd pushed him away since she began fostering Leila. Leila had been afraid of men when she first came home with Sarah. She'd taken one look at Wyatt and screamed until she made herself sick.

He was a big guy, tall and muscular, with dark hair, dark eyes, a skin tanned to a deep olive from his work on the water rescue team. And though he was always kind to Leila, he could be a little intimidating.

Sarah had made him leave; he was pissed at the time, but she could tell he was also relieved. He hadn't signed on for anything more than a good time.

But Leila had been back on an adoption track for months now, and Wyatt had slowly become a part of their life again. Leila began to warm to him, then actually accepted him. Wyatt seemed comfortable with the two of them, and Sarah had begun to breathe. And now, just when it was supposed to be smooth sailing ahead, Carmen changed her mind and could wreck everything. When would Sarah learn that there would never be smooth sailing for her?

"I thought the adoption had gone through. Instead, the bio mother wants visitation rights, and the court granted them."

"Again? What is wrong with those people?"

Sarah shrugged.

Wyatt peered into the backseat. "Where is the little one?"

"At Karen's. I had to call my caseworker and I didn't want to upset her."

He opened the car door.

"I need to get back."

"You can take ten minutes for yourself. Sit on the board-walk with me and regroup."

Sarah shook her head.

"Sarah. Don't start pushing me away again. It isn't good for any of us."

She reached for the ignition. "I can't."

"You can. You just won't." He shut the door before she could even think about changing her mind. "You're not doing yourself or Leila any favors by being wound this tight all the time. Take a good look at the work you do, how many clocks have come in for the same damn reason. Wound so tight they broke."

"I'm sorry." She put the car in reverse and backed out of the parking place. Had to slam on the brakes as two kids on bicycles pedaled past.

Sorry, she thought—Sorry to the kids and sorry to Wyatt—he was a good man. He was still standing there, watching her. She just needed to concentrate on making Leila happy right now.

Sarah knew she tried too hard to keep everything under control. She didn't know why. The one time she *had* let fate intervene, it had brought her to Sam Gianetti and his love of old clocks. And her real family.

Why was it so hard to trust someone now?

REESA DAVIS WAS out of breath by the time she'd followed the four police officers up the three flights of stairs to apartment 3G. The hallway was stifling and smelled like urine and smoke and mold.

She tried to breathe shallowly. She'd been a caseworker for years, but sometimes, things just got to her. This was getting to her.

She'd been sent to a neighbor's apartment earlier. The neighbor had found one of the boys in 3G scavenging food from the trash bins. She'd taken him in and fed him while she called Child Protection.

My God, he looked like he'd come from a prison camp. So thin that his arms were almost skeletal. His cheeks and eyes were sunken like an old man. He said his name was Pete. He'd sneaked out the fire escape to find food for his brothers. The baby wasn't crying anymore.

Reesa had called in a Dodd removal—no court order. The neighbor was frightened, and Reesa had promised to come get Pete as soon as the other two were safely out of the apartment. But it had taken an hour for her to get the go-ahead and for the police to arrive.

The four officers stood back; Reesa stepped up to the door and knocked. Waited for a count of four. Knocked again.

"Ms. White? It's Reesa Davis from the Child Protection office. May I come in?"

Reesa could feel the officers ready themselves for a forced entry. Nobody liked to have to do that. You never knew what you'd find on the other side of that locked door.

Reesa knocked again. "Ms. White? You need to open the door now."

No response.

Reesa knocked again louder. "Ms. White, I need to see the children. If you don't open the door, we'll have to use force to enter. And you will probably be taken into custody."

Finally she heard a chain being slipped out. The door opened a crack. And a hollow-eyed woman stared out at her. "Go away. There's nothing wrong here." She started to close the door.

There was something terribly wrong. Suddenly the woman was yanked away from the door, but before it could slam shut, the officers forced their way past Reesa and into the apartment.

There was screaming and sounds of fighting. Reesa waited outside for the all clear. Minutes later, as two of the policemen dragged a man out and toward the stairs, a third officer motioned her in.

Ms. White sat on a sagging couch. Her face was chalky gray. Greasy strands of hair hung limp at her shoulders. Skinny arms clutched at her middle as she rocked back and forth, whimpering, "Whatcha done with Darrell?" The neighbor had said she was in her thirties, but she looked much older.

Reesa looked quickly around the room. It was disgusting. And hot. An oscillating table fan did little more than push around the stale air and odors.

She should take pictures, but at the moment she was more intent on finding the two children. She crossed the stained shag carpet. Drug paraphernalia was strewn across a coffee table, and beer cans littered every surface. She walked past the kitchen area that was being used for storage or maybe garbage. It didn't look like a place where food was prepared. Definitely a firetrap.

One officer stayed guarding the door, keeping one eye on Ms. White. The other followed Reesa across the room.

She stepped into a second room and gagged. Behind her, the policeman said, "Shit."

He was right. The place smelled like a sewer and was sweltering. It had to be in the nineties.

There were no lights on, so she groped along the wall and found a switch. The light didn't work.

"Can you open a window?" she asked, then covered her

mouth and nose with her hand, while the officer groped his way across the room. He tore away a blanket that they'd tacked to the window frame and forced open the sash, which let in a little air and enough light to show an unmade bed, stained and encrusted with filth, and a boy curled up in a ball, looking at Reesa with dull eyes.

He was so malnourished he couldn't even be afraid.

Reesa had to force herself to move closer. This was the worst situation she'd seen in a long time. If ever.

She didn't sit on the mattress but leaned over to the boy, careful to keep her clothes from touching anything.

"Hello, sweetheart, I'm Mrs. Davis, and I'm going to take you to get some food."

His eyes closed.

"Sweetheart?" Reesa said quietly.

The boy's eyes opened slowly, blinked as if he were emerging from a hypnotic trance.

"Honey," Reesa said. "Can you tell me where the baby is?"

Nothing.

Reesa looked around; there was a crib, but it looked like it was being used as a laundry basket. She didn't want to look more closely, but she had to find that baby.

She moved toward it and forced herself to peer down through the dirty clothes. The child was there, covered in a T-shirt too big for him, no diaper.

Reesa bit back a cry, moved closer. For a terrified moment she thought she was too late. She forced herself to touch the skin. It was warm; the little mouth moved, a slight sucking motion, so minute a movement that Reesa at first wondered if she was willing it to life. She leaned toward it to make sure; yes, the baby was sucking.

"Officer, call the EMTs. We'll need a pediatric harness and an infant carrier."

He was still staring at the kid on the bed, his face twisted in the same emotions Reesa was feeling herself. Shock, disgust, compassion.

"Officer!"

He jolted to life. Grabbed his radio and began giving orders as he walked out of the room.

Reesa forced herself to return to the first boy. He was still alive. But for how long?

And rage bubbled up and tore through her.

She tried to force it back down. Tried to remember the times when things worked out, where parents did care and would be reunited, like last week and the Valentis. A couple who had fallen on hard times but who worked hard and who loved and deserved their children.

She stopped herself. She wasn't supposed to make emotional judgments, but today she couldn't help it. She wanted to lash out, yell at that piece of humanity sitting out on the couch, worried about her boyfriend.

A siren whined in the distance coming nearer and, after an eternity, footsteps sounded on the stairs. Reesa waited by the bedroom door and directed the EMTs to where two children lay near death.

She stepped aside, but not before she saw the revulsion on the emergency workers' faces. They recovered instantly. While one prepared the harness, the other two slid the boy onto the gurney.

A second team came in behind them, lugging an infant carrier. They moved toward the crib as Reesa followed the first gurney out of the room.

The mother just sat there sniffling while they hooked Jerome up to an IV. But when the second EMT came out carrying that small bundle, she threw herself off the couch. "What are you doing? Put my baby back! You can't take my baby!"

One of the policemen restrained her as the EMTs strapped the infant carrier onto a second gurney.

"There's one more at a neighbor's," Reesa told them and started toward the door.

Ms. White broke away from the officer and lunged after Reesa. "You can't take them. You can't take my babies. You bitch! You . . ." She yelled a string of profanity that echoed down the dirty hallway.

Reesa took the stairs down to the first floor where hopefully she would find the oldest boy still alive.

She was almost afraid to knock. But it was her job. "Ms. McKinney, it's Reesa Davis from Child Protection. I'm here to take Pete where he can be cared for."

Ms. McKinney called, "Coming, I'm coming," with a thick Jamaican accent.

The chain rattled, the door opened, and Ms. McKinney opened the door. She was an older woman, with white cottony hair, dressed in a faded housedress and slippers. "Poor children. I didn't know. I didn't see until today." She stepped back to let Reesa in.

"It's not your fault. You were brave to come forward. If you have any trouble because of this, call this number." She handed the old woman her card. "If you fear for your safety, call 911 immediately."

"Always fear for my safety here."

"I'm going to have a colleague of mine give you a call, and see if we can do something about that, okay?"

Ms. McKinney nodded and shuffled back to the kitchen where Pete sat at a scrubbed kitchen table, clutching a loaf of bread.

"Hi, Pete," Reesa said, trying not to let her voice betray her.

"She said I could have it," Pete said, nodding to Ms. McKinney. "I didn't steal it."

"You sure can have it," the old woman said in a lilting way that in spite of the horror of the situation had a calming effect on both Reesa and Pete.

"Your brothers are waiting for you downstairs, Pete," Reesa said. "We're going to a place where you can get cleaned up and eat and stay until everything is better."

Pete shook his head.

"Your brothers are waiting for you."

"Can't go."

"Why?"

"Gotta take care of her."

Reesa froze. "Your sister? Pete, do you have a sister?"

Pete shook his head. "My mama."

Reesa and Ms. McKinney exchanged looks over Pete's head. There were no words.

"Pete, your mama's going to someplace to get help. Someone will look after her."

He seemed to crumple, too tired and malnourished to argue. He let Reesa lead him to the ambulance, but he wouldn't let go of that loaf of bread.

Chapter 3

Ilona Cartwright dropped her files into her briefcase and snapped it shut. It felt good to win. Fortunately she usually did. Actually fortune didn't have much to do with it. She was good. She worked hard for her clients. Harder than most of them understood. And harder than some of them deserved.

Today's clients, armed with hugs and tears and thank-yous, had already left the courtroom, and the next case was ready to take their place.

"Nice work, Counselor."

Ilona nodded an acknowledgment to Barry O'Doul who was up next. She didn't much like Barry, all show and not enough jurisprudence for Ilona's taste. She'd seen him work a jury until they were completely befuddled and doing it without one proven fact. All he lacked was a top hat and ringmaster whip.

He exuded confidence, like he had a case all wrapped up before he even entered the courtroom, but beneath the show, there was almost always flaky evidentiary support.

Ilona didn't have that problem.

"All yours," she said and slid her briefcase off the table.

Another pro bono case cleared. Another family reunited, at least until they fell on the next hard time or got deported. But her work was done.

The only decision she had to make now was whether to go back to the office before she went home and what wine to have with dinner while she read over the brief for her next divorce case.

It was going to be a circus. Lots of money on the table. Several houses to haggle over. Lies and innuendos volleying back and forth. Her client had sued for the divorce, the husband had countersued. And the fun really began.

He was a piece of work; then again so was his wife. At least there were no children to suffer.

Ilona didn't like either of them very much. She would do her best for her client regardless. But she wouldn't lose sleep over the verdict.

She ran into Josie Green, the caseworker for the Sanchez family who had just been given their children back.

"I don't know how to thank you," Josie said.

"They clearly had the right to reunite their family. Let's just hope they don't let us down."

Josie nodded seriously. She was young, white, fired up with good intentions. Ilona gave her eight months. People like Josie with their zealous enthusiasm burned out faster than the ones who didn't really give a shit. Too bad really, but it was the nature of the job.

The elevator came, and the two of them crowded in with the other attorneys, clerks, and caseworkers who were finished for the day or just going out for a smoke.

The smokers got off on the first floor to huddle around the ash cans outside the entry door; the others rode all the way to the parking garage.

"Well, thanks again," Josie said.

"My pleasure."

Josie climbed into an ancient blue Hyundai. *Pitiful,* Ilona thought as she walked to the end of the ramp and beeped open her silver Mercedes. She placed her briefcase on the passenger seat, slipped out of her linen jacket, laid it neatly on top of the briefcase, and slid into the driver's seat.

Two blocks later, she hit the afternoon sun and rush-hour traffic. She didn't have time for traffic. It always put her in a bad mood. On a whim she made the next left turn and drove east. She'd take the ocean road to her condo even though the route took her closer than she liked to her old home. If you could call it that.

All the wealth that money could buy and not one damn drop of love or compassion or kindness anywhere. That was okay. Ilona had made them pay for the privilege of adopting her. She'd worked them for clothes, toys, cars, four years of college, and a law degree from Yale.

Once they started paying, they couldn't very well stop. And they were proud of it. She had the pictures to prove it, and so did every newspaper and magazine on the East Coast.

"Here's to you . . . Mom and Dad." She lifted her hand in an imaginary toast. She'd have a full-bodied cabernet with her filet tonight in their honor.

SARAH FELT PRETTY depleted when she drove away from the beach. The prospect of going to court again was daunting enough and the fact that she'd blown off Wyatt made her feel guilty. And sad. They'd known each other for years. Were good friends. Lovers. She was pretty sure she loved him, but did she love him enough to jeopardize her life with Leila?

Especially if she had to go to court. They'd be looking at everything about her, question everything she'd ever done.

She knew their first commandment was to reunite the child with the birth family.

She could just hear them accusing her.

"Do you have men friends stay over?"

It wouldn't matter that it was one friend, who was a good guy, who saved lives when he wasn't running his dive business. And who would love both her and Leila if she gave him half a chance.

"Do you drink?"

Not how much. Just yes or no. *Just the occasional glass of wine or beer. I never get drunk and never enough for me to neglect my duties.*

"Have you ever taken drugs?"

Not since I got out of child services, Your Honor.

Too bad women didn't have to answer those questions before they had babies.

She took a deep breath. She could see Sam's face like he was sitting next to her. Don't let your anger trip you up or bite you in the ass. Don't worry about the then or the what-ifs. *Fix the now.*

Maybe she was overreacting.

Karen had left a note on the door: *Sarah, we're in the backyard, come on in.*

Sarah opened the door and walked down the hall to the playroom now empty of girls but occupied by fourteen-year-old Rory, who was intent over the controls of a NASCAR video game.

She didn't interrupt his concentration to say hi, but opened the sliding glass door and stepped out onto the brick patio, where Karen sat in a lawn chair while Tammy, Bessie, and Leila, dressed in swimsuits, splashed in a plastic pool.

"You don't mind, do you? Rory wanted the television, and the girls hadn't been out all day."

"It's fine," Sarah said, smiling. Leila was wearing one of Bessie's swimsuits, and it sagged nearly to her knees.

Karen poured Sarah a glass of iced tea and motioned her to the second lawn chair. "Did you get in touch with Reesa?"

"Yeah." Sarah took a long sip of the tea and set it on the table.

"What did she say?"

"She was in the middle of removing three children from their home and couldn't really talk. She just said that it might go to court, and if it did, I would probably need to get a better lawyer."

"Did she think it likely that it will go that far?"

Sarah shrugged, not looking at Karen but at Leila laughing and splashing with the others. "Just that it's best to be prepared and that she knew someone who might consider taking our case. Someone expensive."

"So no Randy?"

Sarah shook her head.

"Who did she recommend?"

"She didn't give me a name. Her police backup came. She said she'd call."

"Bless her," Karen said. "I couldn't do it every day. Several times a day. Several days a week."

"I couldn't either. But you do good work."

Karen laughed slightly. "I'm a good listener and hand-holder."

"Right. You know you do more than that."

"Maybe. But nothing close to what Reesa does. I don't know how she stands it." Karen looked out to the pool. "Five minutes, girls."

"Leila looks so happy," Sarah said.

"That's because she is." Karen put her glass on the table and leaned toward Sarah. "You've done what you can for today. Try to relax. Things will work out."

Sarah sighed. "From your lips . . ."

"Yep, and to prove it, I found some hamburger in the freezer so we won't be stuck with mac 'n' cheese. Stu's picking up rolls and chips on his way home."

Sarah felt like she should say they had to get home. She should cook something healthy that neither of them would enjoy nearly as much as burgers with the boisterous Wolcotts.

"And don't say that you can't stay, because you can. And better to be with this family circus than to brood over stuff you have no control over."

Sarah knew Karen was right. She felt so helpless sometimes. Like all she could do was sit around and wait and she was capable of so much more.

"I saw Wyatt."

"Recently?"

"While I was gone."

"Good for you. Did he stop by the shop?"

"No." Sarah hesitated. She didn't know why she'd blurted out that fact. Now she'd have to explain, and she didn't even know how she felt or what had happened. "I parked down by the beach. He knocked on the car window while I was sitting there."

"And?"

"Seems like I do nothing but piss him off."

"And push him away."

"Well, what am I supposed to do? I don't want any hitches until Leila is adopted. After that we can see what might happen."

"If he's still around."

Sarah's stomach lurched. "What do you mean? Is he thinking about leaving?"

"Not that I know of, but he may move on to someone who actually wants him."

"Well . . ." Sarah sort of wanted him. But she was sure it would cause trouble. Trouble that she didn't need. Besides, she needed to give her total attention to Leila right now. "If it happens, it happens. I can't deal with it right now."

Karen moaned and flopped back on the lounge chair. "What is wrong with you? You can't keep yo-yoing him in and out of your life like this."

"I'm not."

"Of course you are. Both times they sent Leila back to Carmen, you let Wyatt back in, and then you pushed him away when she came back to you. You have room in your heart for a lot of love, girl. It's not going to run out if you love Wyatt, too. We all need a support group. Even you. Wyatt is ready and willing to be part of that group."

"Wyatt rescues people for a living."

Karen sat up. "Is that what this is all about? You think he's hanging around you because he thinks you need rescuing?"

Sarah smiled. "No, we . . . we get along. It's just that Leila was so freaked out by him when she first came."

"She was afraid of all men and most women and children when she first came. She's resilient. *She's* expanded her horizons."

They heard a car door slam. Tammy and Bessie climbed out of the pool. "Daddy, Daddy." They ran toward the patio.

Leila watched for a minute, and she climbed out, too, but her legs were so short it was a struggle before her little body wriggled itself onto the grass and followed after the girls.

A little piece of Sarah's heart broke.

Stu came onto the patio still dressed in jeans and his work boots. Tammy and Bessie glommed on to each leg. "Daddy, Daddy."

"Hey, girly girls." Stu leaned over to give them a hug, saw Leila standing close by. "Hey, Leila."

Leila dipped her chin, suddenly shy.

Sarah instinctively leaned forward to go to her.

Karen stopped her.

Stu held out one hand. "Gimme five."

Leila ran forward, slapped his hand.

Sarah glared at Karen. "If I didn't know better, I would think you had planned that timing."

Karen shrugged and looked innocent. "No more excuses. All right, girls, go get your towels and get dressed for dinner."

Stu came over to kiss his wife, said hello to Sarah.

"Groceries are on the counter. Let me change, and I'll start the grill." He slid the door open. The girls ran into the house and he followed them.

Karen pushed out of the chair and began gathering the tea

things. "Maybe this thing with Wyatt isn't about Leila at all, Sarah. Maybe it's about you."

REESA PULLED UP to the curb in front of her house and turned off the engine, but instead of getting out, she just sat. What a hell of a day.

Attacked by a mother, who screeched and fought and had to be restrained while they removed her children, children she had ignored until they were close to death.

Mary, Mother of God, what was the point?

She didn't understand why someone who didn't bother to take care of her children was so crazed to keep them. Only she did know. They were desperate. It was what they had, what they knew, the only thing that kept them connected to a world spun out of control, what made them feel human.

Most days Reesa could understand. On the days when good floated to the top of the bad, when she felt like she had more energy, more compassion. That she was actually making a difference.

But today had been rough. Really rough. And the two families she had helped to reunite earlier this week were nothing but a dim memory, fading fast. She tried to conjure up the image of their smiling faces, the mothers' tears and words of gratitude, but all she could see was that little boy and his loaf of bread. And the spew of obscenities flung at her by the addict mother.

She got out of the car and trudged up the embankment to her home.

Sometimes she hated this job. More and more she hated this job. Maybe she should apply for a job in a school. Help kids who at least had school to look forward to. Where they came to her office and she didn't have to show up to their homes with a police escort.

Michael was always griping about the hours she put in, the low pay, the toll it was taking. He needed more attention, especially since he seemed to have parked it on the couch as a way of life.

Tonight she was so damned tired, so sick of seeing the underbelly of families, the marginalized, the desperate—she felt desperate herself, and that was no way to face life. Or to help others with their lives.

Reesa stopped with her hand on the doorknob, took a deep breath, let it out slowly, concentrating on driving the resentment out of her thoughts. She needed to lighten up. She was making a difference . . . just not a very big one.

Another deep breath and she opened the door.

As soon as she was inside, she slipped out of her shoes, kicked them toward the closet. Then she felt bad that she'd let the day get the best of her. She looked at her shoes lying on their sides, turned her back on them, and walked down the hall in her stocking feet to where Michael sat in the recliner, his broken leg resting on a pillow.

She stuck her head in the door. "I'm home."

Michael grunted, his eyes glued on the television.

"Did you eat something today?" Reesa asked.

"Nah, wasn't hungry."

Reesa didn't comment, argue, or chastise, just went into the kitchen to see what she could make. If it were up to her, she'd open a can of soup and call it a night. But Michael would want a real dinner on his TV tray since they'd stopped eating at the dining room table years ago.

She found a package of pork chops in the fridge and checked

the date. Still good, barely. She slid them on the counter, then reached back into the fridge for a head of lettuce. By pulling off the outer leaves, she managed to salvage enough to make salad for two. Not that Michael liked salad. She'd have to open a can of green beans.

By the time dinner was ready, Reesa was too tired to eat it. She made Michael a plate and went to shower. She was tempted to just fall into bed, but where she'd been today called for a shower—a hot one—and a shampoo.

After the shower, she shrugged into her old chenille robe and wrapped a towel around her wet hair, retraced her steps, collected Michael's plate, and put the rest of the food away. After a long look at the dirty dishes, she washed them, too.

When she looked into the den, he was asleep in front of the television.

She tiptoed down the hall to bed and was just drifting off when she remembered that she hadn't called Sarah Hargreave.

Tomorrow she'd take the time to look over Sarah's case, contact Leila's advocate, talk with the adoption caseworker, see what things were really going on. She was no longer Leila's official caseworker. Since Leila was in the process of being adopted, she'd been assigned a different permanency caseworker.

That was good in a way because Reesa and Sarah and Sarah's friend, Karen, had become friends. Something that was frowned on in the system. Too hard to make professional unbiased decisions about a friend.

She didn't know this new caseworker very well, and she didn't want to step on any toes, but she did want to make sure he was dotting his *i*'s and crossing his *t*'s.

It was crazy. Reesa was up to her eyeballs in cases. She'd pulled the White case because she was the closest one to the emergency call. That meant she'd probably be handed the paperwork on it. The children would most likely go straight to permanent fostering. And their mother and whoever the man was would be serving time, for quite a while.

She'd probably be called to testify. When all she wanted was to forget. After the ambulance had left and the mother was handcuffed and led away, one officer remained while she took photos of the apartment, the fire hazard that was supposed to be a kitchen, the drugs. The bed and crib where the children had slept. She'd left a written notice that the children had been removed by the Child Protection and Permanency Office.

On her way to the hospital, she'd had to pull her car to the side of the street to throw up on the pavement.

Next she had gone to the emergency room, where she walked into a scene of shouting and hitting. Pete was hysterical and lashing out. He believed they were stealing his brothers; he couldn't be quieted and they wouldn't sedate him until they'd done an initial examination. So it fell to Reesa to tell him the truth.

Truth? What was the truth? That your mother was so strung out that she didn't bother to take care of you. That she'd let you die before she'd give up her drugs? That was the truth, but she didn't have the heart to tell him so. She told him everything would be all right. They both knew she was lying.

Once he and his brothers were admitted, Reesa had gone back to the office to file her report. She would have to justify removing the children without a court order. She was pretty sure she had justification. She certainly wouldn't lose sleep over her decision.

She punched her pillow and closed her eyes trying to recreate the wonderful feeling she'd had on Monday seeing Jamie and Joy Valenti reunited to their family. Sometimes the system did work. Mr. Valenti had a new job, and family services had helped them find an affordable apartment. With a little luck . . .

That's what she was thinking of when her eyes grew heavy.

But she fell asleep on the images of that comatose baby, his brother too weak to move as he slowly starved. Pete and his loaf of bread. And the hysterical woman who kept screaming "don't take my babies."

But tomorrow . . . tomorrow she would be back at the office. And tomorrow she would make certain that nothing bad happened to Leila Rodrigues.

IT WAS ALMOST eight o'clock by the time Sarah stopped the car back at her bungalow. Leila had fallen asleep practically before they were out of the Wolcotts' driveway.

It had been a fun evening, and she'd managed to take her mind off her coming battle for a few hours. And now she had clock repairs to do. Hopefully by the time she went to bed, she'd be tired enough to sleep.

She put Leila to bed, then went onto the back porch that she used as a secondary workshop. It was enclosed but not weatherproofed, which made it pretty hot in the summer and impossible to use during the winter. But since Leila was going to a preschool day-care program five days a week in the summer, Sarah did most of her work in the back of the shop.

Their schedule worked well; it gave Sarah time for the shop while Leila played catch-up to the other kids, still leaving enough mother-daughter time in the afternoons and evenings. Sarah had been very encouraged by Leila's last evaluations. Now if they just didn't have a major setback.

As soon as she sat down at her workbench, anxiety fell away. Clocks had a way of doing that. Steadying the pulse, driving out the fears with their quiet repetition.

Tonight she was working on a black mantel clock that had belonged to the parlor of a Victorian house from the neighborhood. The family was cleaning it out to sell and they'd discovered the clock, wrapped in a sheet and tucked away in a closet. When they brought it in, the inner workings had rattled around on the inside.

Sarah told them she would give it her best shot but didn't have much hope. She'd persevered, though, and now it was close to running correctly. Close but still not perfect.

People brought in clocks that were barely recognizable; they found them in attics, or flea markets, or on street curbs. Sometimes they'd tried to fix a clock themselves and couldn't put it back together, or dropped it and shoved it out of sight until they suddenly discovered it again.

Some repairs seemed effortless; others like they were hardly worth the trouble. But Sarah always tried her best. Because they deserved a second chance.

Sometimes she could almost feel Sam's hands lightly over hers, guiding her movements, steadying her touch. Other times, she was all thumbs with springs popping out in all directions, minuscule screws rolling into oblivion.

At those times, no amount of patience, cajoling, or cursing would make a timepiece run again. Those were sad times, something Sarah considered a personal failure. Then she would remember all the times Sam had patiently helped her through a repair. Even when she messed up, he would undo what she had done and say "try again."

She adjusted the task lamp over her head, put on her loupe magnifiers, and settled down to the minutiae of clock repair. Within minutes she was totally absorbed, her hands steady as she worked.

When Sarah finally shut down for the night, it was after midnight. And that's when she realized Reesa hadn't called back.

It was too late to call her. Social workers carried heavy caseloads and got little sleep. Sarah tried to be the exemplary foster family and not bother Reesa unnecessarily. She chuckled at herself. Sarah Hargreave trying to be exemplary . . . in a good way. After all these years she was sometimes still surprised at how her life had turned out.

She was only sorry that Sam hadn't lived to know Leila. He would have made the perfect grandfather. It seemed like Sarah was always losing someone, someplace, some thing.

She mentally smacked herself. That was so much bull. She'd been lucky. So lucky. And she was thankful for every day, even when it wasn't such a great one. Sam had taught her that, too.

Chapter 4

"Reesa Davis on line one, Ms. Cartwright."

Ilona looked at the intercom. A call from Reesa Davis first thing on a Friday morning boded bad news.

"Shall I tell her you'll call her back?"

Ilona waffled. Reesa Davis was known in pro bono circles as the "Warhorse," which was a misnomer if ever there was one. To Ilona a warhorse was a shiny, black, sleek-muscled thoroughbred. Reesa Davis was more of a bulldog, short, squat, tenacious, five feet of chubby middle-aged Italian with permed hair, ill-fitting suits, and boxy shoes.

"I'll take it." Ilona pressed speaker and picked up the brief she'd been reading. "Reesa," she said by way of hello and turned the page while she waited for Reesa to work her way through the niceties before getting to the reason she called.

Ilona picked up a pen and circled a clause in the divorce papers. *Over the husband's dead carcass.*

" . . . already applied for adoption."

Ilona scribbled a counterpoint in the margin.

" . . . talking about reunification."

"Rights terminated?" Ilona asked and struck out two more lines. This guy had a lot of nerve, but nerve wouldn't get him a nickel in the courtroom.

" . . . But now she's changed her mind."

Ilona paused with the pen poised above the brief. "If the kid's in the adoption pipeline, what are you doing on the case? Where's the adoption caseworker?"

"The foster mother and I have become friends . . . once I was off the case. As a friend, I want to make sure nothing's left unturned. I'm asking you as a colleague."

"You think she should have the kid."

"No question."

"Fax over her paperwork, and I'll take a look. I've got to tell you I'm pretty busy these days, my pro bono calendar is beyond heavy."

"Just talk to her, I think you'll like this case."

"Send her file over and make an appointment. Can I assume you'll accompany the foster family?"

"Single mother, but yes."

"Fine."

"Thanks, Ilona. I appreciate it."

"That's what I'm here for." Ilona hung up and tapped the pen on the paragraph she'd just circled. Then she tossed it on the desk and buzzed her secretary. "Mona, get Sid Ferrelli on the phone." She leaned back in her desk chair. Dollars to doughnuts this rat bastard was hiding money somewhere, and she had just the forensic accountant to nail his ass to the wall.

SOONER OR LATER you met every coffee or tea drinker in town at the Ocean Brew. After Sam died and before Leila came, Sarah looked forward to the morning rush just like the people getting coffee there were her best friends. Truth to tell, Sarah didn't make friends easily. It was even harder to keep them. She'd been out of the system for more than ten years, but the barriers she'd erected there had been built to last.

Sarah could be abrasive when she was scared, which these days seemed most of the time; she also could be standoffish if she was concentrating on something or if she wasn't sure of herself.

She stood on the sidewalk outside the Brew and took a couple of deep breaths. She'd walked Leila down to the school bus stop, then had called Danny Noyes, Leila's adoption caseworker.

She left a message for him to call her. Same with the advocate ad litem. Sarah knew they were busy. But it was hard not to feel paranoid, like everyone was avoiding her because they didn't want to give her the bad news. But then Reesa called her, and Sarah was so relieved that she'd agreed to meet her at the Brew before she remembered that everyone she knew would probably be there. Wyatt would be there.

She needed to apologize to him and she planned to, but she didn't relish doing it with half the town watching.

"Coward," she said and pulled the heavy door open.

The Brew was a low ceiling L-shaped coffee bar. The floors, walls, and ceiling were dark stained wood and reminded Sarah of the hold in some nineteenth-century sailing ship. Not that she'd ever been in any kind of ship.

She shivered at the mere thought. Or more likely because it was always overly cold in the coffee bar during the summer, possibly to counteract the steam machines. And the coffee. There was a line at the counter—there usually was in the mornings—but she saw Reesa sitting toward the back, which would give them at least a nod to privacy. Except as soon as Sarah made out Reesa, she saw Wyatt sitting at the table beside her.

Damn.

Reesa held up a cup, letting her know she'd already ordered for Sarah, so there was no way out there. She walked toward the table.

Wyatt stood and picked up his cup. He seemed to fill the space. "Morning, Sarah. I know you and Reesa have business to discuss, so I'll leave you to it."

Sarah opened her mouth, couldn't think of what she wanted to say. Smiled awkwardly. She knew it was awkward because she felt awkward.

"Wyatt," she blurted.

He hesitated, looked at her.

"I'm sorry for . . . yesterday . . . I was upset."

"I know you were. Reesa, good to see you." He nodded and walked over to talk to the two guys who had just bought the cheese shop two stores down.

Sarah stared after him, then she sat down. "Do you think he knows that was me apologizing?"

"Probably," said Reesa. "But you might want to do it more formally when there is less of an audience."

Sarah nodded. She didn't get why anyone would like her. She'd never learned grace or finesse. She was prickly when she felt insecure, outspoken when she was angry, and had way too many knee-jerk reactions.

It had been different when Sam was alive, but now that

he was gone, it seemed like she was regressing to those days when she had to protect herself every second. And that just made her doubly nervous that she would blow the chance of keeping Leila. Which made her even more prickly . . . which made her—

"Sarah?"

Sarah jumped, almost upsetting her mug. "Sorry. So did you find out anything?"

Reesa wiped the foam off her mouth. She was wearing a light gray suit with a white blouse. Completely out of sync with the shorts and T-shirts, cover-ups, and trendy beachwear of the other patrons.

She pushed her coffee mug to the side, leaned over to get something from the briefcase Sarah knew must be sitting on the floor by her chair. And returned with a manila folder that she dropped onto the table and opened to the first page.

"First things first. I talked to Ilona Cartwright. She's agreed to meet with us; this doesn't mean she'll take the case, but even if she doesn't, she will have some advice. We're meeting her first thing Monday morning, so if you have to make arrangements, do so. We won't get a second chance."

Sarah nodded. She took a breath, then another for good luck. "You make it sound like she might not be interested."

"She'll have to review the case, but this is right up her alley. She spends most of her time pleading cases for people who are just out to get as much from the other person as possible, but giving children a good home is her passion." Reesa frowned.

"What?" Sarah asked suddenly insecure. "You don't think I'll make Leila a good home."

"Oh, for heaven's sake, yes I do. I was just thinking that passion is an odd word in connection to Ms. Cartwright. She's as cold as a Subzero freezer and yet . . . anyway, she's the best and though she's overscheduled, she'll take a look. Monday morning 9:00. Bring all the documentation you have."

"Boxes," Sarah said, slightly embarrassed.

Reesa smiled. Sarah noticed that she looked tired and pale; maybe it was the suit. "Bring the docs from Leila's last two visits to Carmen, how she was before she left, how she was when she returned."

Sarah shuddered.

"And her social and educational milestones."

"Hey, we had a cookout at Karen and Stu's last night. We should have called you, but it was impromptu."

"Thanks, but I couldn't have made it."

"Bad day? I forgot to ask about the kids you were removing."

"You don't want to know. You just worry about your case. And get Danny Noyes in the loop. We won't need him on Monday, but he needs to stay on his toes. I'll try to keep in touch with him, but every summer, my caseloads go through the roof. The heat I guess."

Reesa turned a piece of legal paper toward Sarah. "I've written out some questions I think you should be prepared to answer. In case she asks. She's pretty intimidating, and even though she works for the weak, she doesn't like a show of weakness."

"You trust her?"

"Trust? Trust doesn't really come into it. She likes to win. And she knows how to adapt to every legal situation I've seen her in. Just do what she tells you. And, Sarah, don't be combative."

Sarah circled her cup on the table. "Don't show weakness but don't be combative. Right."

Reesa laughed. "What can I say? But seriously, she needs to

do some yoga or something. And so do you. Do not let this situation get to you, because if it gets to you, it will get to Leila and make whatever happens just that much harder."

"I won't let them—"

"If you're serious about this working out in Leila's and your favor, then you'll chill out. It doesn't do anything but screw things up when you worry about stuff that is out of your hands. We may not even need a lawyer. But best to be prepared. Dress professionally. And go apologize to Wyatt."

Reesa looked at her watch. "Damn." She gulped down the rest of her coffee, leaving a mustache of foam on her lip that she quickly licked away. "Got to be at Probate in twenty minutes. Here's the address for the law office; meet me there at quarter to nine." She gathered up the papers except for the one she handed to Sarah and slid them back in her briefcase. "You have someone to keep Leila?"

"I'll ask Karen or I can ask Alice to come in early and keep her at the store, though she doesn't like to do that. Leila is a bit of a handful."

"You could ask Wyatt; I'm sure he could manage the store and Leila without any problem. If you'd let him."

"Karen already gave me the lecture. I'm trying. I'm going to try again. If he isn't fed up by now."

"Good. We could all use a good man now and then. Monday, don't be late." She hurried out of the coffee shop.

Sarah thought she had just missed something. Reesa never talked about men. She hardly ever even talked about her husband, Michael.

Sarah finished her tea. Stopped by a table to say hello to the owner of the antique shop, then stepped out into the morning sun.

She meant to stop by Dive Works and do take two of her apology attempt. But when she got to the corner and looked two doors down, Wyatt was standing outside talking to a blond surfer chick. He leaned against the doorjamb and laughed. She tossed her hair. Then he pushed the door open and followed her inside.

Sarah changed her mind about the apology. No way could she compete with a blond, tanned, athletic cutie.

And he had been flirting. Sarah stepped off the curb, amazed how her mind was bouncing all over the place today. Places it never went. Places it didn't want to go. Places she couldn't afford to let it go. She had a business to run and a child to protect, and nothing else was worth getting derailed for.

She glanced back at the store, then crossed the street corner to Clocks by the Sea. The day she first stepped into the store, she had laughed at the stupid name. She wasn't even sure why she'd gone inside, except maybe she thought it would be easy to help herself to some contraband. Sarah still laughed at herself and her dismay to find everything safely locked behind glass, out of reach, or too big to carry.

She could remember her initial disappointment. Because the old dude who sat behind the counter was the perfect stooge. He looked like some character from a fairy tale. White hair, kind face, dressed in a button-up sweater and a tie for crissakes.

He looked up, their eyes met. And she knew he knew. She started to back away and he said, "So you like clocks?" She told him the name was dorky, made gagging noises at the prissy Victorian woodwork detailed in green, lavender, and blue.

When he died and the store became hers, she didn't change

the name or the color scheme. And she never would. It was a family business, and she was family.

She'd made a few changes over the years after Sam died. She carried more retail merchandise these days and had moved all the repairs to the back room or to the converted space at the cottage. She could use more space, but space was a rare commodity in the old town. If you wanted space, you went out to the highway.

She would make do with what she had.

Once inside, Sarah began dusting as she did each day before the store opened, starting with the display cases and moving to the mantel clocks, the wall clocks, then the grandfathers and grandmothers, her feather duster moving in counterrhythm to the pervading ticks and tocks of the clocks.

At ten o'clock when the first cuckoo began to chirp the hour, she unlocked the door. By the time the others had joined in, Sarah was sitting behind the counter and Alice Millburn was coming through the door.

Alice was a retired librarian who didn't really care about clocks but was a great counter fixture. Pleasant as long as she could sit and knowledgeable enough to call Sarah from the back room when there was a question she couldn't answer. And she didn't mind Sarah's occasional need to leave Leila with her when no one else was available.

"It's supposed to be a nice weekend," Alice announced in her quiet librarian's voice. "We should hope so. No one wants to buy a clock in the rain."

"Hope so," Sarah said, answering the good part and ignoring the pronouncement of doom, which was the only real downside of Alice; she did love her pronouncements of doom.

"Well, I'd better get to the work on the Kelly's ormolu. They want it by next week and the parts have just come in." Sarah started toward the back. "Oh, and can you open for me on Monday? I have an appointment."

"Oh, dear. Nothing wrong, I hope."

Not as much as Sarah hoped. "There's a glitch in the adoption process, so we may have to go back to court."

"Oh dear." Alice shook her head. *Already imagining the worst,* Sarah thought.

Sarah smiled, and escaping the sympathetic look she knew would follow, she strode into the back room.

She set her alarm and worked for almost four hours, not taking a break, not making a cup of tea, just working, losing herself in the intricate inner workings of the clocks.

When the alarm went off, Sarah was more than ready to take a break and feeling a real need to see Leila. She was waiting at the bus stop when the day-care minibus pulled up. The automated stop sign stopped traffic to each side and the bus doors opened.

The driver held Leila's hand as she waited for Sarah to lift her off the step. In addition to her backpack, she was carrying a rolled-up piece of brown paper.

"I'm big, Mommee," she said. "Wait till you see." She rattled the tube of paper at Sarah, knocking it against her head in her excitement.

"Well, let's go see, then." They waved good-bye to the bus driver and started down the street, Leila chattering about lying on the floor and Mrs. Lester drawing all around her.

"We got to pick our marker. I chose pink."

"Of course you did."

As soon as they were home, Sarah unrolled the life-size outline, while Leila jumped around and clapped and acted like a kid. Sarah said a prayer that it would last. She'd decided not to mention the ordered visit until after the weekend. That would be long enough to "prepare the child for visitation." No reason for both of them to be freaked out for the next few days.

They pinned down each corner of the rolled paper with a book. *Where the Wild Things Are* at the top right by Leila's raised hand, *Hannah's Night* at the right foot, a much taped and re-taped copy of *Wuggie Norple* at the top left, and *Marisol McDonald Doesn't Match* at the last corner.

As soon as it was finished, Leila started to climb on the paper, but stopped herself and sat on the floor. "Shoes off first."

"Right," Sarah agreed. "Shoes might tear it."

Leila frowned. "It might tear."

"It might," Sarah agreed solemnly. "So it's a good thing we have lots and lots of tape to fix it again."

She helped Leila to scoot onto the paper and align herself within the pink lines.

"Ta dah!" Sarah exclaimed. She refused to feel sad, or scared, or anxious. *Fix the now.* She looked heavenward like a baseball player after a home run. She wasn't sure there really was a heaven, but if there was, she knew that's where Sam would be.

"In fact, if we tape it to your closet door, you can see how much you grow."

They carefully removed the books, rolled the paper up, and carried it into the small bedroom that had once been Sarah's.

"We'll have to move Elsa over."

"That's okay."

Leila stood very close, breathing hard with concentration

while Sarah carefully removed the tape from the Elsa *Frozen* poster and repositioned it on the wall next to the *Beauty and the Beast* poster.

Then aligning the feet close to the floor, she taped the Leila outline to the door. Leila stepped in front of it, twisted her body around trying to fit her arm in the raised outline. It took some tries, but at last she was satisfied.

"Take my selfie, Mommee."

Sarah pulled her phone from her pocket and took Leila's picture. Selfies were a great way to document progress, failures, and just plain fun.

Sarah took the rest of the afternoon off, content to let Alice watch the store while she played with Leila. She kept reminding herself not to be too clingy, not to let the panic that rushed up her at unsuspecting times flow out onto her daughter. And soon they both fell into the calm brought by comfort and structure and love.

At six her cell phone jarred her from that total calm. It was Danny Noyes, Leila's adoption caseworker. Holding on to her shred of hope that it had all been a big mistake, Sarah carried the phone into her bedroom and answered the call.

"Sarah. Did you get the papers from the court?"

"Yes."

"I wanted to touch base with you before they came in, but my caseload is into the next state."

"I know, Mr. Noyes. How did this happen?"

"As you know, it's our purpose to whenever possible reunite—"

"No offense, Mr. Noyes, but can we please cut to the chase. I've been in the system longer than you have and I know what this means, someone f— screwed up."

"No, no, it's not like that. Ms. Delgado has been out of rehab for six weeks now."

"This stint."

"Yes, this stint. But you must realize these things sometimes take more than one try."

"Mr. Noyes, my mother died after one of her many 'stints' at rehab. I was eleven and had already been in the system for almost three years. My mother made the right choice in giving me up. If she'd done it earlier, I might have had a better chance of being adopted into a normal family like Leila has."

"Yes, I sympathize, but Ms. Delgado has a new apartment now, and she's looking for a job. She's tested clean for the last six weeks and now insists that she was coerced into signing her parental rights away."

"This was not done in a vacuum, Mr. Noyes. Several people were present, both caseworkers as well as the judge. I hope the department isn't accusing Judge Beckman of coercion." *Stop it, Sarah. Don't be adversarial. Be sympathetic.*

"Of course not, but Ms. Delgado claims her attorney didn't fully explain the meaning of termination of rights. The court feels that we need to revisit the case to ensure we're all on the same page."

Well, we're not, she wanted to say. *There has never been a same page. Carmen is a career crackhead. Pimped by her latest boyfriend and now out to make a few extra bucks off the government.* But Sarah couldn't say that. It would make her look belligerent, and they were all supposed to be so willing to work together.

Sarah knew the drill. She'd given Carmen the benefit of the doubt, twice now. It had been a disaster for Leila and for her—even for Carmen.

"To that purpose . . ."

Here it came. She couldn't stop it. Just couldn't stop it.

"We need to schedule a supervised visit. She wanted a full weekend visit, but we nixed that."

"Thank you."

"I'd hoped to schedule a visit for this weekend."

Before Carmen falls off the sober wagon?

"But I didn't hear from you."

Sarah willed herself to stay calm. "I just received the notification. You probably knew before I did."

"Well, yes, I suppose. How does this coming week look for you?"

Looks like it's going to be hellish with a major chance of setback.

"I'll need time to prepare Leila for the . . ." She'd started to say *disruption in her schedule.* Caught herself at the last second. *Do not be adversarial.* These people are doing what they think is best. Sure, but seeing it from the outside was a whole lot different from feeling it from the other side. " . . . for the visit. Not this weekend. We have plans."

It was the craft fair weekend. Sarah wouldn't be participating; no way was she going to lug antique clocks outside to subject them to the weather and sticky fingers, both sugar and theft-wise. But there would be children's activities and the beach all weekend, and Sarah wouldn't go into the store at all on Sunday.

"Ms. Delgado is available Wednesday after her AA meeting."

"It will have to be after three o'clock, Leila isn't back from school until then."

"Shall we say three then at family services? Room 102. I can pick Leila up and bring her back."

"That won't be necessary. I'll bring her and wait."

"Actually, it would be better if I pick her up."

"Fine." Sarah knew the drill and the psychology. Stay home so that the child knows she will have a place to return to. *Don't blow this because of your own stubbornness.* "Thank you. She'll be ready. See you on Wednesday."

"We really do have the child's best interest at heart."

"Of course you do. And I really appreciate your effort on our behalf."

"Well, then until Wednesday." They said good-byes, very civilized. Sarah hung up, barely resisting the urge to throw the phone across the room. She knew they were doing the best they could with the resources they had—not enough—for more children than they could place, with demands from all sides. Too many files, not enough money, not enough sleep, not enough people who cared. But that didn't make it okay for a kid to fall through the cracks. Not now, not then, not ever.

Dear Nonie

I don't guess you're ever gonna write me back. But in case you read this I just wanted to tell you that my mama died. They came to tell me yesterday. I didn't go to the funeral or anything. Because by the time the system found me she was already buried.

I asked how she died.

They just looked at me all sympathetic. They didn't have to tell me. She died like all users die. I guess I should be sad. Or maybe even happy to know I won't ever have to go back there, not that group home is much better.

I don't mind. The last place didn't work out. Surprise,

*huh? I made sure they got my new address in case you get a
mind to write.*

*Doesn't matter, I guess. I write you even when I don't send
the letter. I think someday you might change your mind and
want to hear from me. I still want to hear from you.*

Well, that's all for now.

Your sister,
Sarah

Chapter 5

Reesa stood at the kitchen sink drinking her first cup of morning coffee and wondering why a garden took so many hours and years of work when nature only took a few weeks to obliterate it.

There had been a day when she would have rushed out first thing on a Saturday morning. Early with the sun and the birds, to hoe and weed and pick the week's anxieties away. It had been great therapy. She could also remember why she had quit.

She drained her mug, put it in the dishwasher, and picked up her briefcase.

Saturday. A day for family, for gardening, for hanging out at the beach. She would be hanging out at the branch office trying to catch up on her paperwork and praying no removals came in that she would have to try to place on a weekend.

"Later," she called to Michael, who had just taken the

morning paper and a bowl of cereal into the family room. She
was almost to the front door before the television began blaring
the sports news.

She walked out the front door, turned around to lock it,
though she didn't know why she bothered; she lived in a safe
neighborhood. Down the front steps, where rosebushes used to
grow, the rhododendrons that had replaced them several years
earlier had begun to straggle. How could you kill a rhododen-
dron? They grew in the wild.

Trying to ignore the feeling that the bushes were an indictment of her life, Reesa walked to the curb, threw her overstuffed
briefcase onto the passenger seat, and climbed in after it.

What had happened to her?

While she was out saving the world, she'd lost herself.

At the Child Protection and Permanency field office, she
parked between a beige Honda and a gray Chevy truck and
went inside. There was always someone working in the Main
Street CP&P office. And it wasn't always the most dedicated
workers. Today two of the newer recruits, fresh faced and clueless, were plugged into their tablets, most likely playing games
or gambling, while they waited for any emergency placements
to come in. Eddie Quinones was sitting at his desk behind a
stack of folders eating a bagel and drinking coffee from a cardboard cup.

Reesa should have stopped for another cup, herself. Actually there was no reason not to go out and get one, except that
her legs felt like lead this morning. What she should be doing
was not cruising Eddie's bagel but running in the park.

"Ha," she said, laughing out loud. Eddie looked up; the two
recruits were oblivious.

"And you find something in this office to laugh about?"

"No, just imagining me in a spandex running suit."

Eddie's eyebrows flew almost to his bald head. "Not really your look, hon."

"Don't I know it," Reesa said, as she slipped out of her faded track jacket and hung it over the back of her chair.

She sat at her desk and booted up the clunker of a computer she'd inherited from an unused cubicle when hers had crapped out five years earlier. While she waited for it to come to life, she called the hospital.

The White boys were still hospitalized. She learned that on the second transfer. But it took three more transfers and a threat to come to the hospital with a police escort before she could find someone who had the authority to give her an update on the boys' conditions. The baby had been moved to an NICU in another hospital. Pete was stable, but there was possible kidney damage in the younger one, Jerome.

Damn, he wouldn't have a chance if he had to be on dialysis for the rest of his life.

Reesa pushed down the anger that even years of futility hadn't quite quenched. That anger, more than anything, was what kept her going.

She pulled their file to the top. Unless a responsible relative came forward willing to take both the older boys and the baby, Reesa was going to advise they be put directly on a permanency track. Maybe even if a relative did show up. In a better world, they would have a family who would take and love the boys, a family who would already have realized they were in jeopardy and done something to fix it. Hell, in the best of worlds, they would be at home with their loving parents.

And Reesa would be out of a job, and that would be fine with her.

There were hundreds of things Reesa could do if she had the time, the money, the energy. Child services ran her dry, beat her down. And just when she thought she would hang it up and quit, a child found a good home, she saved a life—or she'd lose one—and then she knew she couldn't give it up. She just couldn't.

That's when anger kept her going.

ILONA WIPED THE sweat from her brow with her wristband. It was time to put this baby away. She concentrated her energy, bounced the tennis ball a couple of times. Good. She liked the feel of it. She touched it to her racket and in one smooth move smashed the ball into the opposite court.

"Let."

Damn. She pulled the second ball out of her pocket; she hadn't thought she'd need it. Let it fly; the serve was softer, not as powerful. Not as much fun. But it did the trick. Garrett Dunne managed to return it, barely, and she whizzed a passing shot right past his ear. All he could do was grumble.

"Man, you're vicious today," he said, dropping onto the bench where their tennis bags and water bottles were stored.

Ilona laughed. "You're just getting soft. All that politicking to make district attorney."

"I'm in shape." He rubbed his face with a pristine white towel and tossed it on his bag. "What say we clean up and meet in the club bar for a drink?"

Ilona looked at her watch. It was a habit not a ploy. She had nothing to do tonight but go home and read some briefs.

"Sure, a quick one."

"Or two."

"One, I have work at home. Twenty minutes?"

"Do you ever take time off?" Garrett asked.

"Of course, I'm taking time off now."

It didn't take Ilona twenty minutes to look her after-tennis best. It was one of the many things she'd learned from her parents. Always look your best. No holey socks for Ilona Cartwright. No shirttails sticking out. The message was clear. *Don't let anyone see who you really are.*

She walked out of the women's locker room, showered, refreshed, hair just as relaxed and straight as when she'd stepped into the shower. Was she a little overdressed for tennis? White linen slacks, silk tee. Not at all. She hadn't joined the most prestigious country club in the county to dress like a slob.

But she also made sure it didn't look like she tried too hard. Being one of the few black women members, even with skin as light as hers, she made a point of being casually perfect.

Ilona beat Garrett to the bar and took a table on the veranda where there was a hint of a breeze and shelter from the worst of the sun.

She saw a few people she knew. None of whom she really cared about seeing. If they wanted to say hello, they would wander over sooner or later. She shoved away the little niggle of doubt she'd never been able to completely erase. That one day, they might snub her, deride her, might see her for what she really was.

Dear Sarah,

I thought it was going to be nice here. It's beautiful and has a big yard, and a swimming pool and everything. But it isn't very nice. I don't think they'd like you. I'm pretty sure they don't like me.

Remember that movie we saw where the aliens had taken over all the women in town. That was funny. Remember. We laughed till we almost pissed ourselves. But I have to remember not to say words like piss. Well, it isn't funny. I think Mrs. Cartwright is one of them.

She tells me to call her Mom.

I call her Mother instead. She just smiles and it scares me. They don't do anything mean to me. Mostly they don't even pay that much attention to me except to tell me what to do and how to act, especially "in public."

And I do it. Because I've been to places before and I don't want to go back. I hope you don't end up in one of those places. The kind where they tell you how to act and then they hurt you. The Cartwrights don't hurt me, not in any way you can tell. Only in my heart, but nobody can see that.

And it is cushy living here. I just wished they'd love me.

I don't know why they didn't adopt you. At least you're white.

Anyway. It won't be any good you coming here. I'm going to stay if I can. I can get an education here. They're some kind of important people. I'm going to get everything I can from them. Then one day I'll come find you and you won't have to worry about where you're going to live ever again.

Why haven't you written to me?

Your sister,
Nonie

"Did you order anything yet?" Garrett asked, pulling out a chair and sitting down next to her.

Ilona shook her head, momentarily speechless from the unexpected memory. Garrett raised his hand. A waiter appeared at their table. "Gin and tonic with a twist," Ilona said.

"I'll have the same," Garrett said. "Actually," he said, leaning closer as the waiter left to get their drinks, "I'd kill for an icy Bud Light right out of the bottle. But the bad taste brigade would blackball me from the veranda bar."

Ilona laughed. They were all hiding something.

Their drinks came, and Ilona's mind began to wander to her divorce case. The problem with socializing with lawyers was that you could never discuss your work. And she didn't really think Garrett wanted to hear what the latest interior designer had charged her for the brilliant idea of putting a few colorful pillows around the living room to make it "pop."

Ilona felt like popping the designer, but she signed the check and smiled and maneuvered the woman toward the door, while she thought, *Next time I'm hiring a man, and don't have anyone call me for a reference.*

"Oh shit," Garrett said, drawing her attention back.

"What? Are you just realizing that I beat your socks off?"

"No," he said smiling, his glass half raised to his lips. "Your ex just came in, and with the new wife."

"He never comes to the club on Saturday. Saturday is for sailing or polo. Sunday's the club for brunch, Wednesday for tennis."

"Well, he's here today." His smile broadened and he lifted his chin. "He's seen us and he's headed this way."

Ilona shrugged. "And we were having such a lovely time."

"And there's more," he mumbled before he half stood and shook hands. "Kevin," he said in his most jovial voice. "Where you been keeping yourself?"

"Busy," Ilona's ex-husband said.

Kevin Morrissey Blake had been handpicked by her parents. The wedding had been overrun with dignitaries, the dress cost thirty K, and the marriage lasted all of three years.

Ilona didn't wish it back. She wasn't sure she even liked him. Tall, blond, decent enough to look at. A man who knew what he wanted and went after it. And what he wanted was a political career, and the way he went after it was to woo Ilona and then her father.

He still had her father, and he was welcome to him. They were welcome to each other.

She fortified her smile and turned to say hello. But her gaze went right past Kevin's beaming face to his new blond wife. The bitch was pregnant. He'd come to gloat.

But Ilona had spent the last ten years in a courtroom, and she wasn't about to fall for this little piece of malice aforethought. "Why, look at you," she said enthusiastically. "As round as a tomato."

She rubbed the model-thin trophy wife's baby bump.

The woman, whose name Ilona had conveniently forgotten, blushed, smiled up at Kevin for support. Ilona could have told her that was useless; he was watching Ilona, his head tilted slightly, trying to figure out what she was thinking. He would never get it.

"So good to see you two," she continued, like they were all best buds.

Kevin woke up. "Have you seen your parents lately?"

Nice segue, Kev. Ilona's smile stayed securely in place. "Not lately. I'm up to my ears in cases."

"I saw them the other day. I didn't think your mom looked too good. Is she ill?"

Ilona had no idea. They only spoke in public, and they were rarely in public at the same time. Ilona made sure of that. "A little tired; she just got off the garden club circuit. You know how exhausting these house tours can be."

"Well, we'd better get going. Meeting some people for drinks."

Ilona smiled. "Orange juice for you, little mama." She gave the baby bump one more rub. And the couple left.

"Hell, girl, you are lethal. You were rubbing that tummy like you thought a genie might pop out."

Ilona laughed. "And wouldn't that have been something for the veranda staff to talk about. We'd all be blackballed for sure. I think I'll have that second gin and tonic."

Garrett expelled a breath. "I'm going straight for the Bud in a bottle."

REESA DECIDED SHE would knock off and go home at three, but at five till, one of the field caseworkers showed up with a boy, about thirteen, dirty and obese. The caseworker, whose name she remembered was Dominic, looked like he'd had the worst time of it. His shirt was torn, and there was dirt of some kind Reesa chose not to observe too closely on his cheek and hands. As soon as he released the kid, the kid bolted for the door, but he slipped on something, probably whatever was stuck to his shoe, and slammed into a file cabinet.

The caseworker closed his eyes. "Eddie, help me out here."

"I'm not on duty, get Heckle or Jeckle to help you, that's what they're here for." Eddie swiveled his chair so that his back was to Dominic.

Travis, who Eddie usually called Thing One, looked up from his tablet. "Is he talking about us?"

"Yep," Eddie said, not turning around.

"What did you call us?"

"Heckle and Jeckle."

"Who are they?" Thing Two, real name Carl, asked.

Eddie groaned and slid down in his chair until only the bald spot showed over the back.

"Make some calls," Reesa told them. She walked over to the boy. "Hey, I'm Mrs. Davis. What's your name?"

He looked at the ground.

"Would you like to use the bathroom to clean up?"

A minute nod of his head.

"Good. Mr. Hawes will show you where it is."

"And Mr. Hawes will clean up a little himself," Dominic said. "Travis, you can come help out."

Reesa smiled encouragingly. This is not what they thought their job would be back in whatever college they graduated from. She just hoped they stuck around long enough to do some good.

Travis reluctantly followed the other two. Carl waited expectantly.

"You start on the emergency families," Reesa said. "I'll call the group homes."

Fortunately they hit pay dirt with the second group home. They had one bed. Reesa claimed it and sent Dominic, Travis, and the kid over with the paperwork.

Reesa said good night to Eddie who hadn't turned back around and was probably sleeping. The night shift would be coming on soon. Carl could handle things until then.

She considered stopping by the grocery, but she didn't feel like cooking. She'd order out, Greek maybe. Maybe she could convince Michael to get up and go out to the diner or the pub. But who was she kidding; he never wanted to go anywhere.

As she drove home she considered calling Karen or Sarah to see what they were doing. She knew they'd be glad to have her. But Karen had her family, and hopefully Sarah had managed to apologize to Wyatt and would be with him tonight.

Reesa wished she could tell Sarah to just let Wyatt help her. So what if it didn't last forever? But Reesa had been around foster kids long enough to know they very rarely came out unscathed. Sarah hadn't. And she still had serious trust issues. Probably always would. But she was one of the lucky ones.

She had stumbled into a miracle named Sam Gianetti. Reesa had never met him, but she wished she had a hundred more of him to pass around.

As soon as she opened the house door, she heard the ball game. She dropped her keys on the hall table, left her briefcase next to it, and made her way back to the kitchen.

"I'm home," she called into the family room.

A grunt from Michael.

She went into the kitchen for a glass of water. There was an open pizza box on the table. Three pieces were gone, and the rest was a hardened mess. But Reesa was suddenly ravenous. She pulled off a triangle. Took a bite. Spit it out and tossed it back into the box.

"How long has this pizza been here?" she called.

"Lunch."

"You want to go out for dinner?"

"The game's on."

She closed the box, folded it over, and pushed it into the trash can. She sat down at the table and rested her forehead on the heels of her hands.

Her stomach growled. It looked like it would be a can of soup for her tonight.

She opened the cabinet, then changed her mind, went into the hall and opened the closet door. There was a bottle of peach schnapps her sister-in-law had given them for Christmas. She'd never opened it.

But schnapps over ice sounded like a good thing. She stood on tiptoe and worked it off the shelf. Maybe she'd just forgo the soup and really drink her dinner tonight. She'd just returned to the kitchen when she heard the front door open.

"Ma."

"Back here, Tony." At twenty, Tony was her baby. The only one of her children who actually lived nearby. Michael Junior had stayed in Chicago once he graduated from business school, and Evelyn was a stewardess and flew out of Philly.

He came into the kitchen. "Ma, what are you doing sitting in the dark?"

Reesa looked up. "It isn't really dark. It's just that the tree needs trimming. It blocks out the light."

"You look tired."

Reesa noticed he didn't offer to come trim it. "Rough week."

He pulled his hand from behind his back. "Brought you these." He presented a bouquet of roses. The fact that she'd seen bouquets just like them being sold by the guy who accosted drivers when they stopped at the light on Main Street made no difference.

"They're beautiful," she said and took them. "I'll get a vase. Go say hello to your father."

"His Highness still on his butt in the family room?"

She nodded. "He just can't seem to get motivated. Go say hi."

He strode off down the hall. He was back before she finished putting the roses in the vase.

"Is he just going to sit there until he croaks?" Tony said. "He'd better get over his leg not being perfect, and go find some other kind of work."

"I've tried. He's just not interested. I lined up a headhunter, even a therapist, you know, for depression. But he refuses to go. What am I supposed to do?"

"You're supposed to be the great mom you are and enjoy these roses. Then next spring or summer or whenever, we'll plant new rosebushes. How's that?"

"Sounds good." He'd said the same thing last year, but there had never been enough time. "How's work at the garage?"

"Same old, same old. Though we did have a beauty of a Chrysler come in the other day. Nineteen ninety-four. Old man Diggins. Remember him? It's been sitting in his garage for the last ten years doing nothing. Now he wants to sell it."

"Does it even work?"

"It will when we finish with it. If I had the money, I'd buy it myself."

Reesa laughed. "For the purpose of?"

"No purpose at all, just for the heck of it. Well, I've got to run. Meeting some of the guys for a serious night of beer and bowling."

"You good for money?"

"Yep." He leaned over the table and kissed her cheek. "Love you, Ma."

"Love you, too." She walked him to the door.

Reesa locked it after he left, then went back to the kitchen. The schnapps bottle still sat on the table. What was she thinking? She didn't want to sit alone in her kitchen drinking schnapps. Maybe next Christmas she'd invite some people over, have a party. Christmas was a good time for schnapps. She carried it back to the closet and pushed it back onto the shelf.

Tonight she was going to the beach.

SARAH CLOSED UP the shop at six. The craft fair had drawn a lot of customers away from the main business fare. She didn't have anything out on the sidewalk, so it was pretty much the quiet day she'd expected.

Instead of stopping at home, she walked the block and a half to the beach where she'd promised to meet Karen and the kids. Jenny had picked up Leila after lunch, and Leila was probably tired and cranky by now. With the kiddie fair and the food and the beach, Sarah doubted if they'd made it back to the house for a nap.

That was okay. Sarah never went into the store on Sundays. Tomorrow they would take it easy and stay at home. And then Sarah would have to tell Leila that she had to visit Carmen.

If she were honest, she was not just afraid of upsetting Leila. There was a tiny part of her that was terrified Carmen would stay off drugs this time, that Leila would go back and want to stay with her. And Sarah should be happy if that happened. Children belonged with their real parents. Social services were always saying that, how it was important to reunify the family.

Sarah knew that, but she was selfish. And she knew that, too. What would she do if they sent Leila back? She wouldn't think about it. Just let it play out. *Fix the now.*

The beach was still crowded though people were beginning to pack up their gear and trudge back to the street and their cars or bikes. She caught sight of Karen's umbrella, green with big pink polka dots that one of her foster care class members had given her as a thank-you.

Sarah stopped to take off her shoes and roll up her pants even though she didn't plan on getting wet. Over the years Sam had taught her to love the beach, appreciate the ocean, but he'd never been able to convince her to learn to swim.

Karen was sitting in a chair beneath the umbrella. A big straw hat hid her face. Her legs were stretched out in front of her, and she held a bottle of iced tea.

Next to her, Reesa Davis, dressed in gingham clam diggers and a white peasant blouse, cradled a bag of potato chips.

There was one vacant beach chair. Sarah looked out at the sand and found Stu, stretched out on a towel, a paperback open beside him, its pages fluttering with each breeze.

Karen lifted the brim of her hat. "Hey, girlfriend. Are you going to sit down or are you just gonna stand their ogling the hunky lifeguard playing with the girls?"

"I'm going to sit, but actually I was looking at your hunky husband."

"Sure you were."

Sarah sat in the empty chair. "Hi, Reesa. Haven't seen you at the beach for a while."

"Been busy, but I'm turning over a new leaf." Reesa crunched down on a chip hard enough for pieces to explode down her blouse.

"She's having a rough week," Karen said. "So we have to be nice to her."

Reesa reached in the bag and threw a chip at her. It landed on Karen's lap and Karen popped it in her mouth, then reached over and helped herself to more chips.

"Hope it wasn't because of me and Leila."

"Not at all," Reesa said. "You are officially no longer my headache. Now I just care about you because you're my friend. And before you ask, because I know you're dying to, Leila was fine when she saw me. A little wary until she remembered that I no longer have the dubious pleasure of taking her to parental visits and psychology appointments. We're good."

"And the girls are over there practicing for the sand castle competition," Karen added.

Sarah followed a trail of colorful shovels, pails, and containers to where Leila, Bessie, and Tammy were building a sprawling, lopsided sand castle with the help of Jenny and—"Is that Wyatt? I thought you were kidding about the hunky lifeguard."

"It's really Wyatt. I guess they were shorthanded today. So they hit the rescue team for volunteers. Rory nabbed him as he was coming off his shift and begged him to throw the Frisbee. Then the girls stole him from Rory who went off with his friend Billy. See what you miss when you work all day? He and Leila are getting along famously."

"I'll say."

Wyatt was sitting cross-legged next to Leila. He looked good even with his back to her: tanned broad shoulders, that nearly black hair. He excited Sarah and calmed her at the same time. And Leila seemed perfectly fine with him, without Sarah even being there. You just never knew.

As she watched, Leila poured a shovelful of dirt onto his bare knee. Wyatt turned to her and must have made a funny face, because Leila squealed then started giggling.

"See? Fine?"

Sarah bit her lip. "Everybody's fine, but me."

"Pretty much. And you'd be fine if you'd just let yourself be."

"I know. Sam used to always say that."

"And you listened to him. Try listening to the rest of us for a change."

"I *am* trying."

"I know, hon. There's an iced tea in the cooler. Sit down and take a load off for a while."

Sarah accepted both gratefully.

She closed her eyes and gave in to the calming sound of the waves. She was wakened by someone pulling on her eyelids.

"Mommee, wake up."

"Hey, sandy girl." Sarah shifted in the chair so Leila could climb up, which she did, and sat her wet little butt on Sarah's lap.

"Now you look like the rest of us," Wyatt said, coming to stand over her. He was wearing the low-riding red jammers of the beach patrol. A white T-shirt was hanging from the waistband. An ID medallion hung on a silver chain around his neck.

Leila scrambled off Sarah's lap. "Watch what Wyatt taught me."

Wyatt feigned embarrassment. "Aw, don't make me."

"C'mon, c'mon." Leila pulled him to a place in front of the chairs.

"High five right," she squealed.

They high-fived right hands.

"High five left."

They clapped left hands.

"Low five," she yelled even louder.

They turned their palms down and low-fived right and left. Leila's hands disappeared into Wyatt's each time.

"Hokey pokey five," she screamed. They high-fived; both waved their fingers in the air and turned in a circle, wiggling their butts, one small and low to the ground, the other looking mighty fine in red jammers.

When they stopped, Leila giggled and ran in circles around Wyatt until she fell down.

The women exchanged looks, then burst out laughing.

"The hokey pokey five?"

"I had to do something to show Stu up. He taught her high five. I had to come up with something fancy. Anyway, the hokey pokey part was Leila's idea."

Hearing his name, Stu roused from the beach towel and came over, shaking the towel while sand flew everywhere.

"They never grow up," Karen said.

"Just old," Reesa said, and Sarah was pretty sure she wasn't joking.

Chapter 6

Stu came to sit on the end of Karen's chaise, making it sink into the sand. Having recovered from her dizzy circles, Leila climbed back onto Sarah's lap, adding a fresh deposit of sand.

Wyatt pulled the cooler next to Sarah's chair and sat on it. "You should have changed before you came."

"I know. I didn't mean to stay."

"Glad you did."

Sarah looked past him to find Reesa, Karen, and Stu all watching them.

"Me, too. The ocean's calming." That's not what she meant to say. "So you pulled lifeguard duty today?"

"Just a couple of hours. I split the afternoon shift with another sub."

"Sub," Stu groaned. "What's for dinner?"

"Pizza," yelled Bessie and Tammy.

Sarah looked down at Leila suddenly quiet in her lap. She was asleep.

"Looks like this one is ready for a bath and bed," Sarah said.

"The girls have had a big day," Karen said. "We'll just go to the pizza place across the street."

Sarah nudged the sleeping Leila. "Bunny boo, do you want to have dinner?"

Leila made a discontented sigh, snuggled deeper into Sarah's side. "I think we're heading for home. Thanks though. And thanks, Jenny, for watching Leila. See you next week?"

Jenny nodded.

Sarah shifted in her seat. Wyatt stood and lifted Leila smoothly from her lap. Sarah stood and reached to take her back.

"You grab my bag. I'll walk you home."

Sarah was acutely aware of Karen and Stu grinning at them, and Reesa smiling her approval. Leila was draped over Wyatt's chest like a little sea creature, and Sarah's heart gave a thump.

Caught off guard, she grabbed the red duffel bag of the rescue patrol, thankful it was a lifeguard day with no scuba gear inside.

"See you guys," she said. "See you on Monday, Reesa?"

Reesa held up her hand. "Quarter to nine sharp."

Sarah nodded and followed Wyatt across the sand. She felt so blessed to have people who cared about her, and whom she could care about. She wanted to tell them how much it meant to her, but she always seemed to get stuck when she tried to say the words. Even now, there was a dark place inside her that was afraid. Afraid to reach out, afraid that her attempts would be flung back in her face, afraid of finding herself back in the emotional version of a group home.

Wyatt had stopped at the steps to the boardwalk to wait for her. "You okay?" he asked.

"Yep."

They walked the block and a half to her house without speaking. But tonight it was a comfortable silence, a silence where she didn't have to constantly question herself about what she was doing, what she was feeling, whether it would be good for Leila or not. She was sick of second-guessing. Tonight, she was happy to walk alongside Wyatt and Leila. To be a part of something that was sort of real.

The hydrangeas were in full bloom and spilled over the sidewalk so that Sarah and Wyatt had to move closer together. He slipped his free arm around her waist, letting his hand rest on her hip bone. And she was so tempted to lean into him and rest for just a little while.

But that wouldn't be fair. He had his own life to take care of.

They kicked off their shoes on the front porch and went inside. Wyatt carried Leila straight to the bathroom and handed her off to Sarah.

"I'll see what you have in the fridge." And he left before she could say, "Not tonight." Not that she was going to. She wanted to extend this piece of normalcy as long as she could. Who knew what Monday would bring?

Sarah turned on the tub and barely managed to rouse Leila long enough to wash off the sand and change her into pajamas before she was snoring peacefully in her bed.

"Good night, sunshine," Sarah whispered and tiptoed out of the room. She could hear the shower running in the bathroom. She hesitated, caught for a moment between continuing to the

kitchen to check for something to cook or joining Wyatt in the
shower. She glanced back at the semiclosed door of Leila's bedroom. She would be asleep for a while. Dinner could wait.

She turned the knob of the bathroom door and slipped
inside.

"DID THOSE TWO make up?" Reesa asked as she slapped her
shoes together to rid them of sand.

"I don't know that they actually had a fight," Karen said.
"You know Sarah, two steps forward, one step back, sometimes
one forward, and two back."

"Well, if you ask me, Wyatt doesn't help."

"What do you mean?" Stu said, picking up the chaise and
starting to fold it. "He's always doing stuff for her."

"Yeah, doing stuff," Reesa said. "I'm talking about emotional commitment."

Stu stopped what he was doing, looked at her in a cross between *What the heck are you talking about?* and *Duh.* He snapped
the chair shut. "You're talking about Sarah. There's an awful
lot he'd have to commit to. And she doesn't make it easy."

"Has he said anything to you?" Karen asked.

"Guys don't talk about stuff like that."

"The heck they don't," Karen said. "I know your faulty
brains sometimes get stuck on . . ." She looked to see that the
girls wouldn't hear her. "Tits and ass, but I have faith that conversations at the pub sometimes go beyond that."

"Sure they do," Stu said and grinned. "There's work stuff,
basketball, and fantasy league football."

Karen rolled her eyes.

Reesa was envious. Well, not exactly envious. She wouldn't
want to have to do young children again. But she'd love to have

a husband who laughed with her. Made jokes even if they were stupid. Who would do anything except lie around the house and feel sorry for himself.

"I'm thinking about leaving Michael." Reesa froze, appalled at what had just come out of her mouth. She'd never even considered leaving Michael.

Karen and Stu had both frozen and were staring at her.

"Sorry. I don't know why I said that. I must be going crazy." She quickly folded her beach towel and shoved it into her bag. "I'd better get home. I had a lovely time."

She turned to go.

"Wait a minute," Karen said, running to stop her. "You can't drop a bomb like that, then say I had a nice time, see ya."

Reesa bit her lip. She was afraid she might burst into irrational tears. She wasn't thinking about leaving her husband. They'd been married almost thirty years.

"I don't know why I said that. I . . . just had a bad week."

"Well, you're not going home feeling like that. Though I think dinner calls for something more than pizza, don't you, Stu?"

"No, really, you guys go ahead. I'll be fine. I was just being . . . I don't know."

"Stu will take the girls to pick up some dinner. I'll drive with you to our house, where we'll have a grown-up dinner and you can tell us what the hell is going on."

"Yeah," Stu said. "Me and the girls will pick up dinner. Yeah, wow. This is crazy."

Karen insisted on riding with Reesa. She climbed into the passenger seat and waited for Reesa to get in. "I take it Michael isn't bouncing back from his injury?"

Reesa pulled into the street and stopped at the corner. She

looked over at Karen in the passenger seat. "It's hard to bounce when you only leave your recliner to get another beer."

"Is he drinking a lot?"

"Not really. I don't know, actually. I haven't been around that much. It's summer, and for child services, it's the equivalent of the Christmas rush. So many god-awful situations to choose from. Get them quick before it's too late." Reesa waited for a car to pass by, then hit the gas pedal a little too hard.

The car jolted across the intersection. "Sorry. It's just all hitting me for some reason. It's hard enough to see parents struggling, failing, hanging on by their bitten-to-the-quick fingernails, trying to deal with an overworked, underorganized, and haphazardly funded system, and then come home to a guy who won't even get out of a chair while he's complaining about how much I work."

"What does the doctor say?"

"That he probably shouldn't try to work on roofs anymore."

"And that's all he wants to do?"

"He was a good roofer. It paid well. But he used to be interested in other things. Hell, we have some savings; he could buy a roofing company and send other guys up the ladder."

"And that's what it's about, isn't it?"

Reesa nodded. "I think it's all about not being able to do what he could do. Something he was proud of. To suddenly have me making more money than he is just makes it worse."

"Did you suggest he get off disability and get a job?"

Reesa cracked a laugh. "Several times. I researched headhunters, cut out ads in the paper. Suggested he take the civil servants' test. He won't budge. I mentioned therapy—you know, the psychological kind. He nearly snapped my head off. So then I suggested family counseling. His reaction was to pick up the remote and increase the volume on the baseball game. He hardly acknowledges my presence."

"That sucks. Maybe I can get Stu to talk to him."

"No! No. I'm just a little down this week. Forget I said anything. And don't say anything to Stu. If it gets back to Michael, he'll just get mad at me for bad-mouthing him to his friends."

"He *is* a case. Why don't you come stay with us for a few days? Maybe he'll see what he's missing and change his tune."

"Thanks, but I'll be fine. Though I'm beginning to think either the job or Michael has to go; I can't seem to handle them both anymore."

"You're not thinking of leaving until Leila's adoption is complete, are you?"

"It could take years at this rate, but no. I'll try to hang in there. I'm not their caseworker any longer, but at least if I stay, I'll have access to files and info. I'm taking her to see a lawyer I know on Monday. A real barracuda. Excellent track record. Takes no prisoners."

Karen cut her a sharp look. "She doesn't sound very nice."

"She isn't. But she cares more about the children than the wishes of the bio or the adoptive parents. As it should be. If she takes Sarah's case, we'll have a good chance of winning."

"Do you think she'll take the case?"

"If she has space on her docket, yes. Carmen has relapsed more times than I care to count, every time a new man or even an old one enters her sphere. She just can't say no to any of it. I don't see much hope, but we have to get her to try. If Ilona Cartwright has any inkling that Carmen will slide, she'll have no compunction about bringing out the big guns."

Karen winced. "It sounds a bit harsh."

"Really, Karen, reality is harsh. But we have to try to save lives. Now if we could just promise them their new lives will be better than their old . . ."

"Well, Leila's will be."

"Yes, but for every Leila there are hundreds—" She broke off. "Sorry, didn't mean to preach. That's the other reason I'm thinking about changing careers. Half the time when I open my mouth, I sound like a public service announcement."

"You do necessary work."

"Yeah, I do." Reesa just thought maybe it was time to turn it over to someone else to do.

IT WAS MIDNIGHT and Sarah sat on the porch steps, alone. Leila was asleep, Wyatt had gone home half an hour ago. And here she sat, nursing her second glass of cabernet wondering why she hadn't asked him to stay.

Stupid question. He'd picked up the signs, the glances toward Leila's room, the fidgeting. He was getting so good at picking up cues from her that he'd be heading for the door before she even realized she was doing it. And he'd be gone before she could say, "Don't go."

She missed him already. They'd made plans to see each other the next day, but it wasn't the same as waking up with someone you were glad to wake up to. They'd had those times, before Sam got sick, before Leila had come to stay. But Sarah never seemed to be able to multilove. She and Wyatt were good until Sam needed her more.

After Sam died, she gave her love to Wyatt, until Leila came, and even after that until they had started shuttling Leila back and forth from Carmen to Sarah. Each time she returned, Leila would shrink from Wyatt, and Sarah would know Carmen had a man at home who wasn't treating Leila right.

She looked for signs of abuse and fortunately found none. But it didn't keep Sarah from worrying. She knew firsthand how things went. So instead of helping Leila to accept Wyatt, to trust that he would never hurt her, Sarah removed him from the picture.

Now, with Leila's adoption imminent, she wanted to keep them both, but she felt like she was trying to corral soap bubbles most of the time.

So she sat on the steps alone with her cabernet. *Cabernet.* What a hoot; Sarah Hargreave lived long enough to move from strawberry wine and marijuana to cabernet and a medium-rare steak.

She had Sam to thank for that, too.

At fifteen, she'd been hell on wheels until one night she watched a fellow user choke to death. Stood there and couldn't help. And she saw her mother, and herself. And she stepped away. Sobered up.

And became totally obnoxious.

She'd been so afraid of becoming a drug addict and alcoholic, dependent like her mother, that she'd been rigid, and so afraid of losing Sam, that she attacked him for enjoying a glass of wine at night and the occasional cigar.

Sarah blushed hot with remorse at the invectives she'd hurled at him. He took it all, sometimes laughing, sometimes reassuring her, sometimes telling her to bug off. He just let it roll off and kept doing what he was doing.

But sometimes looking back she wondered if she had really hurt him, and she would send him a prayer—on the outside chance there really was a heaven—and tell him she was sorry and that she loved him and . . . and all sorts of things.

Like she'd once written to Nonie, when she had gone.

Sarah wanted to tell Wyatt how she felt about him, before he left, too. For people always left. It was what they did. Moved, died, just drifted apart. She wanted to tell him, but she wasn't completely sure what she felt.

There were moments when she wished they could stay together, be their own forever family. But those moments were quickly followed by her rational mind saying, *Nothing lasts forever, nothing. Depend on yourself. Be happy with yourself. Get used to being alone.*

When she'd finally started looking at life without always waiting for the next rip in her heart, Sam got sick. It took a couple of years for him to leave, all the time preparing her, giving strength to her when he should have been trying to save himself. And when the time came, she couldn't let him go as gracefully as he left.

She was weak. And she had clung to him, even after it was too late to keep him.

Now Sarah started each day with the promise that she would get it together, be happy, not be afraid, and most days she succeeded.

She knew no one could fill the gaping hole she sometimes felt in her heart. Nothing could replace that but her own acceptance of herself.

She finished her wine. Looked at the empty glass. Drugs and alcohol were a walk in the park compared to her real addiction. She was drowning in an addiction to self-doubt.

ILONA WAITED FOR the elevator to close on a satisfied and disheveled Garrett. She smiled, even toodled her fingers at him, which made him laugh. It was a ridiculous gesture, like the cherry on a sickeningly sweet sundae.

He was good enough in bed. Hit all the right places, didn't talk too much. And he did make her laugh.

Tennis, bar, dinner, bed. They had a standing invitation.

And that was all either of them wanted or expected out of their relationship. If she ever married again, though she couldn't imagine why she would ever want to, it would be on her own terms. With her eyes wide open, and to someone who could hold his own without trying to destroy hers.

She put the top back on the gin, added two more glasses to the dishwasher, and turned it on. She yawned; she was ready for bed and the sleep of the truly satisfied. Good match, good food, decent sex . . . She even chuckled as she thought of Kevin's pregnant trophy wife. No sense worrying about her or the percolating kid.

She'd get a good settlement when Kevin chucked her over for the next step of his career ladder. And if she didn't, she could always pay Ilona to represent her in divorce court.

Wouldn't that be a kick. She turned out the light.

Chapter 7

Karen picked up Leila early Monday morning. "We're going to McDonald's before camp," Bessie announced from the backseat, when Sarah opened the car door for Leila to climb in.

Leila stopped. "Am I going to camp?" she asked, her brows dipping into the beginning of a look Sarah knew so well and had tried to banish.

Sarah had explained it twice yesterday. She explained it again. "No, you're going to your fun school, and Bessie and Tammy are going to their camp."

"McDonald's?" Sarah asked Karen.

Karen shrugged. "We were running late."

"Better you than me." Sarah was beginning to feel sick, and she really needed to get ready if she was going to leave plenty of time for traffic.

She gave Leila a quick kiss. "Love you. I'll be waiting for

you at the bus stop this afternoon." She started to close the door.

"Sing my song, Mommee."

"Okay but really, really fast, because you don't want to be late. Sarah started, "You are my sunshine . . ." then slowed down. She wouldn't rush through a minute of life with Leila.

Jenny and Karen joined in from the front seat, then Tammy and Bessie. They were all singing when Sarah shut the door and Karen drove away.

As soon as the car turned the corner, Sarah hurried back inside. She changed into black linen slacks and a nubby cotton shell. It was already hot, so she carried the matching jacket. She opted for sandals. She didn't feel forceful in sandals, but she didn't feel secure in heels.

She'd already carried out a box of documentation earlier that morning. She doubted if she'd need it today, but she wanted to be prepared. She put her purse and briefcase on the backseat, carefully draped her linen jacket over the passenger seat back, and climbed in. She resisted the urge to go back inside to make sure she hadn't forgotten anything. She had everything she needed. Now she just needed to get there.

She backed onto the alley that ran behind the house and stores and headed for the highway. Twenty minutes later she was parked and standing in front of the law offices of Erickson, Cartwright and Hefley.

It was a newer building, modern architecture, lots of large smoky windows and gray stone—or maybe it was concrete. Sarah supposed it was meant to look strong and immovable. But to Sarah it looked like a prison. She thought of her lovely Victorian clock repair store and thanked her lucky stars that Sam hadn't been a lawyer.

She should have asked Reesa more about this lawyer. She could have at least googled her. But she was trying not to get ahead of herself, to just be herself. *Don't worry about the should haves.*

Sarah loosened her grip on the briefcase and concentrated on breathing evenly and trying to relax. It was important to be rational and calm, not let the situation get the best of her. Convince this woman to take her case . . . if it even came to that.

It was another five minutes before Reesa hurried toward her, looking frazzled but determined, and huffing like she'd run a mile instead of across the street from the parking lot. She was wearing the same or similar suit that she'd been wearing on Friday morning.

She stopped when she got to Sarah, held up a finger while she gulped for breath.

"I need to get more exercise," she said, when she finally got her breath back.

Sarah thought she could use a vacation, but she didn't say so. She needed Reesa. Later, she could take a vacation. Actually she could use a makeover and a shopping spree, though Sarah had never seen a fashionably dressed social worker. The work was too get down and get dirty—or worse. Still, Reesa deserved something nice. Maybe she and Karen could take Reesa to one of those one-day spa places—after this was over.

"Now," Reesa said, moving toward the double glass doors. "Just answer her questions in a calm voice. She doesn't go much for desperate pleas or shows of emotion. She wants to know what kind of case you have and if she thinks you're worth it. She may not decide today. I faxed over the particulars. Hopefully she's had time to give them a good look."

Reesa pressed the elevator button. It opened immediately.

"And don't say anything extraneous once we get out of this elevator."

"Okay."

She gave Sarah a quick reassuring nod. Four floors later they stepped off into a large foyer with gray industrial carpeting, a curved reception desk, and several black-and-steel chairs for waiting clients.

The receptionist knew Reesa and they stood chatting for a minute before she told Reesa to have a seat.

"This doesn't really look like a humanitarian-minded office," Sarah whispered as they sat side by side looking out a tinted window to monochromatic treetops.

"It's distinguished. Projecting an image of strong, reliable legal advice. They have clout."

Sarah took a breath. "If you say so."

"Ms. Cartwright will see you now," the receptionist said, as if she hadn't just been chatting with Reesa a few minutes before. She showed them into an office behind a door of wooden grillwork. Reesa gestured for Sarah to precede her, then stepped in after her. The door closed soundlessly behind them. It was a bit intimidating.

The woman at the desk stood. "Reesa, good to see you." She didn't smile but shook hands.

"Ilona. This is Sarah Hargreave, the woman I told you about. I sent over her report."

It seemed to Sarah that time stopped, while she silently repeated, *Fix the now, fix the now.* Then slowly Ilona Cartwright turned to Sarah, and Sarah felt a jolt from the sheer energy of her personality.

She was a tall, light-skinned African American. Impeccably and expensively dressed, she'd been half smiling, the kind of smile businesspeople give to each other, devoid of affection. It stayed on her face as she turned to Sarah.

She didn't blink as she took Sarah's measure.

Sarah had to force herself not to step back. She had no idea what the lawyer was seeing in her or even what she was thinking.

The lawyer finally broke eye contact and rummaged through the folders on her desk. "I've been busy and didn't really have time to look over these, if you'll . . ." She gestured for them to sit down in the chairs opposite her.

She opened the folder and read while Sarah held her breath.

SARAH HARGREAVE. FOR a moment Ilona was afraid she'd lost her mind. There must be hundreds, possibly thousands of Sarah Hargreaves. Because this would just be too much god-forsaken bad luck if this was Sarah.

Sarah was probably dead. At least Ilona hoped she was. That would be the only reason to forgive her for never writing like she promised. All those miserable lonely years . . . Ilona opened the folder, ran down the particulars.

She felt the Hargreave woman shift in her seat. Risked a glance in her direction and there was no doubt, those same gray eyes looking at her like Ilona was gonna—going to—be her savior.

MRS. J GRABBED me as I was getting back from school. "You're gonna get a roommate this afternoon. Be nice."

I'm always nice—at least on the outside. I know how to work the system. I've got plans. And they don't include staying in this group home much longer.

Turns out it's some skinny little white girl, with stringy reddish-yellow hair. Sad eyes, like somebody killed her puppy. Maybe somebody did.

Man, I don't need this shit. It's hard enough keeping myself safe. I can't be worried about some loser white kid. Where the hell are her relatives? 'Cause they all got relatives.

So what if her mother's strung out on some designer drug, crashed the Mercedes, is sitting in some posh rehab hotel; it was stupid to bring her here. They'll finish her.

She doesn't look at me, just sits on the bed clutching some damn backpack. Probably has Barbies in it. I should just take it from her now and save her the trouble of trying to hold on to it.

Already I can see the boys in the other hallway standing as close as they can without coming over to our side. Boys and girls aren't allowed to mix in group home. They do, but nobody notices.

What were they thinking putting her in here? Show her around, Mrs. J said.

I'm not showing her shit. I got studying to do.

I lie down on my bunk and open my English book. I'm not getting stuck here, stuck going back to the hood and getting strung out with the rest of the losers. I got plans and they don't include some poor lost skinny white chick.

I look up and damn if she ain't—isn't—standing right by me looking down at my book. I slap at my ear, the one she's breathing on.

"I know how to read," she says.

"Well, hoo de do. How old are you, kid?"

"Eight."

"I'm eleven. You know what that means?"

"That you'll take care of me?"

Oh shit, she hasn't got a chance.

Ilona forced herself to glance through the pages of Reesa's report, looking for any excuse not to take the woman on as a client. Not to want to care about what happens to her foster kid. Didn't Reesa say the bio mother had changed her mind?

She moved to the second page. There it was. The bio mother had completed rehab, she was clean . . . for a second . . . no, third try; three times was a charm—hardly. Three times and you were pretty much toast. But the Hargreave woman, Sarah Hargreave, didn't need to know that.

All those years waiting for a letter, hoping, every week writing, asking, why don't you write? Now she knew. While Ilona was trying to be someone worth loving, longing for the sister she'd never have, her heart breaking more with each passing week of Sarah's silence, the bitch had been fostered or adopted. It must have been a cushy gig to forget so easily. Her parents must have loved *her*, because she owned her own business. Had a beach house no less. And now she wanted to adopt some poor foster child, pay back to society. How sweet.

Well, she could go for it, but not with Ilona's help.

She closed the folder, carefully placed it back on the desk, appalled that her childhood fears had intruded into the one place she felt totally in control, protected. "I'm sorry, Reesa, this is pretty cut and dried. I don't think I can help you."

She watched Reesa's mouth open, her look of disbelief, the disappointment. Well, she'd just have to be disappointed. No way was Ilona going to help the friend—the "sister"—that had betrayed her so easily.

And the bitch didn't even recognize her.

Ilona stood. Waited. Finally Reesa stood; she still was frowning. Sarah just sat there, just like all those years before, the same damn eyes. But now, Ilona could say no, and she did.

"I can pay." Sarah's voice.

"It wouldn't make a difference."

Sarah looked at Reesa, but Reesa didn't seem to notice her. She was glowering at Ilona. She never brought Ilona stupid cases, useless cases. Ilona had never turned down one of Reesa's cases before. And Ilona would never tell her why she wouldn't take this case.

"I'm sorry."

"Sarah, let's go." Reesa had to pull Sarah to her feet. Ilona was afraid she might pass out and then she'd have to deal with her. She needed her out of her office—now.

Ilona preceded them to the door, opened it. Reesa practically shoved Sarah into the reception area. Ilona returned to her desk but hadn't managed to sit before the door swung open again and Reesa barged in.

"You didn't even look at the case, did you?"

Not a workhorse, a bulldog. "Of course I did, but the mother is out of rehab and has a job."

"And on the second page it shows how many times she's been in rehab and how many times she's lapsed."

"I'm sorry."

"No, you're not. I don't get it. You're not unfeeling. Do you really think you couldn't win? Is that it? You think you can't win, so you won't try?"

Ilona stared at Reesa. "You're losing your cool, girl."

"And why shouldn't I? I had to extract three children this week. They were starving and dehydrated and living in filth because the mother was too busy doing drugs to care. The baby was comatose by the time I got to them."

"Rough," Ilona said. She didn't know how Reesa could do it. "Maybe it's time to take a couple of weeks off."

"Once I see this through, I may just take the rest of my life off."

She turned and banged through the door.

Ilona almost went after her. Then she remembered the other

woman waiting for her on the other side. Even after all these years Ilona would have known her anywhere. But Sarah? Not a flicker of recognition. Those two young girls might as well have never existed.

SARAH JUST STOOD where Reesa had left her. She didn't understand what had just happened. The door opened and Reesa came out, grabbed Sarah's elbow, and pulled her toward the elevator.

"I'm sorry. This was a total waste of time."

Sarah pulled away. "Maybe she doesn't understand that I can pay her."

"No, you can't. Not what she charges. We'll find someone else."

"But you said she was the best."

Reesa stopped dead and turned on her. "Lawyers are no better than their belief in you. No matter how important they think they are." She said the last line so loud that if the door hadn't been so thick, Sarah was sure Ms. Cartwright could have heard it. "She obviously has fulfilled her required pro bono hours this month."

Sarah sucked in a breath. "Don't jeopardize your relationship with her because of me and Leila."

"What relationship? There's only a one-way street to Ilona Cartwright." Reesa practically yelled the last words.

And then Sarah understood why.

Reesa looked past her to the receptionist who was apparently looking for something on her desk. "And you can take that right in to your boss. We're leaving."

Sarah just caught a glimpse of the receptionist reaching for the phone before Reesa propelled her out the door.

And the import of what had just happened hit her full force.

The best lawyer, in the county at least, had refused to take her case, cut and dried she'd said, or something like that.

She and Reesa didn't speak until they were on the sidewalk again. The heat was already oppressive, and Sarah longed just to get back to the store and try to forget the entire morning, the entire situation, but she couldn't.

"Am I being unreasonable?" she asked.

Reesa frowned at her. It was the same expression she'd worn as she'd stormed out of the office, and it hadn't changed. "What?"

"Am I the one in the wrong?"

"What?" Reesa asked more loudly. "Are you just giving up? Is that how much Leila means to you?"

"She means everything to me. But am I being selfish? Deluding myself that I can make her a better home, love her more. Can Carmen change? Should she really have Leila back?" Sarah listened to herself say the words she'd feared, but they had to be said. "Will Leila be better off with Carmen?"

At first Reesa didn't answer, then much more quietly she said, "Send her back and see."

Sarah reared back, physically and emotionally. She was staring at someone she didn't know. Not the positive, nurturing, cheerleading person Sarah knew. But someone with a depth of anger so strong that it rolled from her in heated waves in an already hot atmosphere.

The briefcase fell from Reesa's hand, and she covered her face. "God, I am so sorry. I don't know what's come over me. I never lose my cool. I'm so sorry."

Sarah reached out her hand. Touched Reesa's shoulder. "It's all right. You tried. We'll do something. I'll talk to Randy. Get another lawyer if we have to. If you believe Leila belongs with me. If you don't . . . well, I'll still fight to keep her." *And let them fight to take her away.*

Dear Nonie,

I've been back at group home for a few weeks now. I had a nice family, but they had to move to Connecticut for work. They said they wanted to take me with them, but in the end they didn't. I heard them talking and he said, "There's just too much damn red tape." So I came back.

Now, Mrs. J just came in with the "good" news. I'm going to another home, this will be number four. Nothing seems to work out for me. But don't think I'm whining. I'm hanging tough like you said, though I really wish you would write me. I don't even ask Mrs. J anymore if there's a letter for me, though I still send one to you.

I gotta go pack my things.

Later.

> *Your sister??*
> *Sarah*

Impulsively Sarah dropped her own briefcase and wrapped her arms around Reesa. Just a light hug to let her know she didn't blame her for the morning's fiasco.

But Reesa slipped out of her grasp. "I'm your friend, Sarah. Maybe I'm not seeing this case clearly. Maybe I'm not—"

"Don't," Sarah said. "Don't backpedal. If you don't believe I'm the right mother for Leila, fine. Sort of." Sarah swallowed. It was one thing to fight for Leila's security, or even her own survival but— "I can lose you as a caseworker and adviser, but don't say that you can't be my friend."

"What? You're not going to lose me as an advocate or a friend. We just have to readjust. This situation is not going to happen overnight. There are supervised visits and unsupervised. Then extended visits. A lot can happen before we need to panic. But, Sarah, if Carmen can provide a stable, loving home for Leila—"

"I know. I'm trying to be fair. Abide by what's best for 'the child.' I think I'm what's best for her. But I understand the rationale. And I know that sometimes the foster home is worse than the bio home, but not in this case. And I don't think I'm just being selfish to think that."

"Sarah, you are never selfish. Don't start worrying yet. There is a long way between 'I'm clean this week and I want my child back,' to 'I've stayed clean, kept my job, and I'm able to cope with raising a child to maturity.'"

Sarah nodded. She knew this, but what a toll it could take.

> *PS.*
>
> *I don't know why they make me take everything, I'll just be back again.*
>
> *When they come for me, I can tell they're nervous. That makes me nervous. I make sure they give Mrs. J my new address in case you send a letter. But I don't have much hope.*
>
> *Now I have no friends. Not even the asshole boys who make fun of me and try to feel me up when Mrs. J isn't looking. Now I got this couple. And they're yammering all the time, telling me about their family and how they got several foster children living with them.*

Great, one more monthly stipend coming their way.

"Don't give my bed away," I say to Mrs. J as I pass by.

She frowns at me like she's disappointed in my attitude,

but she knows I'm right. I climb in the backseat of this white

Impala. It smells all musty, and there's a hamburger wrapper

on the floor. They don't even tell me to buckle up.

ILONA DIDN'T SUMMON her secretary until she was sure she could hand her a folder without her hands shaking. It took longer than she expected. She'd seen the intercom light up, but it wasn't Inez's voice that came through the speaker. It was Reesa Davis.

It was a ploy they often used, listening to the conversations of clients as they entered or left. Reesa was usually careful about speaking while in the waiting room. Any good lawyer would be, and Reesa in another life would have been a good lawyer, except her penchant for helping the underdog.

But she'd lost it today. Big-time. Ilona knew she was considered a cold, hard-hearted bitch. She knew they called her "Barracuda" behind her back. She took that as a compliment. But the one-way street barb from Reesa hit its mark. It was true, but people didn't always want to examine the truth about themselves. Not often anyway.

And she'd be damned if Reesa Davis and her lost causes would make her introspective today. Her latest divorce case was heating up. And she had others she needed to prep for.

She shoved Sarah Hargreave's folder to the side. She didn't even try to pick it up. Adrenaline was still coursing through her and she knew her hands wouldn't be steady yet. She didn't want to see it. Another minute or two should do the trick.

Ilona reached for the the divorce case folder; fumbled with

the edge. Spit out an expletive as Sarah Hargreave appeared like the ghost of Marley on Scrooge's front door.

Ilona barked out a laugh at the analogy, surprising herself. She was no Scrooge. She went the extra mile for her clients. She sent money to the appropriate charities. She had a standing date every Saturday. People respected her. Of course they were all lawyers, but still . . .

But still. There was that one dark empty space that never went away. That space had been gouged out by Sarah Hargreave and picked at by Ilona's ceaseless loneliness ever since. And she'd never learned why—until today.

She took a breath, reached for the intercom. Better. She was calm again. She tapped the intercom button. "Inez."

"Yes, Ms. Cartwright?"

She'd meant to make a quip about a good spat giving her an appetite and have Inez send out for a bagel and coffee, but her lips closed on the request. "Get one of the interns to find out what they can about the Sarah Hargreave who just left, and bring me a cup of coffee. ASAP."

"Yes, Ms. Cartwright."

Ilona leaned back in her lush leather chair. She was just curious. Who wouldn't be? She would find out once and for all why Sarah had bailed on her, what happened that made it so easy for her to forget her "sister." And then she could file it away with the rest of her dead cases.

Chapter 8

Reesa waited until she was sure Sarah was calm before she drove to the courthouse. She was on the docket for that morning to substantiate the reasons for her Dodd removal on Thursday and to get a court order for the removal. A no-brainer, if you asked Reesa. One comatose baby, a kid with kidney failure, and another not thriving, the parents in jail for a slew of crimes. She would ask the judge to put the children on a permanency track.

She tried to push away the anger at the unfairness of it all, but it was getting more and more difficult. She needed to find a way to recapture her distance or she'd do no one any good.

Once through the security check, she detoured to the courthouse cafeteria. She hadn't slept well and had awakened with just enough time to dress and have a quick cup of coffee. She still had a few minutes left before she needed to sign in.

Breakfast was in order. Reesa ran her plastic tray past juices and pastries and ordered eggs and bacon. Popped two slices of bread in the toaster and collected utensils and condiments while she waited for the toast. Then she took a table against the wall.

There weren't too many people sitting at the tables. It was after ten and everybody was grabbing fruit and coffee to carry to their respective floors. She saw a couple of lawyers she knew. A couple of caseworkers who looked tired and disheveled. And knew she was looking at herself.

She finished her food and headed for the ladies' room to freshen up her makeup and smooth down her suit. She added extra lipstick then wiped it off. After twenty-three years as a caseworker, she looked like one. Most days she didn't even think about it, but today, for some reason it rankled.

Her poor mother, rest her soul. "Don't let yourself go, or he'll find somebody younger and prettier." Hell, she couldn't even get Michael off the recliner. And as far as finding someone younger—Reesa sighed—she wished he would.

She put the lipstick back on. Surely, she didn't mean that. They'd had a good life. They couldn't give up just because Michael was going through a rough patch and she was burned out at her job. Surely there was more to their relationship than that.

AS SOON AS she'd signed in, Reesa took her place on the bench outside the courtroom. There were a couple of Formica tables and plastic chairs in the wider section of the hallway, but here it was easier to ignore the complaints, the whispers, the negotiations that took place before ever going into court.

Today the hallway was surprisingly quiet. And the people sitting along the bench were wrapped in their own thoughts or paperwork. She reached in her briefcase and pulled out the newspaper she'd picked up from her front door step. She usually left it for Michael, but this morning, she'd crammed it into her briefcase—a little act of passive-aggressive retaliation.

The newspaper rattled as she turned the page. Not a soul looked up, not the processor, not any of the line of people waiting to give depositions, file paperwork, and receive more paperwork in return.

Reesa had to admit as she moved from the sports section to the crossword puzzle, she'd rather be sitting here in the slightly fetid, under-air-conditioned hallway of family court than out on the streets inspecting squalid, hot apartments or even in Ilona Cartwright's sterile offices.

But the morning was marching on, and she hoped the judge would get to her before they broke for lunch. She had a stack of paperwork waiting for her at the office—a stack that never seemed to grow any shorter.

She glanced up at the no-cell-phone notice and realized she'd forgotten to call Tanya Aguda about getting Ms. McKinney placed in a subsidized senior living facility. The older woman had stepped up to the plate to report the abuse. Put her life in jeopardy to do it. And she lived in constant fear. Who wouldn't living in that environment?

Reesa would call in a couple of favors if she needed to. See if she could get her something nice, maybe with a little garden.

She keyed a note to self into her phone, folded the newspaper, and placed it on the empty seat beside her. She doubted Michael would want to read it after she had "messed it up."

She pulled out a yellow legal pad and a manila folder for another case coming up the following week. She read and made notes and glanced at her watch as eleven became noon and her appointment time came and went. Nothing unusual in that.

But if they didn't get to it soon, she'd have to come back for the afternoon. And she'd get further behind.

"Docket number . . ."

At last. Reesa hastily closed the folder. Clutching it to her chest, she grabbed her briefcase, then stood and made her way to the heavy mahogany door. Her knees were stiff, her back hurt; she needed to go to a lady's exercise class, one where they wore sweatpants and oversized T-shirts, not skimpy neon short shorts.

She nodded to the clerk and made her way to the deputy attorney general who was repping the division for the White hearing.

Across the courtroom, the court-appointed attorneys for Mrs. White and "Darrell" looked bored. The Whites were not in the courtroom.

The defendants' attorneys explained that their clients were under indictment for drug possession and child endangerment. They were still in jail, not being able to make bail.

The judge was shown the photos Reesa had taken during the removal. She explained step by step and in detail the timeline of the actual removal. The report of the abuse, the request for emergency removal. The violence of the male resident, finding the comatose baby, the mother's reaction. She followed this with a report of her subsequent follow-up on the boys' health.

"They are all still hospitalized, Your Honor. One may need lifelong continual care."

The DAG presented a police report of the incident.

The defending lawyers had no objections.

The judge okayed the removal, and Reesa was out on the sidewalk before he adjourned for lunch. The first thing she did was call Tanya Aguda and arrange an appointment for Ms.

McKinney, who had saved the lives of two young boys and a baby and who deserved to live without fear.

SARAH WAS GETTING out of the car when she saw Wyatt striding up the driveway from the street.

"Looking very beautiful in your power suit," he said and leaned over to give her a quick kiss. "How did it go?"

"It didn't." Sarah had been driving aimlessly around, wondering why Ilona Cartwright had turned them down without even looking at the case. Worrying about Reesa's reaction and trying to figure out what to do next. Reesa said there was a long time before they had to have a game plan in place. But Sarah didn't like not knowing. She wanted a game plan and wanted to know that it would work. And she wanted it now.

Wyatt smothered her in a hug. He smelled clean and strong and Sarah had to fight the urge to just let down, let someone take care of her for a change. "She just said she couldn't take the case. Then Reesa got very upset. Wyatt, I've never seen her so angry before."

"I think she's been under a lot of stress lately between Michael's injury and her job."

"I don't know, it was more than that." She looked up at him. "How did you know I'd come back?"

"I was going to lunch and saw you drive by." He flicked her chin. "Which still sounds like a good idea. Come on, we'll splurge and go to TailSpin."

"I need to get back to work, then I have to pick up Leila at the bus."

"And you need to eat before you can do any of those things. Humor me."

Hadn't she just been thinking that she wanted someone to take care of her? "Thanks, I'd like that."

They walked back to the street, past the clock shop, and toward the center of town. Since it was Monday, some of the stores and restaurants were closed. But most would be open seven days a week until the season was over. The clock shop was a block closer to the ocean than most of the stores, which meant it didn't get as many browsers as the other stores did. That was fine with Sarah. She wasn't dependent on foot traffic. She didn't sell souvenirs or beach paraphernalia. Just clocks and watches. Most of her merchandise was pricey and not something you'd pick up on your way to the beach.

They strolled down the sidewalk. And Sarah thought how comforting it was to live in a small town where everyone at least recognized one another, even if they didn't know you outright. Despite the influx of summer tourists, the locals still waved at each other, always had time to stop and chat.

"This is my family."

"Who is?"

Sarah looked up at Wyatt, who was frowning curiously at her. "Who is what?"

"You said this is my family."

"I did?" Sarah's stomach twisted. "I meant all of this. The people here. Since Sam died my friends, my . . ."

Wyatt smiled the way he did when he didn't quite believe something but was giving her the benefit of the doubt.

Please don't ask if I mean you, she thought and mentally crossed her fingers. She'd already blurted that stupid thing to Reesa about being her friend. She'd sounded like she was in third grade or something. Anything she might say to Wyatt would be laughable. And she wasn't even sure what she would say. *I love you? I think I love you? I want to love you?*

Sam had loved her. And she had loved him. She'd scored big-time with him, but she wasn't sure she could be that lucky twice in this life. And she was afraid to let go of Sam and take a chance on nothing.

The TailSpin was a nouvelle fish restaurant that catered to tourists looking for a dining experience after a day of sand and sun and residents who were looking for a place to dine away from the rackety noise of the beach.

It was a streamlined space, with curved booths along both walls and two rows of tables in the center of the long room. It was light and airy with aqua-wash walls and a minimalist industrial-shore ambiance.

The hostess, a young girl who only had eyes for Wyatt, showed them to a booth. Sarah slid in. Instead of going to the other side, Wyatt slid in beside her. The hostess handed them menus and went back to her post.

"Let's order, then you can tell me about the nonevent this morning."

Sarah nodded. She'd slipped into a momentary comfort zone, but Wyatt's reminder brought it all back . Her appetite flew south, but he was right, she needed to eat. And, besides, he'd badger her until she did.

As soon as the waiter had taken their order, Wyatt turned to her, "Okay, spill."

Sarah started at the beginning, filling him in about meeting Reesa, about the sterile office and Ilona Cartwright.

"When Reesa introduced me to her, she turned to me with such a weird expression. I tried to look her in the eye, you know, like equals, confident, but it was like looking into a black hole.

I swear. Just blank, grabbing me and pushing me away at the same time. I don't know. We shook hands, I think. She told us to sit down, that she hadn't had time to look at the information Reesa had sent her. She opened the folder. Then suddenly she closed it and said, 'I'm sorry, I can't take the case.' Reesa got really upset. And practically shoved me out of the office. And that was it. It doesn't make sense."

"She didn't explain why?" Wyatt asked and handed her a breadstick.

Unthinking, Sarah broke it in half and took a bite. Swallowed. "No, just that she couldn't help us."

"What did Reesa say?"

"I don't even know. Something about being too close to the case because she was my friend, and I freaked and begged her not to stop being my friend." She dropped the breadstick halves onto her plate. "Like, that was the stupidest thing I could have thought of, like it was even important when Leila's future is at stake."

Wyatt laughed and gave her a quick hug. "Of course it's important. You like to compartmentalize . . . and it may work with clock parts, but life is a lot messier and it doesn't like being put nicely away. Get used to it, love. You'll be a lot happier when you do."

"I am happy," Sarah protested as the waiter placed a bowl of mussels in red sauce between them. "At least I will be when this is all completed." She mentally crossed her fingers. "If it works out right."

"It will or it won't. We'll all do our best. Now let's worry about right now and eat." He'd reached for a mussel just like it was any ordinary day. Like he was oblivious or clueless. But he was none of those.

Fix the now. And right now she was hungry.

"Reesa said the lawyer's pro bono work might be filled for the month," Sarah said when they were halfway through the bowl of mussels. "But I think she was being sarcastic. I told Reesa I could pay. But she said I wouldn't have enough for Ms. Cartwright's fees."

"There are other lawyers. Are you sure you even need a different lawyer?"

Sarah shrugged. "I didn't think so. I thought it was just a matter of the paperwork working its way through the system. Surprise on me. I don't want to be caught unprepared again."

She leaned back while the waiter replaced the mussels with two rectangular plates of broiled flounder and pilaf with a ratatouille condiment.

"If I don't have enough money on hand, I'll have to borrow it." She dropped the fork she'd just picked up. "I don't mean borrow it from anyone or anything like that. I meant take a second mortgage on the house or sell it outright."

"And then where would you live?" He picked up her fork and wiggled it at her, before handing it back.

"Or I could sell the store."

"And become one of the idle rich?"

She speared a piece of flaky fish. "In my dreams."

Wyatt cut a piece of fish, piled pilaf on the back of the fork English style, slid it into his mouth, and chewed, savoring the taste. "Why don't you just hold off on anything extreme until we know how serious Carmen really is."

That stopped her for a second. "Why wouldn't she be serious?"

"She might be. She might really have turned over a new

leaf. But it's just as possible that she has a new boyfriend who is pulling her strings. It wouldn't be the first time."

"No, and I was lucky to even have gotten Leila back after both failed attempts. Usually they just send you to wherever there's a bed."

"I know, hon. You'll figure it out. And you've got a whole crew of people in your court. Your family, like you said. So try not to worry and make this the best time ever."

In case it's soon gone forever, Sarah finished for him.

After a brief skirmish over Wyatt's buying lunch, which he won, they left the air-conditioned restaurant for the heat-pulsing sidewalk. Two blocks later they parted at the corner, Wyatt to return to his store, Sarah to hers. They'd seen each other more in the last few days than they had in a while.

In the back of her mind, Sarah was afraid it wasn't a good idea. It didn't seem fair for Leila to be sent back to Carmen just when she was getting along so well with Wyatt. There were bound to be repercussions when she returned. Either afraid of him or mean to him. He'd make himself scarce for a while and the cycle would continue. Or she wouldn't come back at all.

But Sarah wouldn't contemplate that yet. It would all work out. It had to.

She walked around to the backyard, where she retrieved her briefcase and the box of documentation from the car. It wouldn't hurt her to organize what she had and review some of the incidents she may have forgotten.

After letting herself into the shop, Sarah deposited her brief-case and the box on the floor and walked through to the front room. She normally loved Mondays, when the shop was closed and she could come and go as she pleased. Work all day if she wanted. Or just sit in the quiet.

She stepped out to the center of the room, breathed in the scent of wood and wax and oil. There were no lights on. A few dust motes were suspended in the air near the window where a ray of sunlight sliced to the floor. But that was all. Just her. Alone. And in the silence she could hear it. The ticking of the clocks, steady as a heartbeat.

Could she really contemplate selling this to keep Leila? Could she give up what Sam had loved most in the world? She could still repair clocks without having a retail space, but the store brought in the bulk of her income. And the building was paid for, along with the house; she wouldn't be able to find a place cheaper without leaving the area. And that's not something she wanted to consider.

This is where she had learned to be human. To stop hating and being afraid, to trust and to love. She wasn't sure she could keep all those in her heart if she had to give up her soul, which was forever a part of Sam and his shop.

Sarah smiled for a moment, thinking of Sam, could swear she could hear his monotone humming as he worked in the back room.

She walked around the perimeter of the room, letting her hand run over the carved cabinet of the old Bavarian cuckoo clock, the beveled glass of the grandmother clock that she and Sam bought from an estate sale. It had been in terrible repair but together they had brought it back to life. It was not for sale.

She should have asked Reesa just what amount of money she would need to hire Ilona Cartwright. She'd pay whatever it took, but the cottage and the store were more than buildings;

they were her center, her soul. Surely the sale of a couple of clocks would be sufficient.

ILONA MANAGED TO concentrate for about an hour while her coffee grew cold and she tried not to think about the Hargreave folder sitting unopened on her desk or to be impatient with the intern who was taking a hell of a lot of time researching something that was probably easily found by googling. She could have done that herself.

After an hour, she'd satisfied herself that she really didn't have to open the folder and convinced herself that it was mere curiosity about the case that let her hand slide over and open it.

She'd prepared herself for seeing the name again—she knew right where it was on the page. She steeled herself and read the initial removal report. Birth mother, Carmen Delgado, history of drug and alcohol abuse. Known prostitute. Father, Sonny Rodrigues, deceased. Leila Rodrigues. Seventh of eight children, different fathers, all in foster care. The future didn't look bright for Carmen Delgado.

Like Reesa said. A no-brainer.

In a few years Carmen would probably be dead. Leila would forget her, hopefully.

Ilona didn't remember either of her birth parents. But she'd had Aunty. Aunty was good; she'd made sure Ilona went to school and learned her lessons and her manners. As it turned out, Aunty wasn't really her aunt, but she didn't care. Ilona had thought it would last forever, but the only thing that lasts forever is misery.

Aunty starting forgetting things; sometimes she couldn't remember Ilona's name. She forgot to buy milk, didn't know what the salt was for. She got afraid of Ilona, thought she was trying to steal her social security check. Wandered off and one day the police found her. Alzheimer's, they said.

The service came and got Ilona; she scratched and kicked and screamed, begged them to let her stay and take care of Aunty, but they wouldn't. They pushed her into a car and drove away. Aunty went to a home. Another home that wasn't a home.

Ilona jumped when the intercom buzzed. She reached for it and knocked over the cup of cold coffee. The coffee spread out over the desk blotter. She grabbed all the folders she could muttering, "Dammit, dammit."

She dumped the folders on the chair Sarah Hargreave had sat in and punched the intercom. "Inez, bring some paper towels, pronto. There's a bit of a spill."

It galled her to have to admit it. She never did things like that. Wasn't clumsy. Didn't make messes. Never.

"Ilona, what is wrong with you? How many times do I have to ask you not to run through the house like a hoodlum? Look what you've done."

Ilona looked down at the shards of the coffee cup on the white tile floor, the coffee making a puddle at her feet and the grotesque stain down her mother's white wool skirt. She'd been so excited, she'd forgotten to pay attention to how she was behaving. Stupid. She'd been so stupid.

"So what do you want?"

Ilona hung her head and thrust out the soggy report card without looking up. "I made all A's."

Chapter 9

Usually Sarah could lose herself in her work, but not today. Today she was alternately bombarded with replays of the morning's meeting with Ms. Cartwright and worrying about having to tell Leila about the supervised meeting on Wednesday.

She couldn't put it off any longer. By the time she left for the bus stop Sarah was sick with fear that this would be the time that she would lose Leila forever.

Maybe she shouldn't have taken the book out. The *Everyone Loves Me* book. Photos of Leila with her two families. Sarah had made it when Leila came for the first time. So one day when she became curious about her past, there would be a sympathetic record of her early years. Sarah had put it away after the last failed visit. And it hadn't been out since. Maybe she should try to hide the book when they got home. Talk about the visit then bring it out. She just didn't know what was best.

Sarah was suddenly second-guessing everything she did

or thought and that wouldn't get her anywhere but tied up in knots.

She was smiling when Leila climbed down the steps of the minibus. The bus driver waved and the door closed. Sarah took Leila's hand and they walked back to the cottage, Leila chattering about school and McDonald's and Sarah thinking about the big scrapbook waiting for them on the kitchen table.

They reached the porch steps all too soon. They went straight to the kitchen, where Sarah emptied the contents of the backpack onto the table and washed out the plastic containers of fruit she'd sent for snack. Then she reached into the cupboard for some graham crackers.

When she turned back, Leila was sitting in her booster seat looking at the book.

Sarah put the crackers on a plate and placed them on the table in front of Leila.

"Remember this?" she said brightly, moving the book around for Leila to see.

Leila looked up, took a square of graham cracker, and bit into it. "Milk, please."

Sarah poured milk and put the glass on the table. She pulled a chair close to Leila and slid the book closer.

"Can you read this?"

Leila glanced at the scrapbook. Shrugged.

"Everybody Loves Me," Sarah said, pointing to the words as she spoke. "Remember who's in here?"

Leila shrugged again. Sarah's stomach tightened even further. She opened the book to the first page and a photo of the three of them, Sarah on one side of Leila, Carmen on the other, back in the first days of her fostering, when Carmen was clean for a moment and Sarah was doing her best to be understanding.

Leila was just a toddler.

"See, that's you."

Leila shook her head.

Don't read too much into it, Sarah warned herself. "That's you." She pointed to a much younger, much frailer Leila and quelled the anger that rose inside her. "That's me." She pointed to herself, a little over two years ago; she looked much younger . . . and optimistic.

"And that's Carmen. Your bio mother." She didn't know if Leila even remembered what that meant, though she'd tried to explain it several times. But to Leila, Sarah was her mommee. And Sarah hoped she had no memory of the squalid conditions child services had rescued her from, or the deplorable situation they'd returned her to, twice.

"Mr. Noyes is going to take you to see her on Wednesday."

"I don't want to."

"It's just for a couple of hours. You can take Mickey Mouse. And when he says it's time to go, Mr. Noyes will bring you home."

"I don't want to."

And I don't want you to, Sarah thought. "What color sticker shall we put on the calendar?"

Leila crossed her arms. Scowled. When Sarah got up to get the stickers, Leila threw the book onto the floor.

ILONA SPENT THE evening googling Sarah Hargreave and reading the dossier the intern had compiled that afternoon. Unfortunately he hadn't been able to obtain her foster and adoption record.

But she did find the name of the family she lived with. Gianetti. Sam Gianetti owned a clock retail and repair store. How quaint. And a house next to it, both of which were now in Sarah Hargreave's name.

They must have left her both the house and the business. Not a spectacular outcome, but it sounded comfortable.

All this time, she had been living right here, less than ten miles from where Ilona had lived. For a while after she left the group home, Ilona had consoled herself with thinking Sarah had been taken away to another state, maybe across the country even. That in the move she'd lost Nonie's—Ilona's—address. She'd written to the group home and asked them to send it, but they never had.

She'd imagined all sorts of scenarios. One was that Sarah had been fostered to someone who killed her; then Nonie would cry and say she was sorry that she couldn't save Sarah after all.

Sometimes she imagined Sarah living with people who loved her and she never thought about Nonie. Maybe even wanted to forget her. And then she'd get angry and hope Sarah was dead, and then she'd feel guilty and cry herself to sleep.

Ilona shut down her computer, turned out the lights, and stood at the window, looking out. Beyond the window the sky was black; below it the ocean was blacker; not even the sliver of a moon lit the swell of waves.

Dear Sarah,

Sometimes I wonder where you are. Did you find a family? Are you somewhere where they are kind? Do you give them shit? You could always dish it out for such a scrawny little thing. Remember when you first came? Are you somewhere

where they won't let you write? Where they watch your every move? Maybe it's so you won't embarrass them, maybe it's worse.

Are they mean to you, Sarah? Do they hurt you? Is that why you don't write? I write you every week, like we promised.

Do you think about me? Wonder where I am? I didn't go far. You could probably visit me, except they don't want me talking about before I came. They don't understand, that's who I am, who I'll always be.

Well, I hope you haven't forgotten about me. I haven't forgotten about you. Hang tough. Don't let them get to you. One day we'll be together.

Don't forget, you're my sister.

Nonie

ILONA DIDN'T SLEEP much that night and she arrived at work gritty-eyed and aching the next morning. She had several clients scheduled for the morning. Two new clients and three continuing clients were scheduled for the afternoon. Olivia Sobrato, her newsworthy and embarrassingly gay divorcée, was due at four.

She had to force herself to concentrate during the morning. Her mind kept wandering to that damn clock shop. She'd looked at photos on the Internet the night before until she could remember every little architectural detail.

The morning droned on, while Ilona forced herself to listen to her clients' woes. It wasn't easy, and even though every good sense gene she had was screaming *Stick to your client list,* she knew she could never be free to concentrate until she had seen for herself.

She buzzed Inez and told her she was going out and to re-schedule all her afternoon appointments, except for Olivia's. She'd be back by then—way before then.

Inez hesitated for a second before saying, "Yes, Ms. Cart-wright."

No wonder. Ilona never did things like that. Unplanned things, spontaneous things, not for a long, long time. The fact that she was contemplating it today was unsettling. The fact that she had a pair of flat-heeled shoes on the backseat told her she wouldn't back down.

Still, as she slipped her heels off in the office parking lot, she gave herself one last chance to act rationally. But Ilona Cart-wright was way past rational. Nonie Blanchard had raised her nearly forgotten head and wouldn't go away. She was smother-ing Ilona with unhappiness, with anger, with hate. That had been the only way Nonie had known how to cope with the world, until little Sarah Hargreave had dropped into her life and she was given a reason to care.

It made the betrayal all that more devastating. And if Ilona had her way, Sarah would pay for her deceit, and where it would hurt the most.

Ilona found a parking place a block from the main street in the quaint town where Sarah lived. An auspicious start to her intentions, since it was the beginning of the summer season and already the streets were crowded with summer people and their cars. Ilona never came down this way. Too many memories, most of which she wished to forget, and some she had cherished until they'd finally been buried with the rest of the things Nonie had loved.

The stores were all small and overcrowded. Not the shop-ping experience Ilona enjoyed, but they must be lucrative because they were all crowded. Ilona strolled down the sidewalk, stopping to look in windows, wondering if she would actually catch sight of Sarah today.

Of course, she could walk right into her shop, but she didn't intend to do that. She just wanted to watch, see how Sarah lived. See what kind of kid she was fostering.

Catch her doing something that would indicate that the foster child should be taken from her? Not even Ilona would stoop to entrapment. Would she?

Ilona smiled. The barracuda was out. Of course she would. She'd done more outrageous things to win a case. Nothing illegal, not even anything that wasn't true. But truth was a tangled road, and interpretations were as varied as the interpreter.

Ilona had no scruples using those interpretations to her clients' advantage. Or to her own.

And yet . . .

She didn't remember when she'd finally given up hoping Sarah would write. But she had given it up and she wouldn't—couldn't—forgive. And that made her crazy. It had been a long time since she'd thought of Sarah or of her life in the system.

One moment of not paying attention and the past had slid into her office like the serpent it was and posed expectantly before her, as Ilona watched her world quietly unravel. But no longer. It ended here.

The shopping district consisted of two short blocks of stores housed behind quaint Victorian façades. She knew the clock shop was located on the next block, compliments of Google street view. She'd walk by, careful not to be seen.

Being raised in the social services system had taught her so many skills that she hadn't needed in years, but she had no doubt they would come in handy now. Ilona slowed as she passed the window of the clock shop. *Clocks by the Sea*. How quaint. She gave the window a cursory glance. Saw someone move inside the store. Not Sarah.

She walked past the little house next door. It was all just too damn cute. Perfect for a fairy-tale life. She liked that scenario. She'd be the witch. She'd been called that before, many times, and worse. But she would enjoy being the witch—no, the evil queen—in this tale.

She stopped several houses down, then turned back toward the shopping district. She was starting to perspire. She couldn't continue to stand out in the sun in the height of the day waiting for Sarah to appear. Maybe the coffeehouse she'd seen when she was walking through town had air conditioning and a decent café au lait; she bet she could even see the sidewalk in front of the clock shop from there.

And sure enough, she could. Ilona was contemplating ordering a second coffee when the front door of the clock shop opened and Sarah stepped out. The sight stabbed Ilona right in the gut. The reddish-blond hair, which they'd learned was called strawberry blond, caught the sun, and there was Sarah, the clueless, lost little girl. And Nonie—Ilona—felt a swell of anger and longing so powerful she forgot to take a breath. But not for long.

She threw a dollar bill on the table as a tip and headed for the door.

Sarah was coming toward her, and Ilona had to quickly look in the nearest store window, a toy store, with old-fashioned toys that grandmothers on vacation probably bought for grandchildren back home. Grandchildren who would barely look up from their Androids to receive the toy. Maybe mumble a thank-you, though Ilona doubted it, before going back to their e-world.

Sarah turned when she got to the corner, and Ilona sauntered after her. It took an amazing amount of control not to run after her, shake her until she recognized Nonie, and she'd . . . what? Beg Nonie to forgive her? Hell, she probably wouldn't even remember her. She certainly hadn't recognized her when they were face-to-face.

Sarah crossed the street and Ilona saw a yellow mini school bus pulling to a stop halfway down the block. Ilona smiled slowly, the smile she showed before she cinched a case. It was known in legal circles as her "predatory smile." She was flattered by the nickname from other lawyers, but today it didn't sit well. Still, this was an opportunity she had hoped for.

Sarah was picking up the kid, Leila, Leila Rodrigues.

In a minute the kid would be getting off the bus; there would probably be hugs and kisses, or maybe there wouldn't be. Just because Sarah wanted to adopt the child didn't mean she was a loving mother. She'd been trusting and loving when she'd first come to the system. But the system—hell, life in general— killed trust and love.

Ilona moved closer. They would be returning to their home; they'd pass right by her. She should cross the street, but then their meeting would be hidden by the bus. She'd take her chances. Wait and then cross to the other side where halfway down the block there was a walk-through to the next street. The perfect getaway if it came to that.

The bus driver got off, then he lifted a child down to the sidewalk. She was small for a four-year-old. But sturdy. Sarah had at least been feeding her. Sarah bent down and hugged her, a little desperately, Ilona thought.

She's worried about losing her. And there was a good chance she would. Unless Ilona took the case. And she had absolutely no reason to do that.

Leila wriggled out of her grasp and was looking up, chattering animatedly about something. Ilona wished she was close enough to hear. The kid looked well adjusted and happy. Not that you could tell from a meeting at a bus.

Who was she kidding? Of course you could. Ilona had made a study of body language, starting with how to shoplift without being caught and running the gambit down to which witness was lying.

And she knew she was looking at one happy child and one frightened adult. *Sarah still the scared little rabbit, through and through,* she thought contemptuously.

They began walking her way and Ilona stayed, wanting to get a better look at the kid. She should have had Reesa send a photo over with the rest of the documents. The kid was wearing pink shorts and a T-shirt with a picture that Ilona couldn't decipher. Even the backpack was pink. The kid had dark skin and short hair with cowlicks held by some kind of plastic clips, a round face, and stubby little legs.

At least Sarah hadn't chosen her for her beauty. Not like some people.

They were getting closer and Ilona could hear the kid talking a mile a minute; something about the sound tightened her throat and kept her from beating a strategic retreat until it was almost too late.

Sarah looked up and Ilona turned away. Keeping her face shielded from Sarah's view, she crossed the street. A woman on a day of shopping in no hurry. *No quick movements, don't look around. Just walk away.*

But today Ilona couldn't help herself. When she reached the other side of the street, she did look. Sarah turned at the same time. And they were staring at each other. Ilona slowly turned, walked slowly away, forcing herself not to hurry until she reached the walk-through, then she ducked around the corner of the hardware store and ran like crazy.

SARAH STARTED TO cross the street but stopped. For a split second a woman directly across from her stared back at her. It looked just like that lawyer, Ilona Cartwright. But what would she be doing here?

Leila pulled at her jeans.

"Just a minute." Sarah looked again. As she watched, the woman turned almost in slow motion and began to walk down the sidewalk away from Sarah. There was something . . . something.

You won't get caught if you don't make any quick movements, just slip it beneath your jacket and walk away, no quick movements. Don't run until you find a place to get out of sight, then run like hell.

Sarah snatched Leila off her feet, hoisted her to her hip, and ran.

Chapter 10

Sarah stood at the far end of the walk-through, panting and clutching Leila to her side while she scanned the street for any sign of the woman who she was sure had been watching them.

She didn't find her. She knew she wouldn't.

"Mommee, what's wrong?"

"Nothing, sweet girl. I just saw someone I thought I knew and wanted to say hi."

She was still having trouble believing what she had just seen. Or believing that she'd actually seen anything. She must be losing her mind because of stress or something.

Because when Ilona Cartwright turned and walked away from her, Sarah saw someone else. And when without warning the woman slipped into the walk-through, out of sight, Sarah knew. She knew. Somehow . . . it didn't make sense. And it couldn't be true. And yet it must be.

She'd just seen a ghost. Because she'd thought, wondered, believed that Nonie was dead.

"I want to get down."

"I'm sorry, baby. Was that a bumpy ride?"

Leila nodded. Her bottom lip was stuck out. *Don't cry*, Sarah thought. She was afraid she might join her. And that wouldn't do, not with the visitation meeting on the horizon. Tomorrow.

She wished she could talk to Karen, but this was soccer, ballet, and Brownie day. And Sarah already felt she took too much of her friend's attention. The only thing Sarah could do to help Karen was to occasionally baby-sit when Karen and Stu needed a night away from the kids. Most of the time, help was a one-way street coming toward Sarah.

"How about we go see if Wyatt is at the store and wants to go for ice cream."

"Yeah, yeah, yeah." Leila bounced on her toes. She really had come a long way with Wyatt, especially in the last few weeks. Sarah just hoped that wouldn't be undone once visits with Carmen began.

They started back down the walk-through, and now that there was no emergency, Leila wanted to be carried. Sarah gladly lugged her to her hip, even though she was already beginning to feel the unaccustomed sprint in her thighs. She needed to get more exercise. Wyatt was always telling her so, but she just never seemed to have time.

The idea of Mommy and Me classes ran through her head, and she mentally crossed her fingers. Soon, if God had ears, it would be soon.

Wyatt was in the store just wrapping up an equipment rental to four muscular men who Sarah recognized as members of the rescue team from a nearby town. They'd just beat out Wyatt's group for first place in this year's lifeguard competition—a trophy that Wyatt's team had won three years in a row—and they'd been razzing him about it ever since.

"Don't get too complacent," Wyatt said good-naturedly. "We were working with a depleted crew. We'll get it back next year."

"Big talk," said one of the guys. "We scorched you."

"Enjoy it while you can. Now when are you bringing these tanks back?" Wyatt acknowledged Sarah and Leila with a lift of his chin and helped the men lug the tanks and apparatus out to their trucks.

"So to what do I owe this pleasure?" he said, coming back through the door. It closed behind him. He came straight over and gave Sarah a lengthy kiss.

She was acutely aware that Leila might be watching them, but when she pulled away, she saw that Leila had found the resident boogie board and was squatting on top of it pretending to ride the waves. Then Sarah was sorry she'd pulled away so soon.

"We thought you might like to go for ice cream."

"Ice cream on a Tuesday afternoon. What's the occasion?"

Sarah punched his arm. "I can be spontaneous."

He gave her a look that made her pulse race. He leaned in and said, "I know you can. And I like it when you are." He straightened up. "Of course I like you when you aren't, too."

She punched him again. She watched Leila battling the big waves for a few seconds then said, "There is something else."

"Uh-oh. Hit me with it."

"It's going to sound crazy."

"I can take crazy."

"It was the weirdest thing."

"Sarah."

"Right. Well, when I was picking Leila up from the bus, I saw this woman watching us."

"Are you sure?"

"Positive."

"A caseworker checking up on you?"

"The lawyer who wouldn't take my case."

"That's odd. Maybe it was just a coincidence. She's out shopping and sees you and you see her. Bound to be awkward."

"Maybe, but I got the distinct impression she was spying on me." She hesitated. "That's not all."

He waited.

"We looked right at each other, then she turned and walked away. And this is the crazy part, for a split second she looked just like a girl I used to know. In group home. We were like sisters and then she got adopted and I never heard from her again."

She waited for him to comment, but he didn't. He was good that way.

"So I grabbed Leila and ran after her. She was gone just like Nonie would do when we were . . . when we were shoplifting."

He half smiled. "During your life of crime."

"It isn't funny. I thought she must be dead, because we promised to write and I wrote every week and she never did." Sarah didn't know why she felt like crying. She'd reconciled herself long ago to having lost Nonie. On top of all the other stuff she was going through, seeing her again today was just too much.

"Well, let's see if we can find out and then we'll have ice cream."

At the mention of ice cream, Leila immediately lost interest in the boogie board and ran over to them.

"Just a few more minutes," Sarah told her.

Wyatt moved behind the counter to where he kept his laptop. He keyed in Ilona Cartwright's name. Then her website.

Sarah read over his shoulder as he scrolled down her bio page.

"Yale. Impressive."

"It doesn't go back further?"

"Nope, but . . ." He went back to the search page. Almost four hundred thousand links.

He looked back at Sarah. "This could take a while; can it wait until after ice cream?"

She nodded. Maybe it should wait forever.

Wyatt went to the back to tell his stock boy, Victor, to watch the store. Victor was a fiftysomething-year-old surfer with a long gray ponytail and a selection of surfer logo T-shirts that never seemed to repeat themselves.

"I bet I know what Leila wants," Wyatt said as he swung her up to his shoulders.

"Banilla with sprinkles," she squealed. "Banilla with sprinkles."

ILONA DIDN'T STOP to breathe until she was in her car and blocks away. What had she been thinking? This is not how a well-respected lawyer behaved. And yet she was skulking around the streets like common . . . . street trash. When would she ever learn?

She was a fool.

She barely noticed the red light or car stopped in front of her and just managed to slam on the brakes, stopping a few inches from the car's back bumper. Traffic was snarled into a total gridlock at the intersection, with waiting cars lined up in all directions. And she wasn't even to the highway.

What had she done to heap this day on her head? She hadn't intended to come this way. She'd meant to turn before this and drive up the coast route. But she'd driven away in panic mode, hadn't paid attention to where she was going, and now here she was stuck in traffic in the one place she didn't want to be.

The hood, where they'd hung out between school and curfew. And it was pretty much the same from what she could tell from the interior of her car. Young toughs and their girls were hanging on the street, exuding attitude and cigarette smoke. The guys wore their pants lower, the girls their hair bigger, and instead of boom boxes they had iPod buds dangling from their ears. But they still thought they were so cool. *Man, you're gonna die.*

A car behind her honked.

Idiot. Where did he think she could go?

She dropped her forehead to the steering wheel. She needed to go home.

Dear Sarah,

I skipped school and hitched down to the home to see you yesterday. I was real careful and I didn't go in. I was afraid it would get back to Donnie and June, aka Donald and June Cartwright, my adoptive parents. I didn't see you and when I stopped one of the kids, they had never heard of you. So I guess you got placed.

Donnie and June found out where I went and went all huffy on me. They were very disappointed in my behavior and after all they've done for me. And they said that I was ungrateful.

I'm not ungrateful, but I'll never tell them that. It's like being in prison here, a posh cushy prison, but not a life. I'm like some cheap figurine they dust and put out on display to show everyone what good people they are, so everyone will vote for Donnie.

June likes her little rat dog more than she likes me. Donnie's okay, I guess, just clueless.

I'll stick it out, play the game, because I see the light at the end of the tunnel, I hope. Maybe it's just a big old freight train ready to finish me off.

Sometimes I wish we'd run off before that day. But we woulda never made it.

> *You're still my sister.*
> *Nonie*

Traffic inched forward and Ilona tried not to look anywhere but straight ahead. Had Sarah recognized her? It seemed to Ilona that for a split second, recognition flickered in her eyes, but Ilona hadn't waited around to see what would happen. She'd run, coward that she was.

She reached to the dashboard and speed dialed the office. "I'm stuck in traffic," she told Inez. "If Mrs. Sobrato arrives before I do, tell her I'm running late. I'll be there as soon as I can."

As soon as she got to the next corner, she turned off the congested street. She'd have to take the backstreets to get to the highway. She remembered all the backstreets. Hell, she'd lived on some of them. But first she locked the car doors, not because she was afraid, but to show them she wasn't one of them anymore.

SARAH, LEILA, AND Wyatt were sitting at one of the round sidewalk tables outside the ice cream parlor when Wyatt's phone sounded an alert from the rescue patrol. He looked at it and stood.

"Sorry."

"Be careful," she called after him, but he was already sprinting down the sidewalk to the dive shop where his SUV was parked.

"Where's Wyatt going?" Leila asked.

"Some people need his help."

"Can we go?"

"No, only the rescue team can go."

"I want to be on the rescue team."

"Some day when you're grown up, you can be. But for now how about we walk down to the library?"

Leila nodded vigorously. "And get some books."

"Good idea." Now that Leila was more settled, her reading was improving by leaps and bounds. No worries about her mental capacities so far.

Sarah knew she should start reminding Leila that tomorrow was her visit with Carmen, but she was still shaken from seeing Nonie, and she just wanted a few more minutes with Leila before everything went south.

"Mommee, let's go."

"Right, the library," Sarah said. She cleaned Leila's face and both their hands, then put their trash in the receptacle and they strolled down the side street to the library.

They returned home an hour later with Sarah carrying a book bag filled with at least ten books. Leila would have taken more, but Sarah convinced her that more wouldn't fit in the bag. As soon as they were back inside Leila climbed on the couch and pulled them out one by one. "Read now, Mommee."

"After supper and your bath. You start picking out the ones you want to read first while I make dinner."

"This one." Leila put one down beside her on the couch. "And this one." Soon she was jabbering away, talking to herself, or maybe an imaginary friend, about the merits of each book. And Sarah went to cook dinner.

Leila wanted to bring the books to the table, but Sarah explained about getting food on the books and she was finally convinced to carry them back to her room to be read that night.

The books were stacked neatly on her bedside table when Sarah went to tuck her in a couple of hours later.

Leila climbed into bed. "*Green Eggs and Ham,*" she said and patted the place next to her for Sarah to sit.

"I thought we'd look at this first," Sarah said, bringing out the *Everybody Loves Me* photo album. "Since tomorrow you get to visit Carmen."

Leila frowned. "*Green Eggs and Ham.*"

Sarah didn't have the heart to argue. She dropped *Everybody Loves Me* on the floor. It had been one of those projects that was supposed to help children feel loved and secure. What a joke. It might work for Leila, for a while, but Sarah had no illusions about who loved whom. She opened *Green Eggs and Ham.*

Sarah held the book between them as she read, and Leila joined her on every Sam I Am. Sarah was afraid she'd be upset over the impending visit, but she fell asleep almost as soon as Sarah closed the book.

She tiptoed out of the room and left the door ajar. She usually loved this time at night, with the house perfectly quiet except for an occasional creak or groan. Sarah liked to work in the wee hours. But tonight she had other plans. She booted up her laptop; work and worry about tomorrow could wait while she delved into her past.

It was after midnight when Sarah found an early newspaper clipping of a younger Nonie and her foster parents, Donald and June Cartwright. Donald was a member of the state legislature and on a bunch of committees that Sarah didn't really care about. June, according to the article, was active in many charitable foundations, including foster placement.

His hairline receded slightly giving him an air of respectability. Not a hair of June's platinum pageboy was out of place. Both were impeccably dressed and smiling for the camera. Nonie stood in front of them, dressed in a skirt and blouse that would have had her making barfing noises if they'd seen some other girl wearing it. There was no doubt about it, Ilona Cartwright had once been Nonie Blanchard, Sarah's best friend and sister. She was wearing those stupid clothes. And smiling. *Smiling*.

Just one big happy family, Sarah thought, and anger and hurt swelled inside her. Nonie had lucked out big-time.

She read the article and almost barfed herself at the quote by Mr. Cartwright about race relations and the foster care system and how they wanted to do their part.

Sarah didn't read more. She didn't need to. Nonie had found a great home and forgotten about Sarah. Maybe she was even embarrassed to know her. Maybe she didn't want to be reminded of what went before.

And they had lived twenty minutes away. So close and she never even tried to get in touch with Sarah.

Was that why she'd run when Sarah saw her? Then why had she come at all? Sarah wanted to know. Wanted to confront her and ask her why. Or why she couldn't have just written her that she didn't need her anymore and then Sarah wouldn't have lived so long with false hope. Waiting for the day that Nonie would come and get her and she would have a real family at last.

Sarah yawned. She checked her phone to see if Wyatt had called. She liked him to call when he got back from a rescue mission. Just so she would know he was okay. She didn't always know when he went out. Sometimes he would tell her about it after he'd already returned. Still she worried.

An hour later, Sarah powered down her laptop. She'd learned a little more about Nonie, but as an adult, which stood to reason; the Internet wasn't all that common when they were kids.

She would have to confront her before this was over but not until she'd consulted Reesa and not until this first visit was behind them.

She checked on Leila, a little angel and free of care in her sleep. If only Sarah could promise her a life free from fear and insecurity. If given the chance, she could . . . and she would . . .

SARAH HAD FALLEN into a fitful sleep filled with half-realized dreams and Technicolor nightmares and images that seemed to float between the two. She woke the next morning feeling like she had been sleeping underwater. She didn't remember dreaming, which was probably just as well. She woke Leila, who seemed reluctant to get out of bed. She felt her forehead. No temperature.

During breakfast, Sarah managed to keep upbeat, and so

was Leila. But when it was time to leave for the school bus, she refused to take her backpack. Sarah didn't make a big deal of it, just picked it up and took her hand.

She waved as the bus drove away, then turned to make the best of it until Leila came home and she had to turn her over to Danny Noyes.

She detoured past Dive Works and stopped to peer in the window to see if Wyatt was there. She could see him working behind the counter. Restocking shelves. He was amazing—store owner, rescue team leader, dive instructor, and still he always made time for Sarah and Leila.

With so many things unsettled in her life, she suddenly wanted to make sure he was okay. She tapped on the window.

He looked up, slid a box onto the counter, and came to open the door.

"Hey, what's up?" He was wearing wrinkled khaki shorts and a T-shirt.

He looked concerned and for a second Sarah wondered if she only sought him out when she needed something.

"I was just coming from the bus stop and wanted to know how the rescue went yesterday."

"Fishing boat ran aground. Come on in. I've got a lesson in a few minutes."

"No, I don't want to hold you up, and I've got to get to work. Just wanted to make sure you were okay."

"Thanks. But I have to wait until Victor gets in, and the hires aren't even here yet." He stepped back, and she stepped over the threshold. He turned the Open sign over.

"Skipper broke his leg trying to get her free. Just one of those dumb things."

"Well, I'm glad everything turned out all right."

"So today's the big day, huh?"

"Yeah. I'm trying to stay calm. Maybe we can do this without all the angst and trauma of last time."

He pushed a piece of her hair behind her ear. His fingers lingered there. "You're a strong woman, Sarah Hargreave. You'll come through this."

She smiled shakily. "One way or the other."

The front door opened, setting the entry buzzer off. Sarah turned around expecting Victor. But it wasn't Victor. It was the young woman she'd seen talking to Wyatt the other day. Close up she was even prettier, more fit and blond than she'd been at a distance. She had a dazzling smile. It was trained on Wyatt.

"Am I late?" she asked in a voice Sarah swore was too sexy to be real.

"No. Just right. Here comes my associate."

Sarah slid behind the woman, held up her hand to say goodbye to Wyatt, and walked quickly toward the door.

"Let me know how things go?" Wyatt called after her.

She wiggled her fingers at him and slipped past Victor as he came in the door.

Stupid, Sarah chastised herself as she walked down the sidewalk. She should have been more friendly, or at least not be feeling jealous now. He was teaching the girl—woman—how to dive. Sarah couldn't go out with him because she didn't know how to swim. And had never wanted to, until maybe now.

She didn't have any hold over him. She didn't even want a hold over him. Did she? Then why was she suddenly jealous?

Because she had been taking him for granted. And Karen was right. She yo-yoed him in and out of her life at will. Well, it wasn't exactly at will; it was according to Leila. And that wasn't healthy. Leila needed to learn to trust men.

No, she didn't, Sarah reminded herself. Not until Sarah could protect her.

Men will take advantage, feel you up, rape you if you don't stay vigilant.

Sarah stopped in the middle of the sidewalk. Where the hell had that come from? She didn't think like that. But she had once. And she was still leery now years later. She'd gotten off pretty light in her years in the system. Not that some of them didn't try it with her. She was just good at staying vigilant and running away before she was up against the wall, both figuratively and literally.

Of course that had gained her the reputation of being a flight risk and therefore more difficult to place. That had been okay with Sarah. The group home had its dangers. But there she'd known where they were coming from.

Leila needed to learn to be around men without freaking out, and Sarah would just keep her safe until she could take care of herself.

The morning sun was beating down on the sidewalk, heating the asphalt of the street. Sarah already felt dragged out and the day hadn't even begun. The visit with Carmen was hanging over both her and Leila's heads.

They'd both ignored the calendar that morning. Even though the sun sticker they'd put in the square seemed to grow large and more menacing with each passing hour.

As Sarah stopped to deadhead the begonias that grew in the large terra-cotta pot on the clock shop porch, her cell rang.

Karen's ringtone.

"Hey."

"What time is Leila going to see Carmen today?"

"Danny is picking her up around three."

"Just enough time to get her home and snacked and not enough time for both of you to sit around worrying."

"Hmmm."

"So Reesa and I will meet you at Ocean Brew at ten after."

"I don't know."

"You're not going to sit at home alone making yourself sick with worry."

"You're right. Actually I do have something I want to talk to Reesa about and for you to hear."

"Sounds intriguing. See you then. Gotta run. It's bring your grandparents to camp day. Gotta bribe them with IHOP before we go. See you at three." And she hung up.

Chapter 11

As the clocks ticked their way to the afternoon, Sarah became more and more tense. *It's just two hours, supervised,* she reminded herself. Plus a half hour of travel time. She'll be back by five fifteen.

But Leila was having none of it. When Sarah picked her up at the bus, she stretched up her arms to be carried. Sarah carried her as much for her own comfort as for Leila's. She wanted to make sure that Leila knew how much she loved her.

Sarah had to put her down while she opened the front door, but immediately Leila glommed to her side, her hand fisting in the hem of Sarah's work shirt.

She hadn't forgotten that today was her day to visit Carmen. And it was Sarah's duty to make the transition as smooth as possible.

"Do you want a snack before you get ready for your visit with Carmen this afternoon?"

Leila shook her head and dropped her backpack on the floor.

"What did you do at school today?"

Leila shrugged.

"Okay, then why don't we go to your room and you can put on the outfit you picked out last night?"

Leila pulled her whole body up before huffing out a sigh, letting Sarah know she was not happy.

Sarah tried not to admit it was gratifying. But she'd been here before, and she knew that transitions were the hardest. "It will be fun to see Carmen and I'll be right here when Danny brings you back."

"You go with me."

"Sorry, boobaloo, I can't."

"Why?" A hint of a whine.

"It's the rules. You and Carmen and Danny can visit together."

"Why?"

"Because it's the rules."

"I hate rules."

I know, thought Sarah, *so do I.* These rules anyway. "Well, rules keep people safe."

"Why?"

"Because people, all people, should be safe."

Leila burrowed into her side, and it was all Sarah could do not to snatch her up and drive away with her. But that wouldn't keep Leila or Sarah safe. They wouldn't be safe until this all got sorted out.

Deciding not to push the issue of the clothes, she picked Leila and her backpack up and carried them into the living room where she sat them all in the big overstuffed chair that had been Sam's place. She immediately felt calmer. As if Sam were still giving her strength from the grave. A bunch of hooey, she knew. But she was willing to take even hooey today.

She picked up a book at random and opened it. *Can You Find Me at the Beach?* One of those hidden picture books that Leila loved.

"Crab," Leila said, pointing to the crab peeking out from under a striped beach towel. She took the book in both hands and looked over the picture, her brows knitted in concentration.

The knock at the door startled them both.

"That must be Danny. He's a little early." Sarah went to answer the door. Danny Noyes stood on the porch in baggy khakis and a short-sleeve sports shirt. He was wearing a tie, but it was pulled loose at the neck, and the top button of his shirt was unbuttoned.

"Come in."

They went into the living room, where Leila was standing behind the arm of Sam's chair as if it could hide her.

"Hey, Leila," he said brightly. "Ready to go?"

Leila shook her head.

Danny cast Sarah a disparaging look.

"I did everything the book said."

"Come on, your— Carmen is waiting for a visit. She's excited to see you."

Sarah nodded encouragingly at Leila. "I love you, sunshine."

Leila hung her head. Danny took her hand and escorted her out the door. She frowned back at Sarah as they walked across the sidewalk to Danny's car.

Sarah kept her smile glued in place, even though her jaw hurt and her lips were trembling. It was just a couple of hours. Everything would be fine.

She watched to make sure Danny put Leila in the car seat, watched him go around to the driver's side, watched as they drove away. Even after the car turned the corner and she couldn't see them, she waited. And finally closed the door. She stood in the foyer, fighting the nausea that threatened to overtake her. Leila would come back and everything would be fine.

Karen had been right about her not being alone. She would go crazy pacing the small cottage for the next few hours. She went to her desk and opened the notebook where she documented Leila's progress and setbacks. She logged in the date and time, the event, and Leila's reaction, then grabbed her bag and headed for the Ocean Brew.

She and Karen met at the door.

"Whew," Karen said and hugged her. "Whoever called summer a vacation was bat poop crazy."

Sarah smiled, though she still felt sick and coffee was probably the last thing she needed.

As soon as they were inside, Sarah made a beeline for a free table by the window, so she could see the street in case for some reason Danny and Leila returned early.

Karen gave her a sympathetic smile. "There's a long road ahead, too early to freak out."

"I know. It just blindsided me and you know how it goes, huge backsliding in behavior and learning. It's already starting." She saw Reesa hurrying past the window and waved to her.

Reesa barreled into the coffee bar. "Sorry I'm late. Did everything go okay?"

"So far," Sarah said.

"How about you?" Karen asked.

"I played hooky this morning to arrange housing for an older lady at the senior residence. Aguda found her an available apartment, hallelujah. Sometimes things just work out."

"You've taken on the elderly in your spare time?" Karen asked.

"No," Reesa said as she wrestled out of her summer jacket. "She was the one who sounded the alert for the White boys I just removed. She lives in a building surrounded by drugs and worse. I figured she deserved better."

"Good for you," Karen said.

Sarah dragged her gaze from the window. She couldn't stare out at the street for the next couple of hours, ignoring her friends when they had taken time to help her through. "She's lucky that you pulled the case."

"For my sins," Reesa said.

"I mean, not everybody would have thought about her."

"Any more on the other front?" Karen asked.

Reesa shook her head and turned to Sarah. "At the beach the other day, I blurted out that I was going to leave Michael. I meant it then. But now it seems so extreme. What I think I need is another job."

"Another job?" Sarah said, surprised. "Where would you find the hours?"

"I mean a different job."

Sarah stared at her. "You mean quit being a caseworker?"

"Maybe."

"But what about all those children?"

Karen laid a hand on Sarah's arm.

"Sorry, it's just that you're so good at what you do."

"Except that I'm burned out. Some days I think I can't witness another desperate family, or a battered or neglected child. We're like that story, with our fingers in the dike. God, sorry. We're here to make you feel better."

"Then for starters," Karen said, "let's get drinks and something terribly sweet and caloric." They all went up to the counter and returned a few minutes later with two iced coffees, an iced chai for Sarah, as well as several pastries, a knife, and three forks.

"Well, I have a bombshell to drop," Sarah said.

Karen, who had been dividing the pastries in thirds, stopped.

"Nothing about Leila?" Reesa asked.

"Not directly. But I know why Ilona Cartwright refused to take my case."

Reesa's eyebrows lifted. Karen put down the knife.

"We were in foster care—in a group home—together."

"No. Ilona Cartwright? Are you sure?" Reesa reached for a piece of peach turnover. "I knew she was adopted, but I don't remember it ever being mentioned about her being in the system."

"She was Nonie Blanchard then. And my best friend. Better than my best friend. We said we were sisters." The memory was still like a slice across her heart. "We swore we would always watch out for each other; well, at first she watched out for me mostly. She was older and had been there longer. But then she was adopted, I guess by the Cartwrights. We promised to write every week. But she never did."

The force of that memory hit her so hard that it nearly took her breath away. What had she done to make Nonie hate her so?

"That's crazy," Karen said, putting a piece of turnover on Sarah's plate.

"Neither of you said anything while we were there," Reesa said.

"I didn't know then. She doesn't look anything like she did when I knew her and I never knew her name was Ilona, just Nonie. But she recognized me. She must have. That's why she wouldn't take the case. I don't know what I did that made her so angry at me, but she obviously still holds a grudge."

"Wait. Then how did you figure out that you knew her?"

"She was down here yesterday. I'm sure she was following me. She saw me meet Leila at the bus after school. I saw her standing across the street and when she saw me, she turned and walked away, then disappeared down one of the walk-throughs. I ran after her, but when I reached the end of the walk-through, she was gone."

"And you're sure it was her?"

"As soon as she turned and walked away, I could tell. It's exactly what she taught me to do when we were shoplifting." Sarah grimaced. "Before I reformed. She had me practice so many times and copy her that I would know it anywhere. It sounds crazy, but it isn't. It was Nonie all right. That's why she wouldn't take the case—she hates me. That must be why she came down to spy on me. What do you think she's up to? Trying to sabotage my chances?"

"Stop." Reesa put up her hand, crossing guard style. "You don't know that she has ulterior motives. Maybe she just happened to be shopping when you saw her."

"Then why did she run?"

"You should go talk to her," Karen said. "Maybe it's just a misunderstanding. Her letters got lost. You know how the system is. Someone could have stolen them. Or a thousand things could have happened. I bet if you talked things out—"

Sarah shook her head. "I haven't forgiven her, either. Two years we were inseparable, sisters. Then she left me behind. She promised she'd come back for me, but she never looked back."

Reesa leaned forward on her elbows. "Sarah, you know she wouldn't have been able to do that."

"Maybe not then, but she could have written like she promised to do; she could have looked me up once she was on her own. She never did."

Reesa laid her hand on Sarah's arm. "We may not even need her."

"But you should try to reconcile," Karen said, passing around three sections of a sticky bun. "It's not good to leave things like that to fester. Just talking about it—"

"No. She's had eighteen years to reach out to me. The system knew where I was. And they know where I am now."

"Look," Reesa said. "Let's give it some time, see what shakes out. If it turns out we do need her, I'll talk to her. Twenty years is a long time to be angry. I'll try to convince her to do the right thing."

"Don't bother. You said yourself we had time. I'll let Randy handle it, or I'll find someone else. But not her."

KAREN AND REESA stayed at the coffee bar after Sarah went home to wait for Leila and Danny. They watched her walk across the street, up her porch steps, and go inside. Then they turned to each other.

"It's like she's already distancing herself from us," Karen said.

Reesa nodded. "Detaching. It's a classic reaction. Sometimes the child isn't the only one that regresses."

"But she's pulling away already, like she expects to lose, like she doesn't expect us to stand by her."

"When you're used to losing, losing becomes your default mode."

"Well, it sucks." Karen cut the last chocolate croissant in half and handed half to Reesa. "Gosh, look at me. I've been cutting everyone else's food like I was the mother or something."

"You are and a good one. And so is Sarah if given the chance."

"So what can we do?"

"You've run support groups for years."

"But this is different. Sarah is our friend."

"And we'll be here when she needs us. But she has to come to that realization. We can't just keep butting in. It will make her defensive and less able to cope."

"It's such a mess. Do you think Carmen might really have a chance of getting Leila back?"

"From past attempts, no. But this might be the time that works."

"I should have warned Sarah not to adopt from the system. They make it too difficult."

"Tell me about it. I'd really like to have Cartwright lined up in case we need her."

They both finished their half of the croissant, not talking, each with her own thoughts.

"So what are you going to do?" Karen asked, pushing the cake plate away.

Reesa raised her eyebrows. "About Sarah or Ilona Cartwright?"

"About your life."

"Damned if I know. But something's gotta give or I might end up on the cover of some tabloid."

"That bad?"

"Pretty much."

Karen reached for her hand. "You need a vacation."

Reesa gave her a look. "Me and all the other overworked, underpaid, sleep-deprived caseworkers."

"I mean it. At least take a long weekend. I know. Come stay with us for a few days. It will be mass craziness, but at least it will be good craziness. You can tell Michael you're having a girls' weekend. Even better, we *will* have a girls' weekend. I bet Sarah could use one by then, too. We've got the beach, and I'll con Stu into watching the kids. We'll have Sarah bring Leila over, and the three of us will go have some fun. Goodness knows we could all use some."

SARAH WAS STANDING at the window when Danny double-parked his Hyundai in front of her cottage. He ran around to the backseat and scuttled Leila out of the car seat, swung her to the grass verge, and then hurried her up the steps to the house.

Sarah opened the door and knelt down to give Leila a hug, but Leila pulled her hand away from Danny's and blew right past Sarah without slowing down.

Danny looked apologetic, but spoiled it by glancing over his shoulder to make sure he wasn't getting ticketed.

"This is normal behavior," he said as he began stepping back across the porch. "There's always a little adjustment after visits."

"I know, Danny. Been there, done that. Several times. You'd better go see to your car."

"Yeah, thanks. Next week same time?" He'd asked it as a

question but since there was only one acceptable answer, Sarah didn't bother to say it. He nodded, turned, and sprinted toward his car, just as a black-and-white came around the corner.

Sarah closed the door, took several calming breaths and went in search of Leila. She was in her room sitting on the floor. Her backpack was open and she was rummaging inside.

"Did you have a good time?" Sarah asked.

Leila ignored her. The silent treatment. She'd been pretty good at it herself at one time.

"Want an apple and some almond butter?"

"I want candy."

"We don't have candy. How about yogurt and granola?"

"I want candy."

"We don't have candy."

Leila looked up then, her eyes narrowed, her face scrunched up—her "mean" face—and Sarah smiled.

"Carmen has candy."

"How about Jell-O?"

"Go away."

Leila got to her feet and pushed Sarah toward the bedroom door. Sarah didn't resist or try to change her mind. She just left the room. She heard Leila shut the door behind her.

Sarah sighed. Just like clockwork. It was happening all over again.

ILONA CLOSED HER briefcase as the courtroom cleared. The Sobrato case had just been recessed until next Friday and she wasn't happy about it. She could have gone in for the kill and finished this charade—and the opposing lawyers knew it.

Now they would spend the interim time negotiating and bargaining. She wasn't going to negotiate or bargain. Olivia

Sobrato was going to get a shitload of money or Ilona would go back to law school for a brushup course.

Olivia stood and reached for her purse, leaning in close to Ilona. "We have them, don't we?"

We, nothing, Ilona thought. *The only thing you've done is whine and complain.* "I think we do. Excuse me." Ilona took her briefcase and strode toward Barry O'Doul who was pleading the next case.

"See you on Friday," Olivia called after her.

"Damn," Barry said. "You were fierce."

Ilona smiled her barracuda smile and waited for Olivia to mince her way up the aisle of the courtroom. "I was just doing my job for my client."

"Yeah, you had 'em by the short hairs, that's for sure. Man, the way you wiped the floor with Ken's presentation; my balls headed for the hills in sympathy. Damn."

The clerk called for the next case.

"Good luck," Ilona said and climbed the steps to the back door. Good luck and a dose of histrionics—those were the only two tools in Barry's toolbox.

Her energy lasted as long as it took to get to her car. She reviewed the afternoon and pretended to be pleased—long enough to get out of the parking garage and to the coast road.

Then the courtroom drama fell behind her like the wake of a speedboat, and the hurt and anger she'd been fighting against since seeing Sarah Hargreave rushed over her once again.

She'd made something of her life, had endured, hadn't let anything or anyone stop her from getting what she wanted. She was right where she wanted to be, on her way up in the legal world. Living in a posh apartment, socializing with the up-and-comers.

And in one mistaken decision, one brief encounter, it all came crashing down. Her past staring her in the face.

She stepped on the accelerator and the car tore down the street while Ilona screamed at the top of her lungs.

Dear Sarah,

I hate you. I hope you are dead.

Not your sister anymore.
Nonie

Chapter 12

Sarah and Leila managed to get through the evening, though Leila refused to speak for most of it. Waking up with a tummyache in the middle of the night helped to break the ice somewhat, until Sarah explained that it was probably from eating too much candy. Then Leila turned her back on Sarah, pulled the covers over her head, and finally fell back to sleep.

The silent treatment continued through breakfast, and by the time she saw Leila off at the bus, Sarah was frayed around the edges.

So instead of going directly to the store, she detoured to Ocean Brew. Wyatt was coming out carrying his morning coffee. He was wearing jeans and a stretched-out T-shirt. He looked strong and handsome, but more than that, he looked comfortable.

"Hey," she said.

"How did it go with Leila yesterday?"

"Like you'd expect. Went willingly enough. Came back quiet. Got mad because Carmen had candy and we didn't." Sarah shrugged. "Par for the course, I guess you'd say."

"Well, hopefully this won't go on for too long."

Sarah nodded. "Well, I'd better get to work. I've been sorely neglecting the store lately."

"It's summer." Wyatt grinned, but he seemed a little distant. Was he already expecting her to start pushing him out of their lives? Because that's what she did. She didn't want to. But what choice was there?

Her cell phone rang—Karen's ringtone.

"See you later," Wyatt said.

"Later." Sarah answered the phone as she watched him walk away.

"Hey, girlfriend. Get all your work done. I'm declaring this weekend girls' weekend away."

"Karen, I can't go anywhere, not now."

"Oh, we're not going anywhere, but Reesa needs to have some decompression time. She's going to spend the weekend here. Stu has promised to keep the kids busy and we're going to the beach in the afternoon and to a bar that night and to wherever we want to go. And you're coming, too."

"Maybe for part of the time."

"Listen. Reesa's always doing for other people, now it's our turn to give back a bit. So you can't say no."

"Okay, but I'll have to check on the store sometimes."

"We'll allow that. And you don't have to sleep at my house, unless you want to."

"Sounds like fun. But I do have responsibilities."

"We've invited everyone over to Wyatt's house for a Sunday afternoon barbecue."

"Did you let Wyatt know? I just saw him and he didn't say anything." *And why was that?* she wondered.

"Of course we did. We're bringing the food. The guys will grill."

"Kids, too?"

"Kids, too."

"Great."

"I hope you stir up more enthusiasm than that by Saturday. Reesa needs us."

"I know. I am enthusiastic. I'm just working out the logistics." And wondering if Wyatt was going to invite the blonde to the barbecue. Maybe she shouldn't go.

"Make sure you do. Gotta run." Karen hung up.

Sarah unlocked the store and went inside, stopping to look around like she did every morning. Today she let the steady beat of the clocks calm the beating of her heart. She always found peace among the clocks. Time always passed at the same speed, at least in her world.

You couldn't stop it, you couldn't make it go faster or slower, you could just make the best of it. Sam's words. And he'd laugh when Sarah rolled her eyes at him. Sam had taught her acceptance along with all the other important things.

It hadn't been easy. When she walked into the clock store that first day, she had spent years trapped in a holding pattern of waiting. She'd been living in the system, when you were at the mercy of so many factors, none of them personal, and none of which you understood.

Sarah had never felt in control of her life, her world, until she met Sam. Even then she'd fought him. He never gave up on her; he taught her how to stand on her own feet, stick up for herself in a constructive way, not by fighting or furtive attacks;

he taught her to relax, to enjoy the world around her. And he shared his life's love with her, clocks.

At first he only let her dust, showing her how to lightly reach into the "nooks and crannies, like English muffins," he said. Sarah didn't get it, but she nodded like she did. She didn't fool him. She could tell from his eyes, but he didn't make her feel stupid or anything.

When he finally let her help with repairs, she acted like she didn't care. But she did, more than she could understand. All those little parts, some so tiny that she went all fumble fingers and they would roll and hide until she wanted to throw the whole damn thing in the trash. Sam would just wait for her to calm down, then help her search for the pieces. And when they'd all been returned to the workbox, he'd hand her a magnifier glass, and start her all over again.

She would sometimes complain bitterly, but when she was done, each part, no matter how tiny, was put together in a way that made everything work. Steady, dependable. Like Sam. Like the way life should be.

In the clock shop Sarah felt she belonged, had a reason to exist. Out in the world she was not so sure. Even now, over a decade later.

Now she was stuck in that holding pattern again, at the mercy of decisions made by strangers. She knew there was nothing she could do but wait. Hope, prepare to be disappointed.

Whenever she was depressed or feeling lost, Sam would shake his head and he'd tell her to be her own champion. She sometimes lost sight of that now that he wasn't here to egg her on.

If she was to stay on top of things, she needed to step up to the plate. And she knew just where to start. Because that was one thing she could "do," without waiting for someone else's decision.

The minute Alice walked in, Sarah grabbed her bag. "I have to run out. I should be back in a while." She had no idea when she would be back—a few minutes or a few hours, whatever it took. But sometime before she had to pick up Leila at the bus.

Before she could second-guess herself, Sarah was in her car and driving to the Erickson, Cartwright and Hefley law offices.

She didn't even know if Nonie was there today or if she was in court. Hell, she could be taking the day off and spending it on someone's yacht. Maybe her own. Sarah didn't care; at least she was being proactive. If she had to leave without seeing her, she would, but she'd be back, and she would show up without warning her old friend, her sister, that she was coming. Not give her notice so she could turn her back on her again without hearing her out.

She didn't even know what she wanted to say, mainly she just wanted to know.

ILONA WAS ON the phone to Mr. Sobrato's lawyer. His client wanted to meet. Settle this out of court. Too late, baby. They'd had their chance. She was just about to tell him so when the door opened.

"I'm sorry, I couldn't stop her," Inez explained, following close on the heels of Sarah Hargreave.

"I'll have to call you back." Ilona hung up the phone. "Inez, get security up here. Stat."

Inez hurried from the room.

Ilona turned to Sarah, who looked like an avenging pixie. "Do you think bursting in here will get you anything but arrested?" Ilona said at her coldest. But she was shaken. She'd been off balance ever since seeing Sarah with her foster daughter. Off balance and angry.

Sarah didn't slow down, until she reached the opposite side of the desk. She braced her hands on the top and leaned forward. "I can't believe you have lived here for the last ten years and you never tried to contact me. But I guess I understand it now. You're cold and heartless and you don't care about anything but climbing the ladder to success. To think I actually believed you when you said we were sisters. That we would always have each other's backs. I trusted you. Loved you. And you betrayed me. You left me with nothing, not even hope."

She sucked in her breath on a sob. "I hope you're happy with what you have. I hope it was worth it."

Sarah turned and left as fast as she'd come. Before Ilona had a chance to understand what she was saying. Much less defend herself.

Inez's head appeared in the doorway. "Do you want to file a complaint? Have her arrested?"

Ilona shook her head. "Just have security escort her out of the building. I don't think she'll be back."

Inez nodded, and the heavy door swung closed behind her. Ilona closed her eyes.

Dear Sarah,

I didn't mean it. It's just why don't you write me?

Nonie

SARAH STOOD ON the sidewalk in the sun, breathing hard. Not willing to wait for the elevator, she'd taken four flights of stairs down. She half expected the security team to be waiting for her at the bottom.

What had she been thinking? What if they actually carted her off to jail for breaking or entering or something? She wouldn't put it past the person who used to be Nonie to do something like that. And how would that look on her record at Child Protection and Permanency?

And she didn't even have the satisfaction of seeing Ilona turn back into Nonie and tell her to go eff herself. That's what she would have done before, only she wouldn't have stopped there.

But of course the manicured imitation of her friend inside her air-conditioned, sterile office would never stoop to something so low class. She wouldn't even acknowledge Sarah's presence, much less react to her. Just sat behind her big designer desk with her stony face and waited for her minions to come relieve her of Sarah's unwanted appearance.

Well, to hell with her.

Though to be honest Sarah hadn't given her much of a chance to respond. She had just wanted to get said what she needed to say before she was thrown out. And she had said most of it.

She started walking down the street to where she'd parked the car next to the curb. *Expecting the need for a hasty getaway?* She smiled at the thought. She almost did.

But damn, it felt good to be doing something, even if it made absolutely no difference to anyone else but her.

Her car was stifling, the seat burning from the sun. It was a good thing she hadn't needed to jump in and speed away. As it was, she stood outside while the air conditioner ran, then she got inside and drove away.

It was on the way home that Sarah began to wonder if she'd done something really stupid. Would Nonie be so vindictive as to report her to the child services staff, say that she'd broken into her office and threatened her. That she had anger management problems, that she was a threat to Leila. Sarah wouldn't put it past her. But she had her friends and they would be good character witnesses.

Friends. She had friends. Sometimes in the craziness of her life, she forgot. She had friends. Good friends. Like a family.

Dear Ilona,

I don't need you anymore. I thought I did, but I don't. It was hard but I held out hope that I would see you again. I never stayed with a family for long. One, there were too many children. They didn't do anything but take the money and sit around watching television. Another the man kept trying to get inside my pants. The wife caught him with his hand up my shirt and slapped me. I ran away. There were others, and through it all I kept telling myself to hang tough like you said. That we'd be sisters again one day.

I lost you. But I found Sam. He is the one who taught me how to trust people. How to love. How to expect a good day ahead instead of a bad. I owe everything I am today to Sam, not you.

And to my friends who like me in spite of the socially inept mess that I still am. So go on with your life. And I'll go on with mine.

Your . . . nothing,
Sarah

Sarah went straight to the workshop when she got home. She needed to be with the clocks, to envelop herself in the feel of them, the sound of them. She had friends, but she needed her clocks to keep her sane. To keep her from being afraid. Clocks were good. You knew where you were with clocks.

REESA GRABBED A packaged sandwich and a cup of coffee from the hospital canteen and remembered to get her parking ticket validated before leaving the hospital. The office was still looking for relatives who would be interested in taking the three White children. Until then, Reesa was making sure they were being well taken care of. Pete was resilient and would be ready to leave the hospital soon, probably as soon as there was a bed available in one of the care facilities. Little Jerome was still in intensive care.

Reesa had taken Pete a video game. It had belonged to one of her boys and was pretty out of date, but Pete seemed happy to get it. Then she sat by Jerome's bed, wondering how a boy so small could have so many tubes keeping him alive. It was enough to break anyone's heart.

She drove to the CP&P office where she had to sit in on a team meeting for the White boys. She'd already told them to put the boys on a permanency track. She'd tell them again today. They could talk about it all they wanted and they would. There was always someone who thought they knew best and would argue until the others gave up or shut them down.

And they wondered why caseworkers couldn't get their work done.

She'd heard from Tanya Aguda about an apartment for Ms. McKinney. She'd pulled some strings and found a small unit. It wouldn't be available for another week while it was being repainted, but she could take the older woman over to look at the place before she signed the papers. That's one thing she could do without a committee.

She phoned Michael.

It took him almost ten rings before he answered.

"I was beginning to worry. It took you so long to answer. Were you outside?"

There was silence at the other end. "Michael?"

"I was watching the game. I didn't hear the phone."

Reesa took a deep breath. "It will be after six maybe seven before I'm home; there's chili in the Crockpot and some salad stuff in the fridge."

"What is it with you? Can't I get a decent meal for a change?"

"Well," she said, using every bit of her discipline not to yell. "You could make yourself some chicken. There's a package in the freezer, defrost it in the microwave."

"Maybe I will. It was a strike, you dummy!"

"See you later."

"Huh? Yeah. Ya bum! What are you blind, you—"

Reesa hung up.

She swung out of the parking lot and drove straight to the apartment complex where Ms. McKinney lived. She parked at the curb and walked up the sidewalk to the building. There was a pile of garbage and furniture on the curb and she wondered briefly if it belonged to the Whites. No big deal. Surely there was nothing worth saving, and she wasn't about to look.

She rang the buzzer of Ms. McKinney's apartment, listened to make sure it was working, and waited.

Knocked on the door. "Ms. McKinney. It's Reesa Davis, the social worker who came for the White boys. Are you in?"

She heard the rattle of the chain and the door opened a bit. Ms. McKinney looked out. Then opened it wider.

Reesa gasped. "Ms. McKinney, what happened? Did you fall?"

One side of her face was bruised and scraped. As she closed the door behind Reesa, Reesa saw that she was using a cane to maneuver herself through the apartment.

"Mugged. Those boys. Took my social security money."

"Did you call the police?"

Ms. McKinney shook her head. "They can't do anything but get me in trouble."

"Well, I came to tell you that I've found you an apartment in a retirement community. It's subsidized. And safe. You'll need to come sign some papers and it will be another week before it's ready, if you're interested."

"It's safe?"

"Yes, it has a security guard on duty as well as a buzzer."

The old woman's mouth worked like maybe she was chewing her cheeks. And then tears began to roll down her cheeks. "The Lord is good and so are you, Mrs. Davis."

"I can take you to see it now, if that's convenient."

"Oh yes, ma'am, real convenient."

Reesa knew she should go down to the office to file her report, but protective services wouldn't fall apart if she took an hour to help out an old lady who had helped them. Actually they wouldn't even notice. And probably, neither would Michael.

It was nearly seven when Reesa dropped Ms. McKinney back at her old apartment. She walked her to her door and saw her safely inside. Then, clutching her mace canister, she hurried back to her car and drove home.

Reesa didn't even slow down to take off her shoes when she got home. She marched right back to the den where she found Michael where she knew he would be. She'd meant to sit down with him and talk things out, try once again to get him off his duff and out looking for a job. Hell, at this point she'd be happy if he'd just go out.

But when she actually got his attention over the blare of some sports talk show, she said. "Just so you know. I'm out of town this weekend. You'll have to fend for yourself until I get back."

She walked out of the room and down the hall to her bedroom where she changed into yoga pants and an old gardening shirt.

She shoved her feet into last year's running shoes and was coming out of the bedroom when she met Michael coming down the hall.

"What do you mean you're going out of town?"

"Out of town," she said. "As in, not in town. I should be back Sunday late, or maybe Monday."

She breezed passed him.

"Where are you going?"

"I'm going out to the yard."

"I mean where are you going this weekend?"

She took a breath. "I'm going to a girls' weekend away."

"What the f—? What am I supposed to do?"

"Gee, Michael. I don't know. Why don't you watch some television?"

"Hey, I broke my leg." He followed her into the kitchen.

"That was months ago. The doctor says you're fine. I've tried to be supportive, I've talked myself blue in the face trying to get you going. Now it's up to you." She grabbed a diet soda out of the fridge and headed for the back door and the shed, where hopefully she'd find some forgotten and probably rusting gardening tools.

"I can't go back up on the scaffolding."

She stopped. Turned. Looked him in the eye. "Then get a job on the ground."

She opened the back door.

"Where are you going now?"

"To dig up the dead rhododendrons."

"What about dinner?"

"You'll have to open the Crockpot by yourself."

She started to close the door, but he jerked it out of her hand.

"You sure know how to emasculate a guy."

"No, Michael, you're doing a pretty good job of that yourself."

She went to the shed, pulled open the rusted metal door, bent over, and went inside. When she came out with a shovel and a garden claw, he was gone, the back door was shut.

And Reesa was shaking. It seemed to her she had just started something and she had no idea of where it would end.

Chapter 13

Weekends were always busy for the clock shop. It got more foot traffic from people looking for interesting gifts, so busy that Sarah and Alice both worked a full day.

Sarah had promised to meet Reesa and Karen for a drink Saturday evening. Karen would pick her up and drop off Jenny and Leila who'd spent the day with Bessie and Tammy. At first Sarah hesitated. Leila had been up and down since the Wednesday visit with Carmen, and they hadn't spent much time together since then. Sarah rarely went out at night, and she didn't want Leila to think it was because she was letting her go.

She made all these excuses to Karen, but Karen would have none of it, so finally she agreed to have an early drink at a nearby upscale bar.

The cuckoo sounded for maybe the twentieth time that afternoon. It was the sound that alerted them to the arrival of customers. When Sarah had first come into the store, she'd thought it was the corniest thing she had ever heard. But Sam loved it. He chuckled every time it sounded no matter how many times it went off during the day. Some days she'd want to put her hands over her ears and sing Lalalala until it stopped, but now she loved it, too. It had become so much a part of her that she couldn't imagine a buzzer or a bell instead.

An older lady and her middle-aged daughter were looking for memento mori watches. Sarah didn't carry anything that reminded her of death or how short life really was, so she gave them the name of a dealer who could help them and sent them on their way.

A few minutes before closing, a couple came in who evidently had money and time to burn. After much laughing and dithering, they bought a 1950s "vintage" Swiss wristwatch and Sarah followed them to the door. She locked it behind them and turned the Closed sign over.

"Can you lock up for me?" Sarah asked Alice who had already gotten out the Windex and was cleaning the glass top of a display case from the last customers.

"Going home early?"

"Going out with the girls."

"Oh. Good for you. And who's watching Leila?"

"Karen is bringing Jenny over."

"And you feel confident leaving a twelve-year-old by herself with Leila?"

"We're just going down the street for a drink. I'll probably be back before dark."

"You should go out more often," Alice said. "You're a young woman. You should have some fun."

"I have fun."

"Working all day, and taking care of a child the rest of the time?"

"That's just the way I like it," Sarah said. She really didn't want to get into a discussion of what her life should be like with Alice, who had a way of making even compliments sound depressing.

"You know if things don't work out with Leila, you'll have time to do other things. Could spend more time in the store, more time with your friends. Maybe get Wyatt to propose to you. You know it's hard to get a man interested when you come as a package."

Sarah considered telling her that if she had more time in the store, she could cut back Alice's hours. But she bit her tongue. Alice meant well. Always attempting to make the glass seem half full but invariably making it practically empty.

"Then it's a good thing I'm not looking for a man."

"Wyatt won't wait forever, you know."

Sarah just stared at her. Is that what they all thought? That Wyatt was waiting for her to do what? Dump Leila back into the system? They had never discussed the future. She hadn't thought he was interested in anything but the now. And she didn't have time for anything more. She wasn't even sure she wanted more. Did he? She certainly wouldn't ask Alice her opinion, though she was sure she had one.

"Have a good weekend," Sarah said. "I'll just go out the back."

She showered and changed into capri pants and a boatneck tee. A little dressy for Saturday night at a beach bar, but perfect for the trendy bar in the shopping district.

She was ready when Jenny and Leila came in the front

door. "Mom already fed us and sent us home with Rice Krispie treats," Jenny said. "I'll make sure she doesn't eat too many."

"I know you will," Sarah told her. She knelt down by Leila. "I'm going out for a little while with Karen and Reesa. I'll be back soon."

Leila's lip quivered and Sarah's resolve slipped.

"Mama says you're to go right out to the car, didn't she, Leila?"

Leila nodded.

Sarah kissed her. "You're my sunshine," she said, waved, and left, wondering if this was how ordinary parents behaved or if they would stay at home, considering the situation. By the time she got to the car, she was definitely having second thoughts.

Sarah opened the back car door, but instead of getting in, she looked through the opening to where Karen and Reesa sat in front.

"Oh no you don't. Get in now," Karen said. "We've already prepped Leila about you coming with us. And that you'll be back. Thank you very much. Isn't it nice to have friends with all this professional expertise?"

Sarah nodded and climbed into the backseat.

"It will be fine," Reesa said, craning around to see her from the front. "But don't feel weird; I felt the same way when I walked out on Michael last night." She grinned suddenly, looking years younger and light-years happier.

They found a parking space around the corner from the bar. Several groups were standing on the sidewalk and waiting on the stairs going down to the bar.

"We have reservations," Karen said, as she led them under a green neon sign that read TOOMAY. It was one of those one-name "scene" places, crowded but not so crowded you couldn't find your friends or meet new ones, loud but not too loud to hear the people at your own table or standing at the bar next to you. Plenty of singles but not heavy-handed in the pickup scene. And expensive.

"How do you get reservations in a bar?" Reesa asked.

"I called Larry Swanson and told him to save us a table." Karen smiled a big smug smile. "It pays to know people in the booze business."

Larry was standing at the bar and came to greet them. He was one of the regulars at Ocean Brew. It was one of the things Sarah loved about her town, that all the businesspeople supported one another. And were friends of a sort.

He led them over to a bar table that had a reserved sign on a folded piece of cardboard. It was handwritten. "I made it just for you," Larry explained. "I'm surprised to see you out on Saturday night, Sarah. This calls for champagne."

"Oh no," Karen said laughing. "Tonight we do girly drinks, preferably pink with little umbrellas in them."

"Piña colada with grenadine?" Larry suggested. "Or choose from one of our specialty drinks." He neatly produced a plastic carte for them to read. "I'll send a waiter over posthaste." And he made a beeline for a party who was just entering.

They decided on the piña coladas. They came frozen and pink in large wide glasses with paper umbrellas and a wedge of pineapple on the rim.

They drank and laughed and ordered another round. Sarah felt a little buzz though Karen had told the waiter to go light on the liquor since she had to drive home and none of them were big drinkers.

Sarah would have walked home to clear her head, but

Karen had to pick up Jenny. They made it back to Sarah's without mishap.

When Sarah came inside, Jenny was curled up on Leila's bed. Leila was nestled up against her and Jenny's arm was around her. Jenny's eyes were wide open.

"She had a bad dream. She's okay. She went back to sleep."

"You handled it great, Jenny. Thank you. Your mom's outside."

Jenny eased off the bed. Leila whimpered and opened her eyes. "Mommee," she said, starting to cry, and held out her arms.

"She was okay, really she was," Jenny said.

"I know. She just wants her mommee. See you tomorrow at the barbecue?"

Jenny nodded, still looking worried.

"Really, Jen, It's all right."

Jenny collected her things and left. Sarah gathered Leila onto her lap and began to sing her back to sleep.

REESA WOKE THE next morning without a headache. Which was amazing since after she and Karen came back to Karen's, they polished off half a bottle of wine. She was a little disoriented. It was strange to wake up in a different bedroom than her own.

She never traveled anymore. Michael didn't want to go anywhere except fishing, or bowling or sometimes camping with the boys when they were around. But lately he hadn't even wanted to do that.

Reesa settled back in the bed, enjoying the light green walls and the floral comforter and matching curtains of Karen and

Stu's guest room. It was so cheerful. Her bedroom at home was dark, with a huge heavy bed and huge heavy furniture. What were they thinking when they bought such overpowering pieces? That they'd survive a lifetime of hurricanes?

They'd be lucky if they survived this marriage. But she wasn't going to think about her problems today.

Karen and Reesa had spent yesterday at the beach and Reesa had managed to get a little tan and one strip of sunburn where she'd missed with the sunscreen. *Battle scars,* she thought. She was enjoying herself. At least as long as she could keep the niggle of guilt away. She wondered what Michael was doing, which was stupid. He'd be up by now, would have already eaten a bowl of cereal. The bowl would be lying in the sink for her to wash before she went into the office to catch up on paperwork on her day off.

Today she was playing hooky. Somebody else could do the paperwork for a change. She was going to a barbecue and then . . . then she supposed she'd have to go home. Face Michael's recriminations, if he even noticed she was gone. Of course he would. He'd be making his own meals.

Reesa sighed and pushed the covers away, determined not to let her regular life rain on her weekend. She showered and dressed in blue Bermuda shorts she'd found at the bottom of the bottom drawer of her dresser. And they still fit, though she couldn't remember wearing them in years. And a flowered button-up shirt that was a little frumpy but was colorful and she was going for upbeat this weekend. She even put on lipstick before she padded out to the kitchen to find Karen making pancakes and Stu standing over a cast-iron pan filled with sizzling bacon.

"Hey, girlfriend. How'd you sleep?"

"Like a log," Reesa said. "It felt great. Can I help with something?"

"Nope. We're almost done. You can call the kids in. They're in the den."

Reesa could hear the television blaring.

"Breakfast's ready," she said into the family room. Four faces turned in her direction.

"Breakfast," she repeated over the blare of some superhero fight scene. Rory clicked the remote, and four children and one very large dog padded into the kitchen and took their places at the table in the breakfast nook.

The dog was banished to the backyard.

"Once he ate a whole plate of bacon," Tammy told her.

"And he threw it up on the carpet," Bessie added. All of them but Jenny made upchucking noises. Jenny rolled her eyes.

"So when the bacon comes out, he goes out," Stu said as he set a plate with a stack of pancakes leaning precariously to one side on the table.

"I told Wyatt to expect us around four," Karen said. "I don't want to make too late of a day of it, since the kids have camp tomorrow. He's taking a party out for diving at one. He said if he wasn't back to start without him."

"Are you sure he doesn't mind us coming over there?" Reesa asked.

"No, plus he knows he'll get the leftovers. We'll go to the store after breakfast. Pick up steaks and salad stuff and maybe make some potato salad."

The kids tore through the pancakes and bacon like they hadn't eaten in days and asked to be excused before rushing back to the den where the television immediately resumed to whatever they were watching, only several decibels louder.

Karen shook her head. And began carrying dishes to the sink.

"Stu, will you load the dishwasher so Reesa and I can get an early start at the grocery store? It's bound to be mobbed today. Perfect beach and barbecue weather."

"Only if you'll pour me another cup of coffee."

Karen poured him a cup of coffee. He grabbed her around the hips and hugged her.

Reesa looked away.

"Get on with you. Reesa and I have some heavy grocery shopping to do."

She batted his hand away. "Do we have enough soda?"

"Yeah. Wyatt said he had beer and some wine. But if you girls want something fancier, you'd better pick it up at the store."

THEY DROVE TO a big discount store. One that sold everything from televisions to lettuce and shellfish to cleaning supplies. Even when the kids had been little, Reesa had never shopped in bulk, and it was sort of awe inspiring.

Karen pushed the cart right to the food section, which was as large as any small grocery store. The shelves held condiments all in oversized containers. Gigantic boxes of cereal . . .

"What do people do with a gallon of mayonnaise?" Reesa wondered out loud.

"Make a lot of sandwiches?" Karen returned. "I don't shop here all the time. But I figure with my brood and you guys, and no telling how many Wyatt will invite while he's working today, it's best to be prepared." She grabbed hamburger and hot dog buns and two huge bags of chips.

They moved onto the dairy case for slices of American and blocks of cheddar. And Reesa became aware of a young woman standing at the end of the aisle. She seemed to be looking right at Reesa and Karen.

But Reesa had often stood in the center of a grocery aisle staring off into space trying to remember what she'd meant to buy. And from the pile of food and paper products the woman had in her cart, and the two young children vying for her attention, it would be easy to forget smaller items.

They turned into the meat aisle. Karen picked out a five-pound package of hamburger. "I'll freeze some of this," Karen said. She added a family pack of wieners and moved over to peruse the steaks.

She put four packages in the cart. "Do you know that woman?" she asked, looking past Reesa's shoulder.

Reesa turned. The same woman was looking down the aisle. She smiled tentatively and rolled her cart toward them.

"I don't think so."

The woman stopped her cart next to theirs. She was in her early thirties, thin and wiry. There was a thick scar, like a beige thunderbolt, across her cheek.

And something niggled at Reesa's memory.

"Mrs. Davis?"

"Yes?" Reesa quickly flipped through her mental Rolodex. Young woman, scar, two children. Victim of domestic abuse? She still has her children. Did Reesa help her get her children back? Maybe it was someone she met totally unrelated to work. Fat chance. She hardly ever did anything but work.

"You don't remember me."

"Sorry, I—" She did look familiar, but Reesa just couldn't place her.

"I'm Tanisha Clark. You took me out of my home, oh, about fifteen years ago."

Reesa tensed. Someone she'd removed as a teenager. Now what would happen? Would the woman start screaming obscenities in front of the children, become violent?

Karen stepped into the silence. "Hi."

But Reesa had remembered. Tanisha. She'd been bleeding when Reesa put her and her three sisters under the protection of the agency.

"You haven't changed a bit," Tanisha said.

Reesa breathed out a laugh. "Well, you have. And of course I remember you." Tanisha had fought like a wildcat as Reesa pulled her away from the doorknob she was clinging to. She'd clawed, kicked, spit, and suddenly Reesa could remember it as if it had happened last week.

She swallowed. She had nothing to say, nothing to apologize for. She'd done her job, the best she knew how, and there it was.

"You saved my life that day, Mrs. Davis. I never had a chance to thank you. Well"—Tanisha smiled sheepishly—"it took me a long while to realize it. But you were right, and even though I didn't make it easy, you didn't let me fall. And I just wanted to thank you now."

She started to walk away.

Reesa, who had been gripping the grocery cart in stunned silence, started to go after her. "Wait."

Tanisha stopped and turned; the two kids pulled at her to go, but she waited for Reesa to catch up to her.

"Are these your children?" Reesa smiled at them, a boy and a girl.

"Yes, they are, both adopted. My husband and I both came through the system. We both finished high school. He works up at the hospital and I'm going to school nights for my nursing degree. Right now I take care of kids, five mornings a week.

"We have this cooperative center down on Eighth Street. It's day care and a learning center for working mothers; it's subsidized, but we're always doing things to make more money. It's called Hands Around the World. We call it Halfway to H House, 'cause one way goes to hell and the other goes to heaven and we just sometimes feel stuck in the middle.

"But at least the kids get some food and some learning, and we have a doctor come in once a week. I think you'd like it. I have a card if you're interested in seeing what we've done. If you'd like to come by sometime."

"I'd love to," Reesa said and took the card without thinking. She wanted to hold this moment just like it was. Hopeful that someone she'd tried to help had made good—at least in her own mind. Reesa wasn't sure she wanted to see the reality of Tanisha's life up close.

But before she could start making excuses, Tanisha said, "Great, how about next Thursday?"

You didn't let me fall. The words kept echoing in Reesa's mind as they drove back to Karen's. *You didn't let me fall.*

She'd been falling herself lately. But no more. Somehow, some way, she'd get back to what she wanted her life to be.

Maybe Tanisha Clark was her wake-up call. Thursday, she'd said. It wouldn't hurt to swing by and check out Hands Around the World.

SARAH AND LEILA were just crossing the street to Wyatt's house when the Wolcotts and Reesa pulled up to the curb in front and Stu managed to maneuver his SUV into a space that was more suited to a MINI Cooper.

"Bessie," Leila squealed and tugged at Sarah's hand to hurry.

"We have to look both ways first," Sarah said. They did and then crossed the street. As soon as they were on the opposite sidewalk, Jenny, Tammy, and Bessie piled out of the car, took Leila by the hand, and they all ran up the driveway to Wyatt's backyard.

Sarah stopped at the car.

"Very impressive," Sarah told Stu as he came around from the driver's side.

Karen handed her a big bowl of potato salad. "A man of many talents."

"And don't you forget it, babe," he said and hauled a large red cooler from the back.

"Wow," Reesa said, stopping on the sidewalk to admire the front of Wyatt's house. "Wyatt lives here?"

"Owns it," Stu said.

"Inherited it," Karen added. "And has to rent out the top two floors to pay the taxes."

"Still, it's gorgeous. I would never in a million years think of Wyatt living in a place like this."

Sarah knew what she meant. Wyatt had repainted the house himself; a medium gray with forest green shutters and intricately carved gable boards picked out in burgundy. It fit right in with the rest of the neighborhood until you went inside.

"Yeah, kind of girly for a tough guy like Wyatt."

"I think it's gorgeous," Reesa said.

They walked down the driveway to the backyard. Wyatt's SUV was gone.

"Guess we're a little early," Sarah said.

"We'll just get started without him. He said he'd leave a key." Karen put two bags of groceries on the porch floor and rolled a brass Buddha to the side. "And there it is. Sarah, you want to open the door for me?"

Sarah reached for the key. She didn't like taking liberties like this, especially with Wyatt. And she didn't want anyone to think she had free rein of his house. Which she didn't.

"Are you sure it's all right to do this?"

"Open the door," Karen cajoled. The groceries she'd just picked up were beginning to slide.

Sarah opened the door, and the kids all crowded inside.

"Don't make a mess," Karen said. "Jenny, make sure it's childproofed. Rory, you too. Help Jenny watch the little ones going up the steps." She turned to Reesa. "The turret stairs. There's a little room at the top where you can look out. Total waste of space if you ask me."

She began taking things out of the bags and making herself at home in Wyatt's pristine new kitchen.

"This is amazing," Reesa said.

Wyatt had opened up the front of the house, combining two parlors and kitchen into an open space. The floors were hardwood, the walls were white, and the furniture was wood with beige cushions.

"It's nice," Sarah agreed.

"Nice? That's an understatement. I'd kill for a house like this. And he keeps it so neat."

"Because he's rarely here," Sarah said.

"Ah," Reesa said.

Sarah blushed. Did Reesa think she had reason to know what Wyatt did? Well, she did. And they all knew it. So why couldn't she just accept it? There were two smallish bedrooms in back, one that was hardly big enough to fit the king-size bed and one that served as Wyatt's study, though it was usually filled with extra scuba gear.

But she didn't feel she had the right to mention those.

"What do you want me to do?"

"There's corn that needs shucking, and the salad and potato salad need to go in the fridge. Then I want to marinate the steaks for a bit before we put them on the grill."

The three of them worked and chatted while Stu uncovered the grill, and by the time Wyatt walked in, dinner was almost ready.

"Grab a beer and come out while I grill," Stu called.

Wyatt gave Sarah a fleeting smile before grabbing a beer and heading for the porch.

When the women joined them a few minutes later, two large round tables had appeared on the porch, citronella candles had been lit, and Stu, Wyatt, and Rory were all standing around the grill watching meat cook.

And it was delicious. After dinner they moved over to the sitting area while the kids ran after fireflies on the lawn, and the adults made themselves comfortable to watch the setting sun. Wyatt grabbed Sarah's hand and pulled her down to sit between his legs on the chaise.

At first she sat rigidly upright, but gradually she leaned back into him, settling there. And when he put his arms around her, she thought, *This feels right. Everything will work out.* And for a while she believed it would.

Chapter 14

If Sarah thought that putting a sticker on visitation days would make the transitions easier, she'd been dead wrong. By the time the next Wednesday came, she and Leila were both on the edge.

Sarah's heart tore a little as she watched Leila slow down each time she passed the wall calendar on the way to the table. How her eyes cut toward it as if making sure it was really there. There were times when Sarah wondered if maybe she was looking forward to the visit, and though her stomach turned sour at the thought, she would remind herself that whatever was best for Leila is what she wanted. But what she really wanted was for Leila and her to live happily ever after next to the clock shop.

That's when she really knew she was human. That she wasn't just a leftover piece of flotsam that nobody wanted. Sam had wanted her. Not the way some of the men she'd encountered wanted her.

But like a father wanted his daughter. At least what she

imagined it would be like. Because she knew that was how she felt toward Leila.

When Leila came home from school on Wednesday, Sarah reminded her that it was the day for her visit with Carmen. Leila didn't say anything, merely climbed on the couch and stuck her thumb in her mouth. Another regressive habit.

Sarah gritted her teeth and waited for Danny to ring the bell.

Leila went without argument. She didn't complain, but she also didn't say good-bye, just slid off the couch and went to stand in front of Danny. Danny took her hand and with a quick, "We'll be back," he walked her to his car.

Sarah considered going over to Wyatt's, but she couldn't keep running to him every time she was feeling insecure. And Karen and Reesa had their own lives. Sarah would just have to sit it out. She went back to her back porch workshop.

Mrs. Bridges from the antique store had brought her a late-nineteenth-century Seth Thomas violin clock she'd picked up at an estate sale. The body was in decent shape, but the inner workings were mangled. Sarah had brought part of the inner workings over to work on at night when she wouldn't have any interruptions.

The parts were old and rusty, and some of them were bent; it would take a very steady hand to work them back into shape without breaking them. Oh so carefully Sarah straightened them out with her tiny jeweler's hammer. It was slow delicate work, just what she needed to help the time pass.

Finally the front bell rang, and she rushed to the foyer, but slowed down to appear normal when she opened the door.

Leila walked in and continued right past her.

Danny called out. "See you Saturday, Leila."

She stopped long enough to wave and went straight back to her room.

"Saturday?" Sarah asked. "I told you we have plans that day."

"I know. Didn't anyone call you?"

Sarah shook her head.

"It's Carmen's birthday. She wants Leila to come. I'm sorry, someone on the team was supposed to clear it with you." He shrugged, obviously chagrined. "Leila knows about the plan. It might be upsetting to her to cancel now."

Leila would also be upset to miss the sand castle contest.

"As a matter of fact . . ." Danny reached in his pants pocket and brought out a folded piece of paper. He handed it to Sarah.

She opened it and took a look. A schedule of visits.

"They want to put her on a fast track, if you will. Studies have shown that the transition back is easier if the meetings are more often than once a week."

"She's being adopted."

Danny shrugged. "I'm just doing what the study team is telling me to do. Carmen's caseworker and support team are very pleased with her progress. I think they could use a success story about now," he said confidentially, having no clue to what his words were doing to Sarah.

"So they've set up a schedule, if you can just see if this works for you. It would be twice a week. Wednesdays and Saturday for a longer visit. I'll oversee an in-home visit next week. And then we'll see how it goes from there."

Danny kept explaining, but Sarah was just hearing buzzing. The sound of Velcro ripping open. She tried to make herself concentrate on what he was saying. Tried to focus her eyes on the paper he'd handed her.

"The team understands that some of these dates might not be convenient. If you have a problem with any of the dates, you should call this number." He craned his neck to see the paper and pointed to a number at the bottom of the page.

Oh, sure. It would be one of those numbers that no one ever answered and from which no one ever called back.

"I'm sure you know that reacclimating the child is less painful if it is done with more frequent visits. After all, we want reunification to happen as smoothly as possible, don't we?"

Sarah clenched her fist, and the paper crumpled. They both looked down at it as if it were some defenseless animal she'd just crushed.

"She's on an adoption path. You're her *adoption* caseworker. Have you forgotten that?"

Danny blinked behind his horn-rimmed glasses. "Well, no, and I know you're probably having to adjust to this unexpected development. But if this adoption doesn't work out, there are many more children who need good homes. It's my job to facilitate that if it were to happen."

"Mr. Noyes. Children are not interchangeable. It takes time and work and unconditional love to get a child to accept you. You can't just plug them in anywhere there's a vacancy."

"Ms. Hargreave, please."

"How long have you been in the field?"

"What?"

"How long have you been a caseworker?"

"Well, only eighteen months. But I graduated at the top of my class."

"Well, just so you know. There's a long way down from the top of the class to the rest of us. I won't give her up without a fight."

The caseworker's eyes widened, and he actually stepped back. Maybe he thought she might hit him. And she was sorely tempted.

"Well," he said, backing toward the door, "I'll plan to pick up Leila on Saturday at ten. It's Carmen's birthday," he repeated and fled.

Sarah didn't even know where to turn. Call Reesa? Randy? He'd been totally useless so far. But he's what she had. She'd have to call him. Hopefully he would be in his office even though it was nearly six.

But first she needed to see about Leila.

She was sitting on her bed; *Green Eggs and Ham* was open.

"Did you have a good time?" Sarah asked.

"Go away."

"Are you upset?"

"I don't like you. Go away."

Sarah had been through this before, they both had. She would let it rest for the time being. She closed Leila's door and went to call Randy Phelps.

She left a message. Then she started googling other family law attorneys.

She checked on Leila several more times, but she'd fallen asleep. And Sarah let her be. She was at the kitchen table, drinking a cup of chamomile tea when Leila came in rubbing her eyes. She didn't acknowledge Sarah but went straight to the art supply cupboard and opened it. Pulled out the bag of stickers and went to stand by the wall calendar.

"What day is Saturday?"

IT HAD BEEN three days since Reesa had returned home from her weekend away and nothing had changed. Michael had given her the silent treatment until Monday night when he needed her to get something down from the attic for him.

Then he thanked her . . . begrudgingly. Work hadn't changed either. More and more paper, less and less success.

On Wednesday she'd spent an entire afternoon in another team meeting for the White boys. She didn't mind spending time on their placement, but that was not what was taking up the bulk of time. Several members of the team didn't seem to realize that Mrs. White and her current lover were going to jail, for at least drugs and reckless endangerment. If Reesa had her way—and she probably would be called in to testify—they'd be convicted of attempted murder.

Of course she wouldn't get her way, but she'd make damned sure the court knew just what she'd found in that squalid apartment. She tried to convince the team to give up on reuniting this family. Even resorting finally to "Over my dead body," and stalking out of the meeting.

She felt ridiculous the moment she got outside. Now there was no one in the meeting who knew exactly what had gone on. Sometimes you didn't need a damn team meeting. You just needed to act.

It was simple. Pete White needed a loving home. Jerome would need long-term care. The baby at least would have a pretty good chance of being adopted—if it had no lasting problems. End of discussion.

Reesa didn't go back inside; they could talk all they wanted, but she'd be the one giving testimony at the hearing next week.

She was fed up. She didn't know how she was going to bail herself out of this quagmire. But between her job and her husband, Reesa was slowly having the life sucked out of her.

So instead of going into work on Thursday, she did something she'd really had no intention of doing. She drove down to Eighth Street to visit Hands Around the World.

The building was exactly what Reesa had expected, a dingy little storefront on a block of neglected buildings. And her hope sank. There were the usual knots of people on the street, though she noticed none were standing near the entrance of the center. That was unusual, unless there were some very large security guards inside.

She stepped inside. There was no security at all, just a medium-size room furnished with mismatched chairs and tables and a sagging couch covered by a colorful throw. Old travel posters and construction paper collages by children were the only artwork on the walls.

Reesa felt a stab of disappointment. "Hands" was just another stopgap effort bound to fail or to just fade away when interest waned.

Tanisha spotted her from where she was sitting behind a reception desk, explaining the finer points of answering the telephone and making appointments to a trio of women.

She turned the class over to another woman and came forward with both hands extended. "I didn't know if you would come or not."

Reesa just smiled. She hadn't intended to come. "You have a nice space," she said, deflecting the need to explain.

"Yes. We could use more. Come on back. I'll show you around."

If Dorothy had traveled from black and white to the colorful land of Oz, Reesa stepped from a colorful waiting room into a room with stark white walls, and two rows of tables each with its own computer. The computers were the only imaginative thing in the room and ranged from laptops to old iMacs and everything in between; the women who were practicing on them were just as varied.

"We're gradually updating our equipment," Tanisha explained. "Most of what we have now are donated. But we have a great IT person . . . My husband. And a computer teacher who comes in three times a week. We have about twenty-five women in two levels of classes, and mentoring hours for the more advanced students to help the others. Down here . . ."

She trailed off as she left the room. Reesa quickly followed Tanisha down a hallway where she pointed to additional classrooms, all closed at the moment, and around the corner to another room. The door was closed, but when Tanisha pulled it open, a caroling of noise flooded out. "Day care," Tanisha said proudly.

There were at least fifteen kids in the room. From babies to preschoolers who were being read to by an older woman. "One of our volunteers." Tanisha waved at the woman and ushered Reesa out. "We don't like to interrupt too much. Some of the children are pretty traumatized. We have therapists, but you know how it is. Safety and a sense of security is the most important thing."

"This is amazing," Reesa said. "Are you registered with child services?"

Tanisha frowned for the first time since Reesa had arrived. "They're aware of us, but this is a 'get off your butt and come to us when you're ready to make it' center.

"Most of the women who come here are on their way to a normal life and just need the reinforcement. A place to talk about their fears with their peers. But we also have several apartments upstairs for women and children while the mothers are looking for a permanent job and home. We'd like more.

Actually we'd like to buy the building. We're just renting two of the floors now.

"And before you ask. No men. No drugs. No alcohol. And no hurting. You get three strikes for minor infractions. One for the biggies. No tolerance for drugs or abuse. Do it and you're back out on the street. No exceptions. Not even children.

"You have to be serious about getting your life together."

"Wow," Reesa said.

"Does it sound harsh? Well, it is. Life is harsh. My mama had help. She had services out the wazoo, but she was never held accountable. And she never succeeded. She fell through the cracks"—she smiled—"or because of crack. So yeah, we're harsh. Nobody makes them come here."

"How do you stay afloat?" Reesa asked as they made their way back to the front desk. "The rent alone."

"By hook and by crook. Donations and grants and the families have to pay either monetarily, or by volunteering to teach, or cook or clean. We have a couple of paying positions, and we have an accountant and a lawyer. We also have a couple of part-time administrators, a necessary evil if you want to stay legal.

"We've applied for funds for a development person. Sounds real business-like, but what it means is chief cook and bottle washer. Someone who can write grants and have a vision about how to best use the funds we've got."

"Amazing. And you're going to nursing school?"

"At nights. Hey, you gave me a chance and I tried not to mess it up. I did anyway, but I had some nice families that helped me through."

Reesa met a few of the volunteers and checked out the kitchen before Tanisha walked her out to the street. "Come back any time. We're always open." She grinned again. And Reesa smiled back. She was still smiling as she drove down the street and back to her office.

It only took the ride up the elevator at her office building for her bubble to burst. She never realized before how dingy it looked, and it was by far a newer building than the one she had just left. Of course Hands Around the World was surviving on a shoestring; it was servicing twenty-five families and could go up in smoke any minute. Reesa worked for an agency that serviced thousands of broken families. They didn't have time to put up colorful posters.

ILONA WAS ON the phone to Mr. Sobrato's lawyer again. He'd gotten another recess due to his client's "bad health" and had been stalling her all week. "You know, Ms. Cartwright, he may have to have surgery. Do we want this to drag on for months while he recovers?"

"We can end this right now if he wants. Have him sign the papers and he can go get his surgery with my blessing."

"It will be better for all parties if we settle this out of court."

Ilona smiled, slowly. Too late, baby. They'd had their chance. Now she was going to take them to the cleaners.

Her intercom buzzed. Inez knew not to interrupt calls unless it was an emergency. What could possibly be an emergency? Her cases files were up to date; her court appearances were spot on the money.

"Excuse me. Can I call you back? I have another client on the other line." Let him think it was Mrs. Sobrato. Maybe it was. She was whiny enough to think everything was an emergency. Maybe she forgot to ask for the pet goldfish.

Ilona hung up. "What is it, Inez?"

"I'm sorry, but your father is on line two. He said he really needs to talk to you."

Great. They probably wanted to parade her out to some fund-raising dinner. "Thank you, Inez. I'll take it." Ilona took a deep breath and pressed the speaker as she reached for the Sobrato brief.

"Hello, Dad. How can I help you?"

"I-I hate to have to tell you, Ilona . . . June is dead."

At first she thought he was talking about the month, then understanding slowly seeped in. June? His wife? Her adoptive mother? Dead?

"I know it must be a shock," he continued when Ilona didn't say anything. His voice was shaky.

Hers was nonexistent. "How did it happen?" she finally managed.

"Aneurysm. In her sleep. I woke up and she just—" He broke off and Ilona could hear sounds like . . . crying? They'd never seemed like very loving people to her. Maybe he was worried about being alone. Well, he needn't look her way.

"The funeral is Saturday. I thought you might want to know."

That struck home. "Of course I would. I'm so sorry. I had no idea she was ill."

"No one did. I don't know what I'll do without her."

Ilona looked toward the ceiling.

"I thought if you'd like to come stay here for a few days."

"Sorry, Dad. I have to be in court all day tomorrow, but of course I'll be there for the funeral. Holy Trinity?"

"Yes, 10:00."

So as not to interfere with anyone's tennis.

"Well, I have to make some other calls. How are you, Ilona?"

"Fine. Just fine. I'm sorry about . . . Mother."

Her father blubbered something and hung up.

Ilona disconnected then sat back in her chair. June Cartwright was dead. The only mother she actually remembered. Ilona searched her heart for some feeling. Grief? Relief? Found nothing. Nothing at all. June's passing didn't affect her life one way or the other.

That was sad. The only thing she had ever wanted was love. No, that wasn't entirely true. There were plenty of other things she wanted. But when she was younger, she would have given up the possibility of any or all of them for someone who loved her unconditionally. For a mother and father. A real family. Not one where she felt like a barely tolerated guest.

Her ex had said June was looking unwell when Ilona had seen him at the club. Ilona guessed he would be at the funeral along with his round-bellied trophy wife. He'd probably be standing with her father. Gotta keep one foot on the ladder even graveside. There would be a lot of people she knew or had known once. She supposed she should go to the church early and stand in the receiving line. She hadn't thought to ask her father if she'd even be welcome.

They'd never been that close. You couldn't be that close to someone whose sole purpose in life seemed to be climbing the social, corporate, or political landscape. She sighed, what a waste.

She buzzed Inez.

"Is everything all right, Ms. Cartwright?"

"Yes, fine. Get Mr. Sobrato's attorney on the line, please." Time for them to stop dicking around. She was going to make the bastard pay.

Chapter 15

On Friday the tantrums began. It started with breakfast when Leila demanded waffles. She'd eaten the last of the frozen waffles the day before. Sarah hadn't had time to go shopping. She offered eggs, cereal, peanut butter and toast.

By the time she mentioned toast, Leila was on the floor screaming, flailing her arms and kicking. Sarah pulled the chairs out of the way so she wouldn't hurt herself and walked into the next room. It was hard to watch your child fall apart. And harder still when Sarah knew it was just Leila's desperate attempt to reject before she was rejected.

So Sarah stood in the hall waiting for the storm to pass, waiting to be able to comfort her and chase away her fears.

By the time Leila did settle down, she had missed the bus. Sarah was tempted just to keep her home, but she knew where that would lead. She'd spent too much time and energy to backslide now, even though it seemed like fate and the system were determined to see her fail.

So at ten o'clock she washed Leila's face and hands, gave her a piece of toast and a juice box, and drove her to school. They stopped by the principal's office to sign in. Thank goodness the principal Mrs. O'Riley had dealt with her share of foster children. She offered to take Leila down to her classroom and make sure she got on the bus to come home.

After a sniff and an unhappy look at Sarah, Leila took the principal's hand. And Sarah reluctantly made herself let her go. She waited until the principal was back, thanked her.

"I understand that these mornings happen. She's been doing well," Mrs. O'Riley said. "Anything going on I should know about?"

Sarah told her about the change in status and the revived visits. Mrs. O'Riley just nodded. "You'll see this through."

As soon as Sarah got home, she pulled her notebook out of the drawer and documented the morning. She was sick of documenting their life; it seemed like the bad times were beginning to outnumber the good.

She flipped back through the notebook to reassure herself. Smiled at the entry about going crabbing. Turned to a photo of Leila, her cheeks puffed out as she blew out the candles on her third birthday cake. Then there was the inevitable return to her bio home and the problems and regressions that occurred. At least Leila had been able to come back to her instead of some strange place just because it had a free bed, because even then she'd been on an adoption track.

Sarah longed for the day that this would be over. Then she and Leila could face each day secure in the knowledge that they belonged to each other, when they wouldn't have to fear being torn apart.

She closed the notebook, returned it to the desk. One day

she wouldn't have to document everything. They'd just live. Have the same highs and lows that any ordinary family would have.

She went out the back door and into the shop. It was Alice's day off, and Sarah was late opening the store. And since she had to man the counter, she lost valuable repair time. Then she remembered that Sam would leave a note saying that he was in the back and to ring the bell. Sarah always thought that was just asking for walkaways. But today she wrote out a note and taped it to the door.

Then she went to the back and set about completing the violin clock repairs. And as she carefully restored the pieces to order, the nerves and the hurt fell away, and she gave into another world, a place that worked, that needed to be wound carefully but would go on indefinitely.

It was a place she loved. A place Sam loved. But he'd warned her that it was also a lonely place. She'd only seen it as a place of security, until today. The wooden body felt sleek beneath her hands. Her hands barely shook as she maneuvered the workings back in and tightened the tiny screws to hold it in place.

Putting a clock together was second nature to her now. Except when it wasn't.

The jeweler's screwdriver skipped over a piece of rust, the screw popped out of the threads, and onto the plastic workbox. Sarah tried to catch it before it bounced over the rim—the box tipped and parts flew everywhere.

She snatched off the jeweler's loupe and magnifier, checked her clothes first, found a couple of tiny springs. Carefully placing her feet on the floor, she slid off the stool, listening for any rolling metal.

It took nearly twenty minutes to make certain she had recovered all the parts and returned them to the tray. She'd wasted valuable time. Now she was right back where she'd started, with a gutted clock and a mess of parts waiting for her to make them work again.

She was surrounded by mechanical devices, all in a state of repair or disrepair, some nearly completed, some waiting on parts, some with their guts lying in a tray beside them. Waiting for her.

She pushed the work tray aside, stood up.

Clocks were reactive. They could charm, but they couldn't love you back, couldn't urge you on to better things, or wrap their arms around you when you needed a hug. Maybe that's why Sam had given her a place to land. He wasn't handing out charity, but he'd recognized another solitary soul and took her in to share his life.

And he'd done so much more. He'd taught her to be human. To be a daughter. To be a friend. And she was in danger of losing that. She'd been so caught up in her life with Leila and the prospect of losing her that she'd only been using her friends as a buffer.

How could they stand her? How selfish and self-absorbed she was. But they did. They cared about her. And Sam had loved her. There must be something to that.

She picked up the phone, keyed in Karen's cell.

"Hey, girlfriend. What's up?"

"Nothing, just calling to see how you are."

There was silence for a second, while Sarah imagined Karen wondering WTF.

"Not much. Are you and Leila ready for the sand castle

contest tomorrow? The girls are driving me nuts. Had to go buy new plastic sand tools. I swear they do have their father's genes."

"Sounds great, but Leila has to go to Carmen's birthday party. The team has decided they need to meet more often."

"That really sucks. Is there anything I can do?"

"Thanks, but I didn't call to talk about me and my problems. I was just wondering how you were. So I called. Just to say hi. Not because I'm a needy mess."

Karen laughed. "I don't think that. You just don't call that often."

"I know."

"Well, at least you can come and cheer the girls on. Let Alice earn her keep."

"Maybe I will. I'm getting a little tired of clocks this week."

"Well, that's a first. Good thing you have such scintillating, entertaining friends."

"Good friends," Sarah said, and immediately felt embarrassed.

"Good friends, all of us," Karen agreed. "We'll be in our usual place. And I hear Wyatt is one of the judges."

Sarah smiled. "I'll definitely be there."

BUT WHEN SATURDAY came and Danny finally picked up Leila for Carmen's birthday, all Sarah wanted to do was crawl in bed with the covers over her head. She went to the bathroom to clean up the scratches on her arms and face where Leila had fought getting dressed. She'd have to cut her nails before the next visit, if Randy couldn't get his act together to ask for a temporary stay.

Sarah had pleaded with Danny to give them a pass on this one, that Leila had been looking forward to the sand castle contest, but he was caught in the middle and even though he was obviously nonplussed by Leila's behavior, he picked her up and took her out to his car. "I'll be there the whole time," he called, then climbed in his car with a screaming kid.

Sarah needed to fortify her patience for the coming days, maybe weeks. She and Leila had been through this twice. Leila had been younger then and smaller. Now she was old enough to understand something bad was happening.

Knowing she had three hours until they would be back again, Sarah decided to go to the beach. Someplace where families were happy, where maybe she'd even see Wyatt for a few minutes before returning to the fray. She put on her swimsuit. How was that for optimism?

She grabbed a towel and her sunglasses and stopped by the store to let Alice know she was taking time off. Summer was short; soon the days would be dark early and there would be plenty of time for the store. Clocks didn't stop breaking down because it was winter.

The beach was crowded but it was easy to pick out Karen's polka-dot umbrella amid the sea of umbrellas. They were all there. Tammy and Bessie were playing tag with another group of children. They all wore ribbons around their necks. And plastic gold medallions bounced at the ends as they ran. Everyone under twelve got a medal. And Sarah hurt that Leila would be odd man out. Boy, she knew how that felt.

She put on a smile and climbed down the wooden steps to join her friends. Reesa was there, wearing the same pair of shorts she'd had on the week before. But she looked rested.

Karen and Stu sat in matching beach chairs side by side. Karen looked out from her favorite wide-brimmed straw hat and motioned for Sarah to come over.

Wyatt, who was sitting with his back turned to her, looked over the back of the chair and smiled. Then he frowned and stood up.

"What happened to you?"

"What?" Sarah said. He touched her cheek and she winced. "Oh. Leila didn't want to go."

He led her over to his chair and made her sit. Then he unfolded another chair and sat next to her.

She was touched, but she laughed. "It's only a few scratches. Kitten scratches," she added, but her voice wobbled.

Bessie and Tammy ran over to show her their medals. "Where's Leila?" Bessie asked.

"She's visiting her bio mother."

"She missed the contest," Tammy said. "We wanted her to help us."

"Our castle was huge," Bessie said and spread her arms to show them.

Jenny, who had followed them up to the group, sank down next to Stu's chair and rolled her eyes.

"Daddy took pictures on his phone," Bessie said.

"Then you can show her pictures of your castle. I bet it was fabulous."

Sarah felt Wyatt's hand slide over hers. She was sure he meant it to be consoling, but she was so close to the edge that what emotions she'd held in check while talking to the girls threatened to pour over now. She felt the disappointment as if it were her own.

"There'll be next year," she managed. And hoped to God that was true.

They both nodded. And ran off.

Sarah sat back in the chair, glad of her sunglasses while she blinked furiously. She didn't like to cry in front of people, but she was perilously close this afternoon.

"Is Leila going to have to go back?" Jenny asked. "That's not fair."

"Jenny," Karen said. "Please go see to your sisters."

"But is she?"

"No. Now go."

Jenny reluctantly followed her sisters.

"Well, I don't know what the holdup is," Stu said as soon as she was gone.

"Stu," Karen snapped.

"What? I thought the adoption was a done deal."

"We all did," Karen said.

"Oh," he said.

Sarah had closed her eyes, but she could imagine Karen giving Stu the evil eye to get him to shut up.

"It doesn't seem fair, that the mother can suddenly change her mind," he mumbled and then was quiet.

Sarah bit the inside of her cheek. It didn't help. She was awful at reaching out, and now she was going to make an embarrassing scene if she didn't leave.

"I'd better get back."

"You just got here," Karen said.

"Sarah." It was the first time Reesa had spoken, and her voice sounded weary, not like the advocate Sarah had come to depend on.

Sarah felt her control slipping away. She wanted to be happy, to be able to sit at the beach with her friends and her daughter without worrying.

"You can't keep up this nonstop worry or you'll make yourself sick and won't be any good to Leila."

"I know." Sarah tried to get out of the chair, but Wyatt's hand tightened on hers.

"Stay. It's all going to work out."

She tried to smile, but she couldn't hold it in any longer. "You don't know that. I could lose her. And we were so close."

"Whatever happens," Karen said, "you'll see it through. We'll see it through with you."

"And then what? Leila is everything to me. Everything." She felt Wyatt flinch, but she couldn't stop herself.

"I could lose it all. Better to have left her there instead of giving her hope and then snatching it away. Because of all the stuff that happens, the mean, the dirty, the hurtful, the abuse, losing hope is the worst thing of all."

She yanked her hand from Wyatt's and heaved out of the beach chair. "I have to go." She practically ran for the stairs.

"Sarah!" Karen called.

Sarah didn't stop; she hated herself for being such a mess. Maybe she didn't deserve to be a mother—or a friend.

REESA SAT UP and watched Sarah go. "She didn't mean it, Wyatt. We're all important to her. She's just preparing herself not to feel pain. I see it happen all the time. It's standard issue for system kids."

"And when she's around, can we please be more sensitive?" Karen added.

"Did I do that?" Stu asked.

"No, honey. She's just living on the edge right now."

"Well, it's a damn shame they keep putting her through this."

"It is."

"Give her some space," Reesa said. She hadn't been paying attention to the others. Actually she'd been thinking about herself for a change. And by the time she realized where the conversation was going, it was too late to stop it.

Wyatt stood up. "The hell I will."

"She needs time to compose herself. She won't appreciate it if you find her crying."

He stopped. "You think she's crying?"

Reesa and Karen both just looked at him.

He sank back into his chair. "Oh, hell. Can't you do something? How can the mother just come back after giving up her kid and decide she wants her back?"

"I don't know. This far along in the process it's unusual. But it happens. And if they find something amiss in the legality of the termination or if they think the mother was coerced in any way, they'll usually give her one more chance." Though Reesa thought Tanisha's center had a better way of dealing with things. One strike you're out.

"This doesn't seem right," Karen said. "Leila has been living with Sarah over the eleven-month limit. Carmen gave up her rights free and clear. The father gave up his rights. At least he ODed since then and we don't have to worry about him." She slapped a hand over her mouth. "I can't believe I just said that."

"Well, it's the truth," Stu said. "Why do you people give these people so many chances?"

Reesa smiled ruefully. "I was just asking myself the same

thing, Stu. And I don't know. But put yourself in Carmen's place. Would you stop loving Bessie or Tammy or Jenny or Rory or Amy just because you'd been separated from them?"

Stu scowled. "No, of course not, but it's not the same thing. I have a job, I can give them a good home, I keep them safe."

"I guess the feeling is if everyone had those things, *they* would keep their children safe, too."

"Well, they don't. And maybe it's not their fault. But that begs the question. Are we willing to entrust a child's life to that situation?"

"The hope is that with the proper support system—"

Wyatt stood up so abruptly the beach chair fell over. "People like Carmen can never stay sober. This is so much bull." He stalked off toward the steps.

"Well," Karen said as soon as he was out of hearing distance.

"What just happened?" Reesa asked. "I can tell Wyatt is upset, but does that mean he's going to stand by her or drop the ball and run?"

She and Karen both looked at Stu.

"Are you asking me?"

They both nodded.

"You're asking him to take on a lot of responsibility. I gotta be honest. Sarah alone is a handful. Man, she just can't relax."

"Sarah lost her own mother when she was Tammy's age, never found someone who could love her as a parent should until she met Sam. She was already eighteen. She's not going to be easy to love. But I think she's worth it."

"Well, tell Wyatt, not me. I've got my own handful." He waggled his eyebrows at Karen.

"Stu, this is not the time for your slightly off-color humor," she said. "Though I appreciate the sentiment. So what do *you* think we should do?"

"I think you girls oughta just let Wyatt deal with this himself. Either they'll get together or they won't, but nothing any of us do is going to make one bit of difference in the end."

SARAH BARELY MADE it into the house before she broke down in sobs. She was so embarrassed. *Never let them see you cry.* It was a hard-earned lesson in survival, but now she wished she hadn't learned it quite so well.

She'd actually reached out to her friends and then she couldn't even take their concern. What was wrong with her?

She jumped at the sound of someone pounding on the door. She rushed to it, thinking it might be Danny bringing Leila back early.

She stopped before opening it to wipe her eyes on her shirt.

"Sarah, open up."

Not Danny. Wyatt.

Sarah reached for the doorknob, pulled her hand back. She liked, maybe loved, him so much, but it was unfair to keep dumping stuff on him. They'd had some fun. He was a popular guy in town; neither of them wanted anything from the relationship but a good time.

But it was different now. At least for her. He'd stuck by her through Sam's death and Leila's fostering. She had even sometimes let herself think of the three of them as a family.

Did she have to choose one or the other? Leila or Wyatt? Even though he kept telling her it would work out, she didn't see how it could. He might not want to sign on for the long haul with Leila, and even if she lost Leila, how could she go to him?

He'd think he was a consolation prize and maybe he would be right.

She grabbed her hair and pulled until it hurt. There had been girls in the group home who cut themselves. Sarah never understood how they could do that. Now she did. A sharp pain on the arm or the wrist, to take attention away from the dull ache of despair.

"I know you're in there, let me in."

Sarah shook her head but leaned against the door trying to be closer to him.

"Please, Sarah. We'll see this through."

She rolled her forehead against the wood; she didn't see how they could see it through. She wasn't even able to see it through. She tried to say so, but tears were choking her throat. "Please," she managed. "Just go."

"Why? So I won't see you hurting? I can feel it, Sarah. Through this door. I can feel it."

She moved back. "No."

"Won't work, Sarah. You may be able to push everybody else away, but not me. I'm too damn big, for one thing. And too stubborn for another."

She smiled, but it was twisted, and she knew if she looked in the mirror, it would be ugly.

"Please, Wyatt, I can't do this."

"You don't have to. You think you have to do everything alone, but you don't, nobody can. Not even you Sarah, so you might as well open the door, 'cause I'm not going away."

Open the door, Sarah. She shook her head. *Open the door. Please.*

She wiped her eyes. Peeked out the window to see if he had left or if he really meant it about not going away.

He was sitting on the steps.

She could do this. It was time. Just open the door and go out. Sit down next to him. Tell him she loved him. Ask him to love both of them.

She hurried to the bathroom, splashed water on her face. Her eyes were still red and swollen, but who was she trying to kid? She quickly dried her face, pushed her fingers through her hair, and hurried back to the front door.

Took a breath, unlocked the door, and opened it far enough to slip out.

Wyatt was gone.

Chapter 16

Sarah stared at the place on the steps where he had been, then looked down the street to see if he was going back to the beach or to Dive Works or home. He was nowhere, like he'd just disappeared. Maybe he'd been a figment of her imagination.

She was that crazed. Maybe she had imagined the whole thing, him saying he wasn't going to leave her, that they'd get through it. She was a fool. Everybody left.

Well, hell, it didn't take him long to change his mind.

She went back in the house. Closed the door, locked it. Just because.

She took out a bottle of water from the fridge, pressed it to her forehead until it hurt. Then she drank the whole bottle leaning against the cool surface of the door, smothering Sam's written words, *Fix the now.* So much for that. She'd royally screwed up the now. Left her friends. Hurt Wyatt. Sabotaged her own happiness. Why couldn't she just get it right?

GIRL. YOU'RE NOT gonna last a minute if you keep letting everything upset you. You gotta be hard. If they see you crying like a baby, they're gonna go for you. Do bad things to you. Do you want that? I didn't think so, so quit sniveling and show 'em how tough you are. Always hang tough and they'll stay out of your face and your pants if you're lucky. Be weak and you're finished.

SARAH HAD HUNG tough, stayed strong, and she felt like she was finished anyway. And she'd really tried. She thought of Nonie just a few miles away all this time and her heart broke all over again while at the same time anger swelled inside her. Nonie who was her sister, who wouldn't take her case, who came to spy on her and called the police on her when she confronted her.

Sarah just didn't get it.

Fix the now, dammit.

She went back to the bathroom, washed her face for real, and put on makeup. It didn't hide much, but she could pretend, and by the time Leila returned there would hardly be any traces of tears or scratches left.

ILONA MEANT TO drive her car to the church, be there early to stand with her father, just for show. But her heart just wasn't in it. She drove "home" to the mansion she'd grown up in.

She parked in front of the three-car garage, knowing that people would return to the house after the funeral, and she'd be blocked in. She'd have to stay to the bitter end. Her penance for not being lovable enough, smart enough—just not enough.

She didn't feel sad, not exactly. Not standing in the living room waiting to leave for the church. Everything in its same place except for the one vase she'd broken in a fit of temper.

It had never been replaced. Maybe it was irreplaceable. Like a Ming or Limoges. She couldn't remember what it had looked like. An empty spot had stayed on that side table ever since. An empty reminder.

Toby waddled in, sniffed at her shoes. She nudged him away with her toe. It had never occurred to her that the dog was still alive. His white coat had turned a dirty yellowish color, and one lip seemed to be stuck in a permanent snarl.

Which he did, at Ilona.

"You don't scare me, you lump of lard." He wasn't her dog. He'd always belonged to June. And June cosseted him like . . . Well, Ilona wouldn't think about the dog or the past. She was just here for show. She knew what to do. She'd done it often enough before.

She rode to the church in the back of the black limousine. It felt strange sitting next to her father with no June on her other side. That had been the presentation. June and Donald, compassionate, caring, who believed in the little people, in family values, their loving daughter, adopted from the foster system. Your tax dollars at work.

Ilona swallowed. She felt an almost overwhelming urge to pat her father's hand.

The limo pulled up in front of the church. The two of them sat there while the driver came around to open the door. Her father got out first. Ilona adjusted her sunglasses and took the driver's proffered hand.

A man was there to meet them. A friend? The funeral parlor director? She hadn't gone to the viewing. She'd been in court. Everyone understood. Such late notice.

It wasn't that she was cold and unfeeling, exactly. It was June who had been cold and exacting when she was alive. And

Ilona just couldn't face the chance that she would appear the same in death.

So she'd made it up to her father by playing the grieving daughter. And she had to admit she felt a little empty. She hadn't seen either of them for months; she'd made a point of not seeing them once she realized they were still seeing her ex-husband, that they had chosen him over her. And the new wife. Over their own—not their own—daughter.

Kevin and his wife were the first people Ilona saw when she removed her sunglasses and stepped into the church. They came forward simultaneously as if they'd been rehearsing. He took her father's hand in both of his, and the wife mimicked his actions with Ilona.

Ilona gritted her teeth and smiled, thanked her in a quiet voice, repeated the same with the ex. And the usher guided them down the aisle to the front pew. The church was already packed, and she could feel the eyes of the multitude on her back: old friends speculating about why she'd come, if there had been a reconciliation; strangers wondering if she was her father's new mistress; wives wondering how much her little black dress had cost.

At least there were no cameras, though she suspected there would be some at the graveside. Hidden discreetly out of sight, behind a tree or a car.

The coffin was covered by mounds of flowers. The whole front of the church was filled with flowers, and at first Ilona drowned out the preacher's solemn words by concentrating on not sneezing. She didn't want to hear about how much June Cartwright would be missed. She just didn't.

It wasn't that she was ungrateful. She was. To both her parents. She'd made out really well thanks to their generosity.

And she still found it incomprehensible how they could lavish so much on her and yet withhold the one thing she craved, and which cost nothing, nothing, to give. That was the great sadness in her life.

But she was a big girl. She'd dealt with it. She was even fond of the man sitting beside her, stoically holding back his grief. She'd noticed walking in that he'd grown shorter. She wondered if he had really loved his wife, because now that Ilona thought of it, she'd never seen them exchange affection except in a perfunctory way, and in front of an audience.

The organ swelled, bringing her thoughts back to the funeral. The pallbearers formed a line on either side of the casket and wheeled it down the aisle. Ilona stifled whatever emotion might be lurking just beneath the surface; she had no idea if it would come out as a sob or a giggle.

They followed the casket outside, slipping on their sunglasses at the door along with the rest of the mourners. Got back in the limousine, drove to the cemetery where it was all done again, this time sitting in folding chairs on Astroturf in front of an open grave backed by an inadequately covered mound of earth.

This service was quicker. It was hot, and people had busy Saturdays to get under way. When it was over, most mourners returned to their cars; a few stopped to give their condolences, then they too passed on to their cars. Someone came to get Ilona and her father and led them back to the limo.

Ilona held back, turned to look at the now empty tent, the lone coffin, and quickly lifted her sunglasses and brushed away the tear before it betrayed her.

SARAH CLOSED THE shop early and was sipping a cup of chamomile tea at her kitchen table when the doorbell rang.

She'd been listening for it for the last fifteen minutes and still she jumped.

She hurried to answer it.

"Here she is," Danny said brightly. He looked a little disheveled. He was holding a helium-filled balloon, a cellophane bag of candy, a stuffed monkey.

Sarah opened the door for them to come in. Danny shoved his bundle at Sarah. Before she could take it, Leila grabbed the monkey; it flew from Danny's arms, making him drop the bag of candy, which hit the floor and burst open spreading peppermints, toffees, and lollipops across the hardwood floor.

"Piñata," Danny explained as he knelt to help Sarah pick up the pieces.

"How did it go?" she asked.

"Fine." He frowned slightly. "Not too many people. I was expecting more family."

Sarah had an ungracious thought about where they might be, but she kept it to herself.

They corralled most of the wayward candy and stood.

"Well, until Wednesday," he said.

Sarah nodded.

"See you Wednesday," he called to Leila who had gone to her room. And he let himself out the door.

Sarah went to see what mood Leila would be in.

She was sitting on her bed next to the monkey, which she'd placed on her pillow.

When she saw Sarah, she turned away from her.

Sarah took a patience-inducing breath and came to sit behind her.

"Did you have a good time?"

"Be quiet."

"All right."

Leila turned on her. "Be quiet now, Sarah."

Sarah blinked. Leila looked defiant. Challenging.

Leila never called her Sarah. Should she let it pass? Or should she reinforce what was the norm. And when would she ever get past always second-guessing what would be best?

"I missed you while you were gone." She decided not to mention the sand castle contest.

Leila crawled across the bed and Sarah started to relax. She waited for Leila to climb onto her lap, for things to be fairly calm again. But Leila stopped in front of her. Held her arm up to Sarah's. You could barely see the scratches.

Leila looked at it for a long time. And Sarah was wondering if she should mention the fight they'd had, when Leila said, "Mama says you can't be my mommee because we don't have the same skin. I have my mama's skin. You're just Sarah."

Mama? Sarah was staggered. *Mama.* Blindsided, she looked down at their arms, hers light even with the sun and Leila's dark and rich.

Leila crossed her arms and scowled at Sarah.

"Being a mother and daughter is not about colors," Sarah said. "Your friends Macy and Kendrick's mother doesn't have the same skin color as them. Macy and Kendrick don't even have the same skin color as each other, but they are brothers and she's their mother. There are hundreds of shades of skin. Being a mother and daughter is about loving each other. I'm your mommee."

"That's shit."

"That's not a nice word. Who told you that word?"

Leila shrugged.

"Well, you're not to use it. Do you understand?"

"DeShawn says it."

"Who is DeShawn?" Sarah didn't remember the names of all Carmen's children, but she didn't think any of them were DeShawn. Which meant . . .

"Is DeShawn Carmen's boyfriend?"

Leila slid off the bed and went to the bookshelf, picked out a book, sat cross-legged on the floor, and opened it.

"Is he, sweetie?"

Leila didn't answer. Just looked at her book.

With a sinking heart, Sarah prepared for the long haul. She recognized the signs. Leila was only four and had been living with Sarah for most of her life and yet already she had learned to withhold. And Sarah knew what would come next. The sulks, the lies, the rejection. It came with the territory.

Leila was already building the walls of her protection, and she was using them in the one place she didn't have to. At home with Sarah.

"Leila?"

Leila looked up. Her mean face. "You're not my mama!" she screamed then threw her book at her.

Sarah sidestepped it and rushed to her, picked her up. "It's all right, baby. It's all right."

Leila squirmed. She kicked her, and kept kicking her until Sarah was forced to put her down.

"I hate you!" Leila screamed. "Hate you. Hate you!" She landed a kick on Sarah's ankle.

Sarah saw stars for a second. She tried to stand outside herself. She knew Leila didn't mean it. That this was just a classic reaction to the disruption in her life. Sarah's mind knew it, but her heart . . .

"I hate you."

"It's okay, Leila. I have enough love for both of us."

"Go away. Go away."

"Okay. I'll be out here if you need me." Sarah turned away. Her stomach revolted, and bile rose to her throat. She grasped the doorjamb, stumbled across the hall to the bathroom. And made it just in time before her stomach rejected lunch and tea and what remained of her hope.

At last she straightened up and ran the back of her hand over the sweat on her forehead. She turned on the faucet with shaky fingers, braced herself on her elbows on the side of the sink, and splashed cold water onto her face. Then she just stood there clinging to the sink waiting for her equilibrium to come back, wondering if she really had what it took to see them both through this again.

She didn't know how long she stood there, but she knew she couldn't stay. She would have to face whatever came. When she was more composed, she dried her face and opened the bathroom door.

Leila was standing just outside.

"Mommee?"

Sarah scooped her up and held her tight.

ILONA STAYED AT the funeral repast until the last guest left. But when her father asked if she would like to stay overnight, she refused. She saw his disappointment and, in an aberrant moment, felt sorry for him, but no way was she going to spend a night in that house.

Now, she sat in her apartment, in the dark, on her expensive leather couch, hugging her knees and feeling alone.

She was comfortable alone. But tonight she was unsettled. For the first time in a long, long time, she questioned herself.

She'd managed to get out of a one-way street to failure, had hung in, had lived a luxurious life, gotten a good education, but it had been a shallow existence, one without love.

Yeah, Ilona Cartwright, thinking about love. It was pitiful and Ilona didn't do pitiful.

She'd spent a cold few years inside that mansion. But for the first time, she wondered if it had all been one-sided. Had she brought the cold with her? Had she been impossible to love?

At first she'd tried. So hard. Maybe too hard. Cried herself to sleep over her failures and tried harder the next day. And she just couldn't seem to make it work. So she just turned off, lived her life by rote. Didn't act out or run away, just counted the days until she could get an education and get away.

Tonight in the dark, alone, Ilona wondered if she had tried hard enough. And tonight in the dark, Nonie cried for a life that might have been.

Chapter 17

Sarah and Leila were both feeling a little fragile Sunday morning. The kitchen seemed almost too small to hold them. And yet it felt lonely. Sarah hoped Wyatt would show up with bagels or even empty-handed. They often spent Sundays together if he wasn't working and Sarah wasn't being neurotic, which she swore she was not going to do anymore. What if Wyatt had already gotten fed up and didn't want to be with them anymore?

Even after all the loss, and all of her tough-girl past, Sarah didn't want to believe that he'd actually really walked away. If he'd only waited two minutes longer, if she'd just gone outside with her nose running and her makeup smeared.

If she hadn't waited so long to let him know how she really felt.

Was it too late? Could it really work out? Alice's words kept echoing in her mind: men don't want a "package deal." Sarah didn't want to believe it, but she knew it was true. Maybe it was true with Wyatt, too, and she'd just been fooling herself.

A yelp from Leila interrupted her thoughts. Sarah looked up. Leila's juice glass was overturned and orange juice was spreading across the table and dripping off the edges. Leila just watched it and didn't try to set it straight.

Sarah uprighted the glass and hurried to the sink for a sponge and paper towels. She reached the table just as Leila swept her plate onto the floor. She began rubbing her hands in the sticky juice, then helped it on its way to the floor.

Sarah told herself to stay calm. She lifted Leila out of the booster seat, carried her to the sink, and ran warm water over her arms. Then she carried her to the corner of the kitchen out of harm's way, dried her arms, and said, "Stay here."

Leila crossed her arms, made her mean face.

"That was a naughty thing to do. Do you want to help me clean it up?"

Leila stuck out her bottom lip.

It was hard not to get exasperated even though Sarah knew what this was.

God, Leila's reaction was so classic. Sarah had pulled the same stunt so many times in her line of foster homes. *I know you're not going to love me, so I'm rejecting you first.*

Sarah had thought—hoped—she and Leila might miss the worst of that stage. And they had until now. But Leila was old enough now to know something was happening and also to know she had no control over the outcome.

And Sarah thought about how some things did change. But there were others that not all the love—or therapy—in the world could fix. Today she still felt powerless.

It was all she could do not to scoop Leila up and promise

to always love her. And she would tell her, once the crisis faded and Leila was in a place where she would be able to hear her.

Right now, she needed to know that this was unacceptable behavior.

"You're upset, but you took it out on me. Now I have to clean up the mess. I know you're mad, but we don't act out when we're mad." Sarah reached over and dragged a chair to where they stood. She picked Leila up and sat her in the chair.

"You sit here and think about why you did something so naughty."

Sarah cleaned up the table and picked the plate and eggs and toast off the floor and put them in the sink. She saw Leila start to slide off the seat.

"I told you to stay there. I'm not happy with your behavior."

There was a brief staredown, but finally Leila slid back on the seat.

Sarah went to the closet to get the mop, cleaned the floor, leaned over to pick up a missed piece of toast. And when she straightened up, she came eye to eye with the fridge and Sam's sign. *Fix the now.*

She reached out and touched the saying; let her fingers linger over the letters.

What would you say, Sam? I've made myself sick worrying about losing her, but is it because I worry about her safety or my loneliness?

I thought I knew, but not anymore. I'm so used to being stressed and fearful that I've lost sight of what's important, haven't I?

Have I?

Should I just take each minute that we have together and appreciate it for what it is? Or should I fight to the death for her? Already I see her slipping away. Confused. Wondering who loves her and it breaks my heart. She said "shit" yesterday. That's not what I wanted for her. But if learn-

ing "shit" is the worst it gets, would she be better, feel more loved, by going back to Carmen?

Tell me, Sam.

Even in life, Sam never told her what to do. He just guided her gently until she figured it out. She really didn't expect him to start now. He wouldn't be sending a lightning bolt from wherever he was watching.

Maybe he wasn't even listening, and she was just some nutcase talking to a refrigerator.

She stood, looked around. Leila was gone. But Sarah knew she'd be standing just outside the door—waiting to see what Sarah did.

And what would Sarah do?

She'd start the day again like nothing had happened.

"Morning, sunshine," she called. She waited.

A few seconds later, Leila appeared from behind the doorjamb, quiet, contrite.

Sarah smiled. "Hey there."

"Sorry, Mommee."

Sarah held out her hand, thankful to see that it wasn't shaking as her heart raced. "No more acting mad."

Leila shook her head.

"Then let's get cleaned up and we'll try again."

REESA LOADED THE dishwasher, grabbed her keys, and saying a cursory good-bye to Michael, she got in her car. She intended to go to the garden center, price the rosebushes, check out some perennials. She might even plant some annuals. But somehow she ended up on Eighth Street instead.

She parked and watched a group of young mothers, children, and possibly young grandmothers go into the center.

They were all dressed in their Sunday clothes. Reesa considered driving on, because she really didn't relish sitting through a church service heavy on homily and parables.

But she got out of the car and followed them inside.

The center was already busy. Tanisha and another woman were attempting to carry an unwieldy table from the reception area down the hallway. Reesa hurried over and grabbed one corner. They managed to get it to one of the classrooms, then had to stop to figure out how to get it through the door. By zigzagging the legs through the opening, they soon had it inside and set up next to a half-dozen other tables.

"Classroom?" Reesa asked as they stood back and surveyed the room.

"Life Savers."

Reesa waited for elucidation.

"You know, sewing, small appliance repair, basic first aid. Stuff you need when you least expect it."

"Makes sense."

"Did you have a particular reason for coming today?" Tanisha asked.

"No, just thought I'd see if I could help out. It's my day off." Because even if she did buy plants, she wouldn't have time to keep them alive.

"That's great. There's lots to do. Most people are still coming in from church. We have a hot lunch for them, then story time for the little ones. And share time for the older kids and for the adults. We've been looking for someone who could talk to the kids."

"I can listen."

"That works," Tanisha said. "But let's start with serving lunch."

The kitchen and dining room were at the back of the building near the delivery door that was painted red and bore a big sign that said EMERGENCY EXIT ONLY.

"It only opens from the inside and a buzzer goes off when it's opened," Tanisha explained. "We need a second exit, but we don't want to leave temptation glaring them in the face."

Reesa was surprised to see a variety of tables, round, square, rectangular, all covered in paper tablecloths and set with napkins and silverware. There was an assortment of centerpieces that looked like they had been collected from someone's attic or a thrift store. But it gave the whole room the aura of a giant family reunion.

"Nice," Reesa said.

Tanisha smiled. "Just like home."

They went into the kitchen where several women wearing aprons and hairnets were cooking at two old industrial-sized ovens. A center island held trays of warm biscuits and corn muffins. Stacks of serving dishes were lined up on the counter that ran under a large serving window.

"Someone from each table comes up and gets their food and it's served family style just like at their own homes. Or in some cases like the home they never had. You'd be surprised at the number of women and children we get who have no idea about passing food around. So those families are mentored by more experienced ones."

Tanisha handed Reesa an apron. "The tables are assigned so we have a good distribution. At first we let them choose where they wanted to sit, but it was chaos, with empty places and cold food when the table was finally filled. Not to mention the cliques that formed almost immediately. It was a disaster waiting to happen."

"Where is everyone?" Reesa asked. She'd seen some enter but hadn't seen anyone except the crew since.

"Oh, they're all singing hymns of thanksgiving." Tanisha shrugged. "You don't have to be religious. And we certainly don't push them to believe, though we do encourage them to visit their places of worship. But everybody has to participate in the singing. It's like a prolonged blessing."

She handed Reesa a stack of wicker baskets. "Put a paper napkin in the bottom then put biscuits in one and corn muffins in the other. At the end of the meal they can take the extra bread back home with them."

"Does everyone come here for Sunday lunch?" Reesa asked as she began piling biscuits into the baskets.

"We encourage one meal a week here; a lot come in every day. But it isn't a soup kitchen. They have to pay during the week. Not much, just enough so they remember there is no free ride. Only Sundays are free, but you have to sign up for it and clear any guest ahead of time. It probably sounds kind of like a prison, but some of these women have survived by gaming whatever they could. That's no way to live if you don't have to. So it's really a question of retraining."

"I can tell you've really planned how to approach this."

"Yes, we have. I've got a good staff and a bunch of volunteers with business and not-for-profit experience. We're always looking for more." She gave Reesa a bright smile.

Reesa just bent over her task of filling the baskets.

By the end of lunch, they had served close to sixty people. The cooks retired to a table to eat, and several of the diners relieved them to load the dishwasher and scrub the pans.

Reesa had been surprised to see quite a few men among the diners.

"It's an experiment. The center is for women and children only. But it doesn't seem right that they shouldn't have Sunday dinner with their whole family—if they're drug- and drink-free and are working or actively looking for work."

"How can you get them to abide by the rules? It seems fraught with volatility."

"Peer pressure. Amazing what women can do if they've a mind to."

LEILA'S SECOND BREAKFAST was more successful; the only parts on the floor when it was over were the wayward bits of scrambled eggs that managed to fall off her fork.

Sarah cleaned the kitchen for the second time, washed up Leila, and put her in clean clothes. She was behind in her work but it seemed like today they both needed a personal health day. So Sarah grabbed the play bag, added a big bouncy ball and two water bottles, her wallet, and a towel for unexpected messes, and they went to the playground.

Only a few children were there. Their mothers or babysitters sat on benches while the kids climbed over the jungle gym and ran from one spring toy to the other. Sarah hadn't taken Leila to the child services group play for a while. She'd thought they were past that. But she'd kept Leila at Green Horizons School and Day Care for the summer session. Hopefully by September she'd be pre-K ready.

Leila usually got along with other kids, and Sarah hoped that her new sense of insecurity wouldn't cause any setbacks there. But she needed to be vigilant.

Leila started to run toward the other children but stopped and turned back to look at Sarah.

Sarah smiled encouragingly. "Go play."

"You come." Leila took Sarah's hand and pulled her over to one of the ride-on ponies. When Leila held up her arms, Sarah swung her up. Leila immediately began rocking as fast as she could, and Sarah went to sit on the bench near the other mothers.

They were already talking among themselves, about summer activities and back to school. Sarah didn't join in. She didn't want to have to go through all the explanations of her and Leila's situation. Especially with everything suddenly up in the air.

So she sat watching Leila, holding her breath when she slid off the pony and ran after another little girl. Sarah shifted a little to be able to see them both, since the other mothers seemed to have forgotten they were there.

They ran out of sight for a minute, but she could hear their delighted squeals. Then one head appeared at the top of the sliding board. The little girl swung her legs forward and slid down the board. Before Sarah could move, she saw Leila scrambling over the top of the slide. Sarah's heart leaped into her throat and lodged there. It wasn't a very high slide and Leila could usually manage it, but she always waited for Sarah to come catch her.

Sarah was off the bench and had crossed the distance between them without even thinking.

"Watch me, Mommee!"

Holding on to both sides to push off, Leila slid down, stopping at the end of the slide.

Sarah gave her a thumbs-up, while her heart lowered to a normal rate.

Leila jumped off and ran around to do it again.

"Is she yours?" asked one of the mothers who had come over to supervise.

Sarah nodded.

"Isn't she kind of young to be on the slide by herself?"

Sarah turned to look at the woman, as heat rose in her face. The woman didn't even look as old as Sarah and she was an expert?

"She's four."

"Oh, she looks younger. Megan is four, too." She pointed to the curly-haired girl who was on the slide with Leila.

"She's small for her age." *But growing every day*, she wanted to add.

"Where is she going to school in the fall?"

"She'll be in pre–K."

"Meggy just made it. She'll be going to kindergarten, though I thought about keeping her back just to give her an edge, you know?"

Yeah, Sarah knew all about edges. Not necessarily good things to have. She tried to think of something to say that would be friendly without inviting confidences. "I guess a lot of people hold their kids back."

The woman nodded. "My Benjamin's class has an eighteen-month span, can you believe it? One boy should be a grade up, but his parents kept him back so he'd be good at sports. Benjamin is more interested in music, thank goodness. I shudder every time I see those poor little boys in all that football gear."

Sarah nodded.

"My name's Tyler." The woman smiled at Sarah.

"Sarah."

"You live around here?"

Sarah nodded. "I own the clock repair shop in town."

"Oh, I know the place. I've never been in—we're all hands-free digital in our house—but it looks so cute."

Poor Megan and Benjamin, Sarah thought, not to ever have the fun of winding clocks and the pleasure of watching time circle back to start.

Tyler glanced at her watch. Also digital Sarah noticed. "Meggy, we have to go!" she called. "Nice to meet you." She hurried after Meggy who had rushed to the opposite side of the playground.

Sarah expelled a sigh of relief.

After Meggy left, Sarah threw the ball a few times until Leila said she was hot and she wanted ice cream.

Sarah thought maybe they could stop by Dive Works and offer to buy Wyatt some ice cream, by way of apologizing for freaking out on him the day before. But when they reached the store, it was closed. Sometimes when he had to go out on a lesson or the rescue team needed him, and Victor couldn't come in, he'd just leave a sign, saying what time he would be back.

Today there was no message. Just the Closed sign.

Maybe he just needed a day off. *Maybe he saw us coming and hurriedly turned over the Closed sign so we won't come in.*

She was being crazy. All he had to say was no. He'd probably run around to the Ocean Brew and hadn't bothered with the sign.

"Ice cream," Leila whined.

"Okay." She would call Wyatt from the ice cream store and tell him where they were.

But once they were seated with Leila's vanilla with sprinkles and her own butter pecan, Sarah's call went to Wyatt's voice mail. She hung up. Called back. "Hey, it's me, sorry about yesterday. We're getting ice cream if you're interested." She hung up.

They finished their ice cream, then lingered in front of the toy shop and the fudge store. Wyatt didn't call. Sarah thought he was probably just hung up somewhere and that he'd call back when he got the chance.

Tired out from the playground, the ice cream, and the tantrum, Leila fell asleep in front of the television as soon as they got home, and Sarah went back to her workroom to finish up her neglected timepieces.

She kept her phone right on the table, but no one called. She thought about calling Karen or Reesa, but the one she really wanted to talk to was Wyatt. She considered calling him again, but that would just be pathetic. She'd left a message; he'd call when he could or if he wanted to.

But Sarah couldn't help that little piece of worry from creeping into her consciousness. What if yesterday had finally broken his patience and his love?

The afternoon crept by, but at least she made some headway on her repairs. At six she and Leila had a dinner of chicken and rice and broccoli, neither Leila's nor Sarah's favorite but everybody needed greens.

Bath and bedtime. Wyatt still hadn't called. Maybe he was busy. Maybe he wasn't going to call.

Sarah read Leila two stories, then took out the *Everybody Loves Me* scrapbook. This time Leila didn't object. She was drowsy and snuggled against Sarah. She pointed to the first picture, the one of her with Sarah and Carmen beside her. "That's my mama and that's my mommee," she said.

Sarah took an emotional step back. That was who they were.

Two women who loved the same little girl: Sarah, who could offer her stability and safety and love; and Carmen, who could offer a bio mother's love that people said was different from all others. But if it was so great, how could Carmen have neglected Leila? How could Carmen's love be better than Sarah's?

Chapter 18

Sarah knew the minute her eyes opened that today would be different. It would be the first day of her new life. Maybe talking to refrigerators wasn't so dumb after all. Sam must have talked to her while she slept.

She was optimistic if a little sad. She loved Leila, she loved Wyatt—she would let them both know. And she would do her best by them and her other friends. And she would live with the repercussions, but not without fighting for what she wanted.

Sarah rolled out of bed, showered and changed, not into jeans and work shirt but cotton slacks and a new tee. The store was closed Mondays, and she could always change into work clothes later.

She roused Leila, helped her into the school clothes they'd picked out the night before, and pinned up Leila's hair in several short ponytails clasped by her favorite pink and blue butterfly barrettes. It wouldn't pass the fashion police but it would look fine for catch-up school.

Sarah made Leila granola and yogurt for breakfast and added waffles to her grocery list. She'd have to make a store run today.

She put Leila on the bus with an "I love you, sunshine," then went straight to Dive Works to tell Wyatt the same thing. Her feet started dragging before she'd passed two stores, and when Mrs. Bridges who was sweeping the sidewalk outside the antiques shop stopped her to ask about Leila, she was more than happy to stay and chat.

When she finally got to the dive shop, her heart was pounding. The Closed sign was up. She cupped her hands and peered through the glass window. No movement inside; either Wyatt and Victor were in the back or they hadn't come in yet.

Reprieved.

He'd be at Ocean Brew. She'd meet him there. She wouldn't declare her love in front of everybody but wait until they were outside. But maybe he didn't want her love, just a friendship with benefits? They'd never talked about it. Why was it easier to say I love you to Leila than to Wyatt?

Her old Sarah self was begging her to forget all about it. It could wait. Better not to rock the boat. How embarrassing it would be if he just looked horrified and fled. Maybe he was thinking about dumping her. Maybe he already had.

Across the street to the right was home and safety . . .

She turned left.

The Brew was crowded for a Monday morning. At the height of the season, some of the shops were open seven days a week, so lots of locals were in for their morning jolt of joe and a little of the latest gossip before heading to the sales counters.

A few tourists, their beach gear and bikes piled up outside

by the door, were getting cups to go. Sarah looked around and, not seeing Wyatt, got in line. Once she had her tea she made a quick sweep of the room; several people were using the free Wi-Fi at the counter along the window. A few people chatted around the condiments table, and most of the central tables were occupied.

She didn't see Wyatt. He usually took his coffee to go but she hadn't passed him on the street. Maybe he was running late. Then she saw Victor sitting at a table by himself. He motioned her over.

Sarah couldn't tell if it was an invitation or an order, but she was glad to have a seat, and Victor could tell her where Wyatt was.

He grabbed a chair from the next table and pulled it over for her. She sat down, smiled tentatively. She never knew what to say to Victor; he always seemed to be living partially in some other world.

"Have you seen Wyatt?" he asked.

That had been her question, and it threw her off balance that he'd asked her first. "No. Why?"

"Talked to him?"

"Not since Saturday." Sarah was too embarrassed to say she'd locked him out of the house and only talked to him through the door. "Why? What's going on?"

He looked at her for an awkwardly long time, his expression blank or at least not readable by Sarah.

"You want to know?"

She nodded.

"Are you holding a grudge or do you really not know?"

He was beginning to scare her. "I'm not holding a grudge; he just doesn't want to see me."

"Did he say so? That idiot. It's just like him to— Wait a minute. Do you even know about the rescue?"

Sarah shook her head. Her stomach started to burn. "What happened? Is he okay?"

"He's banged up a bit."

"A bit or a lot?"

"Somewhere in between. Some fools stole a boat to go joy-riding. Overloaded it with a bunch of drunk ass— Anyway, they didn't notice they were taking on water. Boat shoulda never been taken out. Not fit for a bathtub. Lost three passengers."

Lost. "Drowned?"

Victor nodded.

"That's awful."

"Not as awful as it could've been. At least there weren't any children. They lugged four of 'em out of the water. But two guys were trapped in the cabin. They sent Wyatt and Davey Parker down to try and get them out. They pried the door open, but it was too late, and on the way back up the tub shifted and broke up, and Wyatt and Davey got hit with the roll.

"Davey's in the hospital with a concussion and a broken collarbone. Wyatt's home with a bum knee and some heavy bruises. They'll be okay, but it'll take some time. Never did find the last guy, and they searched until almost dawn. Helicopter and everything."

She'd spent yesterday thinking Wyatt had finally dumped her, and he had been called away for a rescue and gotten hurt in the process. "Why didn't he call me?"

"He didn't want to bother you. Said you have a lot on your plate right now."

"That dummy, did he think I can't handle one more thing?"

Victor shook his head. "Well, if you do care—which sometimes I wonder—get your butt over there before that witchy blonde moves in on your territory."

"A blonde?"

"Some girl who came in for lessons. Caitlyn. I called to cancel her lesson for today. *She'd* heard about the rescue and put two and two together." Victor gave Sarah a disparaging look. "I don't know how she found out where he lived, but she hightailed it over there to play Florence Nightingale, before I could call him and warn him."

"Oh," Sarah said. "Maybe he doesn't need me then."

Victor made a nasty noise in his throat. "Is that an excuse so you don't have to be bothered. Sorry I mentioned it."

"Of course not. I just—"

The door opened and Victor rolled his eyes. "Not those yo-yos."

The same four men Sarah had seen at Dive Works the other day parted the clientele as they made their way to the counter—the winning rescue squad.

After they got their drinks, they wandered over to where Victor and Sarah sat.

"Hey, Vic. Heard your boss got banged up the other night."

"Yep."

"He all right?"

"He'll mend."

"Shoulda called our team. We woulda shown him how to do it."

Victor shrugged.

Sarah got mad. "People died," she said.

"Like I said. They shoulda called us. We know how to do a rescue. Got the trophy to prove it."

Sarah stood so abruptly that her chair tipped over. The guy stepped back in sheer reaction.

"What a stupid thing to say. So you did a few exhibitions faster than our team this summer, not a great feat when our team was one man short because he was helping his wife have a baby instead of racing with a rowboat over his head."

She stepped into him, tilted her chin up, and glared at him.

"And where do you come when you need equipment or have yours repaired or when you just need advice? To Wyatt because he knows what he's doing. More than any of you, so don't you dare dis him when you depend on him all the time. Who did you call when you had that kid stuck in the underground cave last year? Huh? Who risked his life to go in and get him? None of you, that's for sure. So just—just shut up."

"Yeah," said someone from behind her.

"Hey, chill. We was just razzing him."

"Really? When he's not even here? That's not razzing, that's defamation. I think you could find a better use of your time. Go practice CPR or something."

"Honey. You just don't understand how rescue teams work."

"I know how they should work."

One of his buddies pulled him away. "Come on, Cliff. She's got you there."

"Yeah," called the barista. "Go on, Cliff, until you got something nice to say."

The second guy stayed behind for a second. "You're absolutely right. Joking sometimes gets outta hand. We didn't mean anything by it. We totally respect Wyatt."

Sarah just gave him a look.

He turned to Victor. "Tell Wy we all hope he and Davey get better soon."

They left and kept walking, but Sarah could see them talking, and she knew the other three were giving Cliff their opinion of his humor.

She turned around and found the entire coffee bar was looking in her direction. Mr. Sykes from the real estate office lifted his cup. "Way to go, Sarah."

"I second that," said Tony Alonso from the bakery. Then everyone was lifting their coffee cups and murmuring support.

Sarah felt the blood rush to her face. What had gotten into her?

She grabbed her chair and sat down hard. Looked over at Victor. "I can't believe I just did that."

"I can't either," he said. "But it's about time you did."

SARAH STOOD ON the sidewalk in front of Wyatt's Victorian. It had been easy enough to decide to go check on the state of Wyatt's injuries when she left the coffee bar. She'd planned to see if he needed anything, groceries or prescriptions or something. That's what friends did.

But she hesitated and felt the same paralyzing fear she'd always felt steal over her.

It was crazy. They were friends. At least she hoped they still were. Maybe she'd tried his patience one too many times, and Saturday had been the final straw.

She reached in her bag. She'd call first. Let him know she was outside. Ask if he wanted company. And then she had a terrible thought. What if that blonde—what had Victor called her? . . . Caitlyn—was already there?

That's why she'd call, and then he could say, no, don't come in.

She lifted her phone out and swiped it open.

He picked it up before the first ring ended.

"It's Sarah."

"I know."

"Are you all right?"

"Good enough."

"I just wanted to know if you needed anything?"

A jagged breath. "I'd really love it if you'd stop standing on the sidewalk outside and come in so I can sit back down."

"You see me?"

"Yeah. I'm watching you from the window."

Sarah looked up and saw him standing on the other side of the glass. He raised his hand slowly, then stepped out of view. She closed the phone and hurried up the walk to the porch.

She had to wait for him to open the door and when he finally did, she understood why.

One side of his face was purple. He attempted a smile, she thought. But it looked more like a grimace. And when he moved back to let her in, he was moving slowly and carefully. He was wearing a T-shirt and gym shorts, and his whole left side was scraped and bruised.

"Oh, Wyatt." Her eyes teared up. Stupid.

"Hey, I probably look worse than I am."

"You look awful."

"Yeah, well, I feel pretty awful."

He turned and hobbled across the entryway and to the couch. The coffee table was covered by glasses, ice packs, several bottles of water, and two prescription bottles that must be pain pills.

He eased himself down on the couch and leaned back against the pillows he had piled against the arm of the couch, using his hand to lift his leg onto the cushions.

"Can I do something?"

"Sit down here." He patted the edge of the couch.

She dropped her bag on the floor and slowly sat down beside him, careful not to jar any part of him.

"How did you get to the window so fast when the phone hadn't even rung yet?"

"I was already there."

"Were you expecting someone?"

Wyatt touched her nose. "You. Victor called to say you were coming. But that you were skittish and might change your mind before you actually got inside. So I was ready for you."

He attempted that lopsided grin and winced.

"I wasn't sure if you wanted to see me. I thought—"

"You think too much." He shifted his weight and cut back a groan.

"It's just when I finally opened the door, you were gone."

"Because I got an emergency call. I didn't have a choice."

"Of course not, I just didn't understand. I thought you were avoiding me or I would have come over yesterday and . . . and . . . brought chicken soup or something." She reached over and gently pushed a lock of hair off his brow. She was afraid any more display of affection would hurt him. "Why didn't you call me? I would have come over, gotten you settled, gone to the drugstore for you."

"Victor did all that. Anyway, I didn't want to bother you."

She stared at him. "After all you've done for me?"

"I don't want to keep score, Sarah. We lost three men. Got two of them out of the boat but it was too late. Never found the third one. Then the boat blew and I thought Dave and I were going to go down with that ship."

Sarah touched his good cheek. "But you didn't."

"No, but it happened really fast. It's funny but I had one

thought in that split second before you know it's going to end. It was you, Sarah. I thought of you. Not my shop, or the other guys, or myself or any of it. Just you." He stopped to take a long careful breath.

"It sounds corny, I know. Then everything went black for a while. And I was on a stretcher, still alive. Dave was alive. And then a bunch of stuff happened that I don't remember so great."

His eyes closed and Sarah thought maybe the drugs were taking effect, but then he opened them again. "I didn't think I was ready for that. You know, for us being something more than we are. I slept most of yesterday, but every time I woke up, it was still there."

He made a sound that might have been an attempt at a laugh. "I decided to wait and see how I felt when I'm back to normal."

"I don't think you're back to normal yet."

"Nope." He was sounding groggy, which was good because Sarah didn't know what to think. She'd come over here to declare her love, but she'd never really thought she would do it. And he'd blindsided her.

Now she was more confused than ever. Would he forget he ever mentioned it once he was completely lucid again? And "us being something more than we are"? What the hell did that mean?

She sat watching him for a couple more minutes then got up slowly and tiptoed into the kitchen. She might as well see if he needed anything from the grocery since she was going anyway.

ILONA CARTWRIGHT WASN'T given to introspection, but it wasn't to show respect for her mother that she decided to take Monday morning off. She had spent Sunday sitting on her couch, knees tucked up, alternately crying and remembering. Remembering June and remembering Sarah. Alternating between feeling sorry for herself and wondering if her own insecurity had made her miss the chance of being loved. And wondering why Sarah had burst into her office and accused her of betraying her? Because she'd been adopted first?

But they'd known that could happen. They'd promised to be sisters. But Sarah had let her down. Ignored her all these years, only to show up now? Is that why she came back? Because Ilona had taught her well. Strike before they can, be the aggressor even if you're wrong. And she had to admit, Sarah had gotten the first lick in with that one.

She couldn't help but wonder if she was missing something. Could she have made June love her more? And then she would cry again, like some disgusting soap opera widow. She couldn't explain why the two women had brought on such an unwelcomed spate of tears.

Barracuda lawyers didn't cry. If they did, they wouldn't last. And she planned on lasting. Actually, what other choice did she have?

So she took the morning off and applied ice packs to her eyes until they looked near to normal. Only Inez would get close enough to see the residual redness. And Inez would be sympathetic. She was always trying to get Ilona to be more compassionate. That's why Inez was a secretary instead of a lawyer. Compassion didn't belong in the courtroom, Ilona knew. But for the first time in her life, Ilona experienced a moment of envy toward the woman who did the most menial of tasks and protected Ilona from the unwanted, the unexpected, and the downright crazy.

By the time Ilona blew into the office around one, she'd pushed all memory of the funeral out of her mind; she'd buried whatever questions she might have posed in the wee morning hours about the nature of love. And she had built back up a slight disdain for her hardworking secretary.

And Sarah? Coming in here, all comfy in her new life but wanting Nonie to bail her out again. After all these years.

The first thing Ilona did when she reached her office was pull out the Rodrigues file. Then buzzed Inez.

"Get CP&P on the line. I need the documentation on Leila Rodrigues." She disconnected, picked up the first page from the file, and leaned back in her chair.

Sarah might have gotten in the first hit, but Ilona would get the last.

Chapter 19

Sarah stayed at Wyatt's until it was time to pick up Leila from school. There had been no calls, and no one came by for a visit. And Sarah thought they had Victor to thank for that.

She didn't wake Wyatt but left a note saying that she and Leila would be back with dinner around six. She left the note propped up against the prescription bottle and hoped she wasn't overstepping.

And thought what a stupid thing to worry about. They'd never had any boundaries. They'd never even discussed boundaries or anything else. Just took things as they came. And that had been enough.

It was enough now, except that she suddenly worried about him not being in her life. That would be weird. And it would leave a big hole. Almost as big as the hole Leila would leave if she went back to Carmen.

When Sarah told Leila Wyatt had been in an accident,

Leila stopped in the middle of the sidewalk, looked up at her, and asked, "Is he going to die?"

"No!" Sarah said, taken off guard. She picked up the backpack. "He just got some owies."

"Can we take him some cookies?"

"I think he would like that a lot."

They crossed the street and instead of heading back to the cottage, they turned left and walked the half block to Alonso's Pastries. Tony Alonso, a third-generation baker and owner of the pastry shop, came out from the back to greet them.

"Wyatt has a owie," Leila told him.

"I heard, and I bet you've come to get him some of his favorite cookies."

Leila nodded.

Tony smiled at Sarah, his eyes twinkling. "And are these going to be from you and your mama, or just from you?"

Leila's brows snapped together, her bottom lip protruding. And Sarah realized what Tony had said, *Mama*. Not *Mommee*. How was he to know? Surely this balancing act would finish soon.

"They're from both of us, aren't they, sunshine?"

Leila nodded, but she was still frowning.

Oblivious to the undercurrents, Tony reached into the back of the display case and brought out a small shell-shaped cookie dipped in chocolate and sprinkles, lifted his brows at Sarah, who nodded, then presented it to Leila.

The clouds parted in an instant, and Sarah breathed again.

Tony packed a box with an assortment of their favorites, then Leila chose a big cookie decorated to look like a smiley face covered with yellow icing with a white piping face.

He put it into a separate box and tied it up with string and presented it to Leila. "You tell Wyatt that we all hope he's feeling better soon."

Leila, whose mouth was full of cookie, nodded. She sprayed a cookie crumb "thank you" to him and they left.

As soon as they got home, Sarah started on the chicken and dumplings she thought might tempt Wyatt to eat. Leila went to the cupboard and pulled out paper and crayons to make him a get well card.

She drew a big red heart on the folded construction paper, and it almost broke Sarah's. She was beginning to realize what people meant when they said the "tapestry of life."

It was scary and wonderful. And might get very, very sad. She smiled and sent a silent thank-you to Sam, who had somehow gotten her off the treadmill of hurt and into a productive loving life.

She spelled out Wyatt while Leila made each letter, the name wobbling from one side of the page to the other and taking a nosedive at the very end. It was beautiful.

"Wyatt is going to love it," Sarah said.

The kitchen soon was infused with the smell of cooking. Leila went to pick out some books she thought Wyatt might like her to read to him, and Sarah gave up all pretense of working that day.

A little before six they climbed in the car, the chicken and dumplings balanced in a wicker picnic basket on the passenger-side floor, Leila in her car seat in back with her library bag filled with books.

"We have to be very gentle with him, because he has a bunch of owies that hurt him."

Leila nodded solemnly. They let themselves in the back

door. Sarah didn't love taking that liberty, but it seemed appropriate for the occasion.

Wyatt was sitting up, one leg still stretched out along the couch, watching a baseball game with the sound on mute. Leila ran toward him, Wyatt braced himself, but she remembered at the last minute to slow down.

She stopped to stand in front of him, then stuck the card at him.

Sarah grabbed her phone and took a photo. It was just too cute to miss. Even if it didn't go into the file. It would look great in the family album.

Wyatt took the card and peered at it. Sarah could tell he was still loopy and was having to concentrate to show interest.

"Thank you," he said. "This is the best card I ever got."

Leila beamed and looked back at Sarah, who smiled, too. Just one big happy, smiling . . . not family but more than not family.

"What smells so good?"

"Chicken and dumplings."

"You cooked?"

Sarah nodded.

Wyatt half grinned at Leila. His face looked even more swollen than before. "We are two lucky people," he told her.

She nodded. "And cookies."

He lowered his leg to the floor, and Leila, her book bag slung over her shoulder, climbed up to sit beside him. She placed the book bag on her other side and frowned at his banged-up knee. "Does it hurt?"

"Not so bad."

"That's him being macho," Sarah called from the kitchen. "So no roughhousing."

Leila patted his arm. "Do you want me to read you a story?" Wyatt leaned back. "I'd love it."

When Sarah brought out a plate for Wyatt, Leila was chattering on and on, making up the words she couldn't sound out and inventing stories that might or might not fit the pictures. Wyatt looked dazed but patient.

He didn't eat much—painkillers did that to an appetite—so Sarah divided the leftovers into containers for him to eat later.

Wyatt walked them to the door but took Sarah's arm as she started to leave. "Vic said you stuck up for me at the Brew this morning."

"Anyone would have. I've just got a shorter fuse."

"We did the best we could. We were too late."

"You did good. No one could have done it better. Shit happens. Just ask me. I know."

He smiled at her, then pulled her close and managed to kiss her in spite of his bruises.

SARAH SPENT TUESDAY running between the store, the school bus, and Wyatt's.

The local paper did an article on the bravery of the rescue team and warned about the danger of boating while intoxicated. The police and the harbor patrol came around to take a statement. Both complimented Wyatt and his team on the quick thinking that saved several people.

But Sarah could tell that the men he couldn't save preyed on his mind.

That night, as he sat watching her clear the table, she called him on it. He denied it.

"Hmmph," she said. "And you call me complicated. Wy, you can't save everybody." And it struck her; that was just what he did do, always the first person who volunteered to help out: lifeguards, rescue squad . . . her and Leila.

Leila definitely needed saving, but Sarah could take care of herself. She didn't need saving. She just needed . . . What did she need? What did Wyatt?

She'd felt right helping him out, cooking, and making sure he had everything he needed. And it was difficult not to look at the three of them and think happy family. If it ever went that way.

Sarah thought about what Alice said, about men not wanting a package, but Wyatt didn't seem to have any trouble with it. Then again, he was used to taking care of people. And he hadn't mentioned anything long term. Ever. Except the one time, when he was loopy on painkillers. He'd stopped taking them after the first few days and he hadn't mentioned it since, so maybe it wasn't even what he meant. He probably didn't even remember saying it.

ON WEDNESDAY, LEILA came back from her weekly meeting with Carmen, loaded down with cheap toys and a letter.

"Just a review hearing in a couple of weeks," Danny told her. "Do you have time to go over some stuff while I'm here?"

"Sure," Sarah said and invited him into the kitchen.

She pulled out the documentation notebook and opened it on the table while he rummaged through his messenger bag to find his notes.

As interviews went it was fairly painless.

Even when she asked him what he was hearing on the system grapevine, he didn't seem concerned. "Carmen seems to be doing fine. And she's definitely petitioning the court to reinstate her parental rights," he added sympathetically, with a quick look out the door to the living room where Leila was sitting quietly by herself.

At least Sarah might be able to get through with the questions and Danny out the door before Leila's reaction from the disruption set in. Though maybe Danny should see the state these visits left her in. Of course, he might take them to be evidence that she should be returned to Carmen.

"It's just a review. It's not really necessary for you to be there. It's mainly just to document Carmen's progress, and report on Leila's comfort level and how she's doing in foster care. And if she's ready for unsupervised visits."

Unsupervised visits? Sarah felt things begin to slip from her hands. "I'll be there. With my lawyer."

It was time to call Randy Phelps and get him up to speed. For a brief second she thought about calling Ilona Cartwright and begging her to take the case, but she dismissed it. Ilona was not Nonie. Ilona was the enemy.

As soon as he was out the door, Leila came to the door, carrying her book bag. "Going to Wyatt's."

"Not tonight, sunshine. He's feeling better and doesn't need—and can get around by himself. We'll see him later this week."

She pushed Sarah to get her to move. "Going to Wy's."

Sarah wouldn't mind seeing him herself. "Okay, but just for a few minutes."

They got in the car and drove over, but as she turned the corner, Sarah saw a little blue sports car turn into his driveway. Caitlyn, the blond diver, got out and tripped up the walk to the door. Wyatt opened it and she went inside.

Sarah's heart slammed shut.

"Wy's house," Leila said.

"Sorry, sunshine. Wy has company."

The whining started before she even made it to the end of the block, the full-blown tantrum by the time she pulled the car into the back parking area of the cottage. Sarah managed to get a kicking, screaming Leila out of her car seat and held her tightly until they were in the house. Then, capturing her arms and legs, she sat down in the easy chair—Sam's chair—and held her until she stopped fighting, and the sobs became hiccups and she fell asleep.

Sarah put her down for a nap and hoped that she would sleep through the night. It had been a long day with school and the visit with Carmen and the thwarting of her dinner with Wyatt, which after two nights had become a part of their routine, it seemed—until Sarah had seen Caitlyn going into Wyatt's house.

There was no reason he shouldn't see Caitlyn; they hadn't made plans for tonight. Still it was as much a disappointment for Sarah as it was for Leila. She'd also felt like dinner with Wyatt had become a part of their lives. Which is what happened when you let your guard down. Well, she was an adult and she could accept that.

Besides, she had plenty on her plate already without changing anything. She would call Randy Phelps first thing tomorrow. It was time he started working hard for the money. And tomorrow she and Leila would have their first Mommy and Me swim class at the Y.

Something to look forward to.

REESA WENT TO bed wondering how she could work so hard and be so dissatisfied. She woke up tired, as if she'd spent the night wrestling with her dissatisfaction. She stood at the kitchen sink drinking a glass of water, too dragged out to even care about coffee. She'd pick up a cup on the way to work. A bagel, too. A bagel with a gob of vegetable cream cheese.

As if that would change anything.

At least she'd been able to help reunify the Washington family yesterday afternoon. Five children, one of them disabled. Father working two jobs, the mother stretched to the limit, they had been evicted and sent to a shelter, where they refused to stay, and who could blame them. But that refusal had landed four of their children in foster homes and the one boy in a group facility.

Fortunately, Mrs. Washington's mother had a home down in Cape May County and was willing to take them in. Mr. Washington had gone down to apply for jobs, Mrs. Washington intended to work part-time, and her mother would watch the children. The grandmother's church was going to help. They'd done it themselves. The only thing Reesa had done was call the grandmother and ask if she would take one or all of the kids.

She was willing to take the whole family, but they hadn't asked. They'd been too proud to admit they needed help. And almost lost their children because of it.

Reesa should have felt pleased, and she was happy for the family, but it just seemed like too near a miss to her. They succeeded, not because the system worked, but because the family had a relative who was able to help. A community who reached out.

Reesa had never taken her life for granted, not working with the people she worked with. But she had thought it was safe. Now she didn't know. The kids were gone and building their own lives. Michael was a stranger and a stranger she didn't like very much at the moment.

She'd lost her temper last night. When she came in and

found him sitting in that damn recliner, she wanted to slash the upholstery. And she just lost it.

"Do you know how many people would sacrifice everything to have our life. Stop feeling sorry for yourself. You belong to a union, for God's sake. They'll get you a job. But you're not going to sit around the house anymore. I've had it with you."

She left him staring after her, interest barely registering on his face.

That night he slept in the recliner and she didn't miss him one bit.

Reesa grabbed her overstuffed briefcase. Only one of the clasps worked. An executive, even a minor one, in any business would buy a new briefcase. They even sold them at the big discount stores. She could afford one, so why did she continue to carry this one around?

She didn't even look into the den to see if Michael was awake. She was afraid that she might take up where she'd left off the night before. She went out to her car, threw her briefcase and purse onto the passenger seat and climbed in after them.

She was halfway to the office when she pulled to the curb and fished in her bag for her cell.

Mrs. Finch, her supervisor, was in the office and answered her phone. Reesa took it as a good sign.

"It's Reesa Davis."

"Good morning, Reesa. Heard things went well for one of your families yesterday."

"Yes." One out of how many? "I called because I'm really not feeling"—*up to the job? can't possibly face it? have had it up to here?*—"well this morning."

"Oh dear. I'm sorry to hear that. Do you have anything scheduled?"

"No. Nothing specific."

"Well, then take the time off. And take care of yourself. We need you."

"Thank you." Reesa hung up. They needed more than her.

She sat there for a few minutes. She never called in sick. But today was different. Today was a mental health day. Maybe a permanent mental health day.

Reesa drove to her favorite deli, ordered coffee and a bagel with extra vegetable cream cheese, and sat down and ate it. Then she drove to Eighth Street and Hands Around the World.

As soon as Sarah returned from seeing Leila to the bus, she called Randy Phelps to alert him to the hearing date, which he already knew but hadn't planned on consulting her about. When pressed for information on why this was even happening, he told her that Carmen had convinced the court that she had been underrepresented by her appointed attorney, that he had not explained things thoroughly about termination of parental rights.

"Which is a crock," Randy said. "Sarah, I don't think we need to worry overmuch. These things rarely go in favor of the bio parents."

"Unless there was some bit of the court order that wasn't correct," she countered.

She could hear him sigh over the phone. And she wasn't even a pro bono case. She expected more from him for her money, but she didn't say so. Now was not the time to alienate her attorney.

"There is nothing on our side that isn't solidly in place."

"So what do you think will happen?"

"I expect it to be thrown out." He paused. "Unless Ms. Delgado has made particularly excellent progress with her rehab and the judge acknowledges the possible mistake in the earlier judgment."

"In other words, the adoption is not a sure thing."

"Not a sure thing, but both factors would have to be compelling for the court to reverse its decision."

"Will you be allowed to present evidence at the hearing?"

"Briefly, perhaps, but it isn't a judgment hearing, just whether to continue on with the appeal and possible reunification. The judge won't make any kind of pronouncement until Carmen's been through unsupervised extended visits and comes out clean."

"That could take months."

"Unfortunately it could. But it also means it allows more time for Carmen to fall off the wagon."

"But—" Sarah stopped herself. She didn't want Carmen to fall back into drugs and poverty and abusive relationships. She just wanted to adopt Leila.

"Let's just wait and see how things shake out. Depending on the judge we pull, the whole thing might get thrown out."

"So should I bring documentation?"

"Not really necessary. The DAG will be there, Carmen's new lawyer, who is a bit of a blowhard, Carmen's caseworker, Leila's CASA advocate—"

"The same one as before?"

"Not sure. I imagine if she's still available. Regardless, since this is an appeal, they'll probably appoint a counsel ad litem to represent her. And if they do, most likely there will be an adjournment in order for the attorney to be brought up to speed on the case."

Which could mean months, maybe a year, before Leila's

future would be decided. "What about Carmen's other children?"

"What about them?"

"Is she trying to get them back?"

"I don't know what she's planning, but those cases are older and pretty decisive. I'm only aware of one baby since Leila, and he was removed at birth. He is in a full-care facility." He sighed. "These crack babies. I don't think she has the desire, never mind the means, to care for him."

"So she's going after Leila because she's the next youngest."

"She's not a predator, Sarah. She's just a mother who wants her child."

"There's a big difference between what you want and being able to love and care for a child twenty-four seven until adulthood."

"True. Whether she's capable of doing that is another question altogether. That's what this round of hearings will decide. If they even decide to go forward with it. Which I doubt. But don't worry. Once this is done, they'll speed you through the rest of the process. You'll get your adoption papers and start on your new life."

New life. It wouldn't be new. Leila had been with her for nearly three years not counting two brief reunifications with Carmen. She was woven into Sarah's life. Tear her away and you tore away part of Sarah. She wasn't sure Leila would survive another round with Carmen. Sarah wasn't sure she could.

That afternoon as Sarah and Leila walked past the dive store on their way home from the bus, Wyatt stepped out from the door.

Leila ran over. "Guess where we're going today?"

"Are you sure you should be working?" Sarah asked, coming up behind Leila.

"Swimming lessons," Leila told him without waiting for him to guess.

"You're going to learn to swim?"

"Me and Mommee."

Wyatt cut a look at Sarah. Smiled.

"I know, but the instructor said I don't have to go in very deep."

"First step, up to your ankles; next step, deep sea diving."

Sarah shivered; she couldn't help it. She didn't know how in the world she could be such good friends with someone whose interests were so different.

"I missed you two last night," Wyatt said.

"Well . . ." Sarah began.

"I told her. And we came but then she said you had company and we couldn't go in."

Wyatt frowned, then he made a face. "Caitlyn."

Sarah shrugged. She could feel her face growing warm; she felt like such a fool.

"Well, you could still have come in," he told Leila, then he glanced at Sarah.

"Didn't want to interrupt."

Wyatt chuckled. "You are too much."

"And we're going to be late if we don't get a move on."

"And we wouldn't want you to be late for swimming, would we?"

Sarah made a face.

"See you tonight?"

She started to say they might be late.

"We can order takeout. I want to hear all about your first day in the pool."

"Yes." Leila lifted her chin, looking up to Wyatt, bending back so far, she almost fell backward.

"Goofball," he said.

They left him on the sidewalk, Sarah acutely aware that he was watching her. But when they turned to cross the street, he'd gone back inside. Good, the way he was acting was making her nervous.

After a quick snack, they donned their swimsuits and drove to the Y for a Mommy and Me swim class. Most of the other children were younger; none of them knew how to swim—including Sarah.

She just took a breath, crossed her fingers that neither Leila—nor she—would freak out when they touched the water, and helped Leila down the steps to the shallow end. The water was warm, and—since the instructor had promised Sarah she wouldn't have to go past the point where she could touch—inviting. Being able to see the bottom and being able to stand on her own two feet made a big difference and she began to enjoy being in the pool.

Leila took to it immediately, kicking her feet and laughing, though she held tightly to Sarah even after the instructor strapped a bubble around her back. As soon as she realized she could float, she eased her grip on Sarah's neck and was content to let Sarah hold her by both hands while the "wheels on the bus went round and round."

Sarah decided that before the next summer she and Leila would both learn to swim. And tried not to think that they might not be together next summer.

Chapter 20

After class and innumerable rounds of "The Wheels on the Bus" and "Five Little Ducks"—which Sarah thought was an odd choice until all the little ducks came back—they showered and changed in the "family" dressing room and called Wyatt from the parking lot.

"So you didn't drown," he said, when Sarah told him they were finished.

"Very funny, and I didn't go screaming down the corridor either." How could she be friends—more than friends—with a professional diver, lifeguard, and water rescuer and be afraid of the water? "Do you still want dinner?"

"Yep. If it's not too much trouble."

"Of course it isn't."

Wyatt said he'd call their favorite barbecue place and Sarah would pick the food up on her way home.

By the time she reached Wyatt's, Leila was snoring in her car seat.

Sarah drove to the back of the driveway and carried Leila up the steps to the porch.

Wyatt insisted on taking her at the door, even though he was still recuperating. But he was looking frustrated and impatient, and Sarah decided it was best not to argue. He only winced a little when Leila wrapped her arms and legs around him.

Sarah went back out for the food; when she came in Wyatt was waiting in the kitchen empty handed. "I put her on the couch so she wouldn't wake up in a strange bedroom."

She smiled. Considerate even when injured. What a guy.

"You know she's accepting me pretty well this time around."

"I know," Sarah said, pulling aluminum tins out of the shopping bags and placing them on the island. "I just hope that won't change with all these Carmen visits. She's already had a couple of full-blown tantrums."

He came around the side of the island and pulled her into a hug. "Promise me you won't shut me out if things get intense."

"Wyatt, I don't want to shut you out ever, but I can't promise. Right now Leila has to know she's safe. I can't put her through that again."

"She has to learn she can trust some people."

"I know." Sarah started to pull away, but he held on to her. "And so do you."

She tipped her head back to look at him. "I trust people."

"Only when it's safe to trust them."

"The food's getting cold."

He let her go and reached to get down plates and bowls from the cabinets.

Sarah piled ribs on a plate. "Wyatt, are you drawn to me because you think I need saving?"

"What? Well, you do need saving, but you could save yourself." He handed her a plate but held on to it. He smiled slowly. "I'm drawn to you, because you're hot." The smile turned into his current lopsided grin.

He looked goofy and tousled and handsome and glorious. And he thought she was hot. How cool was that?

KNOWING THE UPCOMING hearing would take up her time and being determined to spend at least a few hours on the beach on the weekend, Sarah spent the next two days catching up on her work.

The mantel clock was returned to its owners who were ecstatic at having it working again. She prepared several antique watches for sale and took in a grandfather's clock whose mechanisms had been scavenged for parts by person or persons unknown.

Mrs. Bridges's violin clock still thwarted her at every stage, but she had several sections in working order. She was too close to give up now. It would work again if she had to stay up every night to make it happen.

Saturday turned out to be a busy day. While Leila was at her visit with Carmen, Sarah sold two vintage shelf clocks, an art deco alarm clock, several watches, and an Early American tall case clock made from mahogany and walnut burl.

"He must have had his eye on that piece for a while," Alice said as soon as the customer left. "That whole transaction took less than half an hour."

Sarah raised her eyebrows and smiled.

"Are you sure it was priced high enough?"

Sarah's smile slipped a little. "Yes. Enough to pay this year's taxes, maybe a bit of next year's, too."

That night Wyatt came to the cottage for dinner. Leila immediately dragged him back to her bedroom to take pictures of her and her outline drawing to see if she'd grown. When Sarah came in to call them to dinner, they were sitting on the floor, the Candy Land board laid flat between them.

Leila jumped up to go wash her hands.

Wyatt needed a bit of help getting off the floor.

"I owe you," she said as he levered to his feet.

"And you're going to pay me, later tonight."

Leila went to bed soon after dinner. Wyatt stayed until dawn.

WYATT DIDN'T COME back for breakfast since he was giving a diving workshop at a dive place in another town. Sarah didn't think he should be slinging heavy equipment around. He merely said he'd be careful, kidded her about worrying about him. And didn't change his plans.

She suggested he take Victor to do the heavy lifting, but he needed Victor at the store. She gave up.

He'd returned to working at the store but his rescue, lifeguard, and dive instructor work was still on hold. And would be for a while. Sarah could feel him getting more restless as the days went on and he was still hobbling around. He didn't relish nonactivity and she guessed he also wanted to get back on the job to quell any naysaying about the professionalism of the rescue team.

He didn't have to worry. The guy who was talking smack in the Brew that morning called him to apologize. He'd just been razzing, but it was misconstrued. Wyatt told her that the guy had said she was fierce.

"That's right and don't you forget it," she told him. It had been different with Sarah being able to help him out when it was usually the other way around. And Sarah felt herself growing closer to him . . . because of it? In a way it was comforting to see the man out of his element. It made him more human. Not more human, he was always very human, but not so overwhelming. More equal. Which was a joke. She couldn't even swim. Much less save people, or care about her friends enough to run to the rescue anytime one of them needed her.

She was getting better at it though. She'd been so caught up in Leila that she'd lost perspective on the rest of life.

The therapists were always saying you should integrate the pieces of your life into a whole. Sarah preferred the tapestry analogy, herself.

It was a little after three when Sarah and Leila put on their swimsuits, then slathered on sunscreen. They packed up some snacks and bottles of water, stuffed two big beach towels in a beach tote, and walked down to the beach.

"Bessie!" Leila squealed when she saw the top of Karen's polka-dotted umbrella.

Sarah had to grab her hand to keep her from running across the street. Once they had watched both ways for cars and crossed the street to the boardwalk, Sarah let Leila go. She had to slow down to get down the steps, but she managed them by herself, an easy feat for most four-year-olds, and Sarah comforted herself with the knowledge that Leila was beginning to catch up to her peers.

The summer program had been a great idea.

They stopped to take off their flip-flops, then Leila ran across the sand to where Bessie and Tammy were digging.

"We're making pies," Tammy informed her and handed her

a green plastic mold. Sarah unfolded one of the beach chaises and set it up next to Karen under the umbrella.

Karen turned her magazine over on her stomach and pulled her sunglasses down. "I can't believe you're actually wearing a swimsuit to the beach. Is that because Wyatt's meeting you here?"

"No-o-o. Actually he's working."

"Is he crazy?"

"He's giving a workshop on diving. He's going stir-crazy."

"I can believe it." Karen leaned over the arm of her chaise and rummaged in her bag. She pulled out a spray bottle and tossed it to Sarah. "Here, put this on."

"Thanks, but I already sprayed us both before we came, and it's after three so we should be okay.

"Just put it on your face and sit down. Now that you're back to the land of the living, you don't want your skin to look like an old woman."

Sarah made a face at her, but she put on the additional sunscreen.

"I'm even going to learn to swim."

Karen, who had just opened her magazine again, put it down. "Say what?"

Sarah laughed. "You heard me. We're doing a Mommy and Me class at the Y, and in the fall I've decided to sign us both up for real swim lessons. It's about time, don't you think?"

"Everyone should know how to swim."

"So you don't sink," Sarah added. Her eyes caught Karen's for a few seconds. "Thanks for putting up with me, no, for supporting me, when I get crazy."

"We all get crazy sometimes. And you've bitten off a lot for a single woman."

"Is that a hint?"

"Not really. Though it is all over town how you came to Wyatt's defense the other morning at the Brew."

Sarah shook her head. "I can't believe I did that. But, hell, someone needed to shut the guy up."

"They're not bad guys; they just get excited, then go all macho and start bragging. Like kids, only bigger."

Sarah laughed.

"Anything new on the Leila front?"

"Carmen's going through with the appeal. Randy seems to think it's nothing to worry about. I hope he's right."

"He's done a lot of these cases. I'd listen to him."

"I guess. I just wish it was over and I had those adoption papers locked away in the safe."

"Soon," Karen said.

"From your mouth . . . I thought maybe Reesa would be here today. She hit the beach two weekends in a row. That's got to be some kind of record."

"She's coming later. I thinks she's going through some stuff, too."

"About being burned out?"

Karen pulled her chair back up and leaned forward. "I think she and Michael are having problems."

"Because he's out of work?"

"Because he's not trying to find new work. It sounds to me like he's suffering from depression. But she says he won't go to see anyone, just sits watching the baseball channel all day."

"That would be depressing," Sarah said. "So is she planning anything, um, drastic?"

"Well, I don't think she'd mind if I told you. The other night after you left, she said she was thinking about leaving him. She said she couldn't take both him and her job, and one of them had to go."

"Ugh. That sounds drastic."

"She did say she wouldn't quit until she sees Leila settled."

"Well," Sarah said. "Selfishly, that's good for me. And maybe time will help her figure out what to do." She lay back in the chair, closed her eyes.

It seemed she wasn't the only one going through changes. She opened one eye. "Are things okay with you and Stu? I mean, if it's any of my business."

"Of course it's your business and, yes, I'm still putting up with the dude. He and Rory are having a boys' afternoon out on the driving range."

"They play golf?"

Karen laughed. "They swing and try to hit the ball. But they have fun. Whatever works." She looked over at Sarah. "How about you and Wyatt?"

Sarah shrugged. "It's okay, I guess."

"You guess? You don't know?"

"I don't know. Leila and he are really getting along these days, but I don't know if it will last if she keeps seeing Carmen. She's already started with the tantrums. Yesterday when she came back it was the silent treatment."

"Normal."

"I know. I just hate that she has to go through it again."

"Well, if she starts being afraid of Wyatt, we'll know something is going on in the other house that shouldn't."

"Yeah, which I pray won't happen. But . . ."

"But . . . ?"

"I don't want it to be so good that she wants to go back."

"It sucks to be so far along in the process and have this happen."

"But what if Carmen has gotten it together this time long enough to get her back? I don't want to be unsympathetic, but we've been here before."

"Something the judge will take into consideration. I'm actually surprised her appeal got this far."

"Randy said she's saying that her attorney didn't explain that termination meant forever."

"Bosh. If he didn't, the judge did."

"So why are we here again?"

"Damned if I know. I hear the ice cream truck; can children demanding money be far behind?"

Sure enough, three little girls ran squealing toward the umbrella. "Ice cream, ice cream, ice cream."

Karen and Sarah reached for their wallets simultaneously.

"The consolation is that ice cream at the beach mostly melts before they can eat it, saving their teeth and not spoiling their dinner."

They trudged up the sand to the street and got in line.

"Just in time," Karen said.

Sarah turned to see Reesa hurrying across the street toward them.

"Man, that girl could use a day at the spa and then a trip to the mall."

She could, thought Sarah. Reesa was wearing a pair of ancient clam diggers, a Mexican peasant blouse that looked like tomato sauce had been spilled all over it, and she was lugging a heavy-looking canvas bag more appropriate for books than beachwear.

"What happened to you?" Karen asked.

"Lunch at Hands Around the World."

"Is that the place the woman in the store was talking about?"

Reesa nodded.

They all stopped to order their ice creams.

"My treat," Sarah told Reesa.

"Thanks, finding my wallet in this bag has become like the search for the holy grail. I need a job where I can carry a smaller purse."

"Nah," Karen said. She unwrapped the girls' ice cream then started on her own. "Jobs with little purses require very high heels. Not worth it."

"I didn't think about that," Reesa said and bit into her Creamsicle.

They stood on the sidewalk eating ice cream and cleaning up kids, then went back to the beach, where Karen passed out water bottles and the girls sat down on their beach towels in the shade of the boardwalk. Karen and Sarah moved over to make room for Reesa under the umbrella.

"So tell us about lunch at Hands Around the World."

"It's an amazing place," Reesa said. "A cooperative situation. Everybody has to participate in some way. And only mothers and their children. No men. Which quite frankly these days is sounding better and better.

"They have a few paid staff members, but mostly the women are mentored by other women. No drugs, no alcohol, or you're out, no appeal. Tanisha and her husband are pivotal in the operations, but I have to say everyone steps up to the plate.

"Ugh. I'm so inundated with baseball talk I'm using game slang."

Reesa had been animated while talking about the center but at the mention of baseball, she suddenly looked like the tired, overworked woman she was.

Sarah and Karen looked sympathetic, but even Karen didn't have anything to say to that.

"They're looking for a development director."

"Paid?" Karen asked.

Reesa shrugged. "It pays, just not a lot. About half my current salary."

"Whoa. Are you thinking about taking it on as a second job?"

"I'm thinking of taking it on, period."

"You'd leave social work?" Sarah asked, nonplussed.

"For a while anyway. Definitely leave child welfare." She held up her hand. "And don't say I can't because I'm good at it or I do important work. I work hard and sometimes things work out, but just as often they go back to what they were before." She trailed off, then shook herself and said more brightly. "But I'm not going anywhere until we see Leila's adoption through."

Sarah was relieved. It wasn't the first time Reesa had talked about quitting, but Sarah needed her now more than ever. They were too close to lose now.

Chapter 21

The first sign that things might not be going well during the visitations was the skinned knee. Not unusual in children, but Sarah was watching out for any telltale signs that might go unnoticed by a harried caseworker.

"What happened?" she asked Danny when he brought Leila home from the next visit.

"She fell down while we were in the park."

"Which park?"

"The one near Carmen's apartment."

Sarah bent down to take a closer look. Big scrape covered by one tiny Band-Aid. It hadn't even been cleaned out. Carmen's—or Danny's—parenting skills left a bit to be desired.

"Where did she fall?"

"In the park."

"I mean, exactly. Was she running? Fell off the swing, from the monkey bars?"

Danny looked away, just for a second, but the movement

told Sarah everything. She hadn't been shuttled through the system for ten years without knowing every piece of body language. "You didn't see, did you?"

Danny shook his head.

"Were you even there?" She knew that caseworkers sometimes used supervised visits to make phone calls or catch up on paperwork.

"I just turned away for a few minutes to set up my next appointment. And when I got back, she was crying. But Carmen was very attentive, and we took her back to the apartment and Carmen put a Band-Aid on it.

"I assure you, it was just an accident, the kind kids have all the time." He licked his lips. "Which was a good thing in a way."

Sarah waited for him to elucidate. She didn't see how getting hurt was a good thing.

"They've decided to accelerate visits into unsuped—unsupervised—starting next week."

"It's too early."

"Sarah. Things have been going really well."

"And you have too many other cases to be stuck supervising all of them."

"Well, yes. It never stops." He licked his lips again. "Something's gotta give. And since these visits have been going so well, they decided to give it a try."

"But the review hearing isn't until next week. Shouldn't they wait until then?"

"I don't make the decisions," Danny said. "They asked me if things had been going well, and if I thought Carmen could handle a few hours alone with Leila. I didn't see anything so far in our visits to prevent it from happening. She's been fine. Really."

"That's what they said the last two times."

Danny shrugged. "There's really nothing I can do. I shouldn't even be going on these visits."

Sarah bit her tongue. She longed to tell him just what she thought of him and the system, but that would be like shooting the messenger. Plus you never wanted to piss off your caseworker. They held your future in their hands.

As soon as he left she picked Leila up. She hadn't cried, or stormed off to her room, hadn't complained about falling down. Sarah almost would prefer a tantrum. At least it meant Leila was still reacting to what was happening to her. Please God, don't let this be the beginning of total withdrawal.

"Let's fix up your owie."

Then the bottom lip protruded, and Leila started to cry. But without a sound and Sarah held her close and promised herself she wouldn't let anything happen to this precious little girl.

The abrasion wasn't bad in the scheme of skinned knees, but Sarah cleaned it up and blew on it while she applied a bacterial cream to it. Then she covered it with a large Band-Aid. "Now you and Wyatt both have owies."

Leila nodded.

Sarah breathed easier. But after dinner when Leila was in the bath, Sarah noticed the bruising on her upper arm. And she knew they came from fingers. She'd seen and felt them often enough in the past—in Leila's past and in her own past.

She reached for her phone, her hands shaking a bit. "Let's take a selfie and we can send it to show Wyatt. Want to?"

Leila nodded.

So Sarah took a pic of the knee, and while Leila was bent over looking at her Band-Aid, she took another of her arm.

"What shall we say to Wyatt?"

"Say I have an owie, too."

Sarah keyed in the message and attached the photo. Then she turned the phone to Leila so she could press send.

"On its way," Sarah said brightly.

Later she would put both photos in her documentation file. A skinned knee was one thing, maybe the fingers were an accident. Perhaps Carmen tried to stop her from falling and grabbed her too tightly, though somehow Sarah doubted it. The court might be willing to give Carmen one more chance, but Sarah wasn't so forgiving.

She knew Carmen's MO. She wouldn't stay sober or single. She'd have another kid, have it taken away. You'd think after seven children in foster care, someone would figure that out. And yet Carmen got another chance.

Why didn't all those hurt and abused kids get a second and third chance? Sarah had been in more foster homes than she could remember. Some had been okay. Nice even, then one day they'd be at the door to take her away. Send her to another home. Sometimes Sarah knew it was because she acted out, which she did whenever a place was bad, or the father or brother or whoever started hitting on her. But sometimes she never knew why they took her away.

She didn't want that life for Leila. She'd fought to have them guarantee that Leila would be returned to her each time they took her away.

Leila had been on the adoption track almost since the beginning, and still she was not adopted. It was crazy. And it was cruel.

So life was cruel. *Boo-hoo.*

Dear Nonie,

I'd like to run away where nobody would ever find me. But we know what happens to those kids. You can't run away here, somebody just finds you, or hurts you, or kills you.

I hate it here. Why didn't you tell me it wouldn't get better? How come other kids have families that love them and buy them clothes that don't come from a thrift store or from one of the other foster kids, even when they're too old and don't fit right? Why do other kids have their own beds and clean sheets, and good food?

Why can't I have a dad who drops me off at school in his car before he goes to work? It isn't fair. I know, Life isn't fair. Boo-hoo. But it should be.

Does your new dad drive you to school? Do you have your own room? That would be so cool. My new roommate at group farts in her sleep. She's gross.

Everything here is gross. I'd like to run away.

Sarah

"YOU KNOW, MICHAEL," Reesa said as she put a TV dinner down in front of him.

He looked at the food divided into little sections of aluminum. "What's this?"

"Your dinner. You know"—she started again, now that she had deposited the food on the TV tray and he couldn't see her shaking hands—"I've decided you have the right idea. Why work? I don't know why it took me so long to figure it out. I hate my job. It's sucking the life out of me. So as soon as my current case is finished, I'm quitting."

Michael had just speared a piece of meatloaf, but he put it back down. "What the hell are you talking about?"

"Well, I think I might like to sit around all day watching television. Hell, right now I couldn't even tell you the time or day of any program."

"You can't quit."

"Why not?"

"This is about my accident, isn't it?"

Reesa sighed. "No, Michael. It's not about your accident. It's about you sitting on your butt and not looking for another job."

"I'm going to start looking. I meant to go down to the union today."

"Just like you meant to go last week?" Reesa walked to the door, wanting to get out of the room before she said things she might regret.

He threw his fork back on the aluminum plate and pushed the TV tray away. "What the hell do you want me to do?"

"Lose the attitude and the temper to begin with. I've told you what I want you to do for weeks now. You'll feel better if you have something to look forward to every day instead of sitting there like a lump. Michael, there are plenty of things you like to do. You could help Tony at the garage for starters until something bigger comes along."

"Work for my son? When hell freezes over."

"Michael, I can't keep this up. I need a break before I completely lose it."

"Well, just wait until I find work. We have to have one salary coming in."

Reesa shrugged. "I've waited. I've tried to be understanding. I've tried to encourage you. But I can't do it all anymore."

"We'll lose the house."

Reesa looked around. For a second she felt a cold chasm of fear, but it passed. It had been a good house, it had served them well, but now it was more like a ball and chain. "It's up to you."

"That's it. You can quit your bitching. I'm outta here."

"Good. Is the union still open now?"

"I'm going to stay at my brother's until you come to your senses." He stormed down the hallway, barely limping she noticed.

She should feel sorrow, or hurt. She should try to talk him out of going, say that they could work it out. But she just stood by the door listening to him crashing around the bedroom, packing a bag. Just watched as he breezed past her and out the front door without a good-bye.

She should have felt bad or sad, but all she felt was relief.

SARAH KNEW SHE was overpreparing for the court session. It wasn't a trial, merely a review of Carmen's progress.

There would be reports from her caseworker, the therapists, and the drug program rep, and child services would have a lawyer present. Carmen would be there with her lawyer and caseworker. Leila's CASA guardian would probably show, though she had moved onto other cases since Leila was in the process of being adopted.

Lots of people to say how great Carmen was acting. They probably wouldn't ask Sarah to comment. Danny would be there to report on the supervised visits. As Leila's original caseworker, Reesa might be able to respond. She'd promised Sarah she would be there just to support Sarah.

Sarah hadn't pushed her to come. She knew that Reesa was having trouble at home and was preparing for another case, one that had really upset her.

Reesa kept up a good front while she was busy or working. It was when she was relaxing at the beach that Sarah saw the lines of worry, the sag of her shoulders, the unhappiness that lay just beneath the surface of her personality.

Karen was worried about her and so was Sarah. And as soon as this situation with Leila was finished, she was going to really be a good and supportive friend to Reesa. She was going to make sure Wyatt stayed an important part of their lives. And be a real friend to all her friends.

A FEW DAYS before the review hearing, Sarah met with Randy Phelps to talk strategy. He occupied a messy desk in a storefront law office in the next town over, which he shared with several other affordable lawyers.

Randy was young and energetic, that or he ran on caffeine to judge by the paper cups on his desk. He offered Sarah a seat, then sat down behind a pile of papers that partially obscured her view.

Instead of moving the papers, he rolled his chair around to face her.

"Not to worry," he told her.

Too late. She was already worried. "This was supposed to be a done deal," she said, trying to keep her voice from screeching out of control. "What happened? Why the delay?"

"These things happen on occasion."

She just stared at him. He didn't seem at all worried. That made her even more worried. And where was Leila's file? Hidden in that tower of paper? Had he even looked at it lately?

"You said it was finished, and we were just waiting for it to process."

Randy shrugged. "And normally it would have been. But I'm on it. I'll handle it."

She wanted to ask how? When? Maybe if Randy had been more aggressive, this would never have happened and the adoption would be completed by now.

He stood up and she realized a couple had entered and were hovering near by.

Okay, the guy was overworked. But that didn't help her or Leila. He would have to put out for them.

Sarah stood and shook hands. "I'm counting on you," she said, and she hoped he somehow would come through.

THE MORNING OF the hearing, Sarah dropped Leila off at Karen's. Camp had finished for the summer so the girls were home. Leila's school would go through August, but she could miss a day here and there without falling behind. Plus Sarah thought she needed a treat, and she loved playing at Bessie and Tammy's house.

Sarah met Randy and Reesa on the courthouse steps. They went through security and down the hall to one of the smaller family division courtrooms.

She felt the walls closing in on her. Like a bad dream that just kept repeating itself. A loop they could never escape. Patience. *Fix the now.* She was trying, but sometimes it seemed outside her grasp.

They sat in the second row behind Danny, who was sitting with the other professionals who would be giving reports; therapists and drug counselors who would all report on Carmen's adherence to appointments and the results of her drug tests for the last six weeks.

But six weeks wasn't a lifetime, as Sarah well knew. She'd seen it over and over again. First with her own mother, then with other foster kids and already twice now with Carmen. Sarah refused to take the chance of putting Leila in that environment again.

The Child Protection lawyer was sitting at a separate table. And on the other side, Carmen, wearing a skirt and suit jacket, sat straight-backed next to her lawyer. Behind them were two women, one Sarah recognized as Leila's former CASA worker, a volunteer whose sole job was to look out for the interests of the child. She saw Sarah and waved, then shrugged her shoulders as if to say, *Why are we here?*

Randy had explained that since this was an unusual case, brought by Carmen because of "deliberate misleading of understanding" by Carmen's former lawyer, all meetings would be presided over by a family court judge.

Sarah tried to breathe evenly and stay calm, when her whole being was screaming to do something drastic. The room wasn't helping, painted an institutional beige color, with dark furniture. She didn't know how Judge Whitaker could return day after day without growing numb.

The chairs were hard, and the air was overly chilled in deference to the judge, she guessed as he walked through the door and walked up to the bench. They all stood. They all sat.

Carmen stood, but she kept her head lowered as if she were afraid to make eye contact.

The judge opened a folder. "I see we have a full house today." Everyone looked around and smiled, acknowledging his attempt to lighten the mood. "Mr. Costas."

The DAG nodded.

"Mr. Columbine?" The judge looked toward Carmen and her lawyer.

"Here." The lawyer half stood.

"And your client is here?"

Mr. Columbine nudged Carmen, who stood up. "Here, Your Honor."

"And does the child Leila Rodrigues have representation here today?"

The CASA looked around the courtroom and slowly stood.

"Here, Your Honor, I'm Katherine Joyce, I was Leila's CASA on the original case. I was told to come."

"Well, thank you for coming, Miss Joyce."

The judge looked up.

"Mrs. Davis?"

"Good morning, Judge Whitaker."

"I thought that Mr."—he consulted his folder—"Noyes was the child's caseworker."

"The adoption caseworker, Your Honor. I was caseworker on the original permanency track. I'm just here in support of the foster mother, Sarah Hargreave. And to help the court if needed."

"I see. Well, anyone else I've left out?"

Another half smile from the attendees who were all anxious to get to their next appointments.

The back door opened. The judge looked up, frowned, then his eyebrows rose.

"Sorry, Your Honor. My case upstairs ran long. I'm here as attorney ad litem for the child Leila Rodrigues."

"I completely understand. It's an honor to have you in court, Ms. Cartwright."

Chapter 22

Sarah stared as Ilona Cartwright walked down the aisle. She wore a sleek pencil skirt and jacket, silk blouse, and expensive high heels. It made everyone else in the room look shabby.

Then it hit her full force. Ilona Cartwright was Leila's attorney. Instinct took over. "No." Sarah surged from her chair. Someone grabbed her arm and yanked her back down.

"Stay calm," Reesa hissed in her ear.

Calm? The person with the means to sabotage her case had just walked in the door and was representing her daughter.

"What's she doing here?" Sarah whispered. "Did you ask her to come?"

Reesa shook her head. "No, but maybe she's had a change of heart."

"Not Nonie—Ms. Cartwright. She knows how to be vindictive. She's come to pay me back for something I did or didn't do in the past. I can't believe it. She'll undermine this whole case, put Leila in jeopardy just to get back at me."

Reesa took her hand, though whether to comfort her or keep her from running amok in the courtroom, Sarah couldn't tell.

"We don't know that."

Well, Sarah did. If Nonie had the reputation of being a barracuda in the courtroom, they should see her on the street. She shook her head to clear it. That was then; surely they both had left that all behind them.

Except here was Nonie walking down the aisle like she owned the place and from the look on the judge's face, Sarah was pretty sure she did.

Sarah wasn't the only one who was staring. Evidently it was unusual for Nonie to . . . what? . . . stoop so low? Even the judge had said it was an honor to have her in his courtroom. What was with that?

Sarah smelled imminent disaster. She leaned over to Randy. "Did you know about this?" she whispered.

"No. As far as I knew it was Elaine Gardo from the last pretermination hearing."

"Can we object?"

"Why would I?"

Because she hates me, Sarah thought, but a look from Reesa stopped her from saying it.

"Ms. Cartwright is well respected for her pro bono work. Leila will be well represented by her."

Ilona handed the judge a paper and sat down at the table with Carmen and her lawyer. She hadn't even looked at Sarah as she walked down the aisle, and she didn't look at Carmen either, just a quick nod to the DAG and then to Carmen's lawyer, before sitting down.

"As you all know," the judge began. "This is a review to consider extending supervised visits of Leila Delgado Rodrigues with her birth mother, Carmen Delgado, pending the outcome of Ms. Delgado's appeal. It's a given that we are all concerned about the welfare of the child, but may I remind you we're not here today to decide what long-term plan is best for her." He gave the assembled group a sweeping look. "That was already decided by another court, which ruled in favor of permanency. However, while we are waiting for the outcome of the appeal, we are taking the recommendations of the caseworkers about the visitations under consideration."

He looked over to the DAG. "Mr. Costas, when is the scheduled hearing for that appeal?"

Costas rifled through some papers. "Next month, the fourteenth."

"We'll hear the reports from the CP&P now."

The drug counselor began. Carmen had made most of her drug testing appointments, only missing those when she couldn't get off work.

Sarah looked over at Randy. He wasn't taking notes. She shot an urgent look to Reesa, who nodded slightly and patted her hand.

One report followed another. To listen to them, you'd think Carmen was an exemplary success story. But Sarah had been there for her other two exemplary failures.

The reports went by quickly. Everyone was agreed that short unsupervised visits would not place the child in any danger. Sarah understood. CP&P needed success stories. There was so much that was out of their control. They could offer all the services on earth, but if they couldn't get people to take advantage of them, it did nothing but keep them on the streets.

The judge consulted his notes. "Mr. Noyes."

"Yes, Your Honor."

"You are the child's adoption caseworker?"

"Yes, sir."

"And what is your evaluation?"

Danny glanced at Sarah. "The child has been in foster care for nearly three years with the same foster mother. She was originally placed on a concurrent course, until Ms. Delgado voluntarily terminated her parental rights at which point she was transferred to adoption. The child, Leila, has a very close relationship with the foster mother."

"And you have accompanied the child on all supervised visits."

"Yes, sir."

"And were the conditions clean and safe?"

"Well, two were in the CP&P building. But the last two were at Ms. Delgado's apartment, which was clean and safe as far as I could tell. The mother was sober and patient with the child." Danny hesitated. "I've seen no incidences that would lead me to believe the child would be in danger if left alone with her mother, though I would not recommend overnight visits at this time. The child is used to living with her foster mother, she's comfortable there, and she's had every reason to believe she would be adopted soon. She becomes very upset because of the disruption. And since the appellate court date is just a few weeks away, I think it's in the best interest of the child not to disrupt her life more than necessary until the outcome of the appeal is known."

"Our concern today is cleanliness and safety. From your observation, do the living space and the mother fit these criteria?"

"From my two visits, yes."

"Thank you, Mr. Noyes."

"Mr. Columbine?"

"My client was hoping for extended weekend visits, since she works during the week and the child is in school. We feel two hours a week inadequate for necessary bonding."

The judge held Columbine's look. "Your client terminated her rights, which means at this point she has no right to this child at all until her appeal is heard."

"She wasn't advised of the permanent status of termination."

"That is not what we are discussing here, as you well know."

A young woman sitting behind Carmen stood. "I'm Josie Green, and I'm Ms. Delgado's caseworker. And I can vouch that these criteria have been met by Ms. Delgado."

She sat down again.

"Ms. Cartwright. What do you recommend?"

"She's never even met Leila," Sarah said.

"Shh," Reesa said.

"I came to this case recently."

Sarah held her breath. Could it be possible Nonie was going to help them after all?

"But I've talked with the mother's caseworker, and it is my opinion that no harm will be done by granting unsupervised visitation while waiting for the outcome of the appeal."

Judge Whitaker looked over the courtroom, then closed his file. "After hearing the reports of the Child Protection and Permanency staff, the court will allow short unsupervised visits in the home of Ms. Carmen Delgado until the appellate court decision. Thank you all for your time."

Everyone began gathering up their papers and belongings, except Sarah. She just sat, not quite believing that they were going to put Leila and herself through all this again. No one had mentioned Carmen's past failures. How she slapped and hit Leila or left her with men she had living with her. No one even mentioned that.

She was vaguely aware of Ilona Cartwright walking past her, going toward the door. Brisk, in control. She'd won something she knew nothing about.

Sarah grabbed her bag and followed her out.

"Sarah," Reesa called. "Stop. Wait for me."

But Sarah had no intention of waiting. This time security would have to drag her out kicking and screaming, because she was going to have her say.

She reached Ilona as she went through the front doors. Sarah pushed through after her, ran down the steps, and stepped in front of her as she reached the walk.

"Why did you do it?"

"Please, Ms. Hargreave. Do you really want me to have to call security? Again? Perhaps you should do something about your anger issues. I can't imagine a judge would let someone who can't control their temper actually adopt a child."

Sarah's fists clenched. And she was catapulted back to another time. Nonie and her walking back to the home late at night. Sarah was scared, maybe Nonie was too, but that changed when this kid from the streets jumped out and demanded money and more. Sarah started to run, but Nonie grabbed her wrist so hard it hurt. Then Nonie sank onto one hip like she couldn't care less and said to the guy, "Do you really think you can get it up before I run to the end of the block and get the cop car there to put your fat ass in jail? Do you know what they do to fat pervs in jail?"

He made a grab for her, and Nonie kneed him in the balls. They ran, leaving him vomiting in the alley.

The guy never bothered them again.

Well, Sarah had learned from the best. And she wasn't backing off.

"Sarah," Reesa huffed and grabbed at her elbow. "Let's go. There's nothing you can do here. Not today."

Sarah shook her off. Ilona hadn't moved; she just stood there. She hadn't slouched to one hip, but the attitude was there.

"What is wrong with you? You said we would always be friends. That you'd write me every week. But you walked away and forgot about me. I wrote you every week and I never heard from you again. I was alone and scared, and I had lost my best friend. My sister. And I never knew what I did, and I still don't, but whatever it was, you made me pay. Can't you be satisfied? Are you willing to jeopardize the life of a child just to get back at me?"

Ilona just stood there, cold and immovable, a perfect, upscale, tough-ass Nonie. Not Nonie. Nonie was dead.

Sarah swallowed a sob, clutched her jacket with both hands to keep from hitting the cold bitch that stood expressionless in front of her. "If something happens to my child, it will be on your head. See if you can live with that."

She let Reesa pull her away.

When they reached the street, Reesa stopped her. "Wait here." She let Sarah go and strode back to Ilona, who was still standing in the middle of the sidewalk.

Reesa rose to her full frumpy five feet two inches, a head and a half shorter than the immaculate lawyer, and crowded her space. "This was low, even for you, Ilona." She didn't wait for a reaction—which was good since Ilona didn't have one— but turned and strode back to Sarah. Ilona stood frozen to the spot. Cold as ice in the morning sun.

It was the last image Sarah had of her, when Reesa pulled her away and trundled her down the sidewalk to the parking lot.

They were both shaking.

As soon as they got to Sarah's car, they jumped in and locked the doors. The interior was sweltering from sitting in the sun.

"Why is she doing this?"

"I don't know. She's always been an advocate for the children. Not the bio family or the foster family. But unless I've completely lost my judgment, it's a mistake to leave Leila alone with Carmen. She might be fine, until another man comes along or someone offers her drugs. Then it will be back to square one. God, how many times do we have to go through this same scenario?"

Sarah frowned at her. Reesa looked terribly pained. Sarah had been so wrapped up in Leila and her predicament that she forgot that Reesa did this every day and did some things that were even worse. And she was hurting from the futility of it all. Sarah recognized that pain. Had often felt it when she was younger. But that had been when she was on Leila's side of the problem.

"It's okay, Reesa. You did what you could. And I really appreciate it. We'll just have to hope for the best, I guess."

Reesa leaned back and closed her eyes. "I guess."

WHAT THE—? FOR a full two minutes, Ilona stood on the sidewalk trying to process what had just happened. What was the crazy bitch talking about? Trying to turn it back on Ilona, saying she never wrote. What bull. The bitch was getting what she deserved. A kid shouldn't grow up with a lying, crazy, angry mother.

She'd done good today. Set a child back on the road to unification with her bio mother. So Carmen Delgado had had a few failures. She looked like she was in great shape now. She had a chance of being reunited with her child. *One of her seven children,* Ilona reminded herself, and she felt the first niggle of doubt.

She pushed it aside. Reunification of a family while putting the screws to Sarah Hargreave. Not bad for a morning's work. So why did she feel so restless? So . . . Hell, she never second-guessed herself; she realized she was standing in the middle of the sidewalk staring down an empty street. Damn. She wrenched her gaze away and headed to the car park.

But as she drove back to her office, Ilona couldn't shake the feeling that something was off-kilter. What had the bitch meant, she wrote every week? She never wrote. Nonie—Ilona—had been the one who wrote. And wrote and wrote and never received one damn postcard even.

Revisionist history, Sarah. She'd been Nonie's best friend, Nonie trusted her, loved her like a sister, but she was no better than any of the others, pretending to care about her. But they'd just been using her. June Cartwright had never loved her like a mother, hadn't loved her at all. And Sarah? June might not have loved her, but Sarah was the only person in the world who had seen Nonie afraid. One brief second of weakness and Sarah had seen it. Had seen and had betrayed her.

Everything Ilona had thought they were had been a lie. And now Sarah had the balls to stand there and accuse Ilona of never writing, turning things around to make it all Nonie's fault, when it was Sarah who hadn't sent one damn letter.

No wonder June didn't want her hanging out with her old friends from the group home. They were bad influences. Even Sarah. Especially Sarah. She'd made Nonie soft—just a little part that cared about what happened to the younger girl, the frightened kid who breathed on her ear and was annoying as hell. It was just a little piece of soft, but any soft place was an Achilles heel. Fatal for life on the streets.

But she didn't have to live on the streets. She lived in a big old mansion in a rich town on the ocean. She could have been soft there. But she'd left her soft spot behind at the home with Sarah Hargreave.

WHEN SARAH DROPPED her off at home, Reesa didn't go inside; she waited for Sarah to drive away, then she got into her car and drove to the Child Protection office.

It looked the same as it always did, the way it always would. Desks crammed wherever there was space. Computers of every year, make, and model wherever they would fit. Stacks of hard copy folders, papers, printers, photocopiers, fax machines.

A few caseworkers were on the phones or leaning over keyboards. Fingers in the dike.

Reesa bypassed her desk and crossed the room to the door to the supervisor's office. She tapped at the glass. Paula Finch, hair disheveled, glasses balanced on the tip of her nose, a pen behind one ear, a pencil behind the other, looked up. She motioned for Reesa to come in.

"Have a seat."

Reesa moved a pile of folders off a chair and pulled it up to the desk.

She had a moment of sheer panic, the urge to change her mind and run. "I wanted to talk to you."

Mrs. Finch pushed the glasses up her nose and gave Reesa her full attention.

"I'm . . . I've . . . decided to leave child services." She blurted out the last words without stopping to think.

Paula Finch nodded slowly. "I don't guess I can change your mind?"

Reesa shook her head. She felt absurdly close to tears. She'd spent almost twenty years as a caseworker. But she couldn't do it anymore.

"I have some vacation time coming up. I'd like to finish up the paperwork on my open cases and finish the White boys' permanency hearing. But no new cases. Then I'll use my vacation for the rest of my notice."

"That's doable. I'll send you the forms." Paula chuckled. "Forms. We couldn't figure out how to get to the john without them. Ah hell." She sat back in her chair, then looked up at the ceiling and back to Reesa. "I'll hate to lose you, but I'm not surprised."

"You're not?"

"I've seen it coming. You've been a great caseworker, an even better case manager, passionate, indefatigable, and most of all organized and you can type with more than two fingers."

They both smiled at that. It was bittersweet for both of them. Paula had been case manager when Reesa first came to this office. When Paula moved up to supervisor, Reesa moved up to manager. And though they weren't exactly friends, they didn't get in each other's way and between them, they kept things running as smooth as social services could run.

"You were bound to burn out sooner or later. The passionate ones always do. You're smart to know your limit. And even though I hate that you're leaving, I know it's the wise thing to do. We've both seen what happens when people linger too long." She glanced over Reesa's head, and Reesa knew where she was looking, at Eddie Quinones. "It's hard to think of Eddie as a young passionate social worker, isn't it? Now he just puts in his time, takes his paycheck, and tries not to get too involved with his cases."

Reesa tried to remember Eddie being anything but the way he was now. Lethargic, plodding, unruffled by the horror, unexcited by the successes, and perfectly willing to let someone else do his job. Reesa didn't want that to happen to her.

"Have any idea what you'd like to do? I'll give you a reference." Paula smiled. "A good one."

"I do have a few ideas, but I'm going to take some time to do volunteer work."

Paula's smile turned into a grin.

"That's a girl. Then consider something with decent hours and good pay, where you don't have to get down and dirty."

Reesa laughed. "I'll take that under advisement. And Paula. Thanks. We did good work."

"We did, but you're not gone yet. Got anything on your docket other than the White boys?"

"A couple of things. One that I'm just kibitzing."

"Good, I'd hate to think it was that case that drove you away."

Reesa shook her head. "Just the straw."

Paula nodded and pushed the glasses up her nose. "Don't be a stranger."

"I won't. I'll be around another few days."

Reesa went out to her desk. Sat down. Spread her fingers over the surface. Looked over the neatly stacked papers and folders, the stuffed in-box, the empty out-box.

She straightened her already straight desk, throwing out whatever looked redundant or useless. A few things she left.

She'd be back; she had cases to close and to transfer, then Pete and Jerome White, and their baby brother, to place, and then she would pack up what was left.

It was easier to walk away than she'd thought it would be, because in her mind, she had already packed out. She paused at the door and looked back inside. Same as it ever was. Then she drove home, where she changed into slacks and a T-shirt and drove to Hands Around the World.

Chapter 23

That's just crazy," Karen said as she refilled Sarah's glass of iced tea and stuck another sprig of greenery in the glass. "I hope you like mint," she added. "It's taking over the yard."

Sarah took a long sip. "It tastes good."

"You don't think she did it on purpose? It's possible that it just came up on her pro bono schedule?"

Sarah gave her a look. "High-profile attorneys don't usually show up at review hearings. More likely never. She somehow finagled her way into the hearing just to put the screws to me. Regardless of how it affects Leila. Ugh. What's her problem?"

"And you're positive you're not being paranoid?"

"Positive. Ask Reesa. She was pretty upset. She went back and said something to her. I couldn't hear and she wouldn't tell me what she said. But I could tell she was fighting mad.

"And the bit— The woman just stood there, stood there like a statue." Sarah lowered her voice even though the girls were in Tammy's room playing dress-up and couldn't hear. "Now, Leila is going to have to go to unsupervised visits at Carmen's apartment. She won't even let me take her over there. She specifically asked for Danny, because I turn Leila against her. That is such a crock. I go out of my way to be fair. Carmen is the one who says things like I can't be Leila's mother because our skin is different. I'm the only poor dumb schmuck who's playing by the rules."

Karen pulled her chair closer and sat down. "Listen. The appeal is being heard in three weeks. No way is Carmen going to win that. They can't just say oh, she's got a job now, she can have the kid back. They only look at court procedure to see if anything was amiss during the previous trial, and with Judge Beckman presiding, you know there wasn't. Carmen and her lawyer are just posturing."

"How can you be sure? Everything that was supposed to be finished and cleared hasn't been. Every possible glitch has happened. Maybe Nonie, Ms. Cartwright, has been manipulating it from the beginning."

Karen made a face. "Sarah."

"All right, that is paranoid. It just is so unfair. What if something happens to Leila while she's there? We won't even have Danny I-just-left-for-a-minute-to-call-my-next-appointment Noyes to oversee."

"Skinned knees are not signs of abuse, just being a kid. The finger marks, that is questionable. But you documented it, right?"

"Of course. We're the original selfie family. Not easy to transfer the documentation photos to my laptop and delete them before Leila demands to see the regular ones. Which by the way, check this out." Sarah opened the photo app, scrolled through until she found the one of Leila reading to Wyatt.

"Is that cute or what? I call it the long and the short of it."

"Precious. What does he think about all this?"

"He's been a rock. I called him as soon as I dropped Reesa off to let him know how it went. He said the same thing you and Reesa said. Everything will work out."

"Good man."

"I know, but I'm kind of worried about him."

"His injuries?"

"No, up here." Sarah pointed to her temple.

"He's depressed?"

"A little. He doesn't show it, but I think he feels responsible. I mean those men were already dead by the time the team got on-site, but still it's got to be traumatic to see two dead guys floating around and not imagine them desperately trying to get out before the cabin filled with water."

Karen shivered. "Gaw, that creeps me out. Is he going to see someone?"

"Like a shrink? I have no idea. I mean, he's okay. He's just not his usual cool dude self, you know?"

"Hmmm. I'll have Stu talk to him."

"Talk to who?" Stu asked as he walked into the kitchen.

"Hey, hon, I didn't hear you come in."

"Then it was a good thing you weren't saying mean things about me." He leaned over and kissed her.

"Hey, Sarah. How'd it go today?"

Karen stood up. "You don't want to ask. Still on hold until the appeal is heard, Leila still has to make weekly visits."

"Christ, is this what my taxes are going to?"

"Don't start talking about taxes. We're depressed enough. Sarah is worried about Wyatt's state of mind. I thought you might talk to him, see how he's taking all the fallout from the rescue last week."

"There is no fallout. Bastards were out drunk. Hit a jetty, turned the boat over, and drowned themselves. The guys saved as many as they could. End of story."

"Will you just talk to him?"

"Yeah."

"Love you bunches."

"You'd better."

He started to leave.

"Hey, why are you home so early?"

"Not. Louis Raft wanted to borrow my wet saw, told him I'd swing by on my way to the site, and bring it to him." He raised an eyebrow at her. "You're not planning on having me renovate any of the bathrooms in the next couple of weeks."

"No, lovey. For once nothing is leaking, we won't tempt fate."

He saluted and went out the door.

"You guys have a good relationship, don't you?" Sarah asked.

"Yes. Even when he's being the pig in my farm. But yeah, we do. Speaking of which. Word is you've been seen going into Wyatt's quite often these days."

"Well, he was banged up. So I went round to see if he was okay." She winced. "Trying to be a friend instead of a whining self-centered brat."

Karen snorted. "And?"

"And I cooked and brought him takeout. That's what friends are for, right?"

"Right? And?"

Sarah shrugged. "And Victor told me I'd better get my shit together and claim my territory before this blonde named Caitlyn steals it."

"That Victor. He does have a brain cell left," Karen said. "And *is* Wyatt properly claimed?"

"We've never really talked about it, though . . ."

"Though what?"

"This is going to sound like something Jenny would say."

"Spill."

"The first day when he was on painkillers, he did say something about when he got hit and he thought he might die, he thought of me."

"Oh?"

"And not in an I'm-a-walking-disaster way."

"Of course not. What else?"

"And something about he'd been thinking about us being something more than we are."

"Whoa."

"But he hasn't mentioned anything more about it."

"I'll add it to the list of things for Stu to find out."

"I don't think he even remembers saying it."

"So how do you feel about it?"

Sarah drank more tea and considered. "I've already got my hands full with the store, and keeping Leila, and providing her with a good home. It's a lot to juggle."

"An extra pair of hands, especially large masculine hands in all the right places, could really help out."

Sarah laughed. "Oh thank you. I can't remember the last time I laughed over silly stuff. I should do it more often."

"Mi casa su casa, girlfriend. We have plenty of sillies over here any time of day or night."

"And I appreciate it, Karen, I really do. But now I'd better get Leila and get back to the store before Alice thinks I've run away."

They went down the hall and opened the door of Tammy's bedroom to bedlam. The huge dress-up box had been emptied and clothes were everywhere: shiny recital costumes, Halloween costumes, thrift store dresses. Leila was wearing a pink satin tutu and a tiara; Bessie, a cowgirl vest and holster and two big ostrich feathers held on to her head by a sequined headband. Tammy clomped around the room in a pair of high heels over her sneakers, a boa of multicolored feathers around her neck and a football helmet on her head.

Sarah and Karen exchanged glances.

"Ah, the imagination is a messy thing."

"I just wonder what the story is about," Sarah said.

"Okay, girls, time to clean up. Leila has to go home."

After the obligatory *no*s, and *oh*s, and *does she have to*s, the girls, with much help from Sarah and Karen, managed to get all the clothes back into the box.

"Can Leila come to the carnival with us next week?" Tammy asked as they all walked Sarah and Leila to the front door.

"Can I?" Leila asked. "Please?" She made those little prayer hands that told Sarah she was being suckered. Unfortunately, her answer depended on what the new visitation schedule would be.

Bessie and Tammy added her pleas to Leila's. "Pl-e-e-e-ease," like three little cherubs.

"Maybe," Sarah said. "I'll call your mom tomorrow."

Leila climbed into her car seat and Sarah strapped her in.

She backed out of the driveway with Tammy and Bessie waving with both hands and yelling, "Bye, bye, bye!"

Leila waved and called, too, and then they were driving down the street.

"Had a good time?" Sarah asked.

"Yep," Leila said and nodded vigorously.

"I'm so glad."

"You're my sunshine" came from the backseat. "Mommee sunshine."

ILONA WAS CONSIDERING takeout—Thai—or calling Garrett to see if he was free for dinner, when the concierge stopped her as she headed for the elevator.

"Ms. Cartwright. A package came for you today. Hold on a sec."

Ilona walked over to the desk. She hadn't requested any files to be sent over, and she didn't remember ordering anything online that hadn't already arrived.

He returned with a cardboard box and slid it across the counter. "It isn't heavy, but I can have Felipe bring it up when he gets back from his break."

Ilona tested the heft of it. "Thank you, but I can manage." She turned the package around to look for a return address. It was taped and addressed but had no postage and no return address. There was, however, a sealed legal-size envelope taped to the top.

"How did this arrive?"

"Messenger service. Around four o'clock."

Hmm. Ilona didn't get hate mail. Not recently anyway. But an unidentified package was cause for some circumspection.

She lifted the envelope away from the box and looked at it more closely. Then she recognized her father's handwriting.

Now what the hell was this? A get-out-and-stay-out box?

"Thank you, Hector." She took the package, while Hector ran ahead to press the elevator button.

"Have a good evening, Ms. Cartwright."

Ilona carried the box up to her apartment and left it on the entry table while she changed out of her suit and heels. She went into the kitchen and looked in the fridge. Closed the door. Got out ice and made herself a gin and tonic.

Opened the drapes and looked out over the waves. There was a ship on the horizon, no more than a glint of white on the water. A cruise ship or a tanker.

She got out a coaster, put her glass down on the coffee table.

Then she went to the entryway and came back with the envelope.

Sat down. Looked at the writing. Turned it over. It had been sealed.

No mail for me?

No, miss, not today."

"Are you sure?"

"Yes, miss. I'm sure. Maybe tomorrow." The maid looked sympathetic.

Nonie hated for people to feel sorry for her. There wouldn't be anything tomorrow. Everyone knew it. "It doesn't matter."

"Yes, miss."

Ilona put her glass down, went to the writing desk for the letter opener. Her hands were steady as a rock as she pulled out the letter. If she was expecting something dramatic or maudlin, she was disappointed. It was just a note.

Dear Ilona,

The staff was cleaning out some of your mother's things for Goodwill and ran across this box of things she'd saved. I thought you'd like to see them. Hope you're doing well. Give me a call sometime. We'll have lunch—Dad

Lunch? When was the last time they'd had lunch together? That would be never unless he wanted something. What could he possibly want now? She dropped the note in the wastepaper basket and glanced toward the box. *Things she saved.* He was cleaning out June's things. Not him but the staff. What was the rush? Selling the house? Retiring to Florida? Moving his mistress in?

And why send them to Ilona? Unless she'd saved things about Ilona. That's what mothers normally did. Saved things like report cards, prom corsages, graduation photos. Somehow she couldn't see June doing that. Probably legal stuff. And she really didn't need to see any more legalese tonight.

She didn't want to think about law or courts or the look on Reesa's face when she'd said, *This is low, even for you.*

Reesa hadn't even given Ilona a chance to defend herself. As if she needed defending.

This wasn't about her and Sarah, this was about legalities. About families being with their own. Not given up and forgotten about. Not taken away because they were old and infirm. Not because— This had nothing to do with Sarah Hargreave.

Ilona refused to question her motives. It wasn't about winning. Not today. Today was about . . .

What was it about? Ilona walked back to the couch. Sat down. Closed her eyes. Good God, what had she done?

SARAH TRIED TO prepare Leila for her Saturday unsupervised visit as they got ready for bed. Leila was wearing her favorite pink pajamas.

Sarah pulled back the covers, and Leila climbed in.

"It will be like your other Saturday visits, only a little longer and it will just be you and Carmen."

"Danny," Leila said.

"No, this time Danny will drop you off and pick you up later."

"Danny comes."

"He normally does, but this is going to be different."

"You come."

"I can't, sweetheart. It isn't allowed."

"Why can't you?"

Sarah thought about trying to explain how it was to help her bond with Carmen. But she didn't think Leila should have to bond with Carmen. She'd been as fair as she could.

But not this time. This time Sarah was going to fight. And if that didn't work . . .

"Come here." She pulled Leila into her lap and rocked her. "It will all be okay. I promise." And in the safety of the little pink bedroom, lit only by the night-light, the things of childhood surrounding them—storybooks and stuffed animals, toys and puzzles, the Elsa poster and Leila's watch-me-grow outline—Leila fell asleep.

For the first time since Sam took her in and gave her a home, Sarah thought about flight.

Chapter 24

"I'm sorry." Leila was standing in the doorway to the kitchen.

Sarah looked up from the table where she was sitting studying her laptop. "What, princess. Are you ready for breakfast?"

"I'm sorry."

"What happened?" Sarah closed the computer.

"I'm sorry, Mommee. Don't make me go."

Gulping back her dismay, Sarah knelt in front of her. "Sweetheart. You didn't do anything wrong. And even when you make a mistake, I'd never send you away."

"I'm sorry." Big tears rolled down Leila's cheeks. Her little mouth twisted, but she didn't make a sound.

"It's just what the court says we have to do. Just for a little while longer." Sarah scooped her up and held her. "You're my sunshine. I love you. I'm your forever mommee."

"Why do I have to go?"

"Because Carmen . . ." The words stuck in her throat. "Because Carmen is your beginning mother. She loves you, too. Like the book says. Everybody loves you."

Leila shook her head.

"I'm your forever mommee. No matter what."

God, she knew she wasn't supposed to say things like that until it was a done deal. But it should have been over by now. Not this ripping of their lives and their hearts. Maybe if she promised Carmen that she would be a part of their lives, she would give up the appeal.

But Sarah didn't want her to be a part of their lives. And if that was selfish, then so be it. Carmen came with too much baggage, had caused too many frightening memories, jeopardized Leila's safety, and she couldn't be trusted not to slip back again.

Leila clung to Sarah while she tried to make breakfast and finally gave up and poured Cheerios into a bowl. Leila sat but she didn't eat.

"Honey, you'll make yourself sick if you don't have breakfast."

"Then do I have to go?"

Sarah nodded and quickly turned away. "Just for a little while."

Leila refused to get dressed, then hid behind Sam's chair in the living room until Sarah had to drag her out. She kicked and screamed while Sarah carried her into her bedroom.

"Leila, Danny will be here soon. The sooner you get ready, the sooner you'll be back." A lie but Sarah was feeling a little ragged. It didn't work. She set Leila on the bed where she lay stiff legged and armed while Sarah dressed her.

This wasn't right. This was almost as bad as waking up one morning and realizing you're a cockroach. Sarah had read that story in high school. She thought it was so unfair then. Before she knew what it was like to really feel like a cockroach. But that's what she felt like now.

When Sarah tried to pull Leila up, she refused to help. Fine, let Danny come and get her.

"I love you, sunshine. And I'm sorry that you have to go. But you will come back soon and then we'll have some fun."

Nothing.

She walked out of the room. Walked down to the kitchen, drank a glass of water, splashed more water over her face. Glanced at her computer. What was she even contemplating. Was she crazy?

Sam's words radiated from the surface of the fridge. *Fix the now.*

"How, Sam? Tell me how."

The doorbell rang, and her stomach flipped over. *It was just a few hours,* she told herself. Just like she told Leila, just a few hours. Forcing herself to appear calm, to breathe evenly, she went to answer the door.

"Hi," Danny said. He didn't look very happy about being here. Well, he should have made more of a stink. She opened the door far enough for him to come in. What was there to say?

She left him standing in the little entranceway, the place where bad news always seemed to rest. As long as it didn't make its way farther into the cottage—if she could keep it away, they would be safe.

Leila was behind Sam's chair. Sarah knew it, but she didn't find her right away. If Sam had been there, he would have known what to do. He would have told Danny to piss off, told the courts to stop thinking about the unimportant stuff and see the whole child.

But Sam wasn't here, and his chair couldn't protect either of them for long.

"Time to go," Sarah said, not bending down, but just standing where Danny could see her. She looked back at him, looking uncomfortable and helpless, and something snapped. Be an advocate, dammit.

"Come get her." She stepped back out of the way.

He stared at her. He didn't move.

"Sarah, don't make this difficult."

"Me? We were having a perfectly nice morning until you came." Another lie but at this point she didn't really care. "We were having a perfectly nice life until all this bullshit started. So what are you waiting for? I would have gladly taken her to all these visitations, but Carmen didn't want me there. So now it's your duty. Go for it, but don't expect me to make it easier for you."

Danny swallowed, she could see his Adam's apple bobble. He walked over to her, looked behind the chair.

"Hey, Leila. Ready to go?"

She shoved herself farther back in the corner.

"Come on, you don't want to be late." He reached in for her. Her feet started pumping. He jumped back.

"Sarah. Help me out, will you?"

"Why? Can't you see that she doesn't want to go?"

"It's just confusing for her if you don't help with the transition."

Sarah took a step forward. "Don't. Don't even try to blame me for this. I've done everything by the book. Made that stupid book about having two mothers who love you. For what? To have this innocent child traumatized week after week, and then just when you think life will be normal, they make her do it all over again. Did you even read the reports of the last two times we went through this?"

"I'm just doing my job."

"That's hardly an excuse." She pushed him out of the way, squeezed in behind the chair. And sat. Leila had her face to the wall.

"Look, sport, we can't get out of this. But your Mickey clock is in your backpack, and when it goes off it will be time to come home. And Danny will drive you here. And then Wyatt said he'd take us for pizza. Won't that be fun?"

At last Leila peeked out at that.

"I'll be right here when Danny brings you home, and then we'll have pizza. And tomorrow we'll have the whole day to play."

Leila relaxed just enough for Sarah to lift her out, then stagger to her feet with her clinging to her neck.

She gave Danny a look that should hurt. He reacted appropriately and peeled Leila's arms from Sarah's neck.

"You're my sunshine," she called to Leila as he walked to the door.

"You better not let anything happen to her," she added under her breath.

Danny jerked his head back and forth a couple of times.

"See you in a few. I love you forever."

She waited to make sure Danny put Leila in the car seat. Not an easy feat, since Leila didn't help and Sarah didn't offer further assistance.

Sarah watched as they drove away, then closed the door and rested her forehead against the cool wood. She knew she had to go into the store to work or she'd make herself crazy. She could hardly wait to hear what Alice had to say. It was bound to cut to the quick.

She showered and changed and tried to pretend like life was wonderful. And for the most part it was. It would be complete once Leila was adopted. And if Carmen fought back—she thought about the laptop open to her bank accounts—Well, she'd deal with that, too.

THE FIRST THING Ilona thought when she woke up Saturday morning was the satisfaction of a job well done. The Sobrato divorce case wrapped Friday morning. Just in time for the weekend. Ilona had gotten everything she'd asked for. As soon as the hearing was over, she marched Olivia right downstairs to probate and signed her up to have his wages garnished. No easy feat when he owned his own company.

Her forensic accountant had found enough discrepancies in the books to make him sweat. There was no doubt he was taking in more than he was declaring and to avoid the tax man, he'd handed over a wad of cash and two of their homes.

That wouldn't prevent Ilona from giving a little call to the IRS. Good citizen that she was.

She'd gone the extra mile just to nail the bastard, and she was pleased with the outcome. Any qualms she might have had over her role in the Delgado custody hearing were put to rest. Her momentary doubt had been nothing but an aberration brought on by her father's note and delivery of the box.

Which she had shoved into the bottom of the coat closet before going to bed. Did she really want to know what her mother, June, had thought worth saving?

Nothing like pleading a high-profile case to put it all into perspective. As far as Ilona was concerned, she'd gotten a good settlement for one client and a chance to reunite another with her mother. She was pleased with her work on both fronts.

Olivia Sobrato was free to spend her money. Let the courts deal with Leila Rodrigues. They'd asked for her opinion and she'd given it.

There had been that one tiny niggle of doubt. It was mostly gone this morning. And a good hard game of tennis with Garrett would kill whatever residual doubt might be lurking.

It wasn't that she was ambivalent about what she'd done or even how she'd done it. It was the realization that she had, even for a second, questioned her own motivations. Only for a brief moment did she wonder if her actions had stemmed from her belief in the Delgado case, or if it was a knee-jerk reaction to Sarah Hargreaves.

Today there was no question; Ilona Cartwright did not have knee-jerk reactions.

But she did have a date for tennis, dinner, and sex. She was actually looking forward to all three.

TANISHA WAS SURPRISED but delighted when Reesa walked into the center and asked if she'd hired a development director.

"Not yet, but we'll find somebody. Not everybody cares about making a lot of money."

"Well, I'd like to apply for the job."

Tanisha's mouth went slack. "You want to work for the center?"

"For a while, if I have the qualifications."

"Qualify? Oh man, this is great. Are you serious?"

Reesa nodded. "I still have a few things to wrap up at CP&P, but I'll give you what time I can until that work is finished."

"Oh, wow! Really?"

"Yes, if you think I'll be a good fit."

"The best. Let's go tell everybody."

Reesa followed in her enthusiastic wake, hoping she hadn't just blown her retirement and her marriage by a rash act of had enough. Michael hadn't come home last night, nor did he call. And she'd be damned if she'd call him. Maybe his brother could talk some sense into him. And if not, he could have him full-time.

They could put the house on the market and Reesa would find a little apartment somewhere, which reminded her, she should check to make sure Ms. McKinney had gotten moved into the assisted living building.

First stop was the computer room, where twelve young and old women sat before keyboards listening to a heavyset woman explain how to log in.

"Excuse me for interrupting, but I have good news. Reesa Davis has just accepted the position of development director for the center."

Tanisha turned to present Reesa, who smiled and waved, and then Tanisha backed her out of the door.

"This is just so great," Tanisha said as they moved onto the next classroom. Once they'd made the rounds and were standing in front of the main office, Reesa said. "Maybe you should show me what outreach you've done so far."

Tanisha winced. "It's mainly me begging the local businesses to help out. And we did get a couple of grants through the town and one from the state."

In other words, not much. Reesa had her work cut out for

her. But she also had knowledge of the system and where to get grants and who to call for help. Almost two decades in social services had taught her how to navigate the not-for-profit waters.

"There's a little office that you can have." Tanisha frowned, bit her lip. "It doesn't have a window."

Reesa laughed. Really laughed. "That's quite all right. I wouldn't know what to do with one."

The office was maybe eight by nine, with a battered desk and a rolling desk chair whose cushion sagged in the shape of the last person who had called it home. She'd have to bring her own computer and a file cabinet and ask the preschool class for some artwork. But as far as offices went, it looked pretty darn good.

SARAH GLANCED AT her watch for probably the twentieth time that day. Standing in a shop full of clocks, she was obsessed by only one time. Five o'clock—when Leila would be back.

The day, of course, dragged on. It was a brilliant beach day, and not too many people were thinking about keeping track of time. They made a few sales, and Sarah managed to catch up on several small repairs, while wondering how the unsupervised visit was going. But she couldn't seem to make headway on Mrs. Bridges's violin clock. She would fit sections one and two together, but when she connected the next section, it refused to fit in the casing. She took it out again. Tested each section separately, they all fit. Put two together, still fit, added the third. And was stopped again. None of the screw holes lined up and several of the parts didn't sit flush. She took them apart, rehammered the angles . . . would start again.

At four thirty Wyatt came through the door, stopping to flirt with Alice who was not averse to his overtures.

"I've come to take her away," he said. And trundled Sarah out the back door.

He put his arm around her as they walked next door and went in the back. "I meant to get here earlier, but I had a rush on board wax at the last minute."

"Unlike clocks," Sarah told him.

"Slow day?"

"Too sunny and gorgeous to be worried about time," she said, wondering why the violin clock was turning out to be such a challenge.

Wyatt ducked his head to see her better. "Except you. I knew you'd be crawling the walls by now. So I decided to come over and be here to offer pizza and putt-putt and whatever will smooth over the transition."

"Putt-putt?"

"Hey, putt-putt is a real man's sport."

"Uh-huh." She knew he was trying to take her mind off Leila and she appreciated it.

Once they were in the kitchen, he turned her around and kissed her. She let herself lean against him, a temporary haven from the outside world.

"Too bad I didn't get here earlier," he said with a sigh.

Sarah laughed and pushed him away. "How about a glass of hibiscus tea instead?" She went over to the fridge and got out the pitcher of tea. When she turned around, Wyatt was looking at the papers she'd left by her laptop on the kitchen table.

"What's this?" he asked. "None of my business probably, but tell me anyway."

"I was just doing some budgeting this morning before work."

Wyatt picked up the top paper.

Sarah had to force herself not to snatch it out of his hand. "You're awfully nosy today."

"Not really, but you left it out and this looks to me like you're considering some drastic changes. Are you having money troubles? Because—"

"No. Everything is fine."

"Then why does it look like you're planning on selling the store?" He picked up the second sheet. "The house, too?"

"I was just seeing what my assets were."

"Why would you— Sarah, you're not planning on doing something radical."

She shook her head.

"Because if you're thinking you could sell everything and run away with Leila, it just won't work. Is that what all these figures are about?"

Sarah bit her lip. She didn't like lying, and she didn't want to lie to Wyatt. Besides, he would know. He already knew. "I just wanted to see."

He took her by the shoulders. "Listen to me. It won't work. You can't do that to yourself or to Leila. Besides, you wouldn't be able to sell that quickly and the authorities would just follow the money trail."

"Then I could just take her and go."

"Honey, would you listen to yourself? Is that the kind of life you want for either of you? Change your names, living in hiding, not letting anyone get close to you. Is that any way to live your life or raise a child?"

"But what if they give Leila back to Carmen?"

He looked at her long and hard, then pulled her close. "Then you'll have to accept it and figure out how you want to handle it."

"But what if she hurts her?"

"Then they'll take her away again. But you'll have to get on with your own life. You've lived your life completely around her for the last two years. That's not healthy for either of you."

"It's just because everything is always so up in the air."

"And always will be whether you have Leila or not. It's called life."

The doorbell rang.

Sarah jumped away. "It must be them. They're early. I hope everything is okay." She hurried to get the door.

Danny was standing on the doorstep, holding Leila's hand. His expression was stormy.

"Here," he said, ushering Leila inside. "She didn't want to leave."

Sarah's heart broke. She felt Wyatt come up behind her and put his hand on her back.

Sarah roused herself. "Come in."

Danny dragged Leila in. "Good-bye, Leila. See you next week," he said, but his voice lacked any sign of conviction.

"I don't like you," Leila said and kicked him in the shin.

"Leila! We do not hit or kick people. Apologize to Danny."

"No!" She stalked past them.

"I'm really sorry. I'll go get her."

"No, that's okay," Danny said, backing toward the door. "I'll call before next Saturday."

"Do you want me to take her over next week?"

"No, Carmen doesn't want you there. But everything looked fine when I dropped her off. And when I asked Leila if she had a good time, she said yes. Let's just go with the status quo until the outcome of the appeal."

He left and Sarah went in search of Leila. She found her where she knew she'd be, behind Sam's chair. Maybe Sam was protecting her from wherever he was.

"That was very naughty to kick Danny. He's just doing his job and driving you safely to the places you have to go."

Though Sarah had to admit, she'd felt like kicking him and everyone else involved.

"You can tell him you're sorry the next time he comes."

"No."

"Why did you kick him?"

"I don't like him."

"Well, come on out and let's discuss this."

Leila huffed and turned her back on Sarah.

"Please come out now."

A shake of the head. At least she was still communicating, which was better than the dreaded silences.

"Come on out, I'm getting hungry. Aren't you?" When Leila didn't move, Sarah pulled the chair aside and lifted her out. She started kicking the air and Sarah put her down.

Leila saw Wyatt and shrunk back.

Not again. "Maybe we should take a rain check on the pizza."

Wyatt shook his head. And surprised both Sarah and Leila by sitting down on the floor right in front of both of them.

"Now, is that better?" He was talking to Leila. And Sarah realized he was making himself Leila size.

Leila shook her head.

"How come?"

Leila's lip came out. "I don't, I don't, I don't like you."

"Me? What did I do?"

"I don't like you." This time she said it more quietly, and

Sarah held her breath to see if she would dissolve into silence, tears, or tantrum. Sarah wasn't sure how much more of this any of them could take.

Leila pulled on her hand until Sarah sat down on the floor.

Leila knelt in front of her and put both hands on either side of Sarah's cheeks.

At first Sarah thought she wanted to play the bunny wabbit game. Some kind of solace?

But instead she said, "Why does DeShawn have to be my daddy? I don't want him. He's mean."

"Who the hell is DeShawn?" Wyatt asked.

Sarah frowned at him. He winced an apology for his language.

"He shit."

"It's *he's* shit, but we don't use that word."

"DeShawn and Carmen use that word and she say she's my mama now and DeShawn's gonna be my daddy."

"Well, he isn't."

"She say." Leila's face crumpled.

"She may say, but that doesn't mean it's true."

Leila started to cry. "I don't want him."

Sarah reached for her and was relieved when she climbed into Sarah's lap.

"I don't want DeShawn. Why can't Wyatt be my daddy?"

The world winked out for a split second, as Sarah tried to regain her equilibrium. Sarah didn't know what to answer and she didn't dare look at Wyatt.

She just rocked Leila as best she could sitting cross-legged on the floor, murmuring, "There, there," which was the only thing she could think of to say. It had no meaning and didn't help at all.

When she did risk a look at Wyatt, he was still sitting on the floor across from her, looking gobsmacked.

She should say something to let him know he shouldn't take anything Leila said seriously, but she just couldn't say that in front of Leila, who was whimpering in her lap. And Sarah didn't want Wyatt to think that she was taking it seriously but she didn't want him to think she wasn't taking him seriously either. What a mess.

They could talk about it later if it came up. For now, she just gave him a half smile trying to tell him that everything would be cool.

He didn't smile back.

Chapter 25

Wyatt, deciding they had had enough excitement for one day, took Sarah and Leila to Boardwalk Pizza. It was a perfect choice, Sarah thought as she handed Wyatt the keys to her car and she strapped Leila in the backseat.

They could have walked to Boardwalk Pizza, but Leila was tired, still disoriented and upset from her visit with Carmen and DeShawn, and Wyatt wasn't really in shape to carry her for any distance.

He swore he was okay, but when Sarah tossed him the keys to her car, he didn't argue. It was late for the beach crowd, most of whom were already heading home or out to dinner or had finished their pizza and had moved onto the bars a few towns down the road.

BP, as the locals called the pizza joint, was still doing a brisk business. It was a narrow space with an order counter and a single row of tables along the opposite wall, but there were plenty of tables outside on the sidewalk and people even took their pizzas across the street to watch the waves. Sarah found a table outside while Wyatt went in to order.

It was getting dark; the lifeguard stands were tipped over on their sides. A few stragglers were still sitting on the sand. Couples strolled the boardwalk, but mostly it was quiet, except for the occasional rattle of a skateboard passing down the wooden boards. A breeze cooled the air as it often did at night, and Sarah pulled a sweatshirt over Leila's head just as Wyatt returned with a handful of crayons and a paper placemat.

A teenage boy, probably a college student, followed him out with plastic utensils and drinks in paper cups.

Wyatt put the mat and crayons in front of Leila, who yawned but picked them up and began coloring a porpoise red.

Sarah just looked at him in admiration. He was so thoughtful.

"What?"

Sarah realized she had a goofy smile on her face. "Nothing. I just think it's nice that you thought to bring crayons."

"It's no big deal."

"It is. And I appreciate it. I don't always tell you, but I'm really grateful for how you . . . for being such a good friend to me and caring about Leila."

He sighed, a laugh or a sound of exasperation. "Why do you always seem surprised that people care about you?"

Sarah shrugged. "I think once you've come through the system, you never lose that one small fear that someone will come and snatch your chance of happiness or stability away. So . . . well, it's hard to completely trust it. Not your friends but just the situation." She glanced at Leila. "Like if you're not vigilant, if you relax even for a second, it will all go up in smoke."

Wyatt reached across the table and squeezed her hand.

The college student returned with their pizza.

The pizza was good, made better from being eaten in the ocean air. They stuffed themselves, and afterward walked across the street to the boardwalk. Leila was tired but she seemed to have forgotten her earlier visit with Carmen, and knowing that her reaction was bound to resurface sooner or later, Sarah welcomed the chance to put it off for a while longer.

They strolled down the boardwalk away from the lights of the pizza restaurant and sat on a bench to look out to the sea.

Sarah knew that she would have to say something about the daddy bombshell before Wyatt left tonight. But she didn't know what to say. Because if she were to be honest with herself, and she always tried to be honest with herself, it didn't sound so bad to Sarah, either.

She'd liked the way they had been for all these years. Easy, not demanding, on again off again, seeing other people in between. They always got back together, even after Leila came and the game changed. But could the three of them be good together—a forever family?

"Stop it."

"Stop what?"

Wyatt looked down at her. The moon balanced just above his shoulder and for a second he looked like a superhero. Or Lord of the Underworld. "You're overthinking again."

"I can't always help myself." She looked down at Leila wedged between the two of them on the beach, nodding toward sleep. For a moment, Sarah allowed herself to believe in the three of them. She pulled herself together. That was still a long way away, if ever.

She leaned back and rested her head on Wyatt's arm.

Looked up at the sky. It was a clear night and she could see a myriad of stars even with the lights of the community.

The waves were dark and steady; the roll and break lulled her heart. There had been a time, though she hardly remembered it, when she had been afraid of the beach, of the waves. Sam couldn't believe that she had never been to the beach in all the years she'd lived in a group home only a fifteen-minute walk away.

How could she explain that it was safer to walk west, through the exhaust fumes of stalled traffic, past check cashing and liquor stores, the drug dealers and the drunks, than to go east to the beach, where the air smelled like promise but was just a taunt. Because every walk always ended in the same place—group home. She would never have anything better.

So yes, she feared the waves, but she didn't hate them. Actually now they held a special place in her heart. It had been her fear of the water that had turned her toward town where she discovered Clocks by the Sea and Sam Gianetti.

"I'm going to learn to swim," she said into the darkness. She felt Wyatt's muscle twitch beneath her neck. "I know it's crazy that I never learned.

"Sam didn't push me to learn, he said it was enough to sit beside the water and share the energy and peace of its power." She turned her head to look at Wyatt. "Is that what you feel?"

He sighed. "Sometimes, like now, when I'm just sitting. But when I'm diving, or rescuing, or even lifeguarding, it's a challenge." She reached over her shoulder and took his hand. "It can be beautiful but never laid back. There's a whole other world living beneath the surface. A world most people don't experience."

He coughed a laugh. "If they did, maybe they would treat

it with more kindness. And if they respected it more, they wouldn't take a boat out drunk and get themselves killed."

She heard that tiny whisper of bitterness, and she reached over and kissed his cheek. Then she kissed him for real.

"You're squishing me," came a mumble from between them.

"Someone is about to nod off," Wyatt said. "Let's get back and put her to bed."

Sarah nodded. She started to rouse Leila, but Wyatt laid a restraining hand on her shoulder. "And after that, we're going to talk."

REESA STRETCHED TO relieve her aching back. She'd been sitting at the kitchen table hunched over her laptop all evening. The White children's permanency hearing was the coming week. She'd organized her documents, and in case there was any doubt in any person along the info trail, the PowerPoint presentation she'd made this evening would leave all question about reunification behind.

When she finished, it was past time for bed. But she knew she wouldn't sleep with the images she'd revisited alive again in her mind.

Reesa went to the sink, got a drink of water, and came back to her computer. Might as well keep working.

She logged onto the Internet. She'd already run some info searches on available grants for community centers, education, and social progress. She spent another hour checking the deadlines for the ones they might have a shot at, then her mind began to wander to her own predicament. She had a plan . . . of sorts: to work with Hands Around the World on funding and focusing their direction while she beefed up her credentials for work as an elementary-school social worker, if she could afford to go back to school for the requisite coursework. She searched for nearby affordable colleges with classes in psychology and social work.

The kitchen wall clock ticked away the minutes, then the hours.

Other than that, the house was strangely quiet. No television was blaring from the other room. She'd gotten so used to hearing it that it had become a kind of white noise to her life.

Michael hadn't come back—at least not while she'd been there—though she had noticed some of his clothes were gone. Which meant he wasn't planning on coming back soon. And the television stayed off.

Reesa didn't really miss the noise. But she was surprised that she also didn't miss Michael. There was a time not too long ago when she would have felt half of her was missing. But that was before the accident that not only broke his leg but knocked the spirit out of him as well. Now that she looked back on things, she saw they had been leading pretty much separate lives even before then. She went to work, he went to work; she came home and made dinner, and he turned on the ball game.

Or if she was out late on a call, they would order out or run down to the pub for a burger and a beer. At least then they were doing something.

Now, it was just her going to work. And it was just her sitting in the kitchen. She figured he'd come back sooner or later. Or maybe not. Maybe he was just as tired of her as she was of him.

And that made her sad. How many people stayed together just because they couldn't afford to live apart?

The salaries for school social workers weren't much better than what she was making now. She might even have to take a cut in pay since she wouldn't have any seniority in the school system. Was she being unrealistic?

Maybe. But she knew that she couldn't keep doing what she was doing. Her job had sucked the spirit out of her. What a pair the two of them were.

Or not a pair any longer.

Reesa didn't want to leave social work altogether. She just wanted to be on the other side of it. On the side where people succeeded, made something out of their fractured, sometimes broken lives. Running into Tanisha Clark in a store Reesa never shopped in had been the clarion call. Ten minutes earlier, ten minutes later, if she'd just stayed home or gone into the office instead of going to Karen's for the weekend, she would have missed that meeting. And her second chance.

Thank God she had gone. She felt more hopeful tonight than she had felt in many years. Since before the kids had moved out, perhaps.

Hopeful, yet alone.

SARAH AND WYATT didn't talk when they got back to Sarah's. Not at first. Leila barely woke long enough to be carried into the cottage and put to bed in her clothes.

"Go do what you need to do," Wyatt said. "I've got all night." He smiled in a gotcha way and went to the kitchen to get himself a beer. When Sarah came out of Leila's room, he was sitting on the couch drinking his beer. There was a glass of wine for Sarah sitting on the coffee table.

Sarah was suddenly nervous. Like she might be on a date. Not that she'd dated that much—whether she wanted to or not.

It was one of the many things she and Sam had scuffled

over. He'd changed the way she dressed the first week she'd walked into the store; taught her to respect others and herself. Until she ran into a guy from her former life and made the mistake of bringing him to the clock store.

She knew she was testing the waters, pushing to see how far Sam would go before kicking her out. The stakes were getting higher, and she didn't want to leave. But the old urge to fail kept ambushing her.

She'd expected Sam to fly into a rage, kick the guy out. But Sam surprised her. He forced the guy to shake hands then invited him for a cup of tea. Chatted like they were old friends. The guy couldn't wait to get out of there and never came back again.

Sam never said a word and neither did Sarah. He'd proved his point. She really had left that part of her life behind.

There were more times like that, though none as treacherous as the first. Sam was patient, and in the end his good sense rubbed off on her. He'd loved Wyatt. Maybe he thought of him as the son he'd never had. Though he'd never pushed them together. Never even mentioned it. Just stood back and let things take their course.

Fix the now. It was time.

She sat down, took her glass, put it down. "So . . ." she began.

Wyatt just smiled and shook his head. Handed her the wineglass. "Chill. It's all okay."

"But—"

"But it's all okay." And he made it so.

It was close to four when Sarah awoke to crying. Immediately awake, she jumped out of bed and ran across the hall to Leila's room. The night-light was on, Leila was tossing in her sleep, but she was still asleep. Sarah sat on the bed and soothed her hair, rubbed her tummy. And when Leila reached out her arms, Sarah curled up beside her until she was calm again.

When she finally tiptoed back to her own room, it was almost dawn and Wyatt was still there.

Sarah hesitated for a split second.

Wyatt sat up. "Well, do I stay or go?"

She looked behind her to the dark hall and the sliver of light that shone from Leila's room.

"I don't know if Leila . . ."

"What do you want? You? Not what is good for Leila or what she'd want. Not what is good for the both of you. But what you want. That's what I want to know." He looked at her, sleepy and tousled and serious. "And maybe once I know, I'll figure out what I want."

She thought about it.

He pulled her down and kissed her. And she thought she knew the answer. A few minutes later she forgot the question.

Chapter 26

Sarah knew it was morning because Leila was climbing across her and sat on her stomach.

Sarah blinked her eyes open, realized the usual morning empty space beside her was still occupied. And she nearly dumped Leila on the floor in her panic to get up.

Wyatt was still asleep and naked. She was still naked. Fortunately the sheet covered most of them. Sarah grabbed it and pulled it up to their chins, and this time Leila did fall off, in the wedge between them. She didn't hesitate but climbed on Wyatt and pushed his face with both hands.

"Bunny wabbit," Leila demanded.

Wyatt's eyes opened. "Huh?"

"Bunny wabbit," she repeated.

"Oh. Bunny wabbit," he said, his voice low and gravelly with sleep. Leila squealed with delight. "Again." She pushed his lips together again.

"Bunny wabbit and Wyatt."

"More."

Wyatt yawned, groaned, "Bunny wabbit, Wyatt, and . . . and heffawumps and woozles."

Leila narrowed her eyes at him, moved her face close to his. Sarah bolted for the wardrobe and a long T-shirt.

"Come on, bunny wabbit girl; let Wyatt wake up."

Leila looked at Sarah. Back to Wyatt. "How come Wyatt gets to sleep with you and I don't?"

"Because grown-ups get to sleep together," Wyatt said and turned over, dumping Leila on the mattress.

She blinked then climbed back on his side. "Again."

Wyatt groaned and bucked her off again.

Sarah tried not to laugh. Obviously mornings with Leila were more than he was ready for.

Except that the next day he came back for more.

Things went well for the first couple of days, but then Wyatt had to go away to a two-day training course. Leila kept asking where he was, but when Sarah tried to explain that he had to go away for a few days, Leila got confused and started to cry. "Do I have to go, too?"

"Where?"

"Do I have to go away, too?"

"No, sweetheart. No one is going away. Wyatt had to go to school, that's all. He's coming back."

"When is school over?"

"In a day or two."

"Can we pick him up at the bus?"

"He's not on a bus. It's sleep-away school."

"No-o-o-o." Leila started to cry.

The more Sarah tried to explain, the worse it got. She finally gave up with a "Be patient."

When he did show up, Leila ignored him.

"Hey, hokey-pokey girl. Did you miss me?" He bent down to give her a high five and Leila turned on him. "No."

Wyatt looked at Sarah for explanation.

"She thought you had gone away for good."

"Hey, goofball. I'm not going anywhere. Promise."

Leila looked over her shoulder at him. "Promise-promise?"

"Hokey-pokey promise."

She reached out her arms, and he picked her up, shooting a *What just happened?* look toward Sarah.

Sarah just breathed a sigh of relief.

But as the next Saturday came around, Leila became sullen again; cried at the smallest sound, woke with nightmares. She complained that she was hungry, but then wouldn't eat. Refused to get dressed. Everything was a battle of wills. An emotional roller coaster.

Every time she passed the wall calendar, she slowed down, looked, but didn't ask. They both knew there would be another visit.

Sarah began to hate the thing. What had begun over a year ago as a fun way to remember activities had turned into a dreaded enemy. Once Carmen's appeal was—hopefully—denied, Sarah would tear the damn thing off the wall.

And if instead, it reversed the adoption procedure, Sarah would go to plan B. Always have a plan B. Nonie had taught her that. And Sarah had an alternate plan, in spite of what Wyatt said.

ON THE FOLLOWING Saturday morning, Danny Noyes picked Leila up and she went without a word. Came back hours later, the same way. Danny just shrugged and left.

The silence lasted until Wyatt knocked on the door a while later. Sarah went to answer it.

"You look dragged out," he said and kissed her.

From behind them, Sarah heard Leila scream. She whirled around. "What?"

But no catastrophe had occurred. Leila stood in the middle of the floor, fists clenched, screaming at the top of her lungs.

"Stop it!" Sarah demanded. She felt at the end of her strength. She didn't know how she could keep this up. How either of them could.

"Enough already," Wyatt said and stepped toward Leila. He picked her up, and she lashed out hitting and kicking.

He put her down; tried to soothe her, kid with her, distract her, but it only made things worse. "I don't get it. What did I do?"

Sarah couldn't even begin to explain that it had nothing to do with him. She just didn't have the energy. She felt like kicking and screaming herself.

"I think you better go," Sarah managed, holding on to tears of frustration and sympathy for Wyatt who was so good and was being treated abominably.

He hesitated, but on a new spate of screeches, he walked past Sarah and out the door.

Leila stopped screeching immediately. Just frowned at Sarah.

Sarah frowned back. "Satisfied with yourself? He's gone." And this time he might just be gone for good.

That set Leila off again, Sarah snatched her up and carried her kicking and screaming to her room. Dropped her on the bed.

She kicked out and screamed the two bad words she'd

learned at Carmen's at the top of her lungs. "Stay right there until you can calm yourself." Sarah shut her in her room.

At the first crash, she knew she'd made a mistake. She opened the door to find Leila sitting on the floor surrounded by books. She'd knocked all of them off the shelf. Sarah picked her up and carried her into the hallway where there was nothing that she could break and nothing to hurt her. Sarah sat her down on the floor and told her to stay, then sat at the kitchen table and listened.

When she tiptoed out a while later, she found Leila asleep on the floor and Sarah gave into her tears.

ON MONDAY MORNING, Sarah didn't attempt to send Leila to school. Or the next day. She finally called the teacher and told her she was withdrawing her two weeks early.

"Having a hard time?" Mrs. Lester asked.

"Really bad," Sarah confessed.

"Just love her, Sarah, if you can. We'll still be here if you need us before pre-kindergarten. And keep in touch."

"Thank you. You've been . . . Thank you." And Sarah hung up.

Sarah walked around on eggshells. Karen told her just to wait out the storm. One day they would look back on this and hardly remember the pain. Sarah doubted it, but she tried to believe it. Still she called Leila's therapist and made an emergency appointment.

DURING THE NEXT few days, the tantrums alternated with bouts of sullenness and quiet. Sarah couldn't decide which was worse, the little girl who was lashing out her fear and anger, or the one who seemed like she had stopped caring.

Karen sent Jenny over, but Leila didn't want anything to do with her. And Jenny went home in tears. She didn't come again.

"She's very upset," Karen explained. "What happened?"

"I'm sorry. So sorry."

"Sarah, it is what it is. Sometimes we adults just have to hunker in and weather the worst of it."

So Sarah hunkered in and tried her best.

Wyatt called but she didn't answer, and he didn't leave a voice mail. He came to the door, but as soon as he knocked Leila started crying again. As soon as he left, she returned to silence.

Sarah began to wonder if it would ever be normal, their life together. Or whether Leila was already too damaged to ever learn to trust and love.

Then she remembered herself. She hadn't made Sam's life easy. She didn't throw tantrums, but she could be pretty cruel verbally. She defied him, insulted him, tried to make him send her away so that she could say, *See, nobody wants me, not even you.*

But he wouldn't say it. He'd just smiled that wise sometimes sad smile and loved her. Took her out to look at the stars where she would forget to be tough. One night while they were standing on the beach, they saw a meteor shower, like a quick quiet fireworks display.

And she forgot to want to run away, to have the world prove what she already knew: that she wasn't lovable. And over the years she'd forgotten, truly forgotten, that she was unworthy. She accepted his love. And learned in her way to return it.

And while he was alive, she lived with trust, believed that life was good. And when he died, she mourned as she didn't think she could mourn for another human being. And when she was done, she vowed to give to another child what Sam had given to her.

And it was such a mess.

I'm failing, Sam. I don't know what to do. I don't know if I'm cut out for this unconditional love thing. I want to rest, to be able to relax just for a minute and I can't. Maybe I can't do this after all.

And if she couldn't, she'd be throwing his gift back in his face.

Sarah's work fell behind, and Alice had to call several clients and tell them that a family emergency had arisen and it had delayed their repairs. Most were understanding.

Alice was sympathetic. "You poor thing. You're making yourself sick looking after that child."

And Sarah knew she was right. Neither she nor Leila was eating. Sarah could barely force food down. She made Leila meals that she refused to touch. Sarah tried talking to her, promising her that she loved her no matter what, that she'd be her forever mommee, no matter what.

But her bright, willful little four-year-old had already learned not to trust. How to strike out before they struck you. And it broke Sarah's heart.

WHEN SATURDAY CAME and the doorbell rang, Sarah was almost relieved. She handed a sullen Leila off to Danny with barely a word. He frowned at her. "Are you okay?"

She just shrugged. He probably thought she was on drugs.

"She'll be back at five," he said with forced enthusiasm.

"Love you, sunshine," Sarah managed and closed the door.

Seven hours of peace. Sarah threw herself on the couch, curled herself around a pillow, and stayed that way.

She was once and truly effed up. She'd been a fool to think

she could do something useful, helpful, loving on her own. She'd screwed it up. She'd dangled hope in front of a defenseless child and now she couldn't stop it being snatched away. *Better not to have hoped at all.*

At five there was a knock on the door. Sarah had washed her face, put her cell phone in her pocket, ready to cope when Danny returned with Leila and document any bruises or skinned knees. But she wasn't prepared for what waited for her on the other side of the door.

Danny stood holding Leila straight out in front of him. Her face was tear streaked and she was whimpering. She was also filthy and reeked of urine, Her shorts were wet and stained brown.

Sarah stared, not taking in what she was seeing. Leila who she had sent off clean and neat was being returned to her wearing a dirty diaper. She hadn't worn diapers in over a year.

For an eternity Leila just dangled there between them, limp as a rag doll. Then Danny pushed her toward Sarah.

Sarah took her, but as she held her Leila screamed. No wonder, she had obviously been left in this foul state for hours. Her skin was probably raw from the uric acid and whatever else.

"What happened?" she asked Danny through gritted teeth. If she hadn't been in a hurry to get Leila cleaned up, she would have hit him.

"I don't know, they said she got sick and handed her to me."

"They? Who the hell is they?" Sarah used every piece of control not to yell the words at him.

"This guy DeShawn; I think she called him."

Leila wailed and wriggled to get down.

"This ends. Now."

Danny nodded jerkily. "I'm going to make my report. I think you were right not to want unsupervised visits."

"Too late now." Sarah slammed the door in his face. "Come on, baby, let's get you cleaned up."

"Leila bad," she whined.

"No, sweetheart. Leila's my precious girl. My forever girl." *And if I ever see Carmen again, I'll kill her with my bare hands.*

Sarah took Leila into the bathroom and set her on her feet, while she knelt and turned on the water.

"Tubby time?" she said quietly and smiled at Leila, who was no longer sullen—but the same unresponsive, almost comatose child she'd been when she'd first come to Sarah. All that work and building of trust and the promise of love erased in one damnable day with her mother.

In a just world, this would not be allowed.

She took out her phone. "Selfie," she said and fired off two shots. Put the phone on the side of the lavatory.

"Okay, let's get out of these icky clothes."

Leila just stood there, unmoving as a statue. Didn't help but didn't fight as Sarah pulled her T-shirt over her head. Sarah threw it in the corner of the bathroom to be documented.

She pulled her shorts off, and Leila squatted with a cry of pain.

"It'll be better soon," Sarah crooned while anger filled her heart to bursting.

The diaper was too small to begin with, probably left over from one of Carmen's six other children. It had leaked and Leila's legs were streaked with the overflow.

She took two more photos.

"Tubby time," Sarah sang again and lifted Leila into the tub, diaper and all. She pulled away the sticky tabs and carefully removed the diaper from between her legs.

Sarah documented the diaper then pulled it off Leila. It was filthy, and Leila's skin was red from not being changed. Sarah didn't even pretend to be taking selfies, willing her finger not to shake as she documented the state of Leila's skin. Turned Leila around and took more photos.

Another quick shot of the diaper, then rolled it up and threw it in the wastebasket; she'd get rid of it later. "Bye, poopy pee pee diaper," she said in a singsong. "Wave good-bye, Leila."

Leila just stood there shivering.

Sarah cleaned her off with wipes. Leila made an awful inhaling sound each time the wipe touched her. Sarah fought back tears. "Just a few more minutes and it will be better." She reached under the sink and got a pail that they used for washing hair and used it to pour water gently over the child's body.

Leila wouldn't sit in the water, so Sarah unstopped the tub and let the water run, while she held Leila with one hand and washed with the other.

"Owie, Mommee. Owie."

"I know, sweetheart. It won't be much longer."

Leila burrowed her head in Sarah's shoulder. Sarah tried to stay calm, emit love and peace, when all she wanted was to strangle the life out of Carmen Delgado.

Finally Leila was clean enough, and Sarah lifted her out of the tub, still clinging to her neck.

She staggered from being on her knees on the hard tile, but held Leila close. "I love you, sweet girl."

Leila didn't respond, not with movement or sound.

"I love you to pieces."

Nothing.

"You're my sunshine."

Leila let out an animal cry and clung to her.

Sarah wrapped her in a big fluffy towel, fumbled in the bathroom cabinet for some diaper rash ointment that she'd kept in case of emergencies, and carried her into the bedroom.

She laid Leila on the towel and lifted her feet. Just like when she was a baby. But now she was four, and she shouldn't have to go through this.

"Owie, Mommee, owie, owie!" She tried to push Sarah's hand away. But it had to be done.

And by the time Leila was covered in white ointment, they were both crying.

"Okay, done," Sarah said. Her words vibrated out as shaky as her nerves. She got out Little Mermaid underwear and a matching nightgown.

But when she tried to put it on Leila, she started kicking.

"Diaper. Diaper!"

"Lovey, you're a big girl; you don't need a diaper. You're fine. You're home now."

"Diaper! Diaper!" Leila kicked harder. "Diaper!" She choked and started coughing and Sarah became afraid. She picked her up.

"We don't have any diapers. Remember. You don't need diapers."

Leila threw her head back, and Sarah almost dropped her. She began screaming.

Sarah carried her to the closet, to see if maybe there was a diaper somewhere. There wasn't, nor in the bathroom cabinet. She thought about a towel or a pillowcase but knew it wouldn't work.

Leila continued to scream and flail until Sarah was afraid to put her down.

She did the one thing she didn't want to do. She called Wyatt.

At first he didn't answer and she thought for sure she would go to voice mail.

"Hello."

She could hear people in the background. "I'm sorry to bother you. But—"

"What do you need, Sarah?"

She couldn't tell if he cared or if he was exasperated. Leila let out a wail and began screaming "diaper, diaper," over and over. "I need diapers and I can't go out for them. She's out of control. Can you? I hate to ask. But I can't get out."

"I'm on my way." He hung up.

"Okay, baby, Wyatt's coming."

"No-o-o-o. You."

"He's bringing diapers."

"Leila bad."

"Leila's good. You're my sunshine."

Leila grabbed Sarah's hair with both hands.

Sarah bit back a cry. It startled both of them, and in the momentary confusion, Sarah took both Leila's hands in hers and held her close.

It was nearly twenty minutes before Wyatt knocked at the door. Sarah had stood at the window watching for him, holding Leila until her arms went numb. But when she tried to put her down, she started to cry again.

At least the diaper rash ointment had worked its magic so she was more comfortable.

Sarah opened the door with one hand. Wyatt stood there.

"Sorry it took so long, but I was out to dinner, then I couldn't find any toddler diapers, I hope these are okay."

He looked at Leila. "Is she sick? What's going on?"

Sarah didn't answer; she'd looked beyond him and saw the blonde standing on the sidewalk waiting for him. Caitlyn. Sarah's heart—what was left of it—crumbled away.

"I'm so sorry, I didn't realize. You should have told me. I couldn't think of anyone else."

Wyatt glanced over his shoulder. "Don't worry about it. I was glad to be able to help."

"Well, thank you. I'll come by the store and pay you tomorrow."

"Sarah, you don't have—"

"I'm sorry. Thank you." She closed the door on him.

Leila had fallen asleep on her shoulder and couldn't even appreciate the fact that Wyatt had hauled his date out of a restaurant to go look for diapers for someone else's daughter. It would be laughable if it didn't hurt so much.

Sarah considered trying to get Leila into bed without the diaper but when she laid her down, she started crying for her diaper again.

So she got one. "Wyatt brought these just for you. But only for tonight. Tomorrow we go back to big-girl pants. Now get into bed."

Leila grabbed her around the neck.

Sarah lifted her up and sat down in the rocking chair and began to rock, slowly , gently, wondering what tomorrow would bring. Wondering how long she could keep up this constant battle. She began to hum, then to sing, "You are my sunshine."

Sam had sung it to her, tongue in cheek, when she got upset, angry because she couldn't fix some part of a clock, or because someone hadn't treated her nicely. He'd sing it with that twinkle in his eye and it was so hokey—and so filled with love—she couldn't stay angry. She'd hold on to it as long as she could, and when she couldn't stay mad a second longer, she'd roll her eyes and give him a punch on the arm. Because she still couldn't say, you're my sunshine, too.

Finally she felt Leila's muscles go slack; she was asleep. But Sarah didn't relax; she knew that sleep might be ephemeral, and the nightmares might come. And someone, someone, had to sit vigil.

She went back to the living room, considered turning off the light, then noticed movement out the front window. She moved closer, immediately paranoid.

But it was Wyatt sitting on the porch rail. Alone.

She didn't stop to think but opened the door. "What are you doing here?"

"Checking up on you."

"I'm sorry if I wrecked your date."

"It wasn't really a date. Well, it was sort of a date. Oh hell, the girl kept bringing me chicken soup, and I felt like I had to do something to repay her."

"Well, I'm sorry if it didn't work out because of me."

"Really?"

She bit her lip. Shook her head.

"Come here."

She went to him. Leaned into him. "I'm a mess."

"Yep. You are. I know you're doing the best you can by yourself. But you don't have to be by yourself, and before you get all panicky, this is not a proposal, because then I would get all panicky."

That made her smile.

"But you have peeps."

"I know I do, but I don't know why you, any of you, put up with me."

"When are you going to give in to the fact that we all love you? Let us help."

"I try."

He held her close. She didn't realize she'd started to cry until Wyatt's thumb rubbed slightly at her cheek.

She began to relax; Leila started screaming.

"I have to go." She started inside.

Watt followed her to the door.

"Not tonight. Just . . . tomorrow, but not tonight." Tonight she needed to be alone. Not because she wanted to be, but there was something she had to do.

Sarah comforted Leila until she fell back to sleep, then took her cell phone to the kitchen. Opened her laptop and downloaded the latest photos from her phone. She arranged them into some kind of order, though the sight of them made her feel sick and heartsore. When she was finished, she attached them to an e-mail. Added a message and a subject line.

You did this. Can you live with yourself? And pressed send.

Chapter 27

Ilona carried her morning latte over to the window and looked out at the sea. Another sunny day. There were already bright umbrellas pitched across the beach below her. She never went to the beach, something left over from her system days, she guessed. They never walked to the beach in those days. She didn't know why. Maybe because it cost money to get on the beach, money they didn't usually have or if they did, it was spent on something else.

She couldn't remember what. She didn't do drugs. She knew what drugs did. She'd grown up with them all around her. Until she went to live with Aunty. Those had been the happiest few years of her life. Just a shotgun shack on the wrong side of town, but it had been home.

She stepped away from the window. What the hell was she doing thinking about those days? Any of the days before she came to live with the Cartwrights. It must be because of the funeral, because of the box sitting in the bottom of the coat closet, waiting to be opened or tossed out still taped shut.

It was her day off. She could deal with the box. It was as good a time as any. She turned her back on the sand and surf, put her latte on the glass top coffee table, and walked to the entranceway.

She stood at the door of the coat closet. Was she curious? She tried not to be.

Was she afraid of what might be in the box? Possibly. What if she opened it and the things that *Your mother thought you'd like to have* turned out to be a lie. Or what if it were the last cruel joke of the promise of love.

Ilona sighed. Then she picked up the box and carried to the coffee table, where it sat while she went to look for a utility knife to open it. She didn't come straight back but made herself another cup of coffee, then stood at the kitchen counter, drinking it while she checked her phone for e-mails. There were quite a few. Why did people e-mail lawyers on the weekend? Didn't they know that's when they got all their extra paperwork done?

On the other hand, maybe she should clear her cache before she opened the box. Because at this point she knew she was going to open it, and that she was going to think about it until she did.

She dropped the knife on the coffee table and went over to her desk to pull up her e-mail on her laptop. She started with her personal account, systematically deleting and archiving. Read a couple. Nothing that couldn't wait until tomorrow or the next day or week.

Moved onto her business account. Not so many there. She scrolled down, paused, scrolled the cursor back to one with the subject line *You did this*.

She automatically reached to delete it. Even though she was careful about her professional e-mail, there were always a few charities or crazies that slipped through. This one had an attachment. She never opened attachments from people she didn't know. She glanced at the sender address, *clockshop@* . . . She didn't have to read further to know who it came from. She pressed delete.

She continued to scroll down the page. What the hell was Sarah Hargreave e-mailing her about. Obviously a rant because Ilona had just screwed her. Not intentionally, she reminded herself. Just saw the facts and judged accordingly. This was not about Sarah and her, it was about a child who had no one to make sure she wasn't hurt.

Still.

She glanced over to the box sitting on the coffee table, back at the screen. Pulled the e-mail out of the trash and opened it.

This is the way my foster daughter, Leila Rodrigues, was returned to me after the unsupervised visit you encouraged. Wearing a diaper, a diaper she had been wearing all day because her bio mother couldn't be bothered to take her to a bathroom. She hasn't needed a diaper since she turned three. She'd been sitting in her own waste for a whole day and was chafed and raw and crying from the pain.

She called herself Bad Leila and became hysterical when I told her we didn't have diapers at home. Is this the way a competent loving mother would care for her child? Do you even know? Do you even care? Or were you just lashing out at me because of some vague slight you think I committed and for which I have no memory

of? Either way. You are responsible for this. You did this.
Can you live with yourself knowing the way Leila was
treated and knowing it will only get worse?

So she had a little diaper rash, thought Ilona. Sarah was always such a drama queen.

She started to delete the e-mail again. But her finger went to the attachment. A series of photos came up and the aftertaste of Ilona's latte turned sour in her mouth.

Was it possible she had misjudged the situation? She thought back. She'd read the latest files, but only scanned the earlier ones. Because really, it was current behavior that mattered, not the past.

She stopped, blinked. The past did matter. Sarah was accusing her of having an ulterior motive? She didn't. Ilona didn't have to work from revenge. She always worked from what was legally correct.

Or what she could win.

She hadn't even talked to the kid since becoming her lawyer ad litem—since requesting that she become her lawyer ad litem. *And why was that, Counselor?* Irrelevant. She wouldn't knowingly put the kid in harm's way. But she hadn't done much to learn what the kid wanted. Hadn't even talked with the girl, Leila.

And that, she had to admit, she'd done on purpose, to give her the element of surprise. And the reactions had been everything she'd hoped for and more. She'd intended to go in and ask for a postponement until she had time to study the case, but as soon as she walked in, she knew she had them. And Ilona, the barracuda, went in for the kill.

But only because there was no obvious reason for the kid not to visit her bio mother. It was a perfectly legitimate courtroom tactic. The judge agreed with her assessment.

He and Ilona had both spent their careers seeing through other people's emotions.

He'd appreciated that in Ilona. Everyone else had their own agendas. Even the social workers who needed to clear this case so they could get onto their next. They needed a success story to warrant their salaries, make themselves feel like they were doing some good.

Not Ilona. She just wanted to see justice served . . . *Words are cheap, Counselor.* Had she been just or had she let her own emotional entanglement make her decision?

God help her, she knew the answer. Ilona closed her eyes. Swallowed.

She might have misjudged Sarah; but worse than that, she'd misjudged herself.

SARAH INDULGED IN nearly two minutes of optimism when she heard Leila wake up and go into the bathroom. Before she was able to reach her, a wail of rage erupted from inside. The door was open and Leila had pulled down her shorts and seen the diaper. It must have confused her or brought back the memories.

Sarah knelt down and ripped it off her, tried to lift her on the toilet, but it was too late. She could only watch as Leila peed on the bathroom floor.

Sarah gritted her teeth to keep herself from screaming, too. "Oopsies," she said. She lifted Leila out of the mess and into the bathtub. The bathtub she'd stayed up late scrubbing, scouring away the evidence of a terrible day.

Déjà vu. She ran the water and put in the stopper. "Bubble bath?"

"I hate you!" Leila started flailing. Sarah just managed to snatch her out of the tub before she fell.

She carried her kicking back to her room. "Stop it now," she said and shut the door.

It took a few minutes, but Leila stopped crying and screaming that she hated Sarah.

Sarah sat at the kitchen table nursing a cup of coffee that she knew she shouldn't drink. Her nerves were ragged, she was exhausted, and for the first time ever, she wondered if she should just let Leila go. Had there already been too much irreparable damage? Did Sarah have the strength, the money, the time to nurture a troubled girl through to adulthood?

"Fix the now, stupid!" She buried her face in her hands. Now she was yelling at herself.

Fix the now. Life was just a series of nows. "So let's just get to fixing this now," she told herself and marched down to Leila's room. She was sitting on the floor trying to put on a diaper from the box Wyatt had brought over.

Sarah sighed and stepped inside. Stepped on a crinkle of paper. Pieces of torn brown paper were crumpled and strewn on the floor. Where Leila's watch-me-grow outline had been, now only four corners where it had been taped still held ragged scraps of paper.

"Oh, Leila."

Leila ignored her as Sarah dropped to her hands and knees and began gathering the pieces up.

"No." Leila crawled over and tried to tear the paper out of her hands. "Go away."

"I won't go away. I'm going to put your poster back together."

Leila glowered at her. Crossed her arms; huffed. "You shit."

"Well, I'm still going to put this back together. You can help if you want to."

Leila huffed and scooted around so that her back was to Sarah.

"Suit yourself." She carried all the pieces into the kitchen; dumped the torn pieces onto the kitchen counter, found a roll of craft paper in the workroom and several glue sticks in the craft drawer.

She cut a piece as long as the table and weighted it down with kitchen utensils. As soon as she spread out the first piece, she realized that she would have to iron the pieces flat again. She got the iron from the pantry, placed a dish towel on the counter, and plugged in the iron, careful to keep the cord out of reach of angry little hands in case Leila made an appearance.

She ironed each piece and stacked them neatly to be transferred to the craft paper. Then she unplugged the iron and pushed it to the back of the counter to cool.

And she got to work. Slowly the pieces began to form the figure of a little girl who had been so much happier a few weeks before. Now her child was just as torn and ragged as her poster.

She was two-thirds of the way through the repair when Leila silently padded into the kitchen and peered over the top of the table. Then she looked up at Sarah with eyes so sad that Sarah wanted to cry.

Sarah smiled instead. Leila reached up. There was a diaper in her hand. Sarah's hope plummeted. "No can do, sunshine."

Leila shook the diaper at her.

Sarah shook her head.

Leila made grunting noises and pushed the diaper at her.

"Leila, I'm sorry that happened with Carmen. It was a mistake, and it hurt you. But we want to go to the beach and see Bessie and Tammy and Jenny, don't we?"

Nothing.

"And you can't wear a diaper at the beach."

Leila's eyes narrowed and she clutched the diaper to her chest with both hands.

Sarah reached to rub her own aching back. "So when you're ready, we'll have a quick bath, breakfast, and put on our swimsuits."

Leila, still holding the diaper, reached for the edge of the table. At first Sarah was afraid she was going to grab the outline. But she just looked at it. Sarah picked her up. "See, good. as new."

Almost good as new, she prayed.

IT TOOK SOME doing: a fight over the bath, a fight over making her bed and using the potty, a fight over lunch and what DVD to watch while Sarah made a few calls even though it was Sunday. Of course no one answered, so she left messages for Danny and Randy Phelps, telling him he had to do something and to call her back. She checked her e-mail several times on the outside chance that Nonie e-mailed her back. But unsurprisingly there was nothing. She'd been stupid to think Nonie would bother writing now after having ignored her all these years.

A small relapse occurred when Leila insisted that her bathing suit would fit over the diaper. It wasn't until Sarah said, "You know, I don't really want to go to the beach today," that Leila finally gave in and let Sarah help her into a diaperless swimsuit. Maybe she would be sorry later, but right now she would accept any small victory.

Bessie, Tammy, and Jenny were waiting for them by the steps to the beach. Bessie jumping up and down squealing, "Leila, come see."

For a horrible long second Leila balked.

"Come on!"

And finally Leila began descending the steps as fast as her little legs would go.

Sarah held on to the back of her swimsuit until she was on the sand, then went back for the bag.

"You look like you've been through the ringer," Karen said.

"I have." Sarah sat in the vacant beach chair next to Reesa, who was actually wearing a swimsuit, though it was covered up by a beach robe that sort of defeated the purpose.

"Wyatt already came by and told us."

"He did? Is he guarding today?"

"Yeah, just for a couple of hours. He said he'd come by on his way home."

"Good. I need to thank him again. Seems like I'm always having to thank him for something. I had to call him to bring me diapers and I interrupted his date."

"What?" Karen lifted her sunglasses and leaned forward. "He didn't tell us that."

"He wasn't on a date," Reesa said.

Sarah nodded.

"Oh man, man troubles abound." Karen moaned and reached into the cooler and tossed Sarah a bottle of water.

"Not you and Stu?"

"Not today." Karen flicked her head in the direction of Reesa.

"What's up?" Sarah asked.

"In a nutshell . . . Michael moved out—"

"He left you?"

"He left; I didn't try to stop him."

"What's going to happen now?"

"I have no idea."

"But—"

"But there's more," Karen said.

"Good or bad?" Sarah asked warily.

"I gave notice," Reesa said. "After the Whites' hearing tomorrow, and the last of a huge pile of paperwork, I will no longer be employed at the CP&P office." She leaned over and patted Sarah's arm. "But I'm in for whatever you need concerning Leila."

They all looked out to where the three younger girls were throwing water-filled slinky balls at a plastic basket while laughing and falling down on purpose, and Jenny scanned the horizon . . . for boys?

"What are you going to do?" Sarah asked, turning her attention back to Reesa.

"I'm working as development director at Hands Around the World."

"Wow."

"And I'm going back to school."

"I bet they're really going to miss you at Child Protection."

"For a while. But it's time for me to move on and let younger, more agile and energetic workers take over. It won't be long before I'm a dim memory."

"Not to us."

"Thank you for that. And I'll still be doing goody-two-shoes stuff. I'm thinking school psychologist. That's what I was studying before I veered into social work. And it pays more."

"But what about you and Michael. Do you want to get back together with him?"

"Depends. We've been together for a long time, had three kids, probably will have grandchildren soon. He's always been a good man. Good enough, anyway. But I can't stand to be around the lump he's become. I doubt if he likes me much these days. It's not good for either of us. We both have to change. I'm on my way. I don't know that Michael can or even wants to."

"What a weekend," Sarah said and opened her water bottle. She lay back, relaxing in the sun, trying not to worry, trying not to be on edge waiting for the next shoe to drop. Really how many more shoes could drop at this point?

The girls came up for snacks and a few minutes under the umbrella. They had just been given another spray of sunscreen when they saw Wyatt walking up the beach.

Tammy and Bessie cried, "Wy!" And ran toward him. Leila followed after them.

"Poor guy, the girls just love him. All the girls." She lifted her chin toward Jenny who pulled down the leg of her two-piece and tried to look nonchalant.

"It's starting," Karen said. "Boy craziness."

Leila was close to Wyatt when she suddenly stopped. Then she screamed at the top of her lungs and ran in the opposite direction.

"What the—" Karen said.

Sarah was already up when Leila came flying toward her as if her life depended on it. She grabbed her and lifted her off her feet, looked to where Wyatt had stopped cold, the other two girls standing beside him looking toward Leila.

"It's Wyatt, you like him," Sarah said, but Leila was screaming too loud to hear her. She cast a frantic look back at Karen and Reesa. Reesa was immediately on her feet and came over to Sarah.

"Bring her over here and try to calm her." Reesa guided them back to the beach chair and held it while Sarah practically fell into it. Leila tried to climb over her.

Reesa knelt down beside her. "Leila. Stop it, now. You're safe. Stop it."

Leila just tried to bury herself between Sarah and the chair arm.

"Leila, sweetie," Sarah said as soothingly as she could muster. She was completely unnerved. Wyatt had never hurt Leila. He was the kindest, most understanding man that anyone could hope for. He played Candy Land, for Pete's sake. And he'd interrupted his dinner with Caitlyn to bring her diapers.

"Leila, stop crying." Sarah gave her a little shake. "Stop it now. Nothing is going to happen to you. I promise. Now stop it, you're going to make yourself sick."

But she didn't stop.

"What is that all about?" Wyatt asked.

Standing over Sarah, he did seem intimidating. As soon as she thought about it, he knelt down and reached over to tickle Leila's arm. "Hey, hokey-pokey girl. What's up?"

Leila peeked out at him and screamed. Wyatt looked taken aback; Sarah felt like she was drowning. How could she make Leila understand that nothing would happen to her? And after all the progress they were making, and the fun they had when Wyatt was with them.

"Leila," he said.

Leila screamed louder. Sarah began to worry that someone

would call the police, and that would be mortifying to Wyatt, who had done nothing wrong but befriend her and her foster daughter.

"Stop, Leila," Sarah said. "Enough is enough. Look at Bessie and Tammy. They don't know what to think. Just stop this nonsense now."

Leila didn't stop. Just bucked against Sarah until they both almost fell out of the chair.

"Wyatt, I'm sorry."

He shook his head.

"I think you better go."

He stood there looking down at her.

"Please."

He sucked in his breath. "Fine . . . fine." He turned and strode away. She watched him go. Watched him break into a run across the sand.

"Okay, he's gone, Leila. The man you wanted to be your daddy just left because you were mean to him. After he brought you those stupid diapers and did hokey pokey with you. He's gone."

"Daddy?" said Karen. "I'll take Leila. Go after him."

Sarah shoved Leila at Karen and started to run. She hadn't gone a hundred feet when she heard "Mommee!" behind her. Leila was trying to run across the loose sand. Her arms stretched out toward Sarah. Sarah turned to look for Wyatt, but already he was looking small and distant. She would never catch up with him now.

She started back, scooped Leila up. "Be quiet now," she said barely above a whisper. "You're safe. You're always safe with me."

"Sorry, I couldn't hold her," Karen said.

"She socked Mom," Jenny said. "There was no reason to do that. What's wrong with her?"

"I'm sorry," Sarah told Karen. "I'd better take her home."

"No. Stay," Leila cried.

"No. You can't behave properly. So we're going home."

She started to cry. Sarah tried to ignore her, but she was shaking with hurt, mortification, and sheer exhaustion. She was failing.

"No, Mommee. Stay."

"No. You hit Karen and me. You hurt Wyatt's feelings, and he's always been good to you. So we're going home where we can think about how we treat our friends."

Leila sat down in the sand. Sarah handed Reesa her beach bag and picked Leila up.

Reesa slipped the bag over Sarah's shoulder. "Can you manage by yourself?"

"I'd better start, hadn't I?" She turned to the others. "I'm sorry we ruined everyone's day." And she trudged over the sand to the stairs to the boardwalk, aware of the looks and the why-can't-she-shut-that-kid-up stares that followed her.

"WELL," KAREN SAID as she and Reesa watched Sarah's head disappear from view. "You don't think Wyatt . . . ?"

"No. But somebody from yesterday's visit scared her. And from her reaction to Wyatt, I bet there was a man with Carmen yesterday, possibly a tall muscular man. I've seen it happen more times than I care to remember. Still, Sarah needs to figure out how to nip this behavior before Leila understands that she can use it to manipulate Sarah and everybody else."

"I don't remember having that kind of trouble with Amy when I finally got her back."

"Probably because she was staying with your parents in a loving environment, and you visited her a lot. Leila has definitely been mistreated. I don't know about this expedited track or reunification. Six weeks isn't a lot of time for a mother to get it together and keep it together. It's hard enough when she's only got herself to worry about. This may be a question of too much too soon."

"I don't think Sarah or Leila can survive much more of this bouncing around."

"No. I think it's about time someone spoke to Carmen Delgado."

Ilona gave the box a cursory look as she paced before the window waiting for her call to Judge Whitaker to connect or go to voice mail. She would never, ever call a judge on a weekend if it weren't an emergency. This was an emergency.

"Hello, Judge Whitaker. It's Ilona Cartwright. I'm sorry to bother you on a Sunday, but something has come to my attention that I believe needs to be dealt with quickly."

"Ms. Cartwright, think nothing of it. What seems to be the problem."

"The Leila Rodrigues case. I'm the child's legal advocate if you recall."

"Of course I recall. I just wish I could see more lawyers of your caliber in family court hearings."

"Thank you, sir." He wouldn't be saying that for long after he heard her out.

"The birth mother was granted unsupervised visits last week. Her record is clean and all the team members involved were very pleased with her progress. And I concurred."

"Yes, I recall."

"Well, an unsupervised visit was paid yesterday and there are a few details concerning the visit that may or may not be significant but that are disturbing enough that I intend to file for a stay until we've had time to investigate further."

"Abuse?"

"Possibly. And questionable enough to stop further visits immediately until they can be substantiated, and either dismissed as within normalcy, or rectified if they aren't."

"I've got a full docket for the rest of the month and next. And we have to give both sides fair notification of the hearing."

"I realize that, Your Honor. And I mainly need a stay of visitation until we can be placed on the docket."

"Sounds reasonable, though I can guess the bio mother, what's her name, Delgado, will not be happy."

"Better one unhappy mother than a child put in jeopardy."

"True. Call my office in the morning. Have Priscilla draw up the forms for me to sign, then we'll send out notices of the stay in time to prevent the next visit."

"Thank you, Your Honor. I truly appreciate it."

"Not at all; enjoy the rest of your weekend." He hung up. She hung up, placed her cell phone carefully on the coffee table, and picked up the utility knife. It was time to face the contents of the box from her mother.

Ilona flipped open the knife, ran the blade evenly around the edges of the box, wondering if she'd be pleased with the things her mother had decided to keep. She lifted off the top, looked inside.

They were sitting on top. Held together by a rubber band. She recognized her own handwriting.

The room went out of focus as the words swam before her eyes. What were they doing in the box? Had they all been returned? Or . . . Had they never been mailed? Ilona lifted them out with a hand that wasn't her own.

Pulled at the rubber band. It was brittle and it snapped apart and flew across the table. There were a lot of them. June must have saved them all. But she'd never sent them.

A cry escaped from somewhere deep inside her. From a place that had been forgotten and should have stayed forgotten. Everything she knew, that she thought she knew, was wrong. She carefully placed the stack of envelopes on the table. They slid to one side, but Ilona didn't try to catch them.

Something else had her attention. Beneath where they had been was another stack of letters. A different handwriting. And she recognized that handwriting, too. It belonged to Sarah Hargreave.

Chapter 28

The first thing Monday morning, Sarah told Alice that she was closing the store for two weeks.

Alice was concerned, and Sarah had to reassure her that she and Leila were due for a vacation and once she understood that she'd still be paid, she gladly acquiesced. Sarah hung a sign to that effect, including a number where repairs could be picked up. Then she locked up and went home to the cottage—and Leila.

Sarah had no illusions about having any vacation. But she intended to enjoy Leila as much as the stress they were both feeling allowed. And she intended to face whatever would be when it came and not a moment before.

She was tempted to take the calendar off the wall, but that might be too unsettling. And might be futile, so she left it in place, hating the very sight of it.

She didn't go to the Brew or stop by Wyatt's store. Leila had calmed down considerably overnight. She seemed fine when

Sarah reminded her that school was over. No need to tell her that Sarah had taken her out, because it was just too much to have to handle. Besides, Leila could use a break, too.

After breakfast she put Leila in front of *Sesame Street* and called Randy Phelps.

"I was going to call you back," he said before he even said hello.

Sarah had no doubt he was sick of the case. Well, too bad. So was she. She explained about the Saturday visit and the subsequent events. Yes, she had documented everything.

"I'll see how soon we can get a hearing on the docket," Randy said. "But it's getting along in summer and a lot of people are on vacation."

"Just try. I don't want her being exposed to that kind of treatment again."

"Sarah, unless child services deems it a threat to her safety . . ."

"Well, it is a threat. Please do something."

She could hear his sigh even though she suspected he moved the phone away.

"Just try."

She called Wyatt to explain what was happening. Her call went to voice mail. She wondered if that was on purpose. And made herself accept the fact that maybe this time she had pushed him away for good.

She called Danny who was out on a call. She left another message.

She and Leila walked to the library and took back the books they'd checked out except for *Green Eggs and Ham,* which they renewed.

In the afternoon, they made cookies with funny faces.

It wasn't all fun. There were times that laughter dissolved into tears, and sometimes she looked at Leila and saw sheer terror in her eyes, and she'd try to soothe her, to make her feel safe in a world she couldn't control and that made no sense.

And every whimper, every scream, every kick, every scratch and "I hate you" cut to the quick. Hit that place inside Sarah where her own fear and anger were buried so deep that she sometimes forgot they were there. Forever residing within her.

When she'd been a kid, she blamed everyone around her, pushed them away when they got too close, because she knew what would happen. She'd get sent away, or they would show their true colors and hurt her, or turn their backs on her; so she did it to them first.

Now that she was on the other side of that life, she knew Leila's life would always be like that, too. Maybe not as bad because she'd been fostered since early childhood, but it still would be there. Because sometimes Sarah still felt the same way. But now she was the one who could help, who could love, and, if the system let her, could promise to be Leila's forever family. Like Sam who had taken in a girl off the street and become her forever.

Looking back on it, she wished she could go back and change some of the things she'd done. But then she wouldn't have found Sam, and without him, she knew she would have become just another hardened ex-foster kid, screwed up about her place in the world and afraid to let people love her.

Or she would have become a person like Ilona Cartwright. Hard, driven, and uncaring. Is that what happened to Nonie? Had it been too late when she was finally adopted and became a Cartwright to be able to accept their love. Had she just been too old?

Sarah looked over to Leila, sitting on the couch, legs stuck straight out in front of her, "reading" *Thomas the Train*. She was sucking her thumb . . . again . . . At least she'd stopped wearing the diaper.

Was Leila already too old to come out of this unscathed?

REESA SET UP her laptop on one of the tables in the front of the courtroom. She'd just received the strangest call from Ilona Cartwright. She wanted to talk to Carmen and she wanted to meet Leila Rodrigues, and she wanted Reesa to accompany her to both meetings.

A day late and a dollar short, Reesa thought. Or else the lawyer was planning something devious, something that a few months ago Reesa would never have thought Ilona capable of doing. Not until this last case.

She understood that Ilona and Sarah had unfinished business—"issues" as they called them today—and she also knew that people brought up in the foster system had a harder time overcoming some things. But the animosity between Saran and Ilona seemed extreme.

Reesa couldn't imagine what pain they must have felt as young girls. Were still feeling now.

So in spite of her reservations, Reesa made a date with Ilona for the next day. They could talk to Carmen on her lunch break at her work and then drive over to Sarah's to interview Leila. "Leila gets home from school around three," Reesa told her. "I'll have to call Sarah and tell her. It's not fair to just spring this on her."

"Of course," Ilona said, and Reesa tried to read between the lines. With no success.

Now Reesa shoved the conversation out of her mind as she

set up for the Whites' hearing. She didn't know when she'd finally decided to go with a PowerPoint presentation of the White emergency removal. Normally she would print out a few of the more pertinent photos and hand them in to the judge as documentation.

Maybe she had gone a little overboard during the preparation, revisiting that day through her photos, feeling the same horror and revulsion she held felt then. But she had a fire in her gut about this case.

That's why she'd decided to go with the slide presentation for her documentation, instead of passing around a handful of supporting photos that might be looked at quickly by a few of those involved, and then just as quickly be relegated to the evidence table. No one wanted to dwell on the reality. The reality could drive you crazy.

This way everyone would be forced to acknowledge what was going on all around them.

She was early. Only a few others had arrived at the courthouse. But the White hearing was first on the docket, and she was anxious to get it over with.

Over with. For her maybe—this was the last hearing on her bucket list before she left child services. For the boys it was a beginning, but for their teams there was just more of the same ahead.

She'd been in touch with Pete and Jerome's caseworker, Pete's therapist, and Jerome's and the baby's treatment teams. Pediatricians and psychologists. All three children had been appointed guardians ad litem. If the baby thrived, he would have a good chance of being adopted. But the older boys . . . Jerome might never have fully functioning kidneys, and it would take more than most families had to give to see him through. She just hoped they would find him a loving, patient home—hoped, but she didn't have much faith.

Reesa had no illusions about Pete's future. What that boy had been through had marked him for life. Maybe not physically, like his brother, but forever. She'd do what she could for him before she left the agency for good. And she had actually talked about him to one of the volunteers at Hands who had fostered several young boys. Reesa thought they might be a good match. She planned to take him by the center for a trial run just as soon as this case was resolved.

The courtroom began to fill. There were a lot of cases on the docket today and most everyone was ready to get on with it.

Well, half of them anyway, those caseworkers eager to wrap this up and get back in the field. The ones who still had the fire, the passion. And then there were the others who would gladly sit in the tepidly air-conditioned courtroom as long as possible before being pushed into the sometimes sweltering, sometimes squalid, sometimes dangerous investigations in the field.

Reesa guessed now she was one of the latter group. So be it. She was moving on.

Judge Whitaker entered and everyone rose to their feet and sat as soon as he sat. The bailiff announced the first case.

Reesa felt a wave of anticipation, determination, and just a little trepidation. This would be her last case. She wanted it to be successful on so many levels. She didn't see how the judge could fail to grant a permanency track for the three boys.

Then again, look at the problems Sarah was facing.

When Reesa was called, she repeated the details of her Dowd emergency removal. Her eyes kept wavering from the judge, stark in his black robe, but betrayed by his eyes—warm with sympathy and understanding.

"If I may, Your Honor. I've prepared a PowerPoint presentation that will be truer than what my memory might be."

"Proceed."

She walked over to the table on wobbling legs. Powered up the first slide.

"I left Pete downstairs with Ms. McKinney and took the stairs to the White apartment on the fourth floor. The police met me there."

She clicked on the first photo and flinched as the picture filled the screen. The two individuals sprawled on a sagging couch, surrounded by unspeakable filth.

Click. A close-up of beer, drugs, and drug paraphernalia.

Click. The living room. The kitchen. The doorway to the second room.

She slowed to let everyone get the full effect of the photos. At least that's what she told herself. But it was really to give herself time to prepare to relive those horrifying moments over again. Only today it would be even worse, because today she already knew exactly what she'd find.

"The room was dark and hideously hot. The smell was—" She swallowed.

Click. Jerome on the filthy bed, too weak to move.

Her hand was shaking so much she could barely click on the next photo. The crib filled with clothes.

The courtroom was completely silent except for her own breathing. Twenty years of triumphs and tragedies, successes and failures, and the faces of hundreds and hundreds of children and parents paraded through her mind.

"I found the baby underneath the clothes. He was unresponsive, but still alive."

She felt the courtroom exhale. It was her undoing. She managed to grab the back of a chair and sit down before she fell. Next to her one of the guardian ad litems took a tissue from her purse and handed it to Reesa. Used another for herself. And blew her nose.

Even Judge Whitaker looked stunned. Pete, Jerome, and Baby White had ceased to be just another docket number in a slew of docket numbers.

"The children were removed to the county hospital where Pete was given a full physical and psychological evaluation and checked into the hospital. Jerome and the baby were checked into critical care."

The testimony continued. The lawyers for the two parents put up a minimal defense. They were both in jail.

The judge ruled in favor for permanency for all three boys.

All those involved in the case were excused.

Reesa shoved the stack of papers into her briefcase. So much paperwork for such small boys. But today she didn't resent it. She knew as well as most, they hadn't found a better way to run the system. And in its way, the mountains of paper helped them cope with the brutality of their job.

But not for Reesa. Not anymore.

The parties involved in the next hearing exchanged places with those who had just finished, and who for the most part made their way up the aisle toward the coffee shop to wait for their next hearing.

She slid her laptop into her briefcase and lugged it up the aisle to the courtroom door.

A man was standing at the back and opened the door for her. She looked up to thank him.

It was Michael.

"Michael. What are you doing here?"

"I got a job. Temporary but a job. I called your cell, but you didn't answer."

"They're not allowed in the courtroom."

"So I called your work. They said you were here."

Reesa didn't know what to think or how to react. "I'm glad you found work, Michael. I am."

She stepped through the door and kept walking.

He caught up to her. "I didn't know. I'm sorry. I had no idea what you went through every day. I'm sorry."

Reesa kept walking. She was just so tired. She'd reached the street and stopped to wait for traffic to pass.

"I want to come home."

"No one is stopping you." She stepped off the curb and headed toward her car. She just wanted to get out. She didn't want to deal with Michael or the problems with their marriage. She needed to get to the center, no, she needed to go to the beach. Breathe the clean air. Feel the pull of the waves. Why did they never go to the beach?

"I know I've been an ass. I was hoping you'd forgive me."

"I quit my job, Michael. I'm not going back."

"You don't have to."

She stopped. Looked at him. "No, I don't. I don't have to do any of it."

"Including me?"

"Including you."

"What are you saying?"

"That this isn't about your not having a job or about the job I've had."

"Then what?"

Reesa took a breath. "The job thing is a part of it, but it just made me realize that it's about us, Michael, and has been for a while."

"But you could give us another chance."

"I could. But I'm not going back to what it was."

His brow furrowed. She did love him, had for a long time, but she'd just lost it in the other stuff. *But you might be able to find love again. It might be possible.*

"Just say you'll think about it."

"I'll think about it." And she walked away.

"Hey, Rees. Want to go for a walk on the boardwalk to-night? Maybe catch one of the concerts on the beach?"

Reesa stuttered to a stop. Turned around.

"I know you've been going to the beach. We could go there together."

The beach? A concert? Michael? "That would be nice."

"Pick you up around seven?"

"Okay."

He nodded, turned, and walked away.

Reesa watched for a second then headed for her car. Maybe there was hope for them after all.

THAT AFTERNOON RANDY called Sarah back. He was having trouble getting an information hearing scheduled. Like he reit-erated, judges were out of town, a lot of the social service people were taking a much needed break. He finally got something for the beginning of September. Until then they would just have to make the best of it.

Fine. Sarah just wouldn't turn her over to Carmen on the following Saturday. She'd say she had a temperature or some-thing. They couldn't expect the kid to go for a visit if she were sick. That might work for one visit, but probably not more than one. She could take them away—not run away.

Like Wyatt said, that would be hard on everyone, not to mention illegal. But they could drive to Cape May, or Florida for hell's sake. But she'd have to petition the court to be allowed to leave, and that would be more paperwork, and with so many people on vacation it would probably take weeks.

She began to get frantic.

WHEN THE MAIL arrived Wednesday morning, Sarah gathered it up without thinking, then she saw the official envelope. Her world turned upside down, and dread rose in waves of nausea up her body. What could it possibly be this time?

She tore open the envelope, like a bandage on a healing wound. Show no mercy, snatch the skin away when you pull.

It was a court order: a stay on the unsupervised visits. Sarah read it twice. Looked at the date to make sure it hadn't been lost in the mail for months and was out of date.

A stay on visits until the next hearing. Randy had come through, after all. She'd maligned him, and she should have trusted him.

She called to tell him so. "I just received a stay for the un-supervised visits. I don't know how you did it. But thank you."

"What stay? What are you talking about?"

"From Judge Whitaker."

"This is the first I've heard of it."

"You aren't responsible?"

"No."

Was it some kind of sick joke? Sarah looked at the paper again. It looked official.

"You haven't been sent a copy?"

"No. But my mail hasn't come yet today."

But then who? Danny maybe. But did he have the clout to get a judge to reverse his decision, even if only temporarily. Reesa? She might have the judge's ear. Could the judge have possibly done it himself, but why? He didn't know about the last Saturday visit. Maybe he had learned something to Carmen's discredit.

She didn't want to wish the woman ill, but Sarah had had enough. She'd been patient, she'd cooperated, now she wanted to be Leila's mother.

Well, whoever it was, she thanked the person with all her heart. Sarah and Leila had a reprieve, at least long enough for someone to investigate Carmen's most recent activity.

Sarah called Karen and told her the news. Then Reesa. But she had to leave a message because her call went to voice mail. She didn't even know who else to call. She wanted to call Wyatt, but she was afraid to welcome him into their lives again because it was just a momentary stay.

It wouldn't last. And she didn't think either of them could handle another rift. So she kept quiet and hoped he would drop by. He didn't.

Sarah imagined him diving with Caitlyn, who knew how to swim. Her hair probably didn't even look bad when it got wet.

So she didn't call. She just breathed a huge sigh of relief, stuck her tongue out at the wall calendar as she walked by. Then she went back and pulled the sticker off next Saturday's box and took Leila for ice cream.

Her phone rang while they were sitting at one of the tables outside the ice cream parlor. It was Reesa. Maybe she'd heard the good news.

"Hey. I guess you got the notice."

"What notice?"

"The stay from unsupervised visitations until another hearing is scheduled. I called to thank Randy for managing it, but he said he didn't. He couldn't even get an info hearing until the end of the month."

"Wow. That's interesting. That's great. I wonder."

"Wonder what?"

"Nothing. I just called to ask if it would be possible for Ilona Cartwright to meet Leila tomorrow? Around three when she gets home from school."

"She doesn't— Why does she want to meet her?" Sarah asked, suddenly suspicious.

"Because she's her legal ad litem. It's customary to do so. It is usually a good idea for her to get to know the child . . . and see how she's living. It could work in your favor."

Sarah doubted that.

"I'll accompany her, if you like."

Sarah considered. "All right, tomorrow at three. Oh, how did your hearing go?"

"Good; well, as good as could be expected. All three boys go on permanency. The baby might even have a chance of a decent life. Gotta run. See you tomorrow."

"Right." Sarah hung up. Maybe she should hurry home and clean. She stopped herself. Her cottage was clean enough. It was a good place to live, and she had a feeling no matter how much she scrubbed, Ilona Cartwright would make her own conclusions and they'd be based more on her hatred of Sarah than on any state the house was in.

STILL, THE NEXT morning Sarah cleaned house. She sat Leila down and explained how Reesa was bringing another lady over to say hello and that she would probably ask some questions.

She watched as Leila went from calm to wary.

Sarah took a breath. Dare she tell Leila she wouldn't have to go to Carmen's on Saturday? She was just on edge enough, just superstitious enough to be afraid that it would blow up in her face. She took the chance.

"And you can spend Saturday here instead of going to Carmen's. Would you like that?"

Leila narrowed her eyes at Sarah, and for a moment Sarah was afraid she was going to say she wanted to go. But the moment passed.

Sarah made sure Leila took a nap so she wouldn't be cranky and skittish when Ilona came, though the lawyer was enough to make anyone cranky. Sarah took the time to work on an old pocket watch that had been wound so tight that the mainspring had broken. *Wyatt's words.* Clocks broke when they were wound too tight, and so did people.

She pulled the jeweler's loupe over her eye and went to work. The repair went quickly and Sarah found herself reaching for Mrs. Bridges's violin clock. Sarah managed to realign the mechanisms so that they lined up correctly to the brass plate. She carefully screwed the mechanism to the plate, and it slid neatly into the cavity of the clock. Holding the plate steady with one hand, she secured it in place.

The doorbell rang. Sarah looked up. It was only 2:30. They were early. Damn. She quickly finished attaching the mechanism so that it would not shift until she could give it her full attention. With any luck Mrs. Bridges would have her clock back by the end of the week.

She turned off the work lamp, pulled off the loupe, and hurried to the front of the house. The bell rang again.

Leila was still napping. Damn. She would be shy and groggy when Ilona met her. Well, she'd have to offer them tea or something while she woke Leila and gave her time to be fully awake.

She opened the door. "Sorry, I was in the—"

"Where's my baby? Where's Leila?"

Carmen Delgado pushed past Sarah, stopped in the middle of the living room, and called, "Leila, Leila, honey, Mama's here. I've come to take you home."

"Carmen. You can't do this. You really need to leave." Sarah reached in her pocket for her phone to call 911, then realized it was on her worktable in the back room.

"I want my baby."

Carmen's words were slurred. She was either drunk or on drugs. Back where she started. And Sarah felt almost as sad for Carmen as she was relieved for Leila and herself.

Carmen started toward the bedrooms, but the drugs had made her cumbersome, and Sarah beat her to the doorway. She braced her hands on the doorjambs to bar the way.

"Carmen, listen to me. You can't take her this way."

"I want my baby."

Sarah felt Leila come up behind her and press her body into her side. "Go back to your room," Sarah said as gently as she could muster. Leila didn't move.

"Come here, baby. Mama loves you. We can go home, just come with me."

Sarah felt Leila's head shake; she started to tremble.

"Please, Carmen. You're scaring her. We can talk about this later."

"No talk. They sent me a letter. You're all against me. Come here, Leila."

Her slur was getting worse. Whatever drugs she was on were taking effect.

"Give me my baby." Carmen threw herself at Sarah, knocking her backward. Leila screamed and ran past Carmen. Carmen grabbed for her, but Sarah regained her feet and lunged to stop her.

Sarah knew Leila wouldn't be able to get out of the house. The doors were childproofed. From the corner of her eye she saw Leila veer to the left. Sarah knew where she was going. To hide behind Sam's chair.

"Bitch, you steal my baby."

"Carmen, you can't take care of her right now. You need to get yourself straight. You can visit anytime you want." She hoped to hell Leila wasn't listening to this lie. "I'll take really good care of her."

Carmen twisted out of Sarah's grasp. "Leila, get out here. We're goin' home."

Sarah could hear Leila whimpering behind the chair. So could Carmen.

She grabbed the back of the chair and dragged it out of the way. It toppled over, leaving Leila exposed.

"No!" Sarah cried. She rushed at Carmen. Carmen turned, her arm extended, and hit Sarah across her shoulders. Sarah flew back, her head cracked against the wall; she heard the tinkle of glass as a vase hit the floor and the world went black.

Chapter 29

Reesa and Ilona pulled into a parking space outside Sarah's cottage. They'd gone to interview Carmen first but were told she hadn't shown up for work that day. Her supervisor was pretty angry. The company had given Carmen a chance on the recommendation of the Child Protection and Permanency staff.

He was upset. Reesa was worried.

Ilona suggested they go to her apartment, but Reesa convinced her to go straight to Sarah's. They were a few minutes early.

"She may be at the bus picking Leila up, but if she hasn't left yet, it will give you a chance to talk to her."

Ilona nodded.

Reesa wondered what was going on.

Ilona had been particularly quiet since she'd arrived. Sure, the two of them had not parted on very good terms, but it wasn't like Ilona to hold a grudge. They'd had differences of opinion before.

Reesa had tried to talk about it and apologize for her own behavior though she didn't really mean it. And she didn't trust Ilona even today.

Reesa got out of the car, and Ilona reached into the back for her briefcase. Reesa didn't have hers today. Just as well, it would be her beast, to Ilona's beauty.

They went up the short walk to the cottage single file.

The minute Reesa stepped on the porch, she knew something was wrong. The front door was open. Sarah never left the door open.

She held out her hand to stop Ilona and stepped just inside the door. Sarah's favorite reading chair lay on its side, a shelf had been overturned, and broken glass was scattered at its base.

Sarah lay crumpled on the floor nearby.

"Sarah!" Reesa rushed to her, fell to her knees, and felt for a pulse.

Sarah groaned.

"Thank God."

Sarah's eyes opened, shut again. Flew open. "Reesa?" She tried to move, yelped, and fell back. "My head."

"I'll call an ambulance," Ilona said.

"No."

"Too late."

Sarah bolted upright. "Leila."

Reesa looked around. "She's still at school."

"No. She didn't go to school. I took her out for the last two weeks. Leila."

"She was here?"

"Yes. Carmen came. Oh God. Where is she?" Sarah struggled to get up.

"Stay put." Reesa motioned to Ilona. "Check the kitchen and the back workshop."

Feeling a dread that she thought she'd left behind, Reesa went to search the bedrooms. Leila's room was neat, just a couple of books on the bed, but no Leila.

She checked the bathroom, calling Leila's name. She could hear Ilona calling from the other side of the cottage. When she went back to the living room, Sarah had somehow gotten to her feet and was leaning up against the wall. She saw Reesa and staggered toward her.

"We've got to get her back. Carmen took her. She was high and getting higher. She kept saying 'I want my baby.' I tried to reason with her . . ." She trailed off, put a hand to her forehead, which was bleeding into her eye.

Reesa uprighted the chair and sat her down.

"No. I have to find her."

"Ilona has called the police. They'll find her. Sit here and let me get some ice for your head."

"But I have to."

"We will, but you can't do anything in this condition."

Reesa passed Ilona in the kitchen. And for the most bizarre moment, she wondered if Ilona had orchestrated this. She shook the thought from her head. She needed to stay rational. God knew Sarah wouldn't be.

She got ice from the fridge, dumped it into a plastic bag, and wrapped it in a towel.

When she got back, Ilona was leaning down in front of Sarah, holding her hand. Reesa did a double take; she didn't get that woman at all. "Here." She handed Ilona the ice. Reesa heard the siren and she went outside to meet them.

They all arrived at once, EMTs, two squad cars, and a fire

truck. Before they got out of their cars, the sidewalks began to fill with curious people, residents and tourists.

"Inside, in the living room, possible concussion," she said to the EMTs, then stayed to accompany the police inside. She identified herself and explained about the possible kidnapping. "We searched the house, it's the only explanation. The bio mother came and wanted her child. We're pretty sure she kidnapped her."

The officer blew out air. "Can you describe her?"

"Her name is Carmen Delgado, she's about five four, one hundred sixty-five pounds, a known drug addict, who we thought had been rehabilitated. According to Sarah over there, she was back on drugs and demanding her daughter."

"And she's responsible for Ms. Hargreave's injury?"

"Yes, that is my understanding."

He looked past Reesa to the doorway. "I'm sorry, sir, you can't—" His expression changed. "Wyatt. You have an interest here?"

"Two interests." Wyatt said no more, just strode across the room and knelt down by Sarah.

She started to cry.

"I heard the sirens. What happened? Sarah"—he said it sharply enough to make Reesa and the officer turn toward him—"pull yourself together and tell me what happened."

"So that's Sarah," the officer said and left Reesa to listen to what Sarah was saying.

Reesa followed him over, glad that Wyatt knew so many people in town and that he was well respected. He might get them to move faster on finding Leila.

The EMT had bandaged Sarah's head. But when he tried

to put her on a gurney to take her to the hospital, she refused. "Don't ask me to go. I have to find her." She was looking at Wyatt.

He motioned for the EMT to step away. After a brief discussion, the EMT returned with a form for Sarah to sign, then they left, taking an empty gurney with them.

"I told them I would be responsible for you. So I'm sticking to you like glue. No arguments."

The police officer in charge came over to Ilona. "And who are you?"

She told him. He exchanged looks with Wyatt. "You sure fly in high circles," he said under his breath.

"Do you know what kind of car this Ms. Delgado drives?"

No one did.

"I know she takes the bus to work," Reesa said. "I wasn't aware that she had a car."

"Probably borrowed. And you didn't see it?"

Sarah shook her head, winced.

He took some more information, sent another officer to run identification on Carmen and with orders to send another unit to Carmen's house.

"But if she's not back yet, and she sees them, she won't go home. And we'll never find them."

"Yes, we will," Wyatt said.

"I'll send an unmarked to check on it." The officer took everyone's cell numbers, including Carmen's, which Ilona had because she had brought her files with her. He told Sarah to call him if she heard anything and left.

Sarah pushed to her feet.

"Where are you going?"

"To find my keys."

"Wait here. I'll get my Rover. You're in no shape to be running around."

"We'll never get her to sit still," Reesa said. "Get her some water. We'll take my car."

"Somebody needs to stay here in case Carmen comes back."

Wyatt and Reesa turned to look at Ilona.

"Not me. You may need legal advice. I'm coming, too."

Reesa frowned, nodded. And reached for her phone.

Wyatt and Ilona began helping Sarah outside.

Reesa caught up with them at the car. "I called Karen, and she's on her way over. She'll man the phones here, and in case Carmen returns, there will be someone Leila knows. The police will leave someone to watch the house. She'll be perfectly safe."

They settled Sarah in the front seat, and Wyatt and Ilona climbed in the back.

CARMEN LIVED IN a complex of cheap apartments subsidized by the government for people on their (hopefully) way up. They gave a nod to home life by being designed like little box houses attached like paper dolls.

Wyatt scanned the street. "Which one is hers?" he asked.

Reesa pointed it out. The neighborhood was marginal at best, but all seemed quiet for a change.

As they watched, two men in shirtsleeves walked out from behind the complex.

Wyatt leaned forward. "Cops."

"Yeah, I recognize one of them," Reesa said. "They do a lot of work for family services."

"They didn't go inside?" Sarah said. Her voice sounded weak to Reesa. She hoped Wyatt knew what he was doing by not insisting Sarah go to the hospital.

"Not without a warrant or probable cause."

"Kidnapping is probable cause," Sarah said.

"True, but it doesn't look like anyone's home. They'll leave an unmarked to watch the place."

The cops walked to the street.

Sarah reached for the car door.

Reesa held her back.

"I just want to ask them."

"You're a civilian and they'll send you home. Is that what you want?"

Sarah sat back and looked around to Wyatt.

He nodded confirmation.

The unmarked pulled away.

"But hello." Reesa rolled down her window as a skateboarder whizzed by them. "Bobby Carter. Hey, Bobby!"

The kid flipped his board and skated back. Then he saw Reesa, and came to a stop before turning again and taking off.

"Damn," Reesa said. "He thinks he's in trouble."

Wyatt was out of the car before anyone could stop him.

"God, don't hurt him," Ilona exclaimed from the backseat.

Reesa sighed. "Sorry. I scared him. I know him from his foster days. He probably thought I was going to pick him up."

The three women watched as Wyatt ran after the skater, calling his name.

"What's he doing?"

"I don't know," Reesa said.

"I hope he's not planning on physical force," Ilona said.

"Shh," Sarah and Reesa warned.

Wyatt caught up to the boy and ran alongside him until the skater stopped and flipped his board up to his hand.

Wyatt nodded in the direction of Carmen's apartment. The kid shrugged. Wyatt said something. The kid looked around. Wyatt moved in front of him, blocking him from view of the street.

A minute later Wyatt walked nonchalantly back to the car. The kid dropped his board and skated away.

"What was that about?" Reesa asked. "Did you buy drugs from that kid for information?"

"Didn't have to," Wyatt said. "I sell diving and surfing equipment, but I keep spare skate parts for the local kids. I didn't recognize him until you said his name."

"What did you find out?" Sarah asked.

"Carmen's been seeing a dealer, street name Hatch. Real name DeShawn."

"That's him. Oh God, we have to find her."

"Did he know where we can find this Hatch person?" Ilona asked.

"He lives in the projects. I don't have a last name, but the police should be able to run him pretty fast." Wyatt was already on his phone to his buddy on the case, asking him to run a check on DeShawn, street name Hatch.

Sarah was looking at him like she had just had a revelation. "Thanks. You're amazing. You all are."

Reesa pulled away from the curb.

"Where are we going?" Ilona asked.

"The projects," Reesa said. "No arguments."

No one said anything for the next few minutes, but when they turned down Quincy Street, Wyatt leaned over the seat.

"You let me out and keep driving down to the end of the block and wait. I'll see what I can find out. But I don't want you or . . ." He flicked a look toward Sarah. "Around if there's trouble."

Reesa slowed down. Wyatt jumped out. So did Sarah.

Reesa stopped the car.

Wyatt grabbed Sarah as she reached the sidewalk. "Dammit, Sarah, get in the car."

"No. I'm going with you."

"Then so am I." Reesa swerved to the curb and stopped in front of a fire hydrant. She turned to Ilona. "Think you can drive this old heap to the corner?"

"Me? I can, but I won't. You're not going in there without me. God knows what kind of trouble you all will get into."

"Hell, I do this all the time."

Ilona opened the door. "Are you gonna sit here talking or are you going to save that child?"

"Well, hell." Reesa jimmied her CP&P card out of her purse, scribbled Dowd removal, and slapped it on the dashboard. She locked the car, not that that would stop anyone wanting to get in, and followed Ilona, who was already running up the sidewalk as fast as her lawyer shoes would let her.

Ahead Reesa could see Sarah and Wyatt talking to someone who pointed toward one of the doors. Reesa hurried toward them, praying this would not turn out to be a tragedy of déjà vu.

Wyatt and Sarah entered one of the buildings. Reesa and Ilona rushed to catch up, but the door swung closed before they could get there.

"Damn," Ilona said. "Now what do we do?"

Reesa yanked on the door. It opened. The lock was broken—they always were.

Reesa barreled inside, not the smartest move, but she was beyond caring. She heard Ilona gasp as they came to a stop in a dank, fetid hallway. "If you're going to be sick, go outside and wait across the street."

Ilona shook her head but put her hand over her mouth and nose.

The hallway was empty, except for the smell. Reesa took the stairs to the second floor, Ilona clattering up the stairs behind her.

She reached the next floor and saw Wyatt and Sarah at the far end. Wyatt was knocking on the door, yelling Hatch's name.

"Open up now. I want the kid."

Reesa ran toward them, rummaging for her identification. "Child Protection!" she yelled through the door. "Open up!"

No answer. But she knew they were there. She knew it to the very core of her being. "Open this door, or I'll have to call the police."

No answer. Sarah started banging both fists on the door.

Wyatt pulled her away, then pushed her toward Reesa in a move that made them stumble backward.

He took a few steps back and kicked the door in.

It came away in a screech of hinges and screws.

For a nanosecond the three women stared, then Sarah broke for the door.

"Where is she? So help me—"

A man appeared through the doorway to another room. He staggered toward Sarah.

Wyatt grabbed him by the shirt front. "Where's the kid?"

"Yo, man . . ."

The guy was big, but Wyatt lifted him off his feet and shook him like a rag doll.

"Where?"

"Don't know what cha—"

Wyatt tossed him halfway across the room where he hit the wall and slid down to the floor.

Sarah called Leila's name and began searching the room, looking behind chairs, throwing pillows.

Wyatt ran into the back room.

Ilona took the closet and bathroom.

Reesa was dimly aware of the police arriving, cuffing the perpetrator. And still no Leila.

A scream from Sarah. They all rushed toward the kitchen alcove where she was kneeling on the floor. And Reesa prayed they weren't too late.

Leila was tied to the table with a bungee cord. Sarah was on her knees, frantically trying to untie the cord.

Wyatt moved Sarah out of the way and began checking for vital signs.

Leila didn't move. Reesa felt herself crying and didn't even try to control herself. She just kept praying *please, please, please.*

"Wyatt," Sarah pleaded.

"Shh. Call 911," he called to the cops.

"Already on their way."

"Is she dead?" Sarah whispered, her voice a mere scratch.

"She's still breathing, but slowly."

Sarah lay down on the floor beside her. "You'll be all right, now. I'm here. Your mommee is here." She cradled Leila, quietly crying and humming to the child that lay so still, and Reesa was afraid this time she had really failed.

She stared at the back of Wyatt's head as he checked Leila's vital signs. Felt Ilona moving toward the other room. Heard Sarah humming softly as the tears rolled off her cheek onto her child.

And Reesa couldn't move.

Finally, finally, the EMTs arrive.

Wyatt glanced over his shoulder. "I think she's been drugged." He moved out of the way.

Sarah didn't object when he pulled her to her feet. She seemed to know Leila was in good hands. She didn't seem aware of Reesa at all when Wyatt passed her off so he could free Leila from the cords. But as soon as the EMTs lifted her onto a gurney and started oxygen, Sarah stepped forward.

"I'm her mother."

The EMT nodded and let her follow them down the stairs.

"Go with her," Wyatt told Reesa. "I'll come when they finish up here."

Reesa nodded and handed him her keys.

He took them. "I hope your car is okay. You might have a ticket." He tried to smile but didn't manage it.

"If she does, I'll take care of it." Ilona didn't even try to smile. Reesa had a feeling she meant every word.

"Go," he said and turned away.

SARAH AND REESA were sitting in plastic molded chairs in the hospital waiting room when a doctor came down the hall, stopped, looked around, then walked over to them.

"Ms. Hargreave?"

"Yes."

"She was given Benadryl," the doctor said. "She'll be fine once it's out of her system."

And she's out of the system, Sarah thought.

"We'll keep her overnight, maybe a day or two just to monitor her vital signs."

"Can I see her?"

"She's sleeping, but of course. Nurse Taylor will see you down."

Sarah followed the nurse down the hall to Leila's room and stopped in the doorway. Leila was in a modified bed, with side bars all the way around it. She looked small and scarily unmoving, hooked up to a battery of monitors and IVs. And there was just one other bed, empty, in the room.

"I didn't pay for a semiprivate room."

The nurse smiled. "Don't worry. We happen to have extra beds for the moment."

Sarah tiptoed to the bed and looked back at the nurse.

"Just don't jiggle her tubes."

Sarah bit her lip to keep it from trembling, nodded her understanding.

"They look intimidating, but really they're just there to help. She's breathing on her own, but we're keeping her on a steady flow of oxygen just to make breathing easier. The IV is simple fluids, and those round things monitor her heart." She pointed to a screen with green lines. "I can be down the hall and know exactly how she's doing. So don't worry. Oh. She may have a little sore throat when she wakes up, from where we administered medication. Just tell her she gets to eat ice cream."

Nurse Taylor, Natalie according to her name tag, pulled a chair next to the bed. "Just use the call button if you need anything."

"Thank you," Sarah managed and sat down. She reached to touch Leila's little hand, gently traced her finger down Leila's fingers. She didn't stir. She didn't move. Only the blipping of the monitors told Sarah she was still alive. *She's going to be fine, she's going to be fine.* She kept repeating the phrase over and over, willing herself to believe it.

It had been so close. They might not have found her if it hadn't been for Reesa and Wyatt knowing that skateboarder. Sarah smiled slightly. How weird was that? And she could swear she heard Sam chuckling. He always did enjoy serendipity, and the skateboarder definitely qualified.

"Hey, sunshine. Mommee is here." And she began to hum.

LATER—MINUTES OR HOURS, Sarah didn't know which—Reesa poked her head in the door. Sarah motioned her in.

"Everyone is still in the waiting room," she said barely above a whisper. "You wouldn't believe I brought out my CP&P ID, since no one has taken me off the roster yet. Ilona identified herself as the advocate ad litem."

"Nonie's here?"

Reesa nodded.

"What does she want? Why did she come with us to look for Leila? Is she going to take her away?"

"No. No. She's the one who got the stay from Judge Whitaker."

"Nonie?"

"Yes."

"I don't understand. Why would she do that?"

Reesa shrugged. "I have no idea. Maybe she had a change of heart."

"And Wyatt? He broke the door down."

"Yeah," Reesa agreed. "He's still a little pumped. Whew. I've never seen him so intense. And a bunch of people on staff know him, and others shop at his store. We have our own little waiting area, and people have been bringing us coffee and stale donuts."

"You don't have to stay."

Reesa laughed. "Would you stop it? Karen said you'd say that."

"Karen's here?"

"On her way over. She said to tell you three words."

Sarah braced herself.

"We're all family."

Sarah's face crumpled.

"Oh, honey." Reesa put her arms around Sarah's shoulders. "Sorry."

"Don't be. I've already shed a few myself."

They stayed that way, Sarah seated and Reesa standing over her, her arm around Sarah's shoulders. *Like a family portrait,* Sarah thought.

"Did they tell you when she would wake up?"

Sarah shook her head. "I'm not leaving."

"No. You can have the extra bed."

"And I'm not giving her back to Carmen, no matter what."

"No, I don't think they will allow her even visiting rights after this. She left Leila with a known drug dealer. One of them or both gave her drugs to keep her quiet, endangering her life. No. I think we don't need to worry about Carmen anymore. If we ever find her."

"She's gone?"

"Let's just say she hasn't returned. When she does, it will be to a warrant for her arrest."

Sarah jerked. "What if she comes here?"

"She won't get past Wyatt."

"He doesn't have to stay."

"I don't think you have a choice about that. But I'm going to leave now. I called Danny Noyes. I want to write up my report and send it over to him. Get this show on the road, now that we have a catalyst." Reesa looked over to Leila and shook her head. "You'll be okay?"

Sarah nodded. "Thanks. I will." They both would be.

Chapter 30

Sarah spent the night in the extra bed, and slept well, knowing Leila was in good hands.

Leila woke around dawn and called for her mommee and Sarah was there, the way it should be. The nurse appeared seconds later, but Leila had already dropped back to sleep.

"Perfectly normal," the nurse assured her. "The residual drug is working its way out of her system. Your husband left earlier. He said to tell you he was going home to shower and change and he'd be back."

Sarah frowned at her. Her husband. Wyatt? She started to tell the nurse he wasn't her husband.

"And I think you should take the opportunity to do the same. Shower at least. There's a package of toiletries in the bathroom."

Sarah had a hard time leaving Leila, but finally she brushed her teeth and took a quick shower. And when she came out of the bathroom, she smelled coffee.

Wyatt was sitting in the chair holding Leila's hand. Sarah's first thought was to move him away. What if she woke and was afraid of him. What if—

He'd just saved her life. Sarah would make sure she knew what he did for her.

Reesa was sitting in the extra chair, reading the paper and drinking coffee from a cardboard cup. Another cup was sitting on the table. "Thought you might need a real cup of coffee."

"Oh, I do. Thank you." Keeping one eye on Wyatt, she moved over to the table. She looked a question at Reesa.

"He's great with her," Reesa whispered.

Sarah cut a look at Wyatt. He *was* great with Leila. She took her coffee over and kissed him on the cheek. "Thanks. For everything."

THEY WERE DRINKING coffee and watching Leila sleep when there was a knock at the door.

Ilona Cartwright stuck her head in the door. Sarah bobbled her coffee and barely managed not to knock it over.

"Come in," Reesa said and stood up.

Sarah cast a quick wary look in Reesa's direction.

"I'll be outside." Reesa reached for her bag and coffee and started toward the door.

Sarah grabbed her arm and held her back. But she didn't take her eyes off her old friend—more recent nemesis—and wondered what the hell was going to happen now. She braced herself for the worse.

"Reesa said you're the one who got the stay on the visitations to Carmen."

Ilona nodded. "I thought I was helping. I'm afraid I just set Carmen off." She was looking less than put together this morning. Tired.

"Thank you," Sarah said with effort. She wasn't sure she should trust her. "It might have been worse if you hadn't. Who knows what would have happened if they'd had her for a longer time before we found her. But—she looked toward the bed—"she's still sleeping. You don't need to talk to her?"

"No, I need to talk to you."

Across the room, Wyatt stood and walked toward them, but stopped just a little ways off.

Sarah swallowed. Wary. Ready to strike out or do what she had to do.

"Not talk exactly, but I brought something I want you to see." Ilona looked quickly around, saw the hospital tray by the bed, and rolled it over to where Sarah had been sitting. She opened her briefcase and pulled out two stacks of envelopes, which she placed on the table. There were a lot of them.

"What are those?" Sarah asked.

"They were in a box that was sent to me after my adoptive mother died last week. When I opened it, I found these. I was bringing them to show you yesterday." She nodded toward the stacks. "Take a look."

Sarah did, warily. Blinked. Looked again. One stack was addressed to Nonie Blanchard and written in Sarah's handwriting. The other stack was addressed to Sarah.

"I don't understand."

"She never mailed mine, and she never let me see yours. See?" She turned them over, spread them out in two lines. All were still sealed.

Sarah held out her hand as if to touch them, pulled it back. "All these years . . ."

Ilona nodded. "I thought you had deserted me."

"I thought you had betrayed me."

Reesa took Wyatt by the elbow and they quietly left the room.

Sarah turned over the letters she had written so many years ago. Ran her finger over the printed "Nonie" on the first few. The loopy script of the rest. So many letters. All gone unanswered, not because Nonie didn't miss her. But because she never received them.

"Why did she do it?"

"I think she was trying to protect me. I always resented her. I didn't think she loved me. Maybe she didn't, or maybe she did and didn't know how to express it. She didn't want me going back to the old neighborhood. She was afraid I would backslide, get into trouble if I 'consorted' with my old friends." Ilona shrugged. "She was probably right." Her voice wavered. "I wish she hadn't done it."

A whimper from the bed drew their attention.

"Mommee."

Blinking furiously, Sarah rushed to Leila's bedside. "Hey, sunshine. Are you feeling better?"

"Mommee?"

"I'm here, sweetie. Everything is fine. You're safe. I'm never going to leave you." She turned to call Nonie over, but Nonie was gone. And half the letters were also gone. "Just a sec, baby." Sarah ran to the door, looked out. Nonie was just getting into the elevator. The doors shut.

Sarah went back inside and gathered up the remaining letters. All were addressed to her. Was she supposed to read them? Why did Nonie take hers and leave? They could have read them together.

"Mommee."

"Coming." Sarah gathered up her letters, and she was hit

with a bolt of understanding. Once she had accepted the fact of the letters, Sarah had really expected to read the letters together. She knew it would be emotional, traumatic, embarrassing maybe, but she'd been willing to share Ilona's discovery of the letters.

Wow. A big step for Sarah. Willing to let her once best friend, now a stranger, see her at her most vulnerable.

But maybe Nonie wasn't ready for that. Maybe what her letters said would not bring them closer together.

"Mommee."

"Coming." Sarah carried the letters to the bedside, wondering where they would go from now.

She would read the letters that Nonie wrote to her, and hopefully Nonie would read the ones Sarah sent her. Nonie might decide to walk out of her life again. Or they might get to know each other again. They might even become friends again.

There was a knock at the door, and Reesa stuck her head in. "Can we come in?"

Sarah nodded and felt the beginning of a smile. A big, heartfelt unguarded smile.

Reesa came in followed by Wyatt.

A cry from Leila, and Sarah's bubble of euphoria burst. She stepped between Leila and Wyatt. "I'm sorry, Wy. She just needs a little time to get used to you again. She doesn't know that you saved her life. Can you please give us one more chance . . . but later?"

Wyatt ignored her. Walked past her to the bed.

"Wy—"

Reesa stopped her. "Look."

Wyatt stood over Leila looking like a frightening colossus. Sarah tried to pull away and stop him. But Reesa held on.

Leila held up her hand, so small.

"She's afraid."

"Let him try."

Leila said something, stretched out her hand.

Wyatt leaned closer. "What?"

Leila mumbled something.

Sarah wrenched away from Reesa, ready to push him out of the room.

But Wyatt laughed. Softly, hardly more than a breeze.

He took Leila's hand, so gently. Her tiny hand disappeared in his. "High five, baby girl."

ILONA SAT AT her dining table, a glass of cabernet at her elbow and the stack of Sarah's letters organized by date. She'd originally meant for them to read the letters together, but she chickened out at the last minute.

Yes, Ilona Cartwright, barracuda lawyer, was afraid that she might embarrass herself in front of her oldest friend—her sister. Because they were no longer friends, and they were never really sisters.

She picked up the first envelope. Took her letter opener and with a bit of effort managed to get it under the flap. Sliced a line up the fold, then put the opener down and looked at the opening. At the folded paper inside.

She could stop now. Go on with the life she had lived as Ilona Cartwright. But if she opened it, accepted the missing link that lay before her, she knew she wouldn't be able to go back.

Ilona pulled out the paper, unfolded it . . .

Dear Nonie,

*I know it hasn't been a whole week, but I miss you al-
ready. I'm hanging tough like you said. I hope you like your
new home. Maybe they'll want another girl. I hope so.*

Your sister,
Sarah

Ilona folded the letter, placed it carefully back in the envelope. Reached for the next one.

SARAH AND WYATT brought Leila home the next day. She was
clingy and cried as memory came back to her. She kept touching Sarah's face.

"Mommee hurt?"

"No, sweetheart. Just a little owie. I'm fine. Everything is
fine."

"I want to stay home."

"You will. You're my forever girl." Sarah mentally crossed
her fingers. She knew it wouldn't be easy. There were lasting
scars even at this age. But she was ready to deal with them for
as long as it took.

The questions was, was Wyatt?

She'd read Nonie's letters to her and she'd cried for both of
them. One girl left behind, the other torn from the only friend
she had. Sarah began to understand how lucky they both were
to have survived their youth and to have found each other
again.

Or had they?

A WEEK PASSED.

Reesa called to say the police had picked up Carmen wandering the streets, unresponsive to questions. She was taken in for psychiatric evaluation. Sarah tried to be sympathetic but she just felt relief. They'd had a reprieve and if they had to go to court again, maybe she could convince Nonie to take their case.

Sarah reopened the store and finished the repairs on Mrs. Bridges's violin clock. Jenny returned to her babysitting routine. And except for an occasional burst of anger or fear, Leila began to settle into life again. The two of them pulled the calendar off the wall. They would get a new one for fall. One, Sarah hoped, without visitations.

Leila didn't go back to school. She'd enter pre-K in September. That was soon enough. Until then she'd be returning to her regular therapy sessions, and they would continue their Mommy and Me swimming lessons.

She and Wyatt hadn't discussed the future, but he was definitely becoming even a bigger part of their lives.

Sarah hadn't heard from Nonie. She hadn't tried to contact her. After she'd read all her letters, she realized that Nonie hadn't had the cushy life Sarah had thought she had. Oh, she lived in a big house and went to a fancy school. But she didn't have love.

Sarah had been the really lucky one; she didn't have a big house, but she'd had Sam and he was worth the world.

Maybe Nonie didn't want to get to know her now. Maybe her pain just ran too deep. That would make Sarah sad, but she'd respect Nonie's decision. Maybe one day she would change her mind. Until then Sarah would just have to play wait and see. Over the last few years she'd become good at it.

Sunday, she and Leila put on their swimsuits, Wyatt picked them up, and they met the others at the beach.

Karen and Jenny were sitting in two of the chairs. More chairs were set up, more chairs than usual, and Sarah wondered who they were for. Sarah sat in one, while Wyatt went over to help Stu with a big cooler he was lugging toward the umbrella.

"I'm hoping Reesa and Michael are coming," Karen said, explaining the extra chairs.

"I thought he left."

"They're dating," Karen said, and after a struggle, she broke into laughter.

"Forget it," Stu said, positioning the cooler under the umbrellas. "We have too many carpools to think about dating."

Karen smiled smugly. "We'll see."

The girls surrounded Stu and Wyatt begging to go wading. "Mommee, come on."

Sarah immediately tensed. She'd gotten in the pool, and she'd learned to love the beach, but she still hadn't walked in the ocean. Wyatt stood looking down at her, then reached out his hand. "I'll hold on to both of you."

Reluctantly, but with a vague excitement, Sarah let him pull her up. The girls ran ahead with Stu. Wyatt let Sarah take her time. And then suddenly her feet were in the water, the waves rolling over her ankles without warning.

She jumped back, out of sheer surprise, then laughed. When she looked up at Wyatt, he kissed her, accompanied by a chorus of giggles and other sound effects.

Sarah wasn't sure who kicked the first water, but by the time they returned to Karen, they were all wet and laughing. Reesa and Michael had joined Karen while they'd been gone. And so had Ilona Cartwright. She was dressed in beachwear for the rich and famous and looked totally uncomfortable.

Sarah ran up to the group. "I'm so glad you came."

Ilona looked startled.

Sarah stopped in front of her, suddenly wary. "Aren't I? Did you find more letters? Or is this business?"

"Actually, I have one more piece of paper for you." She reached into her ever-present briefcase.

Sarah took an involuntary step backward. Wyatt put a supportive hand on her back.

Ilona stood up to hand her the papers. Their eyes met briefly, and in that moment a history of things felt, said and unsaid, passed between them. Ilona nodded slightly.

Reesa and Karen stood and moved closer to Sarah, demarcation in the sand.

"What is it?" Sarah frowned at the papers, while all the court documents she'd ever opened flashed through her mind. She looked up at Ilona, silently asking the question. A question that held so many questions.

And Ilona smiled. "Adoption papers. Judge Whitaker let me bring them today. You have a court date for next Thursday for the formal ceremony and signing."

Sarah just stared. Tried to take it all in. "Is this for real?"

"Very real."

Karen handed Sarah a towel. She wiped her hands and took the paper.

The girls ran up, curious to see what the grown-ups were doing. Leila immediately grabbed Sarah's leg. Sarah pulled her close with one hand.

"Sarah's going to be Leila's forever mom," Jenny blurted.

Everyone turned to Sarah with congratulations. Only Leila clung to her leg, looking scared. Sarah picked her up. "You're my forever girl now."

For a second, time stood still, then Leila frowned. "I am?"

"Yes, my sunshine, you are. And I'm your forever mommee." Sarah twirled her around. "And this is your forever family."

"Bessie, too?"

"Bessie and Tammy and Jenny and Rory and Amy, too."

"That lady, too?" Leila pointed to Ilona, who had leaned over to pick up her briefcase.

She was leaving? She couldn't leave, not now. "That lady, too. Her name is Nonie." Sarah caught Ilona's eye briefly and found her Nonie she thought she'd lost. "And she's my sister. Your forever aunt."

Leila threw her arms around Sarah's neck. Everyone else moved closer.

"My forever mommee?"

"Absolutely," Sarah said.

Leila twisted around to see Wyatt.

Everyone turned to Wyatt. He looked trapped.

"Are you going to be my forever . . . Wyatt?" Leila asked.

Wyatt broke into a wide grin. "You betcha. I'm your forever, ever, Wyatt."

Leila raised both hands. "Oh boy, hokey pokey five."

THAT DAY AT the beach there was a lot of wiggling of hands, feet, and hips. A whole lot of hokey pokeying going on.

Sarah knew it wouldn't all be easy. There would be times

when Leila's fears and hurts would rise up out of the past and make life hard. But Sarah would be there. And she had her peeps to help. And she knew Sam would be there, too.

Sarah Hargreave was in it for the long haul, rain or shine, for better or worse. She'd fix the now and carry on to forever.

Acknowledgments

There are all kinds of families. The family for this book included Kevan Lyon, Tessa Woodward, Elle Keck, Mary Gilroy, Irene Peterson, Gail Freeman, Susan Calt, Charity Scordato, Lois Winston, and the many foster children and parents who shared their stories.

To all of you, a heartfelt thank you.

Book Club Questions

1. In spite of Sam's love and the security he gave to Sarah, she still has trouble allowing herself to love people and accept their love in return. Why do you think she has trouble with this? Do you think it's because of her time in the foster system? How can Leila avoid a similar fate?

2. Nonie has always had a plan for her life and an unrelenting determination to succeed. How did that single-mindedness affect her personal life? Was she unable to appreciate the present because she was always striving for the future? Do you think that made her *unlovable*?

3. What was it about Sarah and Nonie's friendship that the loss of it impacted their lives for so many years to come and later makes them act the way they do? Do you think they are different from people who are raised with their biological families? What, if anything, do they have in common?

4. After June's death, Ilona begins to wonder if perhaps June did love her, in her own way. What led her to this realization? Do you agree with her? Ilona has always been afraid that maybe she didn't try hard enough to make June love her. Do you think she still tries too hard? What could she have done differently?

5. When the book begins, Reesa has been feeling worn down in her career as a caseworker. What was it about her last case that pushed her over the brink? Do you think she did the right thing to leave this area of social work and find another job? Do you think you could do and see the things she does if it meant you could make a difference?

6. Sarah, Reesa, and Ilona are thrust together because of one little girl. Do you think they could have become friends without Leila? Will they stay friends after this or will they drift apart like Sarah and Nonie did so many years before? Why do you think this might happen?

7. Why do you think Sarah is so adamant about adopting Leila? Is she adopting her for the right reasons? Or is it to fill a hole inside herself? Despite Sarah never having had a mother growing up, do you think she could be a good mother? Is it possible for her loss to make her an even better one?

8. Is there a specific moment that was a turning point in Sarah and Leila's relationship? Or do you think it was a series of moments that created a feeling of normalcy for them? Have you ever experienced this?

9. One of the central themes of this novel is the question of where a child *really* belongs. There seems to be no easy answer. Is the bond between a child and his or her birth mother so strong that no one else can replace it? Do you think adoptive parents can fill that void and even become more to their children?

10. Do you think you could ever become a foster or an adoptive parent? Or if you already are, could you share your experience with the group? How has it changed you? Are there things you've learned about yourself, good or bad, through the process?

Gary Brown

About the Author

Shelley Noble is a former professional dancer and choreographer and has worked on a number of films. She lives at the Jersey shore where she loves to visit lighthouses and vintage carousels. She is a member of Sisters in Crime, Mystery Writers of America, and Romance Writers of America.